The Alpine Obituary

By Mary Daheim
Published by Ballantine Books

THE ALPINE ADVOCATE
THE ALPINE BETRAYAL
THE ALPINE CHRISTMAS
THE ALPINE DECOY
THE ALPINE ESCAPE
THE ALPINE FURY
THE ALPINE GAMBLE
THE ALPINE HERO
THE ALPINE ICON
THE ALPINE JOURNEY
THE ALPINE KINDRED
THE ALPINE LEGACY
THE ALPINE MENACE
THE ALPINE NEMESIS
THE ALPINE OBITUARY

THE
ALPINE
OBITUARY

Mary Daheim

Ballantine Books
New York

A Ballantine Book
Published by The Ballantine Publishing Group
Copyright © 2002 by Mary Daheim

www.ballantinebooks.com

Library of Congress Cataloging-in-Publication Data is available upon request.

ISBN 0-345-45886-9

Manufactured in the United States of America

First Hardcover Edition: September 2002

10 9 8 7 6 5 4 3 2 1

The Alpine Obituary

Chapter One

TUESDAY, NINE-FIFTEEN A.M., publication day for *The Alpine Advocate*. Coffee and a croissant smeared with boysenberry jam. A quiet September morning with the sun filtering through the small window above my desk.

Quiet, that is, until my House & Home editor's hat fell off. She jumped from her chair, ignored the hat, snatched up a couple of sheets of paper, and stomped across the newsroom into my office.

"I've never seen the like," Vida Runkel huffed, slapping the handwritten sheets on my desk. "Believe me, I've seen my share of outrageous obituaries during my years with the *Advocate*, but this one beats all." She crossed her arms over her imposing bust and tapped an agitated foot.

As the weekly newspaper's editor and publisher for the past eleven years, I'd printed some real pips, including leads that read PADDLE YOUR OWN CANOE, ARLO, GEORGIE-PORGIE'S EATING HEAVEN'S PUDDING AND PIE, and AGATHA LEFT HER PIANO TO HER NIECE, BUT TOOK HER ORGANS WITH HER.

I began to read out loud.

"John (Jack) Augustus Froland died Monday night (Labor Day) at home in Alpine after a long illness. Jack, as he was known and loved by all, had turned 80 years young last month. Born Aug. 12, 1920, right here in Alpine, Jack was the son of Augustus (Gus) and Violet (née Iverson) Froland. Jack graduated from Alpine High School in 1938 and went to work at the Tonga-Cascade Timber Mill until his retirement in 1985, when the mill was shut down due to pressure from the tree-huggers."

So far, so good. Well, maybe not very good, but at least not outlandish. I continued as Vida fumed.

"After serving with the Seabees during WWII, Jack returned to Alpine and married June Grandorf in 1948. Their daughter, Lynn, preceded Jack in death in 1967. A son, Max, lives in Seattle. Jack will be remembered as a hardworking, fun-loving man, especially to what he called 'his boys' at Mugs Ahoy Tavern. Funeral services are set for 11 A.M. Friday, Sept. 8, at Faith Lutheran Church. Burial will be in Alpine Cemetery. A viewing of Jack's remains will be held at Driggers Funeral Home, Thursday, Sept. 7, between 7 and 8:30 P.M.

"COME SEE JACK-IN-THE-BOX!"

I laughed. Not loudly, not uncontrollably, and not for long. But at least I laughed. I hadn't laughed much in the past fourteen months, and with good reason.

"We can't run this," Vida huffed. "It's too ridiculous. It's even worse than when Emily Trews wrote her own obituary and viciously attacked most of her relatives and half the congregation at First Presbyterian Church." And though Vida hadn't laughed, she didn't chastise me for doing so. Vida may work for me, but her seniority in years, employment on the *Advocate*, and august demeanor give her the right to take any one of us to task.

"We have to run it," I replied. "Ever since we started charging for space on the Vital Statistics page at the beginning of the year, we've promised to run items word-for-word except for spelling and grammatical corrections. And libelous material such as Emily Trews submitted."

Vida grabbed up the handwritten sheets, stomped out to her desk in the editorial office, and sat down with a thud. "You take full responsibility then," she called to me, whipping off her glasses and vigorously rubbing her eyes with the palms of her hand. "Ooooh," she wailed, "it must have been

June who wrote this up. Jack's wife never did have any sense."

Most people didn't have—much less use—sense as far as Vida was concerned. I smiled in that vague, hesitant manner I'd developed over the past year and more. "Of course I'll take responsibility." I said from the doorway to my cubbyhole of an office. "I'm the publisher, remember?" Sometimes it seemed that Vida forgot.

"I suppose I'll have to go to the funeral," Vida grumbled. "I've known the Frolands forever."

Vida had known everybody in Alpine forever, and in a town of under four thousand citizens, she was related by blood or by marriage to—by my estimate—at least ten percent of them. Nor would she miss a funeral—or a wedding or a christening—unless it was some poor soul who had only recently moved to Skykomish County.

My phone rang, recalling me to my desk.

"Emma Lord here," I said in my acquired robotlike manner.

"I'm going to Rome next month. Want to join me?"

It was my brother, Ben, calling from Tuba City, Arizona, where he is a missionary priest to the Navajo and Hopi tribes. The energy in his crackling voice forced another smile.

"Rome?" I said. "Why are you going there? Is the pope in trouble?"

"The pope's always in trouble with somebody." Ben replied. "I felt like I wanted to get away from here after the summer dust storms settle and before the ice shows up on the roads. Thus, I'm attending a conference on the home missions the third week of October. I'm serious. You could drink buckets of Chianti and put grape leaves in your hair and swim naked in the Trevi fountain while I'm meeting with a bunch of other priests who don't know what the hell they're doing, either. Then we could spend a few days in Paris or London. Take your pick."

I knew that Ben's offer wasn't for his own sake, but for mine. Without his hardheaded counsel in recent months, I might have gone over Deception Falls without a barrel.

"You're serious," I said.

"Sure. Why not? You haven't had a vacation in ages."

I noticed that he wasn't specific about the length of time. But in a generic way, he was right. It was almost two years since I'd taken any real time off from the newspaper.

"You think I should go, don't you," I said, not a question, but a statement.

"Yes, I do." Ben's tone was solemn.

"I don't want to go to Paris," I responded.

"I shouldn't have mentioned Paris. Sorry."

"London would be fine."

"You'll do it?" His voice lightened.

"Give me a few days," I replied. "I'll let you know after the weekend."

"Great," he enthused. "How are you doing, Sluggly?" he inquired, resurrecting his childhood nickname for me.

"I'm doing," I said, trying not to sound glum. "I mean, I really am better than I was, say, a month or two ago."

"Adam thought so when I talked to him after he visited you at the end of July," Ben said, referring to my only son who had been ordained a priest in the spring and was now assigned to an Inuit mission at Mary's Igloo, Alaska, not far from Nome. His ordination had been held in St. Paul, where Adam had attended the seminary. There, in the granite and marble splendor of the great cathedral, I wept tears of joy and sorrow. I was exalted by Adam's achievement, his dedication, his faith. I was heartbroken because Tom couldn't share this proud moment.

"I worry about Adam," I admitted, "when I'm not worrying about me."

"He's doing okay," Ben assured me. "Breaking into the priesthood keeps him occupied. He'll have plenty on his mind when winter comes and he has to fend off the sub-zero temperatures and the hungry grizzly bears."

I worried about that, too. The village was small and isolated. Adam had been candid about his orientation, informing me that every winter at least a couple of people froze to death or were mauled by bears. But that wasn't the only thing that troubled me about my son.

"Maybe," I ventured, "it's just as well he didn't know his father when he was growing up. When he finally met Tom ten years ago, they didn't have much time together. Or am I kidding myself?"

"I can't answer that," Ben said candidly.

"Adam may feel cheated," I said, doodling on a piece of paper. "He should. And it's my fault."

"Hey," Ben said sharply, "knock it off. You had your reasons, and they were pretty damned good at the time."

There was no point in arguing with my brother. It was an old bone we'd chewed between us. When I'd fallen in love with Tom Cavanaugh thirty years earlier, his married status hadn't prevented us from conceiving a child. Tom had been torn between his wife and me. But Sandra Cavanaugh had more than inherited wealth and emotional problems—her trump card was that she, too, was pregnant. I lost the hand, the game, and the love of my life.

"It doesn't matter now anyway, does it?" I asked in that wispy voice I used all too often when discussing Tom. I looked down at the doodles on my notepad. They were teardrops. If there had been room under the desk, I would have kicked myself.

"Jeez, Sluggly, cut it out," Ben rasped. "You're tough. You've been on your own since our folks died when you were twenty. I'm beginning to think you're playing a part. 'Emma Lord, Tragic Heroine.' It doesn't suit you. It's like Jerry Seinfeld playing King Lear. Feeling sorry for yourself is a sin. 'Fess up, I'm listening."

One thing about Ben, he could always get me riled. "I'm not acting, and I'm not feeling sorry for myself," I declared in a far from wispy voice. In fact, Vida had turned toward my open office door and wasn't bothering to conceal her interest. "Admit it, Stench," I went on, dropping a notch in volume and using my old nickname for Ben, "it's not easy to be planning a wedding and a Paris honeymoon with the father of your child and then have him shot to death before your very eyes."

"Well, at least you weren't the one who shot him."

"Ben!" I was shocked, though I knew he was trying to make me laugh.

I couldn't. Not yet.

I had just hung up the phone when Ginny Erlandson, our office manager, approached me with a note in her freckled hand.

"Judge Foster-Klein called a few minutes ago," Ginny explained in her sober manner. "I didn't know how long you'd be, so I told her you'd call back. She wants to arrange a meeting as soon as it's convenient."

I gave Ginny a curious look. "A meeting about what?"

"She didn't say," Ginny replied. "You know how Judge Foster-Klein is—very brisk. She also sounded . . . odd."

Marsha Foster-Klein wasn't particularly odd, but she could be downright acerbic, especially in the courtroom. For the past year and a half, she'd been sitting on the bench in Alpine, replacing our aged and senile superior court judge who thought he was a penguin.

"I'll call her now," I said, curiosity impelling me.

Marsha was temporarily ensconced in The Pines Village apartment complex on Alpine Way, but her office was in the courthouse. Since it was a workday, I was a bit surprised to note that Ginny had given me Marsha's home phone number.

When Marsha answered, her voice was thick and labored.

"Emma Lord here," I said, wondering if she were drunk. It wouldn't be the first time that a local judge had started the day with a quart instead of a tort.

"Emma," she said, then coughed. "Sorry. I've got an awful cold. Every year, just before Labor Day, I get a real pip. Maybe it's the change in the weather."

I expressed my sympathy, then asked the judge if she wanted to wait until she felt better for her proposed meeting between us.

"The sooner the better," Marsha said, and coughed some more. "I'm staying home today. Late this afternoon would be good."

Typical. At her convenience, not mine. Furthermore, I wasn't keen on walking into a House of Germs, but after a brief hesitation, I told Marsha that would be fine with me.

"Okay," she said, and excused herself to blow her nose. "Sorry. I've had this cold since Saturday. They say you can't give it after the second day."

I hoped so. Informing Marsha I'd be at her apartment around five o'clock, I rang off. It was Tuesday, our pub date, and with time off for Labor Day, we'd tried to get the paper filled before the weekend. Only late-breaking news—such as Jack Froland's death—would be included in this week's edition.

My shoulders slumped as I stared at the layout for the front page. I'd saved space for the photos our reporter, Scott Chamoud, had taken of the Labor Day picnic in Old Mill Park. As good as Scott was with a camera, he hadn't been able to rise above his subject matter: the usual three-legged races, demonstrations of pole-climbing, smiling wives showing off their pies, macho men bearing their flabby chests, and happy children running through the sprinkler system that had—as usual—been turned on "by accident."

"You look like you just got thrown out at home plate," said my ad manager, Leo Walsh.

Trying to smile, I gazed up at Leo. "The *Advocate* has become incredibly dull," I declared. "And so have I. My imagination seems to have struck out swinging."

Leo abstained from sitting in one of my two visitor chairs and perched on the edge of the desk. "Except for the six-car pileups with multiple fatalities out on Highway 2, summer can be kind of dull. Things will pick up now that September's here."

"But will I?"

Leo, like everyone else in Alpine, knew the cause of my malaise. But unlike most others, he understood it better. Tom had been his boss and his friend. He'd given Leo a second chance when the World of Walsh was spinning out of control. Later, when Leo resumed drinking and his wife left him, Tom had asked me to give Leo a last chance. I'd agreed, and eight years later, I had no regrets. At least none about Leo.

"You'll be okay," Leo assured me. "You know something," he went on, lowering his voice and leaning closer, "you can mourn all you want for what might have been. But face it, Emma, you can't grieve for what you never had."

It was harsh counsel, but I knew Leo meant well. And he was right. "It's just that I'm not ready to . . ." I hesitated, trying to think of the right word. "To move on. I know that's crazy, but somehow I just can't."

Leo shrugged as he slipped off the desk. "You will. How about dinner after we put the paper to bed?"

I grimaced. "I can't. I have a five o'clock appointment with Judge Foster-Klein."

Leo frowned at me. "What about?"

Ordinarily, he wasn't the prying kind, but I knew what he was thinking: Judge Foster-Klein had handed down the stiffest penalty possible to Tom's killer. Two weeks after being shipped off to the penitentiary at Walla Walla, the S.O.B. had committed suicide. Maybe Leo thought I was crazy enough to ask the judge if there was a way that punishment could be dealt out beyond the grave.

"I don't know," I said. "Marsha's the one who wants to see me."

Leo looked relieved. "Oh. Maybe she's got a hot story for you. Isn't she up for an appointment to the Court of Appeals?"

"She is," I replied. "You're right. Maybe the appointment came through. Shoot—all we have is a bar association photo."

"Can't Scott take a new picture?" Leo asked.

"He could, but if that's the case, we'll miss deadline. Damn." I stood up, drumming my fingers on the desk. "Maybe I should call her back. I never get over how nonjournalists can ignore a local newspaper's publication schedule."

Marsha Foster-Klein didn't pick up the phone. I got her answering machine, which was typically to the point. "I'm unavailable. Leave a message."

Maybe the judge had taken to her bed. I'd try again later. Meanwhile, I scoured the wire service and the Internet for items that might be related—however tenuously—to Alpine. I didn't find much except for a timber story and some traffic revisions around Monroe.

Shortly after three, I got hold of Marsha. "No appointment yet," she said, sounding only half-conscious. "I'll explain when I see you."

At four-thirty, I told our backshop wizard, Kip MacDuff, that we were ready to roll. Kip, who is as good-hearted as he is competent, gazed at the front-page mock-up. "The lead story is ETHEL PIKE WINS LOTTERY PRIZE? But Ethel only won twenty-seven dollars with four numbers."

"Right," I agreed. "Ethel is the bottom of the barrel. What's worse is that she bought her ticket in Snohomish, not Alpine. I couldn't see running all those Labor Day weekend fender benders as the lead. We got lucky this year—or at least the travelers did. No fatalities, no injuries. Wouldn't you know it." Such was the plight of the journalist. Good news for everybody else was bad news for us.

Such was the drivel that passed for news on this late summer Tuesday. I arrived at The Pines Village at precisely five
P.M. Even though it's ten years old, the apartment complex is
one of the newer buildings in Alpine. It has a security system, and after a croaking response from Judge Marsha, I was
buzzed inside.

Her Honor lives in the penthouse apartment, though I've
never figured out why it's been given that designation. The
only thing that distinguishes it from the other units is that it's
on the top floor.

"Stupid," Marsha said to me upon opening the door.
Given her sharp tongue, I hoped she wasn't referring to me.
"Stupid to get this damned cold. But I do. Every year."

I'd never been inside the apartment since she rented it almost a year ago. The hundred-mile commute from Everett
had worn her down.

"Excuse the junk," she said, waving an arm around the
sparsely furnished living room. "I rented this stuff cheap. No
point in buying anything when I don't know where I'll settle
permanently. My own furniture's in storage."

I sat down in an armchair covered in big orange, red, and
purple flowers. It was comfortable enough, but the wild pattern almost blinded me. The judge seated herself in the
room's other armchair, a dull gray.

"Can I trust you?" Despite the croaking of her voice, the
question came through loud and clear.

"What do you mean?" I replied. There are certain conditions under which no journalist can be trusted. It's the nature
of the beast—and the nose for news.

There was a cheap faux-wood end table next to Marsha's
chair. She reached into the single drawer and extracted a
standard-sized white envelope.

"What I mean," Marsha explained, speaking more slowly
than usual, "is that I don't want you putting what I tell you
in a story."

I made a face. "Sorry. That's a promise I can't make."

Marsha's blue eyes narrowed. "Even as a friend?"

I didn't know we were friends. We'd gotten to know each other during the murder trial. We had lunch together twice and dinner once. But it was all business. Or so I thought.

I didn't know what to say. Friends were not easy to make in Alpine when much of the citizenry regarded anyone not born in the town as a stranger. Or maybe it wasn't easy for me to make friends. I'd always had a problem with throwing up barriers. Self-protection, I supposed, and had sometimes blamed it on Tom's betrayal.

"I can't promise anything," I admitted. "Is this news?"

Marsha frowned, blew her nose, and clasped the envelope between her slim hands as if it were a sacrificial offering. Her usually perfectly coiffed blonde pageboy hung lank and listless around her pale face with its highlighted red nose. "I'm going to take a chance," she finally said. "After I've told you about this letter and what I want, you decide."

Great. Toss the ball in Emma's court. Make me feel even worse than I already did.

"Okay," I said with reluctance. "Go ahead."

But Marsha put the letter aside on the end table and stood up. "I forgot my manners. This may take some time. How about a drink?"

"That sounds good," I said. "Are you joining me?"

"Sure," Marsha replied, going to a cabinet in the dining alcove. "A little whiskey is good for a cold. I add honey, hot water, and orange juice. It's no cure—nothing is—but it makes me feel better."

I laughed. Softly. It was a remedy that Adam's pediatrician in Portland had recommended when my son was teething. He told me to rub the concoction on Adam's gums. I'd expressed mild dismay. "But by the time I've mixed all that, there'll be too much for the little guy."

"That's when you drink the rest of it," the doctor had replied. "If it doesn't work for him, then his fussing won't bother you so much."

I recounted the anecdote to Marsha, who nodded in agreement. "I wish I'd used it on my son," she said, handing me a glass of Canadian whiskey and water. "Of course he's making up for lost time at college. Most freshmen seem to major in drink, pot, and sex."

I knew Marsha had a son named Simon who was attending UCLA. I'd never known what had happened to his father, Mr. Klein. Female that I am, maybe I didn't think of Marsha as a friend because she hadn't shared any intimate information with me.

We resumed our ugly armchairs. Marsha rolled up the sleeves of her flannel dressing gown, as if preparing to go to work. In a way, I guess she was.

"What I want is your help," she declared. "I'm in trouble."

I was taken aback. Why me? "What kind of trouble?" I inquired.

"You've run the story about my pending appointment to the Court of Appeals." Marsha paused to blow her nose. Through the tall windows, I could see the sun starting to set above the evergreens in the west. It had been a golden September day, with scattered clouds and the tang of fall in the air. I'd scarcely noticed until now.

"The appointment is a cinch," Marsha continued, picking up the envelope from the end table. "Or was, until I got this in the mail Saturday. Here, you read it." She sailed the missive at me; I missed grabbing it on the fly, but it landed in my lap.

I noted that the envelope was postmarked from Alpine, September third. There was no return, and the judge's home address was written in a small, cramped hand.

Dear Judge Foster-Klein, the salutation read.

> You think you are a big shot. But big shots can fizzle out. You don't deserve that big job you're supposed to get, and you know why. The past has come back to

haunt you. Some of us know your deep, dark secret. If you don't withdraw your name from consideration for that judgeship, everybody else will know, too. And you'll be sorry.

As expected, there was no signature. But there was a photograph attached to the single page, stuck on the back with Scotch tape. The picture, probably taken with an ordinary Kodak camera, was old. Its edges were frayed, there was a diagonal crease in the upper right-hand corner, and it was tinted brown.

"Do you recognize that?" Marsha asked.

The photo was of a wooden railroad trestle. The background showed a clear-cut hill, or perhaps the lower reaches of a mountain. A rope dangled from the trestle.

"It could be anywhere," I said, loosening the photo enough to check the back. It was blank. "What do you think?"

"I haven't any idea," Marsha retorted, as if her lack of knowledge might be my fault. "All I can think of," she went on in a less hostile tone, "is that the rope means something. A lynching, perhaps."

"I've never heard of a lynching in Alpine," I said, reattaching the photo to the letter.

Marsha shrugged. "Whatever. It must mean something to the person who sent this piece of crap."

I agreed. Then I reread the letter. "You honestly have no idea who sent this?"

Marsha shook her head. "Not a clue. Keep the letter and the picture. I know from what I've heard and seen of you that you're good at investigating. It's part of your job. You've even helped solve a few homicide cases in the past. I want you to find out who sent this damned thing and why."

"Marsha," I said, "I'm no detective. Why don't you hand the letter over to the sheriff?"

The judge drew back in her chair. "And have Milo Dodge and the rest of them laugh at me? No thanks. I want discretion. When you find out, the story is yours. If it *is* a story."

"As a judge, you must get all kinds of ugly mail," I said.

"Of course." Marsha's faint smile was ironic. "Usually, they go right in the trash. But this is different. Assuming from the postmark that this is someone right here in town, they can spread rumors. You know how small-town folks love gossip. It can get back to the decision-makers in Olympia. They might ignore such talk. But then again, they might not. I'm not the only qualified candidate for the Court of Appeals. Somebody in the state capital always has a shirt-tail relation or a good friend without baggage who could do the job."

"This really isn't much in the way of baggage," I pointed out.

"It's enough. For me, anyway." Marsha bit off the words.

I remained unconvinced. "Are you sure you can't think of someone from around here who might feel he or she got a raw deal from you? You've sat on the Skykomish County bench for almost two years."

"Everybody who goes to jail thinks they've gotten a raw deal," Marsha responded. "And that's what they say in their letters—before they get to the insults and the threats. This one's different. There's nothing personal. That worries me. Come on, Emma, what do you say?"

No matter how much Marsha coaxed, I wasn't keen on accepting such a responsibility. The judge's request would take time and energy, neither of which I had in great abundance these days. "Wouldn't a private detective be more appropriate?"

"I don't want to do that," Marsha said flatly. "A stranger nosing around Alpine would only attract attention, which I certainly don't want." She paused, staring at me with her reddened eyes. "I'll pay, of course."

"No, no," I responded. "I don't want money from you. I simply don't think I'm the right person for the job."

"Why not?"

"Because I'm not a professional investigator," I said. "I also assume you have a time frame. I can't devote endless hours to finding out—what? Who sent the letter? A crime lab can help you there. What else do you need to know?"

The judge looked affronted. I'd observed Marsha in court when her dignity had been assailed. She became hostile and insulting. I braced myself for a tongue-lashing.

But it didn't come. Instead, Marsha slumped a bit in the chair. "What I need to know is what I've done that's so terrible. Frankly, I've led a blameless life. Or as close to it as most people come."

"Then what have you got to worry about?"

"I told you, I don't need obstacles—no matter how far-fetched—in the way of my appointment. To achieve that, I have to be like Calpurnia, without even the hint of scandal or blame. And the Court of Appeals is a dream I've had for years."

I felt myself weakening. The judge looked so different from her usual well-groomed, brisk, vigorous demeanor on the bench that I had to feel sorry for her. Marsha's plight took me back eleven years earlier, when I was waiting to hear if the deal for the *Advocate* would go through. It meant the world to me then; now it seemed almost insignificant.

But I remembered.

"Let me think about it overnight," I finally said.

The relief that swept over Marsha was visible. "Thanks so much."

"One thing," I added, finishing my drink. "If I do this, I'd like to take Vida Runkel into my confidence. She knows everything there is to know about Alpine."

Marsha rubbed at her nose with a tissue. "True," she

allowed, "but I'm not from Alpine. Her trove of information won't help me."

"Then," I said as I slipped the envelope into my purse and stood up, "we've got a problem."

My purse seemed heavier than when I'd arrived. I couldn't guess that the added content would weigh much heavier on me in the days to come.

April 1916

Olga Iversen rarely gave in to tears, but on this cloudy spring day, she was crying. Seated at the white pine table her husband had made after the family moved from Port Townsend to Alpine, she wrung her reddened hands and didn't look up when her eldest son, Per, touched her shoulder.

"Ma," Per said in Norwegian, "don't get so upset. Jonas is just showing off. He's only sixteen."

"Seventeen, come September," Olga said through her tears. "He should take a job in the mill. He won't study. He needs to work. He has too much time on his hands."

"I'll talk to him," Per said. "Again."

"Your father is sick of talking to him," Olga said, her sobs finally subsiding. "Your father works hard in the mill, he has so much responsibility. I don't want to worry him too much. You remember the last time they talked? They ended up in such a row. Your father felt bad that he had to hit Jonas so hard. His cheek still hasn't healed."

Per went over to the cast-iron stove where a speckled blue coffeepot sat on the ever-present fire. "Beating Jonas does no good. Talking doesn't, either. He has to grow out of this."

Olga rose from the pine chair that matched the table. It, too, had been made by her husband, Trygve. Indeed, the senior Iversen had built all the furniture in the tiny three-room frame house.

"It's not natural," Olga murmured. "Not to do what Jonas did."

"Mr. Rix isn't mad at us any more," Per pointed out.

"He should be," Olga declared, straightening her long muslin skirt. "It's wrong to shoot a dog. The Rix boys loved their pet. I call it a crime."

"Jonas said the dog attacked him," Per said, though there was a note of doubt in his voice.

"I don't think so," Olga retorted, wiping her eyes with a wrinkled handkerchief. "Those chipmunks didn't attack him when he shot them. Jonas should not have a rifle. He has such a temper. He may hurt a person someday."

Per smiled at his mother. "Jonas isn't cruel. He'll grow out of it."

Olga tried to smile back at her son. But she couldn't. "I hope and pray you're right," she replied. "But I am afraid for Jonas. He's not like you or your brother Lars." Tears welled again in her blue eyes. "God help us, Jonas isn't like other people."

Chapter Two

"HOW COULD YOU have forgotten something like Marsha's origins?" Vida exclaimed an hour later when I stopped by her neat little house on Tyee Street. "Either a person is born in Alpine or not."

"Yes, Vida," I said, dutifully hanging my head. "I forgot."

"It makes all the difference," Vida admonished, going to the stove as the teakettle whistled. "Are you sure you want to turn down this rather peculiar request?"

"I don't see that I have any choice," I replied as Vida dunked a pair of tea bags in the kettle. "I honestly don't have time to tackle what sounds like an impossible project. And frankly," I added, looking gloomily at Vida's canary, Cupcake, who was hopping about in his gilded cage, "I don't feel up to it."

I heard Vida suck in her breath. "You don't, do you?" She remained at the stove, waiting for the tea to steep. "Well, now." Vida didn't speak again until she'd poured the tea into English bone china cups with matching saucers. "I don't like that attitude," she said, still reproachful. "That's not like you."

"Yes, it is." I stirred a teaspoon of sugar into my cup.

"No, it's not." Vida was emphatic. "You're moping. You're feeling sorry for yourself. You need to stop. Are you refusing Judge Foster-Klein because she's Jewish?"

"What?" I'd started to raise the cup to my lips but set it down so fast that I splashed tea into the saucer. "Are you nuts, Vida? Have you ever known me to be prejudiced about anyone?"

"Of course not," Vida replied calmly. "That's why I asked. Your refusal seems very odd."

"It's not odd," I said, indignant. "I'm not the right person for the task. Besides, I didn't even know that Marsha was Jewish, and what difference would it make if I had? Carla's Jewish, or have you forgotten?" I said, referring to our former reporter, Carla Steinmetz Talliaferro.

"Certainly not," Vida responded. "Though we've had very few Jews in Alpine over the years. In fact . . ." She stopped and frowned. "Of course. That's how I knew."

"Knew what?" I was still offended.

"That Marsha is Jewish—or part Jewish." Vida took a sip of tea before she spoke again. "Yes, it's coming back to me. There is a connection to Alpine, but it's very tenuous. It came to mind when Marsha began sitting in for Judge Krogstad, after he got so . . . peculiar. Somehow, she's related—though distantly—to the Iversons."

"The Iversons?" I repeated. "As in the same Iversons who are related to the late Jack-in-the-Box Froland?"

Vida grimaced. "The very same." Again, she paused. "But is Klein Marsha's maiden or married name? That is, did she hyphenate her last name when she married?"

I felt stupid. "I didn't ask."

"Then do so," Vida retorted, before assuming a perplexed expression. "I wonder . . ."

"What?"

Cupcake began a merry song. Vida glanced at the bird and smiled. "So cheerful. But it's almost his bedtime." She turned back to me. "Are you certain you ate a proper dinner?"

"Yes," I said resignedly. "I picked up Chinese at the mall."

Vida eyed me critically. "You're too thin. You're wasting away."

"I am not." It wasn't quite true. I had lost six or seven

pounds since Tom died. For the first time since I was in my teens, I weighed under a hundred and twenty pounds.

"Tsk, tsk." Vida shook her head. But when she spoke again, it was not of me, but of Marsha. "I'll have to search my memory. But there may be something there. . . . Would you like a cookie?"

"No, thanks, Vida." Whatever the cookie, it came from the grocery store. For all the recipes that Vida ran on her page, she could barely operate a stove. Vida was one of the worst cooks I'd ever met, but you'd never know it from her trumpeting of exotic fare in the *Advocate*. A month ago, when the various wild berries had ripened on Tonga Ridge, she had run at least a half-dozen recipes featuring huckleberries. Someone—I was never sure who but guessed it was her sister-in-law, Mary Lou Blatt—dared Vida to bake a huckleberry pie for a family function. Vida accepted the challenge and baked two, bringing one to the office. The berry filling reminded me of blue library paste, except that as I recall from my grade-school days, the paste was much better. Ginny told me later that it was wonderful—for stopping a run in her pantyhose.

"We should do as Marsha asks," Vida finally announced. "We owe it to her."

"We do?"

"Of course. Look how fairly she conducted Tommy's murder trial."

I winced, not just at the memory, but because Vida was the only person in the world who'd ever called Tom "Tommy." "I wasn't interested in fairness," I retorted. "Or even justice. I wanted revenge."

"Never mind all that now," Vida said brusquely. "We need to help poor Marsha."

I resented Vida's sudden transfer of sympathy from me to a woman she hardly knew. "Then you help her," I huffed. "You know everything and everybody."

"So I shall," she replied, her tone now blithe as she rose to put a white cloth over Cupcake's cage.

I stood up, preparing to leave. "Are you the one who's going to tell Marsha you're doing the investigating instead of me?"

"If you like," Vida replied, tut-tut-tutting at Cupcake in a game of peekaboo with the white cloth.

"Good luck," I said, starting for the door. "Thanks for the tea."

"Any time. Tut-tut-tutty-too-too."

I couldn't ever recall Vida not seeing me out. Annoyed, and not quite sure why, I got into the Lexus that Tom had given me and drove off down Tyee Street.

But instead of turning left on Sixth and heading for my little log house, I turned right. Even though there isn't a great deal of traffic at night in Alpine, I drove more slowly than usual. I wasn't sure where I was going in more ways than one. But of course I pulled into my usual parking spot at the *Advocate*.

The lights were on in the backshop. I found Kip slaving away, putting the paper together.

"What's up?" he inquired, surprised to see me.

"I'm doing a bit of research," I replied. "Is everything going okay?"

"Sure," Kip answered, looking up from his computer monitor. "Ginny got the classifieds screwed up, though. They're out of numerical order. That's not like her."

"Now that Ginny has two children, she gets muddled," I said. "But it's rare."

"True." He returned to the monitor. "We could use a new layout program. This one is old and slow. Can we afford it?"

"I think so," I said. "Find out what it'd cost and let me know."

"Will do." He moved the cursor around the screen with great aplomb. "By the way, I'm getting married."

"What?" I had started to head back to the newsroom and stumbled over the threshold.

My reaction apparently caught Kip off-guard. "What's wrong? Didn't you think anyone would have me?"

"Of course not," I assured him. "It's just that . . . How could I not have known?"

Kip looked at me with a sheepish grin. "The wedding's set for late November, right after Thanksgiving."

"Who?" I asked, still dumbfounded. Kip was in his late twenties, and though he dated occasionally, I had no idea that there was a steady girlfriend in his life.

"Bev Iverson," Kip replied, now beaming widely. "You know her, she works at kIds cOrNEr for Ione Erdahl."

"Of course," I said, trying to overcome my astonishment. "She's very sweet. Pretty, too." The truth was, I hadn't been in the local children's store in three years. But I'd seen Beverly Iverson around town, and Vida had pointed her out to me. A petite blonde with a pigeon-toed gait, she was the daughter of Fred and Opal Iverson who owned the Venison Inn along with Fred's uncle, Jack Iverson. Thus, I realized, Beverly was also somehow related to Jack Froland and to Judge Marsha. Typical. Sometimes it seemed that Alpine was so inbred that it was a wonder local residents didn't have eleven toes and ears on their elbows.

"Does Vida know?" I asked.

"Sure," Kip replied. His ruddy face darkened. "That is, doesn't Vida always know everything?"

I offered Kip an understanding smile. "Never mind. I suppose you didn't want to tell me about the wedding because you thought it might . . . raise too many painful memories."

Kip hung his head. "That's right. We decided—that is, I thought it'd be better to wait for the right moment. You know, like . . . ah . . ."

"Like when I forget Tom Cavanaugh's name?" I patted Kip's arm. "It's okay. I can't live in a cocoon. Life does go on." But at what a price, I thought.

We chatted some more, then I went into the newsroom. It wouldn't hurt to check out the names of Foster and Klein in our files. Ginny had reorganized us recently, which meant I could never find anything. She, however, could present a birth notice from 1946 within thirty seconds.

It had cost too much to put the precomputer era editions on microfiche, so all the issues up until the early Nineties were in bound volumes. I stared at the well-worn spines and wondered where to begin. We also had a file of names, cross-referenced by families. Even—or because of—Ginny's thoroughness and penchant for detail, they were a nightmare to decipher.

I looked up Klein in search of Marsha's ancestry. There was no one by that name. There was a Foster, Alvin, but he'd worked at one of the mills in the late Thirties and apparently left town to join the military when World War II broke out. He had no family in Alpine, and I guessed that he'd come to town in search of work during the Depression.

Finally, I checked the Iversons, to whom Vida believed Marsha had some tenuous connection. There were two early references, to an Iversen and an Iverson. I had sat down at Leo's desk to peruse the names when I was startled by a noise in the outer office. I could have sworn I'd locked the door behind me.

I was barely out of the chair when Milo Dodge loped into the room.

"Emma," he said in mild surprise, doffing his regulation sheriff's hat. "What are you doing here this time of night?"

"Research," I replied, settling back down in the chair. "You startled me."

Milo gave me his lopsided grin. "Sorry. I didn't notice your car outside. This place is usually dark Monday nights. It wasn't, so I thought I'd better check it out. I used my master key. What's up?"

"For one thing," I said dryly, "it's not Monday, it's Tuesday. Our pub date."

"Sheesh." Milo clapped a big hand to his forehead. "I keep forgetting. These three-day weekends throw me." He put a booted foot up on Leo's visitor chair. "I knew it was Tuesday. I mean, I really did. I had to keep reminding myself all day, and just now, I forgot."

Ordinarily, Milo isn't what I'd call a chatterbox. But in recent months, I've noticed that when we're alone together—which isn't all that often—he jabbers away. I suspect he doesn't know what to say to me. The tragedy that killed Tom also robbed Milo of a woman with whom he'd been keeping serious company. Since Milo and I had once been lovers as well as friends, I figured that he assumed there was an awkwardness between us because our love lives had both been scuttled. Milo is not an introspective type of person.

But he was a native Alpiner. "Let me show you something," I said, reaching into my purse. I fumbled a bit as I detached the old photograph from the back of the letter that had been sent to Judge Marsha. "Do you recognize this trestle?"

Milo's hazel eyes squinted at the picture. Holding it in the palm of his hand, he studied the scene for a long time. "Is it supposed to be some place around here?"

"I don't know," I answered honestly.

"Where'd you get it?" His gaze was still fixed on the photo.

"From a friend," I said. "She wants to know where it was taken."

Shrugging, Milo handed the snapshot back to me. "No idea. It probably dates back at least seventy years. Those brown tinted pictures—they stopped doing that in the Twenties, I think."

"That's so," I said, studying the photo once more. "You're sure you don't recognize the background?"

Milo started to shake his head, then took the picture back from me. He was silent for some time. "Well . . . those boulders in the background—they do look kind of familiar. See that cleft in the one at the left? It looks like some fat guy's rear end. It could be the old trestle that used to run over Burl

Creek just before it got to the river. But the trees have all been cut, and by now this whole scene would be second- or even third-growth timber. The boulders might all be gone from a slide. Anyway, I'd have to think about it."

Again, I palmed the photo. Milo was a hunter and a fisherman. It didn't surprise me that he knew every rock, creek, and other formation in Skykomish County. Besides, it was his job to know the local turf.

"If you think of anything," I said, "let me know."

"Sure." Milo reached into his jacket pocket for a pack of cigarettes and offered one to me.

I accepted. I'd started smoking—again—after Tom was killed. As of September first, I'd quit—again. But it wasn't official. I'd decided that the long weekend had given me a grace period.

"Who wants to know?" Milo asked.

It wasn't his professional inquiry tone, but I didn't like lying to Milo. "A woman in Everett," I replied, hedging my bets.

"Oh." Milo shrugged. Like other natives, he wasn't interested in outsiders.

"Why are you working tonight?" The sheriff pulled night duty only during the investigation of a serious crime.

He gave me a sheepish grin. "Because of the holiday." Which he'd forgotten. "Jack Mullins took last week and most of this one as his vacation, and Dustin Fong took an extra day to visit his folks in Seattle. Believe it or not, we were shorthanded over the weekend."

My reaction was to speak sharply to the sheriff. "You didn't tell me that? It's a story, dammit."

Milo looked surprised. "It is?"

"Of course it is," I said, glaring at him. I turned in the direction of the door to the back-shop. "It beats the hell out of Ethel Pike's crappy lottery ticket."

"Hunh." Milo gazed at me through a puff of smoke.

"Well, I wouldn't want it all over the county that we were at half-speed during a major holiday."

"But it's over," I countered. "The news is that you got through it without any problems. It makes you look like a . . ." I winced at the next word. "Genius."

"Hunh," Milo repeated.

"I'm going to run the damned thing, front page," I declared. "Give me a quote."

"Like what?"

"Like . . ." I booted up Leo's computer, then started typing. "It speaks well of the community and our law enforcement agency in Skykomish County that even though we operated at less than full manpower over the Labor Day weekend, our deputies and staff members were able to meet all the challenges that a national holiday presents."

Milo frowned. "That doesn't sound like me. I'd never say that."

"How about if I put in a couple of 'duhs' and an 'aw-schucks'?"

Milo glowered down at me from his impressive height of six-foot-five. "You're making fun of me, Emma. Don't piss me off."

"I'm making fun of you," I said in a cross tone, "because you and the rest of population don't understand what's news around here. For one thing, names make news. After we get the law enforcement information out of the way, we can get personal. Dustin's visit to his parents. You, having to work an extra shift. And where did Jack go on his vacation?"

"Salmon fishing, up at Glacier Bay," Milo replied, looking only slightly assuaged. "The run's still on, from what we hear."

"Ah." I gave Milo a bogus smile. "That, too, is news in these parts. All of it. Now go away and let me finish the damned story."

With a shake of his head, Milo started to lope out of the

newsroom. But at the door to the front office, he turned around. "By the way, Nina Mullins went with Jack. She bought the Alaska trip at some Catholic auction in Seattle last spring, but she kept it a secret from Jack until now. Sunday was their fifteenth anniversary."

I gave Milo a bleak look. "Thanks," I said with a straight face. "I can use that, too."

I didn't add that I could also use more sources who could figure out a news story from a nail file.

I abandoned my research project that night, having been required to help Kip redo the front page. Ethel Pike was now below the fold, which was just as well, since the photo showing her holding up the twenty-seven-dollar lottery ticket bonanza also revealed that one of her front teeth was missing. Scott had begged her not to smile, but happy old Ethel couldn't resist.

By the time Kip and I finished, it was going on nine o'clock. I was tired, so I went home. Alone. As usual.

Since it was two hours earlier in the part of Alaska where Adam was now residing, I thought about calling him. But phoning to such a remote site as Mary's Igloo involved many obstacles, including the call itself, which was transmitted on some kind of radio relay and caused frustrating delays at both ends of the conversation.

Instead, I dialed Marsha Foster-Klein's number. When she answered, she sounded worse than she had a few hours earlier.

"I took to my bed," she announced, "but I can't sleep, even propped up on pillows. I cough more when I'm recumbent."

I offered sympathy, then posed the question that Vida had asked: "Which is your family name, Marsha? Foster or Klein?"

"Both," Marsha replied. "It was my mother who hyphenated her name—which was Klein—and my father's name of Foster. Why? Have you changed your mind about helping me?"

I hesitated. "I don't feel right about turning you down."

"That's up to you." Marsha coughed three times in a row, taking some of the sting out of her remark.

"What puzzled me," I went on, "is that I thought one of those names might have belonged to your husband."

"I never took his name," Marsha said. "I'd already started practicing law when we were married. Anyway, he died a year later, right after our son was born. Phil had a brain tumor."

"I'm sorry," I said, and meant it. Marsha and I had something else in common besides Tom's murder trial.

"You don't need to apologize," Marsha responded. "You didn't cause the tumor." She coughed steadily for almost a minute. "I'm hanging up now," she gasped.

I heard the click at the other end of the line. After a few minor domestic chores, I took a long bath, went to bed, and tried to read myself to sleep. But sleep didn't come easily these days, even when I was dead tired. Shortly after eleven-thirty, I put my book aside and reached for my handbag, which I kept next to the bed.

I didn't re-read the letter to Marsha, but instead, stared at the old snapshot. What was important about it? Why had it been taken in the first place? Was it because of the trestle—or the rope?

I must have hypnotized myself with that long stare. Five minutes later I went to sleep with the light still on and the photo having slipped onto the floor.

Buddy Bayard's Picture Perfect Photo Studio has always been our version of a photography lab. The next morning I told Vida I was going to show him the snapshot to see if he could identify it. Buddy and his wife Roseanna have an extensive collection of old Alpine pictures.

"An excellent idea," Vida declared. "So you've changed your mind. That's wonderful."

"Marsha's a widow." I almost added, "too." Somehow I thought of myself as a widow. "She has a son, you know."

"Yes, he's college age," Vida remarked. "I'm glad you're doing this. It's good for you."

"It is?" I was dubious.

"Of course," Vida said. "That's why I didn't call Marsha last night to tell her I was stepping in for you. I was sure you'd come 'round."

Which, I assumed, was also why Vida hadn't shown me to her door. She was giving me time to think things through. Darn her hide. She was rarely wrong about people.

"I was thinking of checking the *Blabber* files," she said, ignoring my bemused expression.

The Alpine Blabber was the precursor of the *Advocate*. It was more newsletter than newspaper, published on an irregular basis from the end of World War I to the closure of the original mill in 1929. A gap in local news coverage had existed for almost three years before Marius Vandeventer's father founded the *Advocate*.

"Good idea," I told Vida. "By the way, last night I looked at the index cards on the Iversons. There were two spellings. I take it there must have been two different families in the early days."

Vida was sitting at her desk and wearing one of the more bizarre hats from her collection, a black high-crowned affair with a small gilt-edged picture of a Victorian lady stuck in the satin band. It was reminiscent of the Mad Hatter's headgear from *Alice in Wonderland*.

"No," she said slowly, "that's not the case. The original spelling of Iverson was -*sen*, but they changed it to -*son* years ago. Now let me think why." She rested her cheek on her hand and appeared to concentrate. "It wasn't a family feud. I believe it was because of some scandal. Alas, it was well before my time, and I can't recall it offhand."

"Do you remember how Marsha Foster-Klein is connected to the family?" I inquired.

Vida shook her head. The Victorian lady swayed precariously. "I plan to ask someone tonight at Jack Froland's wake."

I stared. "You're actually going to see Jack-in-the-Box?"

"Duty calls." Vida spoke with a martyr's air.

So did curiosity. "Let me know what you find out," I said and left to seek Buddy Bayard's photographic counsel.

It was another fine September day. At the lower levels where deciduous trees flourished among the evergreens, the cottonwoods, maples, and alders sported bright patches of gold and orange. A few wispy clouds cruised across the sky. In autumns past, I had relished this time of year more than any other. But not the previous year, three months after Tom's death, and not this year. If anything, the beautiful signs of autumn seemed to mock me.

Roseanna Bayard did not mock or chaff. She offered me her gaptoothed smile and a warm welcome. Buddy was in the darkroom, she told me, and offered coffee. I declined, having fulfilled my caffeine requirement for the day.

"Too bad about Jack Froland," Roseanna said as she sorted negatives behind the counter in the waiting room. "I didn't realize he was that sick."

"Cancer, wasn't it?" I replied, admiring the latest Bayard portraits, displayed with soft lighting.

"Yes," Roseanna said. "Colon, I think. But the last I heard, Jack was doing fairly well."

"He was eighty," I pointed out.

"True." Roseanna turned as Buddy emerged from the back. "Here's Himself now."

Buddy's greeting was less enthusiastic than his wife's. "What did we screw up this time?" he asked, the corners of his mouth turned down inside his graying blond goatee.

"Nothing," I replied. "You hardly ever screw up, Buddy."

"But when I do, I hear about it." Our darkroom maven seemed in an uncharacteristically bad mood this morning.

"I want your advice," I said, taking out the snapshot,

which I'd detached from the letter. "What can you tell me about this?"

Buddy scowled as he studied the photo on the counter. "You mean what is it? How would I know? Call the Burlington-Northern office."

The Burlington-Northern & Santa Fe was the railroad company that now ran on the original Great Northern tracks. Amtrak's passenger train also passed through Alpine.

But even as I accepted Buddy's advice, he had one eye focussed on his magnifier. "I know this shot. That is, I've seen other photos taken of the trestle. It's at Burl Creek, even though you can't see it from this angle. That's Mount Baldy in the background. In fact," he went on, no longer grumpy, "I've got a similar shot in my archives. Hold on."

Buddy disappeared again into the back of the studio.

Roseanna grinned at me. "Buddy's a butt today. He's mad because he has to take pictures of Jack Froland in his casket tonight at the viewing. Buddy hates dead bodies."

"I'm not keen on them, either," I admitted. "Does Buddy often get asked to photograph corpses?"

"You'd be surprised," Roseanna replied as Mayor Fuzzy Baugh could be seen about to enter through the glass-paned door. "There are more fools in Alpine than you might imagine," she added, lowering her voice as His Honor entered the studio.

"Well, well," Fuzzy called out in a voice still tinged by his Louisiana roots, "two of our city's fairest ladies are here to greet me. Emma." He offered his hand. "You brave thing."

I'd probably run into the mayor three dozen times since Tom's death; on every occasion, he said the same thing. I tried not to wince as he gave me his perfunctory office seeker's handshake.

"And Roseanna," he said, beaming as he approached the counter. "Lovely as ever."

Judging from the fixed smile on Roseanna's face, I assumed she had heard that salutation at least a hundred times.

"Eleven-thirty," she said to Fuzzy. "You're right on time for your portrait sitting."

Fuzzy had his picture taken every year, and each time Buddy used more filters, more airbrushing, and more touch-ups. But it was good business, since the mayor ordered several dozen copies to be placed in various city, county, and business sites.

"Hey, Fuzz," Buddy called as he reemerged from the back. "Get your butt into the dressing room and make pretty. I'll be right with you."

The mayor continued to smile as he nodded deeply at Roseanna and me before heading off to serve his vanity. Buddy, meanwhile, had laid out three photographs of varying age and size on the counter.

"There you are," he said to me. "This first one is virtually the same shot, same time period, but during the winter."

I gazed at the picture, which was mounted on heavy gray cardboard. It was tinted brown like the snapshot, but there was snow in the background, not deep, only in patches, as if the picture had been taken in late autumn or early spring.

The second photo was a standard black-and-white eight-by-ten, with three men standing on the trestle. Judging from their work clothes, they looked as if they were railroad workers, probably during the Thirties. There were trees on the face of Baldy, perhaps ten to twenty years old. The trestle itself looked different.

"It is different," Buddy replied. "It's new. The Great Northern rebuilt the tracks in the Twenties." He pointed to the third and final photo, which was also an eight-by-ten, also black and white. "I took this one myself about eight years ago. You're looking at third-growth timber. I think it's due to be harvested in another five or six years. If it's allowed."

I hoped it wasn't. At a somewhat higher elevation, the stately evergreens were visible from my house. I supported the loggers, but I didn't want to look at a clear-cut gouge.

"So where is this trestle exactly?" I inquired.

Buddy gave me a curious look. "You don't know?"

"I'm not sure. It could be anywhere along the line outside of town. There aren't any buildings or landmarks in your more recent shot."

"That's the angle I took it from," Buddy explained. "If I'd gone a little lower—which I did in some of the other shots—you'd see Burl Creek. This was taken about a hundred yards from the college's new computer lab."

"Ah." I gazed at Buddy's trio of photographs, then looked again at the snapshot from Marsha. The background had changed over the years, but the railroad tracks were constant. The biggest difference was the rope in the picture I held in my hand. I couldn't see the lower end.

I wondered if it was a noose.

May 1916

It was raining, a typical June day in Alpine. Most of the snow around the town had melted, and the nearby creeks—Icicle, Burl, Carroll, Deception—were discolored and overflowing their banks.

The Alpine Lumber Company's owner stood on the mill's loading dock and surveyed the river flowing two hundred yards below him. "The Skykomish could flood before the week's out," Carl said to his superintendent, Floyd Duell. "The runoff from the higher elevations is coming down much too fast."

"If it does," Floyd replied, "it won't be a problem. The high-water mark has never risen beyond Old Mammoth." He pointed to a huge cedar stump, the flat top of which could have been used as a table for twelve.

Carl, a handsome man of middle age whose bearing was less of a woodsman's and more like the Stanford University alumnus that he was, nodded slowly. "You're right. We have other things to worry about. I don't like the way the strike is dragging on at the Everett shingle mills."

"Carl," Floyd declared with a smile and a shake of his head, "that won't hurt us. Your workers love you. You're a fair employer. They think of you as a father, not a boss."

"I know," Carl said, brushing at the raindrops, which had dripped from the brim of his slouch hat. "It's those blasted Wobblies. They like to stir up trouble. Look at all the mills where they've agitated and created terrible problems. I don't

want them coming anywhere near Alpine. They bring hatred and violence."

Floyd frowned at the mention of the infamous Industrial Workers of the World, whose radical philosophy and intolerable demands went far beyond mere Marxism. "They're the devil, all right," John agreed.

"And they're not far away," Carl said. "They're in Everett, I hear, stirring up trouble since the shingle weavers went on strike."

"That's eighty miles from here, Carl," Floyd pointed out. "That's pretty danged far away."

Carl didn't respond immediately. When he did, his face looked as gloomy as the heavy gray skies. "It's not far enough."

Chapter Three

IT WAS ALMOST lunchtime when I drove out to Burl Creek to study the railroad trestle firsthand. I'd driven past it innumerable times during my years in Alpine. As I got out of my car and looked up, the tracks took on a new meaning. They had a story to tell. I wished I knew what it was.

There was no dangling rope, of course. But across the creek some thirty feet away, I could see the boulders in the original photograph. The cleft was visible, though partially covered with moss. I realized why Milo had recognized it: The creek took a sharp turn on the other side of the trestle and the boulders flanked a decent riffle where trout might lurk. But fish in the local streams were as elusive as any clue to the snapshot's importance. It had to be the rope, which was long gone. If only a noose had been included in the picture. . . . Was it possible that it had been around someone's neck?

Feeling frustrated, I went back to the office where the first calls of outrage over the current issue of the *Advocate* were coming in. Dot Parker was irate because two years ago she'd won twenty-nine dollars with four lottery numbers and we hadn't put it in the paper. Tweeter Hedberg berated us for not publishing the name of the Snohomish store where Ethel Pike bought her lucky ticket. The Rev. Otis Poole from the Baptist church chastised me for promoting gambling.

Vida didn't have time to go through the old issues of *The Alpine Blabber* until mid-afternoon. I was about to volunteer my assistance when Spencer Fleetwood breezed into the newsroom.

"I'm here to issue an invitation," Spence said, leaning against the door frame of my office cubbyhole. For once, he'd shed his Gucci sunglasses, but the rest of his uniform of tailored slacks, cashmere sweater, and gold chain was in place. "Radio Station KSKY celebrates its second anniversary at the end of September. We're throwing a party and you're invited, along with the rest of your staff."

I tried to express enthusiasm. It wasn't easy. The radio station was the newspaper's rival, not only for news—where the *Advocate* was automatically the loser because of our publishing schedule—but for advertising. Despite Leo Walsh's considerable efforts to maintain our ad revenue, we had suffered some setbacks since Spencer Fleetwood's arrival in Alpine.

"When and where's the party?" I inquired with a stiff little smile.

Spence, as he prefers to be called, sat down in one of the visitor chairs, one long leg thrown over the armrest. "Saturday, the thirtieth. It'll be at the ski lodge in the Rufus Runkel Room."

Rufus Runkel was Vida's late father-in-law, and one of the men credited with saving Alpine when Carl Clemans closed the original mill. Rufus and a couple of other old-timers had decided to get in on the growing craze for skiing. The first lifts had been opened in 1931, and the lodge followed a year later.

"We'll do a remote broadcast that evening starting at six o'clock," Spence continued. "We should get a big crowd, so we'll have live interviews, live music, and plenty of delicious, dead fish."

I forced another smile. "It sounds very festive."

Spence turned away just enough to show off his profile. The strong chin, sharp, almost hooked, nose, and high forehead reminded me of a vulture. I suspected that he thought his side view was eaglelike. Either way, Alpine's Mr. Radio struck me as a bird of prey.

"Let's hope it's the party of the year," he said. "Face it, Alpine's usual idea of a big evening involves bowling shirts and half racks."

"May I quote you?"

Spence looked straight at me and chuckled. "No. But you and I are city people. We're a bit more sophisticated than your average Alpiner."

"I wonder," I remarked. Spence was inclined to brag about having lived in Los Angeles, Chicago, Boston, Dallas, and various other major cities. "I've been here eleven years. Maybe I've turned into a real rube."

"Not possible," Spence assured me. "It's how you were raised, not where you end up."

I considered telling Spence that when I was growing up in Seattle, it was still a virtual backwater in the eyes of the rest of the country. But there was no point in arguing. KSKY's owner always had an answer.

"How come you waited until after the paper came out to tell me about the party?" I inquired.

Spence tried to look ingenuous. "It's not official. I won't announce it on the air until Tuesday. The formal invitations to public officials and Chamber of Commerce members won't be mailed until then."

"So why not wait a day? Then I can have the story at the same time you do."

"Hey," Spence responded, looking genuinely surprised. "Why not? Okay, I'll broadcast it late morning, Wednesday. How's that?"

I, too, was surprised. "That's great. Thanks. I appreciate that."

"Then let's celebrate with a drink after work," Spence suggested. "I'd like to talk over some joint promotion plans. What do you say?"

I tried not to recoil. The one and only time that the *Advo-*

cate and KSKY had combined forces for a multimedia promotion was during last year's summer solstice parade when Tom had been killed. The memory jarred me once again.

I guessed it showed. Spence leaned forward and reached out a hand. "Emma, I'm sorry. I know what you're thinking. That's why I haven't mentioned joint promotions until now. Please don't be angry with me."

"I'm not angry," I said stiffly. "I'm just . . . upset."

Spence's brown eyes actually looked sympathetic. "Look—I don't mean to sound harsh, but by the time people get to our age, we've all suffered some kind of terrible tragedy." He saw me open my mouth to protest but waved the hand he'd held out to me. "I know, I know. You're right up there with Jackie Kennedy in Dallas, holding tight to your martyred loved one."

Like the weather, Spence seemed to be mocking me. "What a horrid thing to say." My voice was dry and cracked, like a dead leaf.

"Forget it," Spence snapped, getting to his feet. "I thought you were a businesswoman. When you climb out of that emotional ditch you've dug for yourself, give me a buzz."

With his usual irritating aplomb, Spencer Fleetwood walked away.

I don't cry easily, but my lower lip trembled and my fists shook. Granted, Spence had been very kind to me immediately after Tom's death. I'd begun to think he wasn't an entirely self-centered monster. But if he was one part compassion, he was nine parts phony. It's a wonder he hadn't claimed to have covered the Kennedy assassination.

Vida, of course, had been listening at her desk. When Spence had safely departed, she all but vaulted into my office.

"Oh, dear!" she exclaimed. "You're distraught! Whatever happened?"

For once, I couldn't speak. I merely shook my head,

caught my quivering lower lip in my teeth, and forced my hands to relax.

"Later, maybe," I finally murmured.

Vida nodded. "Of course." She paused. "I've finally gotten through the early issues of the *Blabber*. They're very gossipy, you know."

"You've read them before," I noted, sounding more normal.

"Oh, yes, but years ago." Vida straightened her red bowler. The color was so bright and shiny that it looked as if she were wearing a Chinese cachepot on her head. "Have you a moment? I'll bring some of them in here."

"Sure," I said. I had a feeling that the rest of the day wasn't going to be very productive. After Spence's visit, I felt intellectually as well as emotionally depleted.

The Alpine Blabber had been printed on cheap stock, though it wasn't newsprint. Ginny had carefully slipped each copy into a plastic sleeve for the sake of preservation. Still, the issues—which usually were made up of four six-by-eight pages—had suffered neglect. Some had been patched, many had been taped, and all were yellow with age.

"The *Blabber* is not to be confused with the Alpine Lumber Company's yearbook," Vida cautioned. "Those are all in a bound volume. Of course the original name was the Nippon Lumber Company, which Carl Clemans kept until the end of World War One."

"I know," I replied. The town's early name was Nippon. Carl had changed that, too, but much earlier. "I went through the books a few months ago when I was doing research for an article on early logging."

"What I should have said," Vida amended, "is that the yearbooks are strictly factual. Plenty of news in the sense that they relate all the births, deaths, marriages, moves, and so forth, along with the social and cultural life of the town."

"I know," I repeated, hoping that Vida hadn't embarked on

a lecture. "Features, too, like the article on the Dawson sisters who were born a year or so apart but graduated from high school at the same time. 'Alpine's fairest flowers,' or something like that."

"Yes," Vida replied. "Frank and Mary's girls. The Dawsons had six children, you know. The eldest, Monica—who was nicknamed Babe—returned to Alpine in the Twenties as a bride. I suppose she just couldn't stay away."

I couldn't resist the question: "I take it she remained here for the rest of her life?"

"Well . . . no," Vida admitted. "Her husband was a seagoing man. He got a job on a ship and they moved back to Seattle. Babe was born there, so I suppose she was used to the city." Vida all but shuddered at the notion. "Her father, Frank, was an Englishman, and he had some very queer ideas. When Babe and . . . Katharine, I believe, graduated, he thought they should return to Seattle and go to secretarial school. He was afraid that they might have too much time on their hands in Alpine and get into trouble. Imagine!"

An image of Babe and Katharine standing outside the pool hall with rolled stockings and beaded bags raced through my mind's eye. But all I said was, "That was before your time, right?"

"Considerably," Vida agreed. "Oh, here's an early mention of the Iversens—that's with an *e*—in the *Blabber* from May, 1914 'Trygve and Olga Iversen arrived at camp April 30. Trygve will be the new assistant superintendent of the mill. The Iversens bring with them their four children, Per, Karen, Jonas, and Lars. Per, who is a sturdy lad of twenty-two, will work in the mill as a loader.' " Vida picked up a pencil and made some notes on a white ruled tablet. "A family tree," she said with satisfaction. "We'll be able to see how Marsha might be related. Not to mention"—she winced—"Jack Froland."

I found the next Iversen reference in the second edition of the *Blabber*. "Per, that sturdy young lad, takes a bride in the

September issue. Susan Wicks of Seattle. They were married at a Lutheran church in Ballard, like any good Scandinavian of the era."

"Ballard," Vida murmured. "That part of Seattle was almost exclusively Scandinavian until rather recently, wasn't it?"

"Yes," I said, "but the ethnic groups have diversified in the past few years."

"Trygve Iversen was born in Norway, as was his wife, Olga," Vida recalled. "My mother once told me that Olga never really learned to speak English. Indeed, she rarely spoke at all. Tsk, tsk."

We remained silent for several minutes, perusing the fragile newsletters. "Are we looking only for Iversen/Iverson references?" I finally asked. One more euphoric comment about Mrs. De Bie's Belgian waffles or Head Cook Patterson's flapjacks and I was either going to sleep or going to eat.

"At this point, yes," Vida replied. "I'm still trying to make the connection with Marsha."

"Why don't we ask her?"

"I thought she didn't know," Vida replied, looking puzzled. "I suppose we could ask again."

I dialed Marsha's home number but got her machine. Next, I tried the courthouse and was put through to her chambers.

"I dragged my butt in for the morning session," Marsha said, sounding somewhat better. "Now I'm about to go home and take to my bed again. What's up?"

I related that Vida believed Marsha was somehow connected to the Iverson dynasty. "Does that ring any bells?" I asked.

"The Iversons," Marsha repeated. "Don't they own the Venison Inn?"

I said that was so. "Jack and Helene owned it for years, but when his nephew, Fred, got hurt in the woods, Jack brought him and his wife, Opal, in as partners. Jack's been threatening to retire."

"My Aunt Josephine was married to an Iverson," Marsha said after a long pause, "but they lived in Mount Vernon. Uncle Burt was killed during World War II, and Aunt Jo remarried a few years later. Frankly, I lost track of her. The last I heard, she was in a nursing home in Port Angeles or some place. She must be ancient."

I gave Vida a high sign. "Was your Uncle Burt from Alpine?"

"I'm not sure," Marsha responded. "He'd been dead years and years before I was born. We were never close with that side of the family. Aunt Jo was my dad's sister. My mother and Uncle Burt fought over politics, I think. Anyway, I hardly remember seeing Aunt Jo except at the wedding of one of my brothers. She didn't come to mine."

Vida was making wild gestures with her hands. I became so distracted that I had to terminate the conversation with Marsha. "Sorry, I've got to go. There's a whirling dervish in my office. Get well."

I hung up and gave Vida an exasperated look. "What?"

"Burt Iverson," Vida said, her gray eyes glinting. "He was one of Per's children. Burt had married before the war and moved away, then he went in the army and was killed in North Africa. Kasserine Pass, as I recall. Since he'd grown up here, a big fuss was made when we got the sad news. You'll see his name inscribed on the war memorial at the courthouse."

"So that's the Iverson connection to our judge," I remarked.

"Tenuous, at best," Vida said, adding onto her family tree, which she had transferred to a large sheet from the tablet Leo kept for manually laying out ads. "Josephine—his widow—married a Bergstrom after the war. They lived in Sultan for years, then he died, and Josephine came to live with her daughter. Now what was her name?" Vida thought for several seconds. "Marjorie. Marjorie's husband—dear me, I forget his name—took a job in Port Angeles. Josephine went into the nursing home here, but left on her own and went to join Marjorie over on the Peninsula. Don't you remember that Josephine was reported as a missing person about four years ago?"

"Vaguely," I replied. "She wasn't missing for long."

"Of course not," Vida replied. "Marjorie came to the nursing home to collect her mother's belongings. Then we heard where the crazy old fool had gone. Port Angeles! All those ferries you have to take to get there."

"What a scamp," I murmured as Scott Chamoud squeezed into the office.

"There's a forest fire up on Martin Creek," he said. "Do you want pictures?"

I gazed—as always with pleasure—at my handsome reporter. "How bad is it?"

Scott shrugged. "Not too bad right now. But the woods are really dry. Look at all those wildfires we've had over in eastern Washington. The arrow on the Skykomish Ranger Station sign still points to 'extreme danger.' "

It had been a terrible summer for fires, not just in Washington, but across the entire country. Until now, Skykomish County had been spared.

"Do they know how it started?" I asked.

Scott was loading film into his camera. "A ground fire broke out early this morning. Careless campers, maybe."

"They should be imprisoned," Vida said.

I agreed. "Go ahead, Scott, but be careful. Have they brought in a fire crew?"

"Yes. They're digging trenches to contain the fire. It's only about two or three acres. Depending on how the wind blows, the fire could move northwest, right into Martin Creek." His handsome face looked excited. Scott was still young enough to be enthusiastic about a new kind of assignment, particularly one with a hint of danger.

"How are you going to get there?" I asked.

Scott gave me a puzzled look. "In my Jeep. There's an old logging road. The fire's at the twenty-eight-hundred-foot level, just south of where Kelley Creek goes into Martin."

I glanced at Vida who looked blank, and no doubt sorry for it. I'd never been on that particular road, and I guessed she hadn't either. There was nothing in the area that couldn't be seen from a nearer, safer vantage point.

"Can't you get a ride up there with one of the Forest Service people?" I asked, feeling like Scott's mother.

Scott cocked his head to one side. "Emma, we're not talking about a conflagration. I don't mean to disrespect you, but it's not like Yellowstone or one of those other mammoth fires like they have in eastern Washington."

"Okay," I said, "but be careful. We haven't had much rain lately. The fire could get out of control in a hurry."

Scott saluted, then dashed off to seek his thrill.

"They intended to burn Alpine to the ground, you know," Vida said with a dark expression. "Without Mr. Clemans's mill, the town had little reason to exist. Thank goodness for my father-in-law and Olaf the Obese."

I paid brief homage to the old-timers' entrepreneurial spirit, then leaned back in my chair and stretched a bit. "What are we doing, Vida?"

"Research." She frowned at me. "Why do you ask?"

"Because I don't think the *Blabber* or early copies of the *Advocate* are going to tell us much about Marsha Foster-Klein's great sin. Whatever that may be."

I expected Vida to be annoyed, but she wasn't. "Maybe we've found out everything we can from these old issues. At least we know there is a connection between Marsha and the Iversons."

"Which gets us nowhere." I yawned. The afternoon had grown quite warm, and the sloping tin roof over my cubbyhole raised the temperature inside by at least ten degrees.

"It's a start." Vida stood up, tugging her print dress down

over the hem of her white slip. "Surely we'll find some-thing."

By five o'clock, Scott Chamoud hadn't returned from Martin Creek. I stood on the sidewalk outside of the *Advocate* office and looked northeast. Sure enough, I could see billows of dark smoke in the further reaches between Mount Baldy and Windy Mountain. A small plane circled overhead, probably a Forest Service lookout. The wind had changed, now coming from the north. I could smell the smoke. That was not a good sign. The fire would be fanned in the direction of Highway 2 with only Deception Creek—which was very low this time of year—in its way.

I told myself that Scott was probably having the time of his life. He'd been gone only a little over an hour. Putting my worries aside, I went home.

Such was my state of mind these days that I had sunken to eating TV dinners. But lately, I'd made a small effort to improve my lifestyle. I no longer microwaved the dinners but actually baked them in the oven. One day at a time.

While waiting for my feast—Mexican tonight, olé!—I drank a glass of bourbon and 7UP and watched the Mariners play the Blue Jays in Toronto. The three-hour time difference meant that I could eat during the last two innings.

By the time I'd finished dinner and the Mariners had finished the Jays, the smell of smoke had permeated the log walls of my house. I went outside to see if the fire had spread.

There seemed to be more smoke. My view from above the town showed a haze over the business district six blocks below. The wind had died down; the air was quite still. This wasn't the first forest fire I'd watched in Alpine, but there was something ominous about the quiet that had settled over the town along with the haze. The entire population couldn't have gone to see Jack-in-the-Box.

The phone rang just as I went back inside. It was Scott, calling on his cell.

"Hey," he said over a connection that was marred by static, "I got some great pix. This thing has spread toward Embro Lake, but the fire crews expect to have it out by morning."

"You're okay?"

"Sure." He laughed, or maybe the sharp sound was static. "I'm kind of warm, but this is really cool. If you know what I mean."

"I do." I'd gone back to the front porch where I gazed again at the billowing clouds of smoke. "Exactly where are you?"

"Well . . ." Scott sounded uncertain. "I'm on Department of Natural Resources land, according to my buddies here. We're off the road about a quarter of a mile." He paused. "What's that?" Apparently, he was speaking to someone nearby. I could hear another voice, very faint. I could also hear what sounded like the snapping of branches and more dimly, the fire itself. "We're at about the forty-five-hundred-foot level."

"When are you coming down?" I asked.

"What? I can't hear you very well."

I raised my voice and repeated the question.

"Not right . . ." There was a loud noise, like a champagne cork, and then nothing but static. Apparently we'd lost the connection. At least, I hoped that was all we lost.

Maybe, I thought, I should be at the fire scene, too. But if Scott was right, by the time we ran the story in the next issue, it might be relegated to page two.

For the next two hours, I puttered around the house but kept my eye on the fire across the valley. As darkness settled in, I could see several pockets of flames. The smell of burning wood is usually a pleasant, comforting aroma. But the smoke was thickening over the town and turning acrid. I closed all the windows and considered going to bed.

The phone rang again just as I was heading into the bathroom.

"Emma." It was Vida, sounding perturbed. "What are you doing?"

"Nothing, really. Why?"

"I'm calling from Driggers Funeral Home. Can you come over to the Froland house?"

"What for?"

I could hear her take a deep breath. "Something's amiss," she said, lowering her voice to its familiar stage whisper.

"Don't tell me Jack got out of the box."

"No, no, nothing like that." There was a long pause. "June Froland is in a state of collapse. She insists that Jack was murdered."

June 1916

The mail had arrived as it always did, on the ten-thirty Great Northern freight train. Mary Dawson had picked up the family's delivery at Alpine's general store. There was a postcard of the Isle of Wight from her husband's family in England, the new Sears Roebuck catalog for fall, and a letter from her in-laws in Seattle. Bad news, Mary thought. It was almost always bad news when Fred and the other Mary wrote to their son and his wife.

Her two older daughters, Monica, nicknamed Babe, and Kate, met her at the door of the family's small house above the Great Northern railroad tracks.

"Can we see the catalog, Mama?" Kate begged, trying to elbow Babe out of the way.

"If you behave like young ladies instead of hooligans," Mary replied, handing the big book over to Babe. "Here. Don't get any big ideas."

Mary sat down in a spindle-back chair by the window. She read the postcard first: "Fine weather here, fishing tomorrow. Watched the yachts off Cowes yesterday. Will walk the chalk downs Sunday."

Reluctantly, Mary opened the letter from the senior Dawsons. Did they need money again? With five children and possibly—Mary wasn't certain yet—another on the way, it was hard enough to make ends meet on Frank's salary at the mill.

But this time Fred and Mary didn't want to get anything

from their kinfolk. They wanted to give. And that was worse news than a request for twenty dollars.

"Dearest Frank and Mary," the letter read. "With summer upon us, it is very difficult to keep young Vincent occupied. We thought it would do him good to stay with you for a while in Alpine. He is a good boy, but restless, and sometimes makes Mary very nervy. If it is all right with you, he will arrive next Monday on the four o'clock train. We bless you for your kindness to your poor orphaned nephew.

"Your Papa and Mummy send their love to all."

Mary slapped the letter down on her apron-covered lap. "Nervy, my foot," Mary said under her breath. "The woman's crazy as a loon."

"What did you say, Mama?" Babe asked as Kate yanked the catalog out of her older sister's hands.

Mary smiled guiltily at the girls. "Nothing." She paused as little Frances toddled into the room on chubby pink legs. "How would you like to have your cousin Vincent for company?"

Babe clapped her hands. "That sounds wonderful!"

Kate made a face. "I don't like Vincent. He's no good."

Frances, who had just turned four, turned blue eyes on her sisters and spit up all over her cotton pinafore.

Chapter Four

VIDA GAVE ME the Frolands' address, which was on Spruce Street across from the high school football field. I got there in under five minutes, recognizing Al Driggers's black funeral car out front.

Apparently Al had just arrived. He got out of the driver's seat as the Reverend Donald Nielsen emerged from the passenger's seat. Each man opened the rear door on his side of the limo. As I approached from my parking spot a few yards away, all I could see were their bent backs.

But I could hear high-pitched shrieks coming from inside the funeral car. I was approaching with caution when Vida pulled up in her Buick. I waited for her to join me while a third man backed out of the limo's rear compartment. As more and more of his black-suited figure appeared, I could see that his hands were gripping a woman's ankles.

"That's Max," Vida said in her stage whisper as she appeared at my side. "The son. I don't think June wants to get out of the car. Oh, dear, listen to that! My ears are about to burst."

Vida wasn't entirely exaggerating. The piercing screams cut through the smoky air as Max and Al forcibly removed the stricken woman from the limo. Her stout legs flailed, her flabby arms waved, and her vocal cords were strained with hysterical cries.

For the first time, I noticed a half-dozen people congregated in the Frolands' front yard. Vida saw them, too, and with one hand on her beribboned black hat, she marched up to the paved walkway.

"What are you doing here?" she demanded of the group. "Didn't you see what happened after the viewing?"

Bessie Griswold, who was, to put it charitably, six ax-handles across, set her fists on her wide hips. "What do you mean, Vida? Jack's kid said there was coffee and cookies at the house. We left the funeral parlor then. What else do we need to know?"

"Yeah," chimed in George Engebretsen, one of our aged county commissioners. "June makes those real good ones—krumkake, filled with whipped cream."

Vida pointed at the funeral car where Al Driggers and the others were still grappling with June. "There's no coffee klatch tonight. June is overcome."

To prove the point, the bereaved widow let out a blood-curdling shriek.

"Good God," exclaimed Jack Iverson, Jack Froland's nephew and namesake. "Auntie sounds pretty bad."

"She is," Vida declared. "Go home. Now. You'll have to wait for your treats until after the funeral tomorrow."

Bessie Griswold shot Vida a dirty look. "You better not eat all those cookies tonight," she warned, as she started down the walk. The others trailed behind her. They stopped, however, on the sidewalk as three or four neighbors came out of their houses to see what was going on. June Froland was drawing quite a crowd.

Reverend Nielsen, with his long-legged step, had hurried ahead to the front porch where he opened the door. Max, who was carrying his mother's lower extremities, momentarily stumbled over the threshold, causing Al to trip on the porch's top stair. They bobbled their burden but righted themselves as June Froland emitted a groan that sounded like a cross between that of a wounded bear and a hoot owl.

I'd started to follow, but Vida put a hand on my arm. "Wait

a moment," she said, gesturing at an approaching car. "I called Doc Dewey. Here he comes now."

"Has June gone off her rocker?" I asked as Doc's modest dark blue sedan pulled in ahead of the limo.

"That's a relative thing with June," Vida said. "I've always thought she was a bit mental."

Since Vida thought that of many Alpine residents, I didn't take her diagnosis seriously. With a windmill-like wave, she called to Doc Dewey.

"Yoo-hoo! They've taken June inside. It might take a while to get her in bed."

The onlookers, who now numbered more than a dozen, moved closer to the doctor.

"Is June done for?" called George Engebretsen.

Doc, who was carrying his medical kit, gave the county commissioner a mild look of reprimand. "June's upset. She'll be fine." He turned to Vida and me, nodding and smiling. "Not uncommon after a loved one has died, I'm afraid." He paused, his expression even more kindly than usual. "You were very brave after Tom died, Emma."

"I was drugged to the eyeballs for a week," I replied. "Four Valium and a quart of Wild Turkey work wonders."

"I didn't prescribe the whiskey," Doc said, wagging a finger. "That was your brother's doing."

"I think he drank most of it," I murmured as we headed into the Froland house, where June's wails could be heard in the distance.

"I know the way," Doc said, leading us past the living room and down a narrow hall. "I visited Jack here a few times."

I knew June Froland only by sight, a plump little person with a dour manner. As we crowded into the small bedroom, I was shocked by her anguished appearance as she heaved convulsively on top of the covers.

Reverend Nielsen's eyes were cast toward the ceiling. I assumed he was praying. Al was attempting to hold June's hand, but she kept snatching it away and began hurling words of abuse at the undertaker.

"Fiends!" she screeched. "Go away! I can feel the evil! Murder! Oh, God!" She turned her face to the wall and began to sob again.

"Ma," Max said in a pleading voice, "please. You're making yourself sick."

But Max's ma kept screaming incoherently. Doc moved closer to the bed, then spoke quietly to the rest of us.

"It might be best if you'd all leave the room," he said. "There isn't much space in here. And make sure those people outside don't try to get in the house."

I immediately turned to leave, but Vida grasped Doc by the arm. "Don't you need help?"

Doc shook his bald head. "No, Vida. I've done this before. You go along with the others."

Doc Dewey must have been one of the few people on the planet who could make Vida obey without an argument. She did sniff slightly but followed the rest of us into the hall.

"Emma," she said, gesturing at Max, a bearded man of middle age with sharp brown eyes, "this is Max Froland, Jack and June's son. I remember him as a little boy, playing with his hula hoop up and down Sixth Street."

Max looked pained but forced a smile as he shook my hand. "It wasn't a hula hoop. It was a ten-speed I won in a Chamber of Commerce drawing. I was fifteen."

Al, wearing his usual mournful expression, motioned at Max. "Do you mind if I leave, Mr. Froland? I don't think there's any more I can do here, and I have to make preparations for the service tomorrow."

Max held out his hand. "Go ahead, Mr. Driggers," he said in a deep, husky voice. "On your way out, could you disperse the gawkers?"

"I'll do my best," Al promised. He nodded at the rest of us and took his leave just as Doc entered the living room.

"I've given June a sedative," Doc said quietly. "She's

already calming down and should go to sleep in just a minute or two." He shook his head. "Poor woman—I guess the viewing was too much for her."

"Does she have a history of hysteria?" I asked.

"No," Doc replied. "She's never been an emotional woman. June's always had remarkably good health. I've been her physician since my father died ten years ago."

Gerald Dewey, known as Young Doc, had inherited Cecil Dewey's practice. The senior Dewey, of course, was known as Old Doc. Alpiners still referred to Gerald as Young Doc despite the fact that he was now well into middle age.

"She's a woman of great faith," Pastor Nielsen declared. "She must know that Jack is with our savior now."

Vida, who was Presbyterian to her toes, shot the Lutheran minister a sharp look. "It's how Jack got there that seems to have disturbed her."

Pastor Nielsen gave Vida a kindly smile. "That's not the real point, is it, Mrs. Runkel?"

"Oh, bother," Vida huffed, then beckoned me into the kitchen. "Let me tell you what happened. I'd rather that Max didn't overhear. This must be very hard on him."

I recalled the obituary with its list of survivors. There had been only one, the son who lived in Seattle. Max's sister, whose name I'd forgotten, had died years ago.

"After the viewing," Vida began, "Max invited everyone back here for coffee and cake. But suddenly June, who'd been holding up rather well, started to cry. Not sobbing, but more like hysterics, wailing and thrashing about. Naturally, Al Driggers took charge. He did his best to calm her, as did Max, but she wouldn't quiet down. Finally, she shrieked that Jack had been murdered. That's when I called Doc Dewey. I honestly believed June had become unhinged. Max announced that they wouldn't be hosting any kind of do at the house."

"I shouldn't think so," I put in.

Vida looked miffed. "Yes, but those greedy pigs outside

had already raced off to get here first. No doubt George Engebretsen didn't want to be cheated of his krumkake. But I digress." Vida glanced out into the living room. "Pastor Nielsen is leaving. Good riddance." She paused, scanning the kitchen counters. "I wonder where that krumkake is. Indeed, I wonder if June actually made any."

Vida was looking in the cupboards when Doc came into the kitchen. "I told Max that his mother will sleep for a few hours," he said, rolling down his shirtsleeves. "I'll be on call, so I let Max know that if she wakes up and resumes her hysteria, she should be hospitalized."

Giving up on her search, Vida nodded. "Very wise, Doc. Thank you for coming so quickly."

"That's my job," Doc said with a weary smile. Like his father before him, the younger Dewey still made house calls, at least to his elderly patients. He'd finally gotten some help at the clinic in the form of Elvis Sung, a young physician originally from Hawaii. But Dr. Sung's skin wasn't a pure white shade, and he'd been in Alpine for less than two years. Naturally, the locals still preferred Doc Dewey.

Doc shrugged into his jacket and eyed me closely. "When was the last time you paid me a visit, Emma?"

"Umm . . . a year ago?" I'd been in the hospital for almost two days after Tom was killed. I'd checked in with Doc a week after the funeral, then had seen him once more, in early August. There wasn't much he could do for a broken heart.

"You look peaky to me," he said. "Make an appointment for next week. Promise?"

"Okay." If nothing else, it might make Doc feel better.

His stalwart figure moved out of the kitchen, though he stopped for a word with Max Froland.

I turned to Vida. "As you were saying?"

"You know the rest. Al drove her here in the funeral home car. Max and Pastor Nielsen rode with them, and I gather that June was incoherent for the entire trip. Of course it's only five blocks." Vida eyed the teakettle next to the sink. "I really could use a cup of tea."

The kitchen was small, with outdated appliances and worn linoleum flooring. It was not very tidy, but I couldn't fault June Froland's housekeeping. As I well knew, death has a way of disrupting routine. There was no sign of preparations for a post-viewing get-together. Maybe June and Max had planned to wing it.

I cleared off an aluminum-backed chair and sat down. "I assume June's accusation was unfounded. Did she say who'd murdered Jack?"

Vida shook her head. In her black swing coat and a bonnet with its ribbons streaming over her shoulders, she looked like something out of Dickens. "June kept repeating—between screeches—that Jack had been killed." Vida sat down across from me, waiting for the water to boil.

"That's it?" I said. "She made no accusations or mentioned how Jack might have been killed?"

"Not that I heard," Vida replied. "Of course I was on the phone to Doc for a short time."

"Weird." I stared at the soiled cotton cloth on the small kitchen table. "June was aware that Jack's condition was terminal, I assume."

"I'm sure she was," Vida replied. "She always went to the doctor with him. Or so my niece Marje Blatt told me."

Marje, the receptionist at the clinic, was one of Vida's many sources who were also related to her. I sometimes thought her news network rivaled CNN.

"June's in denial," I remarked as Max Froland rather diffidently came to stand in the kitchen doorway.

"May I?" he asked.

"Goodness, yes!" Vida cried, the black ribbons swinging at her shoulders. "This is your home, isn't it? Would you care for some tea?"

"Yes, thanks." Max looked wistful. "My parents didn't drink alcohol. Frankly, I'd prefer a stiff vodka martini."

I was about to agree with Max, but Vida intervened. "Your mother is an abstemious woman. In my opinion, that's a virtue."

"Pa wasn't so virtuous," Max said with a droll expression. "But Ma wouldn't let him keep liquor in the house. That's why he spent so much time at Mugs Ahoy."

I remembered the line from the obit that mentioned Jack Froland's drinking partners at the local tavern. "It doesn't seem that drink killed your father," I noted.

"No." Max shook his head sadly. "I think it kept him going. In fact, I came up here to visit two weeks ago. He seemed better than he had in months."

"Perhaps he'd gone into remission," Vida said, finding some mismatched cups and saucers in a cupboard. "Cream or sugar?"

"Neither," Max replied, leaning against the counter by the stove. There were only two chairs in the kitchen. There was no dining room, and I wondered where the Frolands entertained. Maybe they didn't.

"I don't know about remission," Max said after Vida had handed him his tea. "My folks never mentioned it when I was here. To be candid, they weren't quick to pick up on medical terms, even with Pa's cancer. They were old school, the kind of people who never question what the doctor says and don't ask for explanations."

"So foolish," Vida murmured.

"I agree," Max said. He had the burly build of his father, but his mother's dark coloring. In physical terms, I could imagine the son following the father into the mill. But he hadn't. Max looked comfortable in his dark suit, pale blue shirt, and tasteful tie. I suspected he was some kind of professional man.

"So," Vida said, also still standing, "do you believe your mother was out of line when she said your father had been murdered?"

"No," Max replied. "I assume she meant murdered by cancer. Or the medical profession that couldn't save him."

"I see." But Vida sounded dubious.

Max caught the tone in her voice. "Do you mean you put some stock in her rantings?"

"N-o-o," Vida answered slowly. "But it did strike me as a strange thing to say."

Max's smile was ironic. "You mean my mother wasn't a particularly imaginative woman."

"Nor fanciful," Vida allowed.

Max set his cup and saucer down on the counter. "That's true. But why would anyone murder Pa? It's absurd. My parents had nothing except for this house, Pa's pension, and a bit of savings. I live alone, I don't need money. Except for the usual bickering with his coworkers before he retired. I can't think of any enemies he might have had. You don't kill over who doesn't pony up for a round at Mugs Ahoy."

It would have been tactless to ask if Jack and June got along, so I kept my mouth shut. Vida, of course did not: "Your parents seemed to live separate lives."

Max chuckled. "Are you hinting at a love triangle, Mrs. Runkel?"

"No," Vida responded, "of course not. But your father spent his spare time at the tavern or watching TV. Your mother was a member of the Burl Creek Thimble Club. She crocheted and read romance novels. I don't recall them ever taking any big trips. I interviewed them only once, six years ago when they drove to Spokane for a family wedding."

"They didn't like to drive," Max said. "Not after Lynn was killed in that accident up at the summit."

Lynn. I recalled the name of the late Froland daughter from the obituary. I didn't recall the accident. It must have happened before I arrived in Alpine.

"Yes," Vida said, "I can see how such a tragedy might affect them. But of course that was in the winter and there was black ice on the road. Your family has had its share of sadness. Especially you, Max. It seems like only yesterday that your wife passed away."

Max lowered his gaze. "Jackie was only thirty-two. We'd been married less than five years. You don't expect such a young person to die of an aneurysm."

"Such a loss," Vida said with a sad shake of her head. "And then to find out that she was six weeks pregnant. How did you bear it, Max?"

Max gave Vida a grim look. "Is there a choice other than putting a gun to your head?"

"No." Vida glanced in my direction. "You have to be strong. And you have been, Max. I greatly admire you for it."

I turned away, reaching for the sugar bowl. I didn't feel strong. And I certainly wasn't admirable.

Maybe I really was a grief diva.

Maybe it was time to change.

Vida insisted that I attend Jack Froland's funeral the following morning. "Don't you want to see what happens next?" she demanded.

I started to reply that I'd attended one too many funerals already but thought of my resolve the previous evening. "Do you really expect that something will happen?"

"Who knows?" Vida retorted. "That's the interesting thing about funerals." She suddenly blanched. "Oh dear, I shouldn't have said that! Never mind, you don't have to go if you don't want to."

I searched my conscience before making a decision. "The truth is, Vida, I've got a paper to put out. Yesterday we wasted half the afternoon going through those old issues of the *Blabber*. I think I'd better stay close to the office and figure out an interesting feature for Scott and an electrifying editorial for me."

"You have the fire story for your lead if nothing more current comes along," Vida said. "Scott must have taken some excellent photos."

Scott had come to work late, which had worried me. But instead of being turned into toast at Embro Lake, he'd merely been tired. The fire was still burning, but under control. Scott had waited for the formal announcement, which had come shortly before five in the morning. Four hours sleep hadn't affected his looks, however.

"So how did the fire start?" I asked after Vida had returned to her desk and begun two-fingered typing on her old upright.

Scott was pouring himself a second cup of coffee. "They don't know. Careless campers are always good suspects, but there's no good place to pitch a tent in that area. Hikers, maybe, stopping for a smoke or a toke."

Leo Walsh, who had been on the phone, slammed down the receiver. "Dammit, Fred and Jack Iverson are pulling their standing ad for next week. Fred says he's doing it out of respect for Jack Froland."

"Hey," Scott put in, "aren't there too many Jacks in this town? Whatever happened to originality?"

Vida looked up from her typewriter. "Both Jack Froland and Jack Iverson are actually named John. Indeed, Jack Iverson was named for his uncle. Both Jacks were grandsons of Trygve Iverson, though born fourteen years apart."

Scott shook his head. "I don't know how you keep everybody in this town straight, Vida. Why don't they just call all the guys Swede?"

"Because the Iversons are Norwegians," Vida said.

I perched on the edge of Leo's desk. "Couldn't you talk Fred and Jack into running an In Memoriam ad?"

Leo made a face. "I tried. No go. By coincidence, Fred and Opal are going on vacation next week. They're closing the Venison Inn for repairs."

"Then hit them with a big reopening ad," I said.

"I will," Leo replied, looking determined. "The upside is that they're also pulling the Venison Inn ad from KSKY."

"That restaurant could use some work," Scott remarked. "It looks like it hasn't been renovated since the Sixties."

"That's correct," Vida said. "They closed down after President Kennedy was killed in 1963. That's the last time they remodeled."

"They could use a new menu, too," Scott said. "There's only one decent place in town for a really nice meal, and that's the ski lodge."

"Don't forget Le Gourmand out on the highway," I said. "They often make the top twenty lists of best restaurants in the state."

"But it's way out of my price range," Scott responded, no doubt blaming me for his less than opulent salary. "A meal for two costs close to a hundred bucks if you want a couple of glasses of wine."

Scott was dating a professor from Skykomish Community College, a somewhat older beauty named Tamara Rostova. Even college instructors made more than Scott, an economic fact that no doubt embarrassed him.

"We need more ad revenue," I declared, with a glance at Leo.

"We need more advertisers," Leo shot back. "Since when don't I work my butt off scrounging up ads?"

"Of course you do," I said, "but maybe we should come up with a special promotion to tide us over between now and Halloween."

"The college," Scott suggested. It was hardly a surprise, since I figured his mind was there much of the time. "Unlike the other schools, they don't start fall quarter until the end of the month."

"We included them in the Back to School edition," Leo pointed out.

The newsroom went silent until Ginny came in with the mail. "What's wrong?" she asked, looking alarmed. "Did something awful happen?"

Leo waved a dismissive hand. "No. We're thinking. It's done best when not talking. You got any ideas for a new kind of special edition?"

Ginny handed Vida her mail. Our House & Home editor was always first on the delivery list.

"Autumn," Ginny said, moving to Leo's desk. "What about things people do in the fall?"

"How many pictures of leaf raking can Scott take?" Leo asked dryly.

Ginny, whose scarcity of imagination is rivaled only by her lack of a sense of humor, frowned at Leo. "People do other things. Like prune. Oh—and dig up bulbs and tubers that won't winter in this climate."

No one said anything for almost a minute. It was Vida who finally spoke up: "That's not really a bad idea, Ginny. Leo could get large ads from Harvey's Hardware and Mountain View Gardens and some of the other stores that provide plants and tools and such."

Scott was fingering his chin. "How about a tie-in with the environment? Energy conservation, too. Preparing your house for winter and all that."

"Well . . ." Leo paused to light a cigarette while Vida, as usual, stared him down. "That does have some possibilities. Let me think about it. Thanks, Ginny."

"I like it," I said. "Fall officially starts September twentieth." I looked at Leo. "Do we have enough time to pull it together for the edition on the thirteenth?"

"I'll see," Leo replied, his weathered face showing no expression.

"Do that," I said as a spur. I had the feeling that despite his polite words to Ginny, he wasn't entirely sold on the project.

Half an hour later, Vida was off to attend the Froland funeral. I worked on a list of possible features for the proposed autumn edition. The more I thought about Ginny's idea, the better I liked it. The broadness of scope meant that there were plenty of advertisers to tap. Home improvement. Yard work. Energy. Fashion. Food. "An Alpine Autumn." That sounded good to me.

By noon, I was so pleased with the concept that instead of

eating in, I decided to call Milo and see if he wanted to meet me for lunch at the Venison Inn. I was told, however, that the sheriff wasn't in. Feeling slightly deflated, I walked down Front Street to the restaurant. There I encountered a CLOSED sign on the door and a handwritten message taped to the glass.

THE VENISON INN WILL BE CLOSED BEGINNING FRIDAY, SEPT. EIGHTH, UNTIL MONDAY, SEPT. EIGHTEENTH, IN MEMORY OF
JOHN AUGUSTUS (JACK) FROLAND.

I'd forgotten about the closure. Annoyed, I started to cross the street to the Burger Barn but stopped just short of the curb. It was twelve-ten, about the time that Jack Froland's funeral would be over. Vida would probably go to the cemetery. I could meet her there and see if she wanted to go to lunch. Ordinarily, Vida wouldn't miss a post-funeral get-together, but I figured that after the fracas the previous night, any socializing at the Froland home would be cancelled.

I drove down Front Street, all the way to Highway 187, or the Icicle Creek Road as it was unofficially known. Smoke still hung in the air, and the sky was overcast. The temperature was close to seventy degrees, which wasn't all that warm, yet the hazy skies spread an oppressive air over the town. Perhaps it was my imagination. I hadn't attended a burial since Tom's, which had been held not in Alpine but in San Francisco, where he had lived for years with his family.

"Damn!" I said aloud as the steep road curved ahead of me. Can I do this?

"You damned well better," said a crackling voice inside me. It sounded like Ben. I kept driving and finally entered through the cemetery's open iron gates.

It wasn't hard to find the Froland mourners. The cemetery is built on hilly ground. The road at the entrance dips down, so I slowed enough to spot the line of cars pulled up on the verge and the cluster of people under a green canopy.

I parked behind the last car. To my left I saw the Runkel monument, a solid granite monolith that marked the graves of Rufus Runkel and several other family members, including Vida's late husband, Ernest. She had told me that she would be buried beside Ernest and that the headstone was already in place. She'd bought it when Ernest died over twenty years ago.

"It was such a bargain," she'd said. "I couldn't turn it down."

I'd never looked closely at the Runkel family plot. I couldn't bear to see Vida's name there, even though in my lighter moments, I'd wondered if she'd have a periscope installed with her so that she could keep track of the local happenings even from the grave.

At least two dozen cars were parked alongside the road. I trudged across the grass, which showed ominous patches of brown, a reminder of our tinder-dry surroundings. As always, I noticed the strange markers that looked like sawed-off tree trunks. I'd finally done some research and written a feature about them, explaining that they were a favored cemetery item from the turn of the last century and represented the Tree of Life. They were often the choice of people who had worked in the timber industry, though their popularity wasn't exclusive to job or class, and they had been sold through the Sears Roebuck catalogs.

To my surprise, June Froland was at the graveside, seated in a sturdy chair. Her chin rested on her bosom and her hands were slack in her lap. I wondered if she was so medicated that she'd fallen asleep.

Pastor Nielsen was praying over the pale blue casket as I sidled up to my House & Home editor.

"Well," she said in her stage whisper, "you came. Now why is that?"

"Lunch," I said under my breath. "Do you want to eat with me after this is over?"

"Oh, dear," Vida replied. "I brought lunch because I heard there's no post-burial function. June barely made it to the funeral. I understand she's heavily sedated."

As the casket was being lowered into the ground, several people turned our way. Vida's sister-in-law Mary Lou Hinshaw gave us a dirty look and put a finger to her lips in a shushing gesture.

"Nitwit," Vida breathed.

Al Driggers handed Max a shovel. The son was about to put the symbolic dirt on his father's casket when a siren cut through the air, startling us all.

Everyone turned to the road where Milo Dodge's Grand Cherokee was coming to a stop in front of the hearse. The siren, which the sheriff—in an uncharacteristic flight of fancy—had ordered through Harvey's Hardware, was the wah-woo-wah-wah sound of the British police. Milo had sent for it not long after we broke up. I figured it was the masculine equivalent of the feminine change of hair color following a broken romance.

Max stood stiffly with the shovel in his hand. June's head slowly lifted. Pastor Nielsen looked annoyed. Fred and Opal Iverson, standing with several other kinfolk, eyed the sheriff with curiosity. Only Al Driggers—ever the professional—showed no emotion whatsoever.

"Hold it!" Milo shouted, loping awkwardly to the grave site. He winced as the widow Froland scowled at him. "Sorry, June, sorry, folks." The sheriff removed his regulation hat. For at least ten seconds, he shifted from one foot to the other, looking like a student caught in class without an answer.

Finally, turning to Al, Milo spoke. "I hate to tell you this, but you've got to take Jack out of the box."

July 1916

The mill at the Alpine Lumber Company was running full-bore. Harriet Clemans could smell the smoke from the saw-dust burner a hundred yards away. It was a sweet, heady aroma, but sometimes it made her eyes water. Looking to her right and then to her left to make sure that no trains were approaching, Harriet crossed the tracks to the three-story wooden building that housed the general store, the social hall, and the community center.

Her husband, Carl, was just coming down the wooden steps. "Your trunks are here," he said, taking his wife by the hand and leading her past the flower bed next to the building where dahlias grew almost as tall as the couple. "Isn't it awfully soon to start packing?"

Harriet, a tall woman with a patrician profile, shook her head. "There's so much to do before the girls and I leave for Iowa at the end of August. We have to spend almost a week shopping in Seattle." She stopped as she saw the stricken expression on Carl's face. "Oh, you're being silly! You won't miss us that much. And you know perfectly well that it's time for the older girls to start college."

Carl's smile was wistful. "And you want to finish your degree."

"Of course." Harriet lifted her chin. "I've always wanted to do that. It was my goal before we married."

Carl nodded slowly. "I know. I admire you for it." He

paused as Ruby Siegel came out of the company store. Carl tipped his hat, and Harriet smiled.

"I'm running out of scrip already this month," Ruby declared, juggling her parcels. She was a petite redhead with a mischievous twinkle in her green eyes. "Louie says I'm a poor manager."

"You have three growing boys," Carl pointed out. "They must eat you out of house and home."

"They do," Ruby admitted. "Louie's not one to talk. He's got a big appetite, too." She puffed out her cheeks in an imitation of her husband's round face. "Oink, oink."

Heedless of her long skirts, which brushed the dirty ground by the railroad tracks, Ruby headed for home.

"What were we saying?" Carl asked, looking a bit befuddled.

"That you won't miss us," Harriet replied in a dry tone.

"Yes, I will," he asserted. "I'll miss you especially."

Harriet's eyes were following Ruby down the tracks. "No, you won't, Carl. I'm sure you'll find ways to keep occupied."

Chapter Five

ＡL DRIGGERS LOST his customary composure. His jaw dropped and he seemed as speechless as Milo had been a moment earlier. It was Max Froland who broke the silence, moving slowly toward the sheriff.

"I don't understand," he said simply.

Holding his hat to his chest, Milo grimaced. "We got wind of foul play regarding your dad's death, Max. We have to do an autopsy."

"No!" Max bridled at the sheriff's words.

June let out a little shriek. Her head slumped forward and the white rose she'd held her lap tumbled onto the ground.

Vida had stomped up to Milo. I felt obliged to follow.

"How did you hear about the possibility of foul play?" Vida demanded.

Milo put his hat back on and scowled at Vida. "It's all over town after last night. The phone's been ringing off the hook."

"Rumors!" Vida breathed. "It's nonsense, Milo."

"Could be," the sheriff admitted. "But we still have to look into it." He signaled for Al to start putting the coffin back in the hearse. "Let's go, let's move."

Fred Iverson marched up to Milo. "This is stupid. Since when did you start listening to the rantings of a crazy woman?"

"How do I know if your Aunt June's crazy?" Milo retorted. "I'm just doing my job."

Fred's brother, Rodney, came to stand by his kinsman. Both men were totally bald, though barely into middle age. "Do you mean we have to go through this whole damned thing again?"

I could tell by the tightening of his jawline that Milo was growing impatient. "That's up to you. When the autopsy's finished, you can have Jack cremated and save yourself a trip to the cemetery."

"But," put in Opal, who had joined her husband, Fred, "June's paid for the plot. We'll have to come for the burial."

"Easy for you to say," growled Rodney. "You live here. I have to come all the way from Tacoma."

"What's the argument?" Jack Iverson demanded, pushing his younger kinsmen aside. "Let Dodge do what he has to do. Even if June's cracked like an egg, the sheriff has to follow the rules."

Fred, Rodney, and Opal all deferred to the older man. Maybe it was because he still had some hair; maybe it was because he was Jack Froland's namesake. In any event, the threesome backed down but muttered among themselves.

"Drat!" Vida exclaimed. "I should have brought my camera. Do you have one in your car, Emma?"

As the worst photographer in Skykomish County, I shook my head. Rarely did I bring a camera with me. It was pointless. The photos either didn't turn out or I ended up with pictures of my feet.

Vida gave a fierce shake of her head, which was covered in funeral mourning, anchored by a satin turban featuring a matching black rose. "That's what I get for having good taste and being thoughtful. Not being in the habit of taking graveside photos, I don't have my camera when the burial turns into a news event."

"Maybe Scott can take a picture of the empty grave site," I suggested as the coffin was rolled away to the hearse.

Vida didn't respond. Instead, she started toward her car.

"I'll see you at the office," she shouted before getting into the driver's seat.

My next stop was lunch. Dutifully waiting for the hearse, the family funeral car, the rest of the mourners, and Milo's Grand Cherokee to pull out, I ended up last in the slow-moving line. It took ten minutes to reach my usual parking spot in front of the *Advocate*, and another thirty seconds to dash across the street to the Burger Barn.

I ordered a burger, fries, and vanilla malt to go, then stood by the takeout counter surveying the other diners. They were a familiar sight, from Mayor Baugh to Deputy Sam Heppner. Not wanting to get waylaid, I avoided eye contact with all of them. The mayor, however, was not to be ignored. He rose from his booth in the middle of the restaurant and headed in my direction.

"I've had a brainstorm, Emma," he announced, not forgetting to smile and nod at everyone within his line of sight. "I've had a look at those new portraits Buddy took of me, and a mighty fine job he did. It struck me as a good idea to run the official one—I haven't made up my mind yet, the little woman hasn't seen them—on the front page of the *Advocate*."

Fuzzy occasionally managed to catch me off-guard, but not this time. "Gosh," I said, hoping to sound genuinely regretful, "we can't do it in the next edition. We've got those dramatic forest fire pictures."

"Oh." The mayor looked disappointed but not defeated. Obviously, he was wrestling in his mind between Fuzzy vs. fire. "What about the week after next?"

"It's impossible to predict what could be front page news by then," I temporized.

"Hmm." Fuzzy shot me a quizzical glance. "You haven't had much in the way of big stories lately. No offense, but the paper seems kind of . . . mundane."

"That's true," I admitted, then challenged the mayor on the

very ground he'd been trodding. "What would be the news peg with your picture?"

Fuzzy took umbrage. "Isn't the mayor always news? That is, I've a twenty-four-hour-a-day job keeping this fine city running."

Since Mayor Baugh's most recent contribution to Alpine's welfare had been conserving water by turning off the sprinklers in both of the town's parks and thus creating a fire hazard of its own, I wasn't about to reel from his accomplishments.

"Have you some big plans?" I inquired innocently.

"I've always got big plans," Fuzzy replied with a smug smile. "But you know how it is, Emma—between trying to convince the city council and coordinate with the county commissioners, it's like pulling teeth. The wheels of progress turn slowly in a town like Alpine."

I had visions of running Fuzzy's mayor's new portrait with the cutline, WHEELS OF PROGRESS AND MAYOR'S BRAIN MOVE AT SNAIL'S PACE: ALPINE STALLED SINCE 1988.

Back at Fuzzy's booth, his companions, Henry Bardeen, manager of the ski lodge, and Deputy Mayor Richie Magruder, were on their feet.

I pointed out that fact to Fuzzy. "They're leaving without you. Let me know when Irene decides which photo she likes best," I added, wondering how Mrs. Baugh put up with Fuzzy on a daily basis. But then again, she hadn't for many years. The Baughs had married young in Louisiana, divorced not long after their arrival in Alpine, and remarried just before Fuzzy's first electoral campaign. I figured Irene could only stand Fuzzy for fifteen-year stretches at a time.

The mayor gave me his bogus politician's smile and hurried off to join his buddies. I was breathing a sigh of relief when Marsha Foster-Klein came through the door a moment later and spotted me at the takeout counter. The judge zeroed in like a mosquito going for a bare leg.

"Well?" Marsha said without preamble. "What have you found out so far?"

I tried not to look defensive. "We're still working on it."

"Hey—it's Friday," Marsha said, her voice, if not her disposition, improved since I'd last spoken with her. "We're running out of time."

"Marsha," I began as my order was called, "time is what this takes. It'd help if you had some inkling of what the letter writer was talking about."

Fretfully, Marsha rubbed at her forehead. "I don't, dammit." She saw me turn to pick up the white bag with the red barn logo. "You're not eating here?"

"No," I replied. "Unless you want to join me and have a think tank session."

The judge glanced at her watch. "Court's recessed until two. I have a short meeting before that. It's just after twelve-thirty. Let's sit."

With some reluctance on my part, we headed for a booth that had just been vacated by Harvey Adcock of Harvey's Hardware and the Bank of Alpine's Stilts Cederberg. Not only was Vida expecting me at the office, but she would also be miffed at being left out.

I asked Marsha if my House & Home editor could join us.

"Why not?" Marsha retorted. "She's Mrs. Know-It-All, isn't she?"

"You might say that." I dialed the *Advocate*'s number on my cell phone. Apparently, Ginny had gone out to eat; the call went straight through to Vida's extension. Naturally, she would come right over. The hardboiled egg and cottage cheese, along with the celery and carrot sticks, could wait.

Marsha had ordered without consulting the menu. "A secret's not a secret if it's been published in the newspapers, right?"

"Of course it's not," I agreed. "Why do you ask?"

"I've been thinking," she replied, allowing her coffee mug to be filled by the latest in a long series of young blonde waitresses. "What if the letter doesn't refer directly to me, but somebody else in my family?"

"You have a candidate in mind?" I inquired as Vida flew in through the door.

"Maybe," Marsha said as Vida marched up to our booth.

"Ladies," she said with a nod of the black turban. "Would you mind, Emma?" Before I could budge, she sat down next to me. I edged over a few inches to accommodate her.

I recounted what Marsha had just told me. Behind her big glasses with their bright orange frames, Vida's eyes widened. "A family member? Who?"

Marsha sighed. "My grandfather on my mother's side. His name was Yitzhak Klein. He was a Jewish immigrant who settled in New York where he married my grandmother, Esther. They moved west around 1915."

Vida's face was blank. "I've never heard the name."

"Probably not," Marsha conceded. "Grandpa Klein was a Communist and a labor agitator. During the big Red Scare back in 1920, he was arrested in Seattle and went to prison for three years. Maybe that's the secret I'm supposed to have."

Vida considered. "Dubious," she finally said, then turned to pinion me between the wall and the back of the booth. "What do you think, Emma?"

I agreed. "I assume he never lived in Alpine?"

"Not that I know of," Marsha said. "My mother was also politically active, but she never got arrested. She was a born rebel. When she decided to marry my father, Grandma and Grandpa Klein had a fit. Dad wasn't Jewish. It wasn't that Mom gave up her religion—though I wouldn't call her devout—but she hyphenated her name with Dad's. It was pretty unusual to do that back in the late Forties. Anyway, that's how I got to be Marsha Foster-Klein. I kept my maiden name for professional reasons. My husband's surname was Barr. Marsha Barr sounded frivolous for an attorney."

"A little," I remarked. "Are your parents still alive?"

Marsha shook her head. "Dad's been dead for fifteen years. Mom died two years ago this coming November."

"It's possible," Vida said, seemingly out of the blue.

Marsha and I both stared at her. "What is?"

"The arrest. The prison term. Being a Communist," Vida replied as Marsha's order arrived. "That is . . ." Vida leaned out of the booth and called to the waitress. "Toby? It is Toby, isn't it?" The young blonde nodded and smiled. "Toby dear, could you bring me a small salad? With ranch dressing?" Toby nodded again. "And perhaps a fishwich with those lovely chips. Now don't be stingy on the tartar sauce." Vida wagged a finger in a jocular manner. Once again, her calorie count had been abandoned.

"Nobody cares these days about someone being a Communist way back when," I pointed out.

But Vida disagreed. "Some do, particularly the old-timers. See here, Marsha, you don't know who wrote that letter. It could be some pigheaded person with a long memory, someone who holds a grudge against radicals. Or it could simply be some fool who might think you'd be embarrassed by your grandfather's shenanigans."

Marsha absorbed Vida's ideas. "You could be right." She grimaced. "Of course, there's always anti-Semitism."

"Dear me," Vida said, "I suppose there is. Really, except for the Middle East, isn't that out of vogue these days?"

Somewhat to my surprise, Marsha uttered a small laugh. "You'd like to think so," she said. "But unfortunately, it's one of those awful things that never goes away."

"Have you received anti-Semitic hate mail before this?" I inquired.

"Oh, yes," Marsha replied. "I've also been called a nigger-lover, anti-Catholic, a Jap-basher, a lesbian, too liberal, too conservative, and a lapdog of modern science. I could go on, but you get the picture."

I nodded in sympathy. "I've been tabbed many of those

things, too. My favorite was 'Popish running-dog left-wing Finn-hating whore.' I'm still trying to figure out what it meant."

Marsha gave a shake of her head. "That's pretty wild. Do you know who wrote that?"

"Oh, sure," I said. "I usually do even when the letters are anonymous."

"The post office," Vida said suddenly. "Marsha, have you inquired at the post office to see if anyone there or on the mail routes knows who sent the letter?"

"No," Marsha admitted. "Why would they?"

Before Vida could respond, Toby delivered the salad with a generous covering of ranch dressing. In fact, the lettuce was barely visible, with only an occasional hint of green poking through, like treetops after a heavy snowfall.

"Thank you, Toby," Vida said with a toothy smile. "Just the way I like it."

"What Vida's saying," I put in, "is that in a small town like Alpine, the postal workers pay more attention to the mail than in a city like Seattle or even Everett. They, too, are curious about their friends and neighbors." I ignored Vida's owlish stare. "How many people mail handwritten letters within the town every day? Frankly, we should have thought of this before now."

"Yes, we've been remiss," Vida acknowledged between munches and crunches of salad. "I shall go to the post office as soon as I finish lunch."

I'd finished my meal and Marsha had put the remnants of her turkey sandwich aside. She was due at the courthouse to talk to the opposing attorneys in an insurance case.

"I'm going back to the office, too," I announced, waiting for Vida to move so that I could get out of the booth.

"You can't," she asserted. "Here comes Toby with my fishwich. You know how I hate to eat alone."

Marsha, who was on her feet, leaned down to Vida. "Then

eat fast. I'm running out of time." Heaving her handbag over
her shoulder as if it were a rifle, the judge marched out of the
Burger Barn just as Milo Dodge came in.

"Milo," I murmured to Vida. "You can interrogate him." I
swiveled around as best I could and waved at the sheriff.

Vida harumphed, but she slid out of the booth so I could
escape. I encountered Milo halfway to the cash register.

"You're leaving?" The sheriff looked disappointed.

"I have work to do," I replied. "I called earlier to ask you
to have lunch with me, but you weren't in."

"I'd gone to the funeral at Faith Lutheran," Milo said, "but
they'd all left for the cemetery. I was hoping I could stop
everything before they got to the burial site."

"You caused quite a stir," I remarked.

"It's probably a bunch of bull," the sheriff said. "I talked
to Doc Dewey this morning. He hadn't seen any sign of
trauma on Jack Froland's body. The only way he could have
been killed was if he was poisoned. We're shipping him over
to Everett where they can run the toxicology tests, but it'll
take time. Maybe before they get the results, June will have
gotten over her nutty idea."

"You don't think Jack was murdered?" I stepped aside as
the local GM dealership owners Skunk and Trout Nordby
came down the aisle.

Skunk stopped to speak to the sheriff. "You been out
lately?"

Milo shook his head. "No time."

"You should take a couple of days, go down to the mouth
of the Columbia," said his brother, Trout. "We'd go but the
new cars are in."

"I might try the Peninsula later," Milo said. "Maybe the
Humptulips and the Bogachiel."

"We're thinking Cowlitz in November," said Skunk. "See
you."

The brothers moved away. Only a local would know they
were talking about rivers and fish.

Milo saw Vida, who was leaning out of the booth and making wild motions. "I'd better go suck up to your House & Home editor," the sheriff said.

"So do you really think it's murder?" I persisted.

"Hell, no," Milo said over his shoulder. "But I have to go by the book."

Of course. Milo always did.

There were still tongues of flame visible in the hills a mile to the north, but the smoke had drifted away from the commercial district. We'd been lucky so far. The terrible wildfires that had devastated eastern Washington hadn't yet struck Skykomish County.

I glanced down the street at the post office. It was almost one-thirty, and about the time that my home mail was delivered. Vida could handle the other postal workers, but I decided to track down our mailman, Marlow Whipp.

Sure enough, as I cruised along Alpine Way, I saw his little truck parked at the corner of my street. On pleasant days, Marlow preferred to walk some of his route. Driving slowly, I passed the RV park and the modest condos that had been converted from apartments years ago. In another two blocks, I came to my house. The flag was up on the mailbox. Marlow had already passed this way.

I spotted him by the cul-de-sac and caught his attention with one beep of the horn. He stopped at the curb, eyeing me curiously.

"What's up, Emma?" he asked. "Did I give you the wrong mail?"

"I haven't even looked," I said. "Hold on while I pull into the cul-de-sac. I've got a question for you."

Marlow, who had recently sprouted a goatee, waited patiently until I got out of the Lexus. "What kind of question?" He was a very literal man, no doubt from years of matching names to addresses, of sorting each delivery, of walking the same streets day after day after day.

"Think back to last Friday," I said. "Did you work that day?" I felt obliged to be literal, too.

"Last Friday?" Marlow reflected. "No. It was the Labor Day weekend. I had four days off. Seniority has its perks."

"Who took your route around town?"

"That new kid, Sean Corson. You know—Delphine's son."

I knew Delphine, who was the local florist. I hadn't realized that her son was old enough to have a job. The last I remembered of Sean Corson was when he made the news by crashing his skateboard into a tree on First Hill and broke his leg. He'd been about fourteen at the time.

"What about Thursday?" I asked. Even though the letter had been postmarked Saturday, September third, it might have been mailed earlier. The postal employees in Alpine didn't always rush, especially with a holiday on the horizon.

"Oh, sure. I worked Thursday," Marlow replied. "I hate Thursdays. That's magazine day for me. Then there's all those darned catalogs this time of year. Would you believe I've already delivered a bunch aimed at Christmas?"

Having received at least two holiday catalogs, I nodded in sympathy. "Most of them end up in the recycling bin," I said.

"Crazy," Marlow declared. "What do people in Alpine want with catalogs from all over the country? Don't we have stores right here? It's not fair to the local merchants. Not to mention the post office. There ought to be a law."

"I thought there was," I said. "I mean, regarding bulk mail."

"You're talking media mailings if you mean the newspaper. Check out regulation 3.0 under parcel post where you'll . . ."

"I meant the catalogs," I interrupted. "But that's not my question."

"Oh." Marlow looked surprised.

"Last Thursday," I began, "do you recall picking up any handwritten letters along your route?"

Marlow bowed his head. His back was already bowed

from carrying heavy mailbags for the past twenty years. "Let me think. You mean, letters that were left out in the boxes for me·to pick up, right?"

"Exactly."

"It's been over a week," Marlow said, sounding apologetic. "Handwritten, huh?"

"Yes. Stationery-sized envelope."

"A number three," Marlow mused, finally looking up. "White?"

"Off-white," I said. I'd have called it ecru, but maybe that was too literal even for Marlow.

"Eggshell or ecru?" inquired Marlow.

I tried not to smile. "Ecru, actually."

"How thick?"

I frowned. "The envelope?"

"The letter, the whole thing."

"A single sheet, with a small photo attached."

"Gosh." Marlow was thinking again. When he finally spoke, it was with a shake of his head. "Nope, I don't remember anything like that. Check with Sean Corson. Gotta run, Emma. The Thorstensens across from you complain like crazy when their mail's late."

"Hey!" I called after Marlow who was already across the street. "Where will I find Sean?"

"He's doing the rural routes today," Marlow shouted. "He won't get back until after five."

I surrendered and went back to work. Vida didn't return from the post office until two o'clock, and when she showed up, she was frustrated.

"Honestly," she exclaimed, sitting down with a thud, "people simply don't pay attention any more. They're all wrapped up in their own little worlds. Why can't they be more interested in their surroundings?"

"No luck?" I inquired.

"None." Vida removed her glasses and rubbed vigorously at her eyes. "Ooooh! Roy Everson has become an absolute robot. If I didn't know he was only fifty-one, I'd say it was time for him to retire as the local supervisor. There he is, at the very nerve center of the town's communications, and he acts as if it's just another job. Wouldn't you think he'd take a more personal interest?"

"The others weren't any help, either, I take it."

"Certainly not," Vida retorted. "Hopeless, just hopeless."

I told her about my equally fruitless encounter with Marlow Whipp. "It seems that Sean Corson is our last resort," I said as Leo came through the door.

"Sean Corson's a half-wit," Leo declared.

I didn't take the statement seriously. Leo had dated Sean's mother, Delphine. After they broke up, my ad manager had griped that her son was partially to blame. Sean was a teenager then and jealous of any man who made a claim on his mother's affections.

Vida also ignored Leo's comment. "I stopped at Posies Unlimited on my way back from the post office. I had Delphine send flowers to June Froland," Vida said as she regained her calm. "It was the least I could do."

Leo was unwrapping a double-truck ad layout for the Grocery Basket. "I hear June's gone over the edge. If Jack Froland was murdered, she'd be my prime suspect. I got the impression those two didn't live together, they coexisted. And not always in peace."

"There's some truth to that," Vida allowed. "In their later years, after the children were raised, Jack and June had very little in common. The death of their daughter, Lynn, only seemed to widen the gulf between them."

"Was that a car accident?" Leo asked.

"Yes. Up at the summit. Lynn had been skiing." Vida hesitated. "There were rumors, of course."

"What kind?" I inquired. I'd known almost nothing about Lynn Froland until the last few days.

"Well." Vida put her glasses back on. "Lynn was very young, about twenty, as I recall. She'd gone up to the summit to ski, but I heard there was more going on off the slopes than on them. Drinking, you know. So foolish, so unnecessary. The tragedy occurred on that terrible curve where the Cascade railroad tunnel begins."

"Was there an investigation?" I asked.

Vida sniffed. "Cursory. That incompetent fool, Eeeny Moroni, was sheriff then. You'd hardly expect thoroughness from his sort."

Milo's predecessor had a tainted reputation in Skykomish County. Vida, of course, had always insisted Eeeny was no good. As is often the case, she'd been right.

"I really should visit June," she went on, "but I understand Max is staying through the weekend at least. He teaches at the University of Washington. Classes don't start until the end of the month."

"Duchess!" Leo exclaimed in mock surprise. "I didn't know you were so self-effacing. How does a mere grieving son prevent you from cross-examining the bereaved widow?"

"Don't be so exasperating," Vida shot back. "And don't call me Duchess. You know I despise that nickname."

"But it's so fitting," Leo asserted, all mock innocence. "Look at that turban. You remind me of pictures I've seen of Queen Mary."

"Queen Mary wore a toque," Vida snapped. "That's not the same as a . . ."

Mercifully, we were interrupted by the arrival of Scott Chamoud. "I've got the fire photos," he announced, waving a manila envelope. "They're pretty spectacular, if I do say so myself."

Scott was right. He'd taken both color and black-and-white. He had several excellent frames of the firefighters in action, but what caught my eye was a wide-angled shot above the trees at Embro Lake with the glowing orange sky so bright that I could almost feel the heat.

"Great, Scott," I enthused, passing the photos on to Vida

and Leo. "We can do a whole spread with these and not run text, just cutlines." I turned to my ad manager. "Do you think we've got enough advertising to support twenty-four pages next week?"

Leo punched numbers into his calculator. "Not yet, but we'll make it. I'm going on a road trip this afternoon, to ply my trade with the merchants of Highway 2."

"Brilliant," I said. There were several businesses between Alpine and Monroe that could provide autumnal goods and services.

"I've got an idea for a feature on the firefighters," Scott said. "Especially those they call the pounders." He pointed at some shots of dirty, gritty men and women braving smoke and flames. "They're the ones who work on the ground. Their gripe is that all the glory goes to the smoke jumpers. No glamour in their job, they say, but it's really tough. They're the grunts."

"That sounds terrific," I said with a big smile. Scott wasn't always a self-starter when it came to story ideas. "We can put the feature along with a couple of photos on a separate page from the big spread."

The issue was coming together. I didn't feel light-hearted—I hadn't felt that way since before Tom died—but I experienced a sense of relief. Sometimes I felt like a trapeze artist, working without a net. Would we have enough advertising for our regular sixteen pages? Could we expand to twenty-four on short notice? Was it possible to publish thirty-two plus an eight-page insert every Christmas, Easter, and Thanksgiving? Could we survive at all? I often felt as if I were continually holding my breath, at least in a metaphorical sense.

Yet the impromptu special edition's progress was reassuring, thanks to Leo. I went back into my cubbyhole and tried to decide on an editorial. Maybe it would be fitting to laud the firefighters. I could combine the singing of their praises with dire warnings about careless campers and hikers.

Before I could make up my mind, the phone rang. It was Marje Blatt, calling from Doc Dewey's office.

"Doc told me you were supposed to call and make an appointment," Marje said in her nasal voice. "We haven't heard from you, but Doc just had a four-thirty cancellation. Is that convenient?"

"Um . . ." It was convenient, but it didn't please me. I knew that Doc was going to give me a lecture. "Okay," I sighed, "I'll be there."

I spent the rest of the afternoon writing what seemed like an insipid forest fire editorial. Fits and starts, changing leads, switching emphasis from the doughty pounders to the shiftless campers. Speculating, too, about more fires before the fall rains set in.

ARE WE OUT OF THE WOODS YET?

I stared at the editorial headline. I was the one who wasn't out of the woods. Maybe I should get reckless and call for a complete closure of the surrounding forest land. Logging had already been curtailed. Why not ban recreationalists as well? The idea didn't seem unreasonable.

The phone rang again just as I was getting ready to leave for the clinic. It was Milo.

"You're going to be mad at me," he said. "Fleetwood's got another scoop."

"About what?" I asked, sounding cranky.

"We just got word that somebody was killed in that fire up by Martin Creek."

My hand tightened on the receiver. "Who?"

"Can't tell," Milo replied in his laconic manner. "The body's burned to a crisp."

August 1916

It was hot in Alpine, with a cloudless sky and no hint of a breeze. Frank and Mary Dawson stood by the railroad tracks, awaiting the Great Northern's Empire Builder. Frank removed his cap and wiped perspiration from his high forehead.

"Don't say it," Mary warned.

"What?"

"What you usually say," Mary replied, cocking her head at her husband. " 'Hot enough for you?' It drives me crazy. One of these days, I'm going to hit you with a flatiron."

Frank smiled faintly, then turned away from Mary as the whistle of the oncoming passenger train could be heard from a half-mile away.

"Vincent better be here today," Frank muttered. "I wonder what his excuse will be for not showing up yesterday or the day before."

"You can't blame the boy," Mary said. "Your parents probably didn't have the train fare. I suppose they were waiting for money from England. As usual."

Just as Frank and Mary caught sight of the locomotive, two young boys ran down the hill to join them.

"Do you think Vincent's aboard?" Louie asked, out of breath.

Frank shrugged at his eldest son's question. "Who knows?" He put one hand on Louie's shoulder and the other on his nephew Billy's. The boys were eight years old and vir-

tually inseparable. "Keep clear," Frank warned them. "This train's wider than some of the freights."

The train slowed to a crawl as it approached the water tower. From the cab of the locomotive, they could see Harry Geerds leaning out and waving.

"Sorry, Mrs. D.," the engineer called, "I can't stop for pie and coffee today. They've got me harnessed to the passenger train. See you next week."

"Blackberry or huckleberry?" Mary called back.

Harry grinned. "Doesn't matter, as long as you or Mrs. Murphy bake them. You two sisters are the best cooks from Seattle to Chicago."

"Oh, go on!" Mary laughed as Harry Geerds and the locomotive moved up the line.

The train finally stopped. Several crewmen got out, but there was no sign of passengers. Scowling, Frank approached the conductor, who was lighting his pipe.

"Have you got a youngster on board?" Frank asked. "Sixteen years old, reddish dark hair."

The conductor, whom Frank didn't recognize, took two pulls on his pipe. "Yes, I think I do, in the last car. Is he supposed to get off here?"

"He sure is," Frank retorted. "What did he tell you?"

"That he was headed for Minnesota," the conductor replied, then frowned. "Come to think of it, he didn't show me his ticket. Hold on."

The conductor climbed back onto the train. Mary, along with Louie and Billy, had joined Frank.

"What now?" Mary asked, annoyed.

"Vincent's pulling some stunt," Frank sighed. "Good God, I hope he isn't taking after his worthless father."

The conductor reappeared toward the end of the train with a boy who struggled in his grasp. "Here's your kid," the conductor shouted, and unceremoniously dumped Vincent Burke onto the ground. "He's all yours, and you're welcome to him."

Frank hurried to his nephew. "Vincent! Here, do you need a hand?"

"No!" Vincent shouted, getting to his feet. "I don't need anything from you! I want to go to Minnesota! You'll see," the boy went on, red in the face. "I won't stay here! I hate this place! I hate all of you!"

Vincent ran past Frank's outstretched arm. The heedless youth didn't see Billy Murphy extend his foot. A moment later, Vincent was once more sprawled in the dirt.

He was crying.

Chapter Six

I'D BEEN A step away from exiting my cubbyhole when Milo called. Now I sat down again. "I don't get it," I said, grabbing a pen. "Are you saying that the body was someone not known to be at the fire scene?"

"Everybody from the Department of Natural Resources, the Forest Service, the national parks, the firefighters, and even the volunteers has been accounted for," Milo replied. "I suppose it could be a curiosity seeker or even a hermit."

"You don't have any missing person reports?"

"Nope."

"Maybe it's too soon," I ventured.

"You mean," Milo put in, "some hiker or camper who planned to be gone for several days and nobody's worried yet?"

"Exactly." I posed another question. "The body's that of an adult?"

"As far as we can tell," Milo said.

I glanced at my watch. It was twenty-eight minutes after four. The two-minute warning for my doctor's appointment went off in my head. "Do you know of any hermits or recluses in that area?"

"No," Milo replied. "The fire started fairly close to what those mountain men call civilization."

"Male or female?"

"Not sure."

"Teeth?"

"Yeah, the body has teeth. Jeez, Emma, why do you need to know all this crap? The paper doesn't come out until next week."

I gazed up at the ceiling. "Gosh, Milo, maybe I'm just curious. You find somebody who's been turned into a French fry up on Martin Creek, and I'm supposed to be disinterested?"

"You know damned well I'll give you the details when I get them," Milo countered. "Right now, I've got to run these stiffs over to Everett."

I was taken aback. "Did you say 'stiffs' or 'stiff'?"

"Stiffs," Milo reiterated. "We've still got Jack Froland here. The Snohomish County M.E.s are backed up in Everett. They won't get to Jack until next week. Still, I'd like to move him and this other corpse out of here before the weekend. So unless you drive a hearse, I'll see you later, Emma."

The sheriff hung up. I was used to Milo's crass detachment when it came to death, knowing it was the only way he could survive in his job. But ever since Tom had been killed, I couldn't help but wince at the sheriff's synonyms for the deceased. Even in death, Tom had never been "the body" as far as I was concerned. He was still Tom. With a small shudder, I left the office and started for the Alpine Clinic.

Passing Mugs Ahoy, I could see that the door was open. It looked as if the owner, Abe Loomis, had drawn quite a crowd on this late Friday afternoon. Most of the regulars were probably hoisting a stein in memory of their boon companion Jack Froland.

Despite being almost ten minutes late for my appointment, I still had to wait for Doc Dewey. From behind the reception desk, Marje Blatt inquired rather archly if I'd purposely been tardy.

"Some of our patients are deliberately showing up late," she said with a sniff of disapproval that reminded me of her Aunt Vida. "I realize that when Doc was alone at the clinic, the wait could be over an hour, but that's changed now that Dr. Sung is here."

"Honestly, I intended to be here at four-thirty," I responded. "I got held up on the phone."

Marje's expression was skeptical, but she said nothing, merely holding up two fingers, indicating the number of the examination room I should take. Five minutes later, Gerald Dewey appeared.

"How do you feel, Emma?" he inquired after sitting down in a blue swivel chair.

"Physically?"

Doc smiled and shook his head. "Not really. Though of course that's important, too. I'm more concerned with your mental and emotional health."

I sighed. "You don't expect me to have gotten over Tom's death, do you, Doc?"

"No," he said simply. "You never will. That's why I asked you to see me. I think you could use a little help."

I was wary. "What kind of help?"

"How are you sleeping?"

"Fairly well." It was true, but I was in the habit of taking four Excedrin P.M.s every night.

"Nightmares?"

"Some, but not like at first." I bit my lip. The horrible sleep-induced visions I'd suffered the first few months after Tom had been killed were slowly being replaced by dreams of him still alive and the two of us happily in love. I almost preferred the nightmares; at least I didn't have to awake to the grim reality of loss. It was as if I had to go through the shock of his death over and over again.

"That's good," Doc said. "It's normal for your dreams to change."

"I'd rather not dream at all," I said.

"That can't be helped," Doc responded, then smiled in the droll manner that was so reminiscent of his late father. "I'm more concerned about when you're awake. By nature, you've

always been a pretty enthusiastic sort of person. I don't see
that any more. How do you feel when you start the day?"

I shot Gerald Dewey an ironic glance. "You mean once I
wake up and realize that Tom's really dead?"

"Yes."

I avoided Doc's gaze. "I feel dead, too."

Out of the corner of my eye, I saw Doc nod. "That's a sign
of depression. In fact, you're exhibiting several symptoms.
What would you think about trying Prozac or another of the
antidepressants?"

My head jerked up. I'd always considered antidepressants
as one step above illegal mind-altering drugs.

"I'd rather not," I declared.

Doc chuckled softly. "I had a feeling you'd say that. We're
not talking about witchcraft, Emma. Depression can be
rooted in physical and chemical disorders."

"Mine's not," I said sharply. "If I'm depressed, it's because
my entire future died with Tom Cavanaugh. I've got every
right to feel God-awful."

"Speaking of God," Doc went on in his mild way, "have
you discussed this with Father Kelly?"

Dennis Kelly was my pastor at St. Mildred's. "Some," I
replied. "But mostly I've talked with my brother, Ben. Father
Kelly tends to be more intellectual in his approach. Ben's the
practical kind. And neither of them are the sort of priests
who hand out comfort pap with titles like *Lift Me Up Lord,
I Feel Like Bird-Doo*. Furthermore, I don't blame God for
what happened. I'm not a theological ninny."

"I'm glad to hear that," said Doc, who was an Episco-
palian. "It means you're a sensible person. Which should
also mean that you have some faith in science as well as religion. What have you got to lose by trying an antidepres-
sant? And by the way, I don't hand them out the way some
physicians do. They're not a cure-all, and in my medical
opinion, they're prescribed too freely."

I made a face. "I don't know, Doc. . . . If I start taking the pills, it'll be surrendering. It's as if I lack the moral courage to fight my problems."

Doc chuckled again. "Most people fight with weapons. That's what antidepressants are. Weapons in the war on depression."

I rubbed my forehead several times. "I don't know what to say."

"I'm the doctor, remember?" Doc reached out to pat my arm. "Emma, you aren't you any more. You've had a terrible loss, but you still have so much. Your son, your brother, your friends, the newspaper—what would happen if you decided to give up the *Advocate* and go off to mope some place? Do you want Spencer Fleetwood to buy you out and take over the news in this county?"

Doc had pushed the right button. "Of course not!" I cried, my head jerking up again. Then I laughed. "You sly fox."

"Well?" There was a twinkle in Doc's eyes.

"Okay," I sighed, "I'll try it."

Doc nodded slowly, then picked up a prescription pad from the desk at his elbow. "You can take this to Parker's Pharmacy now. They don't close until eight."

"What are you prescribing?"

"Paxil," he replied. "It doesn't have as many side effects as Prozac and some of the other drugs. But once you begin taking it, don't stop. It doesn't jump-start you. Give it time, up to a month."

"Okay," I said as we both stood up and Doc handed me the prescription. "By the way, I have to ask you one more time— were you surprised that Jack Froland died so suddenly?"

Doc was ushering me out the door of the exam room. "At eighty, and with colon cancer, you can hardly be surprised. I will admit, he seemed more chipper lately." Doc paused, fingering his round chin. "Feisty is more like it. But then Jack was always feisty."

"When did you see him last? That is," I amended, "before the night he died?"

Doc reflected. "The last week of August. That's when I noticed he seemed in a better mood."

"Did you ask him why?"

Doc gave me a puzzled look, then gave a nod. "Oh, I see what you mean. Yes, I suppose I did. I don't recall exactly what he said, though. I think it was something about believing he could still beat what he referred to as his 'gut buster'. I'd removed some of his colon, you know. He'd been pretty angry when he had to wear a colostomy bag. That was a low point, even when we found the cancer had recurred and was inoperable. But once he didn't need the bag after the colon healed, he cheered up."

I was doing a backward shuffle down the corridor to the waiting room. "I gather you didn't feel he was at death's door the last time he came to see you?"

"No, I didn't," Doc said slowly. "But at Jack's age and given the prognosis . . ." He stopped and narrowed his eyes at me. "Emma, you're not taking this silly rumor about foul play seriously, are you?"

"Not really," I said.

"Good." He patted my arm again. "Don't forget to stop at the pharmacy."

I thanked Doc, gave Marje a wave as I passed her desk, and headed out into the sunlit afternoon. I'd parked in the clinic's small lot across the street from the hospital. Parker's Pharmacy was on Front Street, in the block between the *Advocate* and the sheriff's headquarters. As I turned the corner from Third Street, I saw the metal hands on the sidewalk clock outside of the bank click to exactly five-thirty. Traffic on the town's main drag was as heavy as it ever gets, which meant I could count at least twenty vehicles within a four-block stretch. Hardly gridlock, but what annoyed me was that a car was parked in my usual place outside of the newspaper office. I was forced to take a left off Fourth and come around the other way to see if there was a space by the drugstore.

While I waited behind two cars at the four-way stop, I realized that the usurping car looked familiar. It was a black BMW. Moving up a spot, I could see the front vanity plate, which read MRKSKY.

Sure enough, Spencer Fleetwood was coming out of the *Advocate* office. I honked as I reached the intersection. Spence—and another half-dozen pedestrians—turned in my direction. I took a left and pulled up by the fire hydrant on the corner. MRKSKY walked toward my car, his tanned face wearing a big grin along with the inevitable Gucci sunglasses.

I rolled the window down on the passenger side. "Were you looking for me?" I asked.

Spence leaned down, the gold chain around his neck dangling above the car's window frame. "In a way," he said. "When Leo Walsh told me you'd left early I thought maybe it was to avoid me. We didn't part on chummy terms the other day. Would you care to drink and make up?"

I hesitated. But I was curious as to why Spencer Fleetwood had come to the newspaper office. "Okay," I said. "The Venison Inn's closed. How about the ski lodge?"

"Sure thing," he replied, giving my Lexus a couple of raps on the door frame. "See you there."

By the time I went around the block, I ended up following Spence out Front Street to the Burl Creek Road. We both slowed down as we wound up the slope of Tonga Ridge, over the bridge that spanned the creek, through the tall grand and Douglas firs, the western hemlocks, the red cedars, the Sitka spruces, and the white pines. I rolled all the windows down to savor the scent of the evergreens. It was like having Christmas in my car.

In a gallant gesture, Spence opened the car door for me. "I'm surprised," he said. "I didn't think you'd come. In fact, I figured you'd probably prefer to run over me in the middle of Front Street."

I wasn't amused. However, I felt I should meet my competitor halfway. There were, as he had pointed out, occasions when we could join forces to benefit the newspaper and the radio station.

On a Friday evening, the ski lodge's Norse-accented bar was crowded. Heather Bardeen, the daughter of the lodge's manager, was acting as hostess. She was also ostentatiously flashing a diamond ring on her left hand.

As she seated us in an upholstered booth for two by the woodcarving of Odin, I pointed to the ring. "Is that new—or news?"

Heather blushed, a rather charming reaction for a thirty-year-old. "Both. The formal announcement is being made Sunday at a dinner in one of the lodge's private dining rooms. Just family and close friends. Trevor and I plan to be married next June."

"Trevor?"

Heather nodded. "Trevor Bavich. He's in the restaurant supply business in Everett. Would you believe his great-grandfather worked in Alpine years ago?"

"No," I responded. "I mean, yes, I could believe it. So many of the descendants of the old Alpine timber workers are still scattered around the region." What I couldn't believe was that Vida had given no hint of the engagement party. Her longtime companion was Buck Bardeen. Henry Bardeen's older brother. Surely Vida would be included among "friends and family." Now that I thought about it, she hadn't mentioned Buck for the last few weeks. And I'd been so wrapped up in my own gloom that I hadn't noticed.

"Congratulations," Spence said, moving smoothly to take Heather's hand. "Does your impending marriage mean you'll be leaving us?"

"No," Heather replied. "We're going to live in Monroe. A compromise, you see. Trevor travels fairly often in his job, so we'll both have to commute a bit from work to home."

"Good news," Spence declared, releasing Heather's hand.

"Come Monday, we'll air your engagement on Rings 'N' Things."

Scooped again, I thought. Rings 'N' Things was a canned feature—one of many broadcast over KSKY—devoted to weddings, anniversaries, and engagements. How to give a shower, nuptial color schemes, planning the menu for a fifti- eth anniversary celebration ("Go easy on items that are hard to chew—you don't want the happy couple losing their den- tures on that special day," chirruped the show's hostess, Myra Sweet), and as a tag-on, Spence or whoever was filling in for him would announce impending local events. I rarely listened to the program but had caught it a month ago when one of the community college communications majors had read the names of an engaged couple who planned to wed the following Saturday ". . . unless their baby arrives sooner, in which case the ceremony will be cancelled."

Permanently, I'd wondered?

Heather personally delivered our drink orders to the bar. Maybe she was overcome by Spence's charm.

"You beat me again today," I remarked, trying not to sound annoyed.

"That's radio," Spence said, removing a pack of Balkan Sobranie cigarettes from somewhere inside his oatmeal- colored cashmere sweater. He proffered the gold-tipped cig- arettes. "I forget, do you . . . ?"

"Yes," I shot back and took one out of the pack, which was actually a box, black, with gold lettering. A very tasteful way to kill oneself. I hoped they cost at least a buck apiece. I planned to smoke several of them.

"What do you think?" he inquired, leaning over to light the cigarette for me. "A hermit? A hiker? A poor lost soul?"

"There's no way of knowing until an ID is made," I said.

"You can speculate," Spence said. "Not in print, of course."

I shook my head. "It's pointless. It could be anyone. A berry picker, a mushroom gatherer, a treasure seeker with a metal detector. That's not uncommon around here. But you know that."

Spence, who had finally removed his sunglasses, managed to make his brown eyes twinkle. Maybe he had batteries in his head. "Oh, I've picked up a lot of local lore in the past two years. I'm good at that. I absorb things, like osmosis."

Grudgingly, I admitted that I understood. "In journalism, you have to be a quick learner. When I came to Alpine, I was overwhelmed by all the names I needed to know. By the time I got out my first edition, I could breathe a little easier. Having Vida helped immensely. But eleven years later, I still can't keep track of who's related to whom, not to mention the exes and stepchildren and the family feuds."

"In some ways," Spence said, "it's easier in a big city. There, you only have to know the VIPs. The rest of the news makers come and go."

"That's true," I agreed. Then, because the story we'd done on Spence when he arrived in town had been deliberately cursory, I asked which big cities he'd worked in over the years.

"I started out in Salinas, the lettuce capital of the world," Spence replied, his gaze fixed not on me, but the glass mural of the northern lights behind the bar. "Over a period of five years, I made the circuit of small-town California radio. Finally, I caught on with an FM station in Sacramento."

He paused as Heather presented our drinks, a bourbon and water for me, a dry martini for Spence.

"How long were you in Sacramento?" I asked after Heather had gone back to her post by the bar's entrance.

"Three years," Spence replied. "Frankly, I didn't like doing FM. It was a classical station, and in those days, you had to sound very highbrow, almost effete. Like this—'Now we have Dmitri Shostakovich's Symphony Number 5, Opus 47, performed by the London Symphony Orchestra, Pierre Monteux conducting'."

Spence recited the announcement in a mid-Atlantic voice

I barely recognized. I couldn't help but laugh. "So you returned to AM radio?"

He nodded. "In Milwaukee. I had the morning drive-to spot. It was the post-Woodstock era. Everything was crazy. I got a little crazy, too." He stopped, glanced at me, then stared at his glass. "This tastes more like vodka than gin. Can you see who's tending bar?"

I twisted around in the booth. Behind the artificial trees that flanked the bar, all I could see was a white-shirted arm. Heather, however, was eagle-eyed: She rushed over to ask if something was wrong.

After Spence stated his complaint, Heather apologized. "The regular bartender took the week off. You know, to extend the holiday weekend. Fred Iverson's taking his place, since the Venison Inn is closed right now. Frankly, I don't think Fred's much good at mixing drinks, even if he does say he subs for Oren Rhodes at the inn."

I vaguely recalled seeing Fred behind the bar when Oren was sick or on vacation. As co-owner of the Venison Inn, Fred usually ran the kitchen at night.

Heather was back in a flash with the proper martini. She apologized again, but Spence gallantly soothed her and sent her on her way.

"Milwaukee," I said, resuming our conversation where it had left off. "Where did you go after that?"

"Chicago," Spence answered, carefully studying his drink. "How about you? I understand you worked for a long time in Portland at *The Oregonian*."

"Almost twenty years," I told him, a little surprised that he'd gotten off the subject of himself. "I was in a rut, and when the chance to buy my own weekly came along, I jumped at it. How did you get from Chicago to Alpine?"

"It wasn't a direct route," Spence said, again staring at the mural, which depicted fjords and trolls and other Norse symbols. "Mainly, I got tired of working for other people. Like you, I suppose, I was in a rut."

"It couldn't have been easy," I pointed out. "That is, there was no radio station here until you started KSKY. You had to apply to the FCC for the license, buy the property, build the plant—that takes entrepreneurship."

Spence shot me a sly look. "And money? That's what you're really thinking, isn't it?"

I tried to look innocent. "I inherited the money to buy the *Advocate*. Raising a child on my own didn't give me the luxury of socking away serious savings."

"I had a windfall, too," Spence replied, then held up his drink. "Now this is a real martini. Beefeaters, I think." He looked straight at me again. "What's going on with this story about Jack Froland getting murdered?"

"June Froland temporarily lost it," I said. "That's my guess." I glanced at the bar where I could see Fred Iverson serving Cal and Charlene Vickers. After Labor Day, Cal always closed his Texaco station at six o'clock. If your needle was hovering on empty during the evening, your only hope was Gas 'N' Go by the Icicle Creek Tavern. "I suppose we could ask Fred what he thinks."

"He's pretty busy right now," Spence said, "especially for a guy who can't tell vodka from gin."

"You're right," I said. "Let's discuss our mutual media situations."

"Ah." Spence paused to eat one of the two olives Fred had put in his drink. "Why not do that over dinner? They serve in the bar."

I accepted another expensive cigarette from Spence, which gave me time to consider the offer. It was Friday night, I was already here, and so far Spence hadn't annoyed me very much.

"Fine. We split the tab."

"Of course." Spence looked amused. "This is an alliance, not a partnership."

"What's the difference?" I tried not to cough. The Sobranies were stronger than the ultra lights I smoked. When I smoked. When I wasn't quitting.

"The difference?" Spence again gazed at the mural. "A partnership would mean we're in this together, all the way. An alliance hedges our advertising bets. We'll still be trying to cut each other's throat some of the time."

"What do you have in mind?" I asked, raising my hand as a waitress I didn't recognize came away from the table next to us. More and more of the local restaurants seemed to be drawing on the labor pool provided by the community college students. "Menus," I said to the dark-haired girl. "We need menus."

She nodded and scurried off.

During the meal we discussed ideas and strategies. Combination ads for radio time and newspaper space. Discounts for the upcoming holiday season. Attempts to get more national advertising to promote mail order catalogs. And—something Kip kept nagging me about but I put off— a joint Web site on the Internet.

"I can't believe you haven't done that yet," Spence said as the bill arrived in a tasteful green folder with a pen that featured a troll on top. "I had a student at the college put ours together a month ago."

"So why isn't it online?" I inquired.

"There are still a few bugs," Spence replied, scanning the bill. "Besides, I've been meaning to discuss a combination site for some time. I didn't want to rush you. That is, I knew you had other things on your mind." He paused and looked up from the bill. "You owe thirty-two dollars including tip."

"I'll have to write you a check," I said. "I don't have that much cash on me."

"That's fine, I'll card it." He reached into his wallet and withdrew a platinum Visa card.

I wrote the check and handed it to Spence. "I appreciate your thoughtfulness," I said stiffly. "I mean, about not . . ." I couldn't quite get the words out. Maybe the second drink had made me emotional.

Spence shrugged and stood up. "I'm not a completely insensitive boob. Besides . . ." Now he stopped, then shrugged again and put on his sunglasses. "We'll touch base Monday, bring Leo into the loop. Okay?"

"Sure," I said as we nodded farewell to Heather. "Leo's very good at what he does."

"I've noticed," Spence said as we exited the ski lodge. It was almost dark. "If Leo weren't so good, I wouldn't have to worry about the competition."

Spence walked me to my car. "It's a funny thing," he said as I clicked the remote door opener. "When I first got into radio thirty-odd years ago, I wondered why. It seemed as if television was taking over the airwaves. But radio's survived and come on even stronger."

"It's the print media that's a dinosaur," I said, slipping into the driver's seat. "I meant to ask you—why Alpine?"

Spence looked up at the clear night sky with a trillion stars so close they seemed within reach. "Oh—just lucky, I guess. Good night, Emma."

He closed my door and strolled off to his Beamer. I had been pleasantly surprised by our dinner together. Maybe Spencer Fleetwood wasn't as big a jackass as I'd thought he was. There were qualities in the man that I hadn't yet seen until tonight.

But there were also many things I didn't know about him. That bothered me, because I realized that Spence had eluded several questions during the course of our get-together. I wondered why.

I arrived home at a quarter after eight.

I'd forgotten to stop at Parker's Pharmacy and get my prescription for Paxil.

September 1916

Bert Stites was running as fast as his short, stout legs could carry him. By the time he reached the office of the Alpine Lumber Company, he was so winded that he couldn't speak.

"What's wrong, Bert?" Carl Clemans asked, looking up from the paperwork on his desk.

Leaning against the door frame, Bert took several deep breaths before he responded. "It's those damned Wobblies. They're headed this way. Word's come down the line from Sultan."

Carl stood up, his manner calm, but a spark of alarm in his eyes. "Are you sure?"

Still panting, Bert nodded. "I heard it from a couple of the section men working the tracks. Mike Flood and Johnny Steppich. You can count on them. They're two of my best men."

Carl studied his railway construction foreman. Bert was a good man, reliable and not given to panic. "Are the Wobblies armed?"

"I don't know," Bert replied, moving a few steps from the door. "Some have been arrested during the shingle weavers' strike in Everett."

"I know," Carl sighed, pacing the cramped quarters of his office. "But the Wobblies were only giving speeches, trying to rile up the strikers. Some of those so-called deputies from Everett's Commercial Club are pretty hotheaded, too. They're working strictly for the mill owners."

103

"What should we do?" Bert asked, his red face wearing a plaintive expression.

Carl picked up his hat from a peg by the door. *"Let's talk to Floyd Duell and Tom Bassen. The fire danger's high. We might as well shut down, at least for the rest of the day."*

The conference, which was held under the warm late summer sun on the loading dock, lasted less than five minutes. Floyd hurried off to sound the mill whistle, signaling a work stoppage. Several more mill workers had gathered around Carl and the others.

"We don't want them goddamned Wobblies here!" Rufus Kager shouted. *"We got no complaints!"*

"You're damned right!" agreed Ben Napier. *"If other camps got lousy grub and crummy bunkhouses, that's too bad. Let those Commie agitators go somewhere else to stir up trouble."*

More men began pouring out of the main mill and the shingle mill. In the distance, the sound of trucks and logging rigs could be heard, headed back into town. Across the river, on the slopes of Mount Baldy, Carl could see the occasional gleam of metal as the vehicles drove down the switchbacks from the logging sites. He glanced at his watch. It was almost three o'clock.

He turned to his woods foreman, Tom Bassen. *"If the Wobblies were in Sultan a few minutes ago, they should get here in less than an hour. That's when the next eastbound freight is due."*

Tom ran a hand through his thick dark hair. He was a sharp-faced man with keen eyes and a deceptively relaxed manner. *"How many, I wonder?"*

"We can't be sure," Floyd Duell replied. The mill superintendent looked worried, his eyes fixed on the railroad tracks. *"Even if we check in by telephone, more could hop on along the route."*

Several of the wives and children had joined their menfolk on the loading dock.

"So we're going to have some excitement around here," Ruby Siegel said to her brother, Rufus. *"Where's Louie?"* She stood on tiptoes, searching the crowd for her husband.

"He's not down from the woods yet," Rufus replied. *"Listen, you and the other women and the kids should stay put. This may get ugly."*

"I should hope so!" Ruby exclaimed, her eyes dancing. *"I'm going to get my big cast-iron skillet and show those Wobblies a thing or two!"*

"Ruby," Rufus said in a mild tone of reproach, *"I thought you liked some of those Bolshie ideas."*

"I do," Ruby retorted, *"but not here. Besides, those Wobblies aren't true Marxists. They go way beyond that. I know, I've read up on them."*

Rufus gave his sister a dubious smile. *"I suppose you have. I'll be darned if I know why."*

"The world's changing, Rufe," Ruby declared. *"Look at the war in Europe. Look at what's going on in Russia. Look at what's happening in Mexico."* She paused, pointing down the railroad tracks. *"Look at what's happening right here. You can't ignore change, not even in Alpine."*

Carl Clemans came up behind Ruby. *"Go home,"* he said softly. *"Get the other women and the children together and go home."*

Ruby swung around to face Carl. She was a full head shorter than the mill owner, but her entire being vibrated with an energy that would have befitted men twice her size. *"Why should I? Why should we?"* she demanded. *"We aren't cowards."*

"That's not the point," Carl said quietly. *"You don't want the children to get hurt, do you?"*

Ruby glanced around the loading dock. At least two dozen youngsters milled around, talking mostly to each other. There were three babes in arms. There were teenagers, including Jonas Iversen and the new boy, Vincent Burke. Those two had their heads together. They looked as if they were spoiling for a fight. But some of the younger children, among them Ruby's sons, looked frightened. Several of the mill workers had sought weapons at hand: Axes, knives, baseball bats.

"Maybe you're right," she finally said as the first of the logging trucks stopped by the main mill. "But what are you doing to do?"

Carl's smile was faint. "Wait."

Chapter Seven

ITOLD MYSELF I hadn't deliberately forgotten about the antidepression drug. It was just that I'd gotten caught up in promotional plans for the paper and the radio station. Besides, I was curious about Spencer Fleetwood. In the past, I'd backed away from getting to know him, perhaps hoping that by ignoring his presence, he might evaporate into the airwaves. The irony was that after spending over two hours with him, I had more questions than answers.

The red light glowed on my answering machine. Before checking the messages, I changed into my robe, got a Pepsi out of the fridge, and glanced through the mail that Marlow Whipp had left in my box.

A couple of bills, a bunch of ads, and yet more fall catalogs were my lot from the post office. I threw out everything but the bills, then turned to the answering machine. There were three calls that I listened to in reverse order. The most recent was from Vida:

"Where are you? It's almost eight. What happened at the doctor's office? You aren't hospitalized, are you?"

The second call was from Marsha Foster-Klein:

"I don't mean to nag, but is there anything I can do to help you with our project over the weekend? Call me back ASAP."

The third message was delivered by Max Froland, who, after identifying himself in formal terms, asked if he could stop by this evening to discuss an article about his family.

Despite the professed urgency of the other calls, I looked up the Frolands' number and phoned Max first.

He sounded diffident. "This may be a bad idea," he said, "but some of the family members think it might be nice to run a piece on the Iversons and the Frolands. My dad's passing signals the end of an era, in a way. I'm staying through the weekend, so I could help you put something together."

It occurred to me that I could combine the research into Max's Iverson side of his family with Marsha's project. Not that I really believed it would help her. But the article would fill up more space for our special edition.

"Okay," I agreed. "How do you want to start?"

"I've spent a few hours going through Pa's mementos and such," Max replied. "Ma helped, but she's asleep now. Doc Dewey prescribed some medication to settle her down. When do you want to start?"

"How about at the *Advocate* office tomorrow around ten?"

"That's good. I'll be there. Thanks so much."

Judge Foster-Klein didn't answer. I left a message, telling her that there was the possibility of new leads. I didn't add that they might be coming from the souvenirs in Jack Froland's attic.

Vida answered on the first ring. "What happened to you?" she demanded. "Are you all right?"

"Of course," I replied, then told her about running into Spence.

"You dined with the enemy?" she cried.

I explained about Spence's ideas for joint promotions. Vida simmered down a bit, but not without a warning.

"I wouldn't trust that man an inch," she declared. "What about Doc? Did he give you a checkup?"

"No, we just talked." I decided against mentioning the Paxil prescription. "By the way, Heather Bardeen is sporting an engagement ring. Did you know about it?"

There was a long pause at the other end. "I knew it was imminent," Vida finally said in a strained voice.

"I assume Buck told you," I remarked.

"Yes."

I was puzzled. Vida never responded with one-syllable words. "How long have you known?"

"Oh—a few weeks."

"Vida," I said firmly, "what's wrong?"

"I don't want to discuss it over the phone."

"Vida . . ." I began, then switched gears. "Let me ask the questions. You can say yes or no. Okay?"

"We'll see."

While Vida insisted on knowing everybody else's business down to the last nuance, she was intensely private when it came to her own personal life. I respected that, I honored it, but sometimes it was frustrating.

"Are you going to the engagement party Sunday at the ski lodge?" I asked, slipping into my reporter's mode.

"No."

"Were you invited?"

"Yes."

"By Buck?"

"Yes."

"Did you decline?"

There was a long pause. "Not at the time."

"You changed your mind later?"

"Yes."

"Because of Buck?"

Another lengthy pause. "Yes."

"Have you two broken up?"

This time, there was a heavy sigh at the other end. "I can't say more. Not on the phone."

"Vida, who do you think is listening in?" I demanded. "There are no party lines in Alpine any more, and the switching equipment is automatic. When was the last time you cranked your telephone?"

"There are ways to cut into conversations," Vida said cryptically. "Crossed lines. You know that happens, particularly with cell phones."

"You're not on a cell phone," I pointed out.

"We'll discuss this later," she said. "In person."

I was forced to surrender. "Okay, I'll meet you for breakfast at the Heartbreak Hotel Diner at nine."

"Not in public!" Vida exclaimed. "Come to my house. I'll make a lovely omelet."

Vida's omelets, like all of her cooking, were to be avoided. "Better yet, you come here. I'll make French toast." I knew Vida was fond of French toast.

"Oh. That sounds very nice. I'll see you then."

After I hung up, I sat lost in thought for several moments. Vida and Buck had broken off their long-standing relationship, I was certain of that. But why? I'd expected them to marry eventually. He was a widower and she was a widow. Their children were grown, indeed were approaching middle age. Buck had a house off Highway 2 in Startup. He'd been talking about selling it and moving to Alpine. Maybe he'd proposed and been rejected. Vida cherished her independence. Perhaps she saw no future for them and had called off the relationship. Or if Buck had been turned down, he might have ended it.

For the first time since I could remember, I went to sleep that night without grieving for my lost love. Instead, I was filled with curiosity about Vida's apparently punctured romance.

Misery loves company. Perversely, a friend who also has a broken heart may help mend one's own.

On Saturdays, I usually slept in, sometimes as late as nine-thirty or even ten. But on this September morn, I was up at eight-fifteen and in the kitchen by eight-thirty.

Vida was customarily punctual. I noted that she looked a bit drawn and didn't have her usual bounce. Had she been like that for several days, even weeks, and I'd been too caught up in my own woes to recognize the change? I hoped not.

As soon as we reached the kitchen, I began frying bacon. The batter for the toast and the coffee were ready. I offered her a mug.

"I believe I will," Vida said, though at work she usually drinks only hot water.

I didn't try to question her until I'd finished cooking breakfast, which didn't take long. At ten minutes after nine, we were pouring syrup over the French toast and sprinkling salt and pepper on our scrambled eggs.

"Okay, Vida," I said after she'd taken her first bites of food, "what's up with you and Buck?"

Rolling her eyes, she set down her knife and fork. "It's just too much. I'm not sure I can even talk about it."

I tried to suppress a smile. "There's nothing you can't talk about, Vida. Come on, let's hear it."

"Oh, very well." Vida took another bite of eggs before she began. "I may have mentioned a month or so ago that Buck put his house on the market. He didn't get any offers until a week ago when he got two. Both were slightly below the asking price, but he decided to accept one of them. The couple—from Everett—wanted to move in as soon as possible, but Buck hadn't really looked for a place here in Alpine. You know how men are—they put things off." She stopped to sip at her coffee.

"In any event, he asked if he could move in with me, at least for a time. Naturally, I wanted to help, but I told him I simply didn't have room. As you know, my house has three bedrooms, but one's reserved for Roger when he stays with Grams."

Roger was Vida's dreadful seventeen-year-old grandson who occasionally bunked with her when his parents went out of town. "Isn't Roger old enough to stay alone?" I asked.

"Certainly," Vida responded, "but that's not the point.

Roger likes staying with me. We have such good times together."

What Vida meant was that she spoiled the kid so much with special treats and extra pocket money that despite jeopardizing his status among his peers, he couldn't subjugate his opportunistic nature.

"What about the third bedroom?" I inquired, offering Vida another piece of French toast.

"Thank you, Emma." She paused to butter the fresh slice. "That room's not usable."

I gave Vida a quizzical look, then realized I'd never seen the third bedroom. "Why not?"

Vida stopped with a piece of bacon almost to her mouth. "That's where I keep my hats."

In all the years that I'd known her, I'd never really thought about where Vida's millinery was stashed. Certainly she had dozens of hats—hundreds, maybe.

"Your hats?" I said stupidly.

Vida nodded. "Yes. They're all in boxes. I don't want them to get dusty between wearings."

"Your hats," I repeated. "How many are there?"

"I'm not sure," Vida replied. "Three or four hundred, I suppose."

I was dumbfounded. If Vida hadn't been my House & Home editor, she certainly would have made the *Advocate*'s pages as a feature.

"There's no room to store them in the basement," Vida said. "It's unfinished, you know. And I certainly couldn't have Buck sleep in my room. People would talk."

Admittedly, I had never known if Vida and Buck slept together. More specifically, if their relationship was of a sexual nature. But I had my suspicions. Buck was a vigorous man of late middle age. And if Vida's appetite for food was any indication of her appetite for more sensual delights . . .

On the other hand, I didn't really want to think about it.

"So Buck got angry when you turned him down? His request to room with you, I mean," I added hastily.

Vida frowned. "Yes. He felt I was being unreasonable."

"Were you?"

Vida's gray eyes traveled to the ceiling. "I'm not sure. Now that school's started, I wonder if I've been a bit hasty. That is, Roger doesn't stay with me as often when he's in school. This is his junior year, and he has to prepare for his SATs."

For reform school? I thought, but made no comment.

"Besides," Vida continued, "Amy and Ted have no travel plans in the near future."

No doubt they were sticking around to help their son prepare for his SATs. Like teaching him to read.

"I gather that you and Buck quarreled over your . . . refusal," I said, offering Vida another slice of French toast.

"I'm afraid so." She paused to sip her coffee. "That's why I'm not going to his niece's engagement party."

"But if Roger isn't going to be staying with you for a while," I pointed out, "couldn't Buck use the room until he finds his own place?"

Vida heaved a big sigh. "I've considered that. But ever since Roger was a baby, that has been his room. I don't want him to think his Grams is being frivolous and letting someone else stay there, even temporarily. Not to mention that I might be setting a poor example for Roger. Living with someone, you see."

Since in the not-too-distant past Roger had bragged— falsely—that he'd gotten a teenaged girl pregnant, I found the last part of Vida's argument ludicrous. I folded my hands on the table and looked Vida straight in the eye. "Have you considered yourself in any of this?" As Vida opened her mouth, I held up a hand. "Stop. Think. I know how much you love Roger. But you spoil him." She started to speak again, but I kept talking. "You have other grandchildren, and even if they don't live in Alpine, has it occurred to you that they might be resentful?"

Vida's eyes were hot with anger. "The others don't know. They live in Bellingham and Tacoma. What they don't know can't hurt them. I'd spoil them if they were here. That's what grandmothers do." The look she gave me said, "And you will never know because you will never be a grandmother."

I took a deep breath and kept from lashing out. "You also have to think of yourself. And Buck. I thought you were fond of him."

"I am," Vida replied, lifting her chin. "As he is of me. That being the case, why can't he take an apartment until he finds a house to buy?"

"Because he'd rather be with you?"

Vida actually looked surprised. "I . . . shouldn't think so. That is, Buck's very independent. As am I."

"But where he lives has become an insurmountable issue, right?" Once again, I didn't wait for an answer. "You're mature adults, Vida. Why is this an all-or-nothing situation? Why can't one of you give a little? What happened to compromise?"

Vida pursed her lips. The glint in her eye that I'd taken for anger now looked more like tears. "One thing led to another," she said, dropping her voice. "We've had arguments, but we've never quarreled until now. Things were said. . . ." She blinked back what surely were tears and gave herself a shake. "I'm not certain it can ever be the same."

I presumed the sticking point had been Roger. But I had to allow for obstinacy on Buck's part. He was a retired Air Force colonel, used to giving orders and probably rigid in attitude.

"I don't know what to say," I admitted.

"I don't either," Vida said, staring beyond me to the window above the sink.

I wanted to tell her not to throw away anything as precious

as love. All the wasted years Tom and I had spent apart came rushing over me. But I said nothing. Vida, being Vida, would chart her own course.

"I should be going," she said, carefully wiping her mouth with a napkin. "I should have told you about this earlier, but you've had problems of your own."

I must have looked upset, because Vida rose and wagged a finger. "Don't feel guilty. This is a small matter compared to your loss."

I also got to my feet. Her insinuating look about grandmothers still stung, but I had to let it pass. The truth always wounds. "It's not a small matter for you and Buck. That's what I've been trying to say."

Vida was getting into her car when I suddenly remembered my appointment with Max Froland. I rushed out of the house, shouting and waving my arms.

"Do you want to join us?" I asked after explaining my plans for the rest of the morning.

Without hesitating, Vida said she'd be at the office in half an hour. It was almost ten o'clock, and she had some errands to run.

I arrived at the office ten minutes early to make coffee and clear some space on the table in the newsroom. Vida and Max joined me within a minute of each other. Max was carrying photo albums and a shoe box.

"How is your mother?" Vida inquired as soon as we were seated at the table.

"She's sleeping a lot," Max replied, accepting a mug of coffee from me. "Whatever Doc Dewey gave her has certainly knocked her out."

"Just as well," Vida said as I handed her a mug of hot water. "Now tell us what you have so that we can complement it with articles from our files."

Max tapped the album that sat on top of at least three

others. The one he indicated and the one under it were smaller and older, with black covers and black pages. The two underneath were larger and newer.

"These are family photos from both sides," Max said. "A few of the pictures go back to my maternal great-grandfather's day."

"That would be Trygve Iverson?" Vida put in.

Max nodded. "His daughter, Karen, was my grandmother."

Vida moved backward in Scott's swivel chair. "I started a family tree," she said, then quickly added, "I often do when a longtime resident passes away. Let me make sure I've got it right, and to make additions you may have."

Vida propelled herself a few feet to the coat closet where she'd put the family tree. Scooting back to the table, she unrolled the big sheet of paper in front of Max, who studied her notations in silence.

"This is right—as far as it goes," he finally said. "You've got a gap here under Trygve and Olga Iverson's children."

Vida leaned over the paper. "You mean I don't have wives or descendants for Jonas and Lars?"

"Yes, but . . ."

Vida swung the family tree into her purview. "Do you have names, dates?"

"Lars was married just before the crash in twenty-nine," Max said. "It was an old family joke—his wife, Alice, had been very extravagant, and Great-Uncle Lars was a tightwad. He insisted his bride quit spending so much money. The rest of the family claimed that Alice's sudden thrift affected the economy and caused the Depression."

"Alice . . . ?" Vida bestowed a coaxing look on Max.

"Gough," he said, then spelled out the name. "They've both been dead for several years. They were Uncle Jack Iverson's parents."

"Oh, yes." Vida made the appropriate notations. "They lived in Wenatchee, didn't they?"

"They'd retired there," Max agreed. "They wanted to be in a larger town. Medical resources, transportation—all the usual reasons older folks sometimes have for moving out of a place the size of Alpine."

Vida gave Max a sharp glance. "Most stay here."

As an expatriate, Max seemed aware of how defectors were viewed. "That's true. My own parents stayed in Alpine."

Vida accepted the statement as an apology and resumed looking at the family tree. "That takes care of Lars for the moment. What about Jonas?"

"That's what I was going to say earlier," Max said, looking away. "He's a bit of a mystery." He removed the lid from the shoe box. "I haven't gone through all of these postcards and letters yet."

Vida gazed at Max from over the rims of her glasses. "Who else in your family is interested in a newspaper piece?"

"Uncle Jack and Aunt Helene," Max responded. "My cousin, Fred, and his wife, Opal. My other cousin, Doug, over in Leavenworth. They thought it'd be appropriate. It's a new century, so much has changed, especially in the timber industry. The fact is, as far as the Froland part of the Iverson descendants goes, the line ends with me."

Vida offered Max a sympathetic look. "You still could remarry, Max. You're only—what?—fifty?"

Max smiled faintly. "I never wanted to be married to anyone except Jackie. Even after almost fifteen years without her, I still don't."

"That's a shame," Vida declared, then added, "I was somewhat older when I was widowed. But I must confess, I always felt that if I found someone else, it would be like replacing Ernest. Somehow, I couldn't do that." Abruptly, she turned away.

I intervened to change the subject. "Why don't you leave the letters and such here, Max? Vida and I can sift through them later to see what might be usable for the article. We're not going to muckrake, I promise."

Max grinned sheepishly. "I didn't really think you were."

"It's a reflex reaction on our part," I explained. "Journalists always jump on a story's worst aspect, especially if there's any mystery to it."

"I understand," Max said. "Let me show you some of the photos. Assuming, of course, you'd want to use any of them."

"Oh, we love family pictures," Vida asserted, once again her usual self. "Our readers do, too. Let's see them."

Max opened the first album and turned it so Vida and I could study the photos. "Some of these are quite old," he said. "I don't know how they'll reproduce."

"Buddy Bayard can work with old pictures," I said. "He's very good at tweaking them to register well."

Max gave a nod. "This," he said, pointing to a portrait that took up the album's first page, "is my grandparents' wedding photograph. Trygve met Olga in his hometown of Trondheim, Norway, when she was only fourteen. He came to America to work in the Minnesota north woods. By the time he'd saved up enough money to go back to Norway and marry Olga, he'd decided they should move further west, to Washington State. This picture was taken in Trondheim where they were married in 1891."

In the sepia-tinted portrait, Trygve Iverson—or Iversen, as he was then known—was a bear of a man with a heavy beard and piercing eyes. Olga, who was seated in front of her groom, looked as if she might have been pretty when she smiled. But people didn't smile much in photos of that era. Olga appeared sturdy enough to out duke a musk ox.

"That's a lovely veil," Vida remarked. "Handmade, I should think."

I sensed that Vida was hard pressed to give a compliment. The white veil and the bouquet of lilies were the only indications of wedding finery. Olga's dress was dark and quite plain. The suit that Trygve wore looked too tight for his husky frame. Judging from their expressions, the couple looked like they had scheduled back-to-back root canals instead of celebrating a wedding.

"What do you remember about them?" I asked as Max flipped the page to a grouping of old snapshots.

"Nothing." Max wore a half-smile. "They both died long before I was born. Grandpa Tryg wasn't much older than I am now when he passed away. Grandma outlived him by over twenty years. It's family lore that they both died of broken hearts."

Abruptly, Vida looked up from the photos she'd been studying. "How so?"

Max shrugged. "I'm not sure about Grandpa. With Grandma, it was Uncle Burt's death during the war in North Africa. She died a year to the day that he was killed."

"That was Burt Iverson," Vida said softly. "He married a woman named Foster, didn't he?"

"Aunt Jo," Max responded. "She's still alive. I think she moved to a nursing home in Port Angeles where their daughter lives. Marjorie—I don't know her married name—was not quite two when Uncle Burt died. Aunt Jo remarried one of the Bergstroms."

"Yes," Vida said. "I knew that. But your aunt wasn't from Alpine, was she?"

Max shook his head. "No. She was from Everett, I think. I didn't know her very well. For some reason, my grandmother never liked her."

"Why not?" Vida asked.

"I honestly don't know," Max replied, casting a wary eye on Vida.

I was looking at the pages of old snapshots. I saw Tryg and Olga standing in front of a small frame house with tulips and daffodils blooming by the picket fence. Olga held a baby draped in a fringed blanket. Someone with fine printing skills had labeled the photo with a gold pen. "Per Iversen, two weeks old, May 14, 1892."

"I think," Max said, following my line of sight, "that was taken in Port Townsend. My grandparents lived there until they moved to Alpine many years later."

"In 1914," I said, remembering the mention of the Iversons' arrival in Alpine. I took a last look at the picture of the young couple with their baby. Vida had told me that Olga never really learned to speak English. Perhaps she hadn't wanted to come to America but couldn't resist Trygve's entreaties. It couldn't have been easy for a girl probably still in her teens to leave the familiar circle of family and friends behind in Norway. I wondered if she'd been happy in her new life.

Max looked surprised. "So you've been reading up on the family already?"

"Well," I replied, trying to recover from my slip of the tongue, "we often do background checking when an old-timer like your father dies."

"Tell me," Vida said, leaning her elbows on the table and addressing Max, "why did the family change the spelling of their last name?"

Max looked blank. "It was always Froland. F-r-o . . ."

"No, no," Vida interrupted, shaking her head. "The Iversons. It was originally spelled with an *e*."

"Oh." Max rubbed at his beard. "I found Pa's birth certificate when I was going through his things the other day. His mother, Karen Iverson, had spelled it with an *o*."

"I've always thought," Vida continued in a musing tone, "that the s-o-n was more of a Swedish spelling than Norwegian."

"Generally, yes," Max said, "but there are exceptions. Border crossings, and all that," he added with a wink.

I'd resumed looking at the photos. They were typical— adults posing in their Sunday best, more babes in arms, kids riding horses, kids playing ball, kids under a Christmas tree. The second album started out the same way, though there were no new babies and the kids were getting bigger. Trygve and Olga were bigger, too.

Halfway through the snapshots, the backdrop changed. Now they were in Alpine. I could see Mount Baldy in the background, a small frame house above the railroad tracks, the bunkhouses below. One large photo was familiar. It showed the entire population of Alpine on the mill's loading dock with the American flag they'd won for selling the most Liberty Bonds per capita in the state of Washington.

I turned the page. Three men identified as Per, Lon, and Oscar stood in front of an enormous fallen cedar tree. Per, I assumed, was Trygve and Olga's firstborn. He was a tall, strapping young man, and unlike his parents in their wedding portrait, Per was grinning at the camera.

There were more photos taken in the woods, but it was the one on the facing page in the lower right-hand corner that grabbed my attention.

It was a snapshot of a rope dangling from a railroad trestle.

September 1916

The first face that Frank Dawson saw belonged to Harry Geerds, who was leaning out of the big locomotive. Harry looked grim, his ruddy cheeks smudged with coal and his broad shoulders slumped. Even before Harry's brakeman had come to a complete stop by the water tower, men began to jump from the slow-moving boxcars.

"Goddammit," Harry shouted to Frank and the others, "I didn't want to bring this bunch to Alpine, but I don't have much choice."

"Don't worry," Frank called back. "We'll make short work of them."

One of the new arrivals had already commandeered a packing crate and was standing on top of it. He was a tall lean man with a black scruffy beard and black scruffy clothes to match. In one hand he held a small red book. At least two dozen other men surged around the bearded newcomer, many also holding a similar red book.

With a dignified calm, Carl Clemans approached the group. "Is that your leader?" he asked one of the newcomers.

The man, who had bright red hair under his shabby cap, raised a fist. "We're all leaders!" The others, including another dozen or more who had descended from the freight cars, chorused the same reply.

Someone handed a red flag to the man on the packing crate. As he unfurled the banner, the Wobblies waved the little red book and raised their voices in song:

"The people's flag is deepest red,
It shrouded oft our martyred dead;
And ere their limbs grew stiff and cold
Their life blood dyed its every fold."

"Bullshit!" cried Tom Bassen, the woods foreman. "Get back on that train and get the hell out of Alpine!"

Shouts of "Commies!" "Reds!" and "Traitors!" rent the smoky September air as more millworkers and loggers poured onto the platform.

But the man with the scruffy beard and the scruffy clothes had a powerful voice that carried above the hostile Alpiners' shouts. "Don't be fools!" he cried in an accented voice. "You're being gypped! You should join your Everett brothers and strike! You work for greedy capitalist pigs who will drain you of your lifeblood!"

"No! No!" several of the men responded. "Not us! Not here!"

Frank, with his brother-in-law, Tom Murphy, stood back a few yards from the other mill workers. "Why did they come here?" he murmured. "There are plenty of other camps where the conditions are bad. But not with Carl. He's fair and generous."

Tom nodded. "I know that. We all know that. But I guess these wild-eyed radicals don't."

Close to fifty I.W.W. members had now exited from the train. Harry Geerds wasted no time in starting up the locomotive again. "Good luck!" he called from his engineer's perch. Slowly at first, then gathering momentum, the freight continued on its eastern journey.

"The fat cats who own the mills and the woods and the camps don't want to give you a fair shake!" the bearded man declared, still waving the red banner. "We working stiffs got to stand together! Solidarity forever!"

As he paused to catch his breath, a small object hurtled

through the air. It caught the man on the cheek, just above the line of his beard. He staggered slightly, then glared in the direction from which the missile had been thrown.

A rock, Frank thought. Along with everyone else, he turned to see who'd struck the Wobbly speaker. No one stepped forward. The men who were in the vicinity all looked around, too.

"Cowards!" the speaker cried, as a trickle of blood ran down his cheek. "You're fools and you're cowards!"

Shouts went up from both sides; scuffling broke out. And then real blows were exchanged.

The caboose had just passed by the loading dock. At least a dozen fistfights spilled over onto the now-vacant tracks.

Tom Bassen held up a two-by-four. "Okay, men, let's go!"

The rest of the workers who had not yet joined in the melee surged forward. Even Carl Clemans had discarded his navy blue suit jacket and rolled up his sleeves. He held no weapon but led the charge from the loading dock ramp with at least sixty men right behind him.

Tom Murphy wielded a baseball bat. He was first-generation Irish from New York State, and knew what it was like to be treated as an inferior. He'd come west to seek his fortune in the Yukon, but the golden dream had eluded him. Now he had a wife and two children, and no damned rabble-rousers were going to spoil the claim he'd staked to a better life in Alpine.

Frank Dawson also picked up a baseball bat, but his gaze wasn't fixed on the violence directly in front of him. Instead, he looked up the hill a few yards, then shook his head. He thought he knew who'd triggered the brawl. Frank turned just in time to see a fierce Wobbly descend on him with a pine club. Frank ducked, fell to the ground, and rolled over. The club hit so close to his nose that he could smell the wood's sweet scent.

Someone—Frank thought it was one of his other brothers-

in-law, Louie Siegel—was grappling with the man who'd swung the club. Louie was no more than average height but built like a bull. With his baseball bat, Frank clubbed the Wobbly on the shoulder. He fell with a loud yelp of pain. Exchanging satisfied glances, Frank and Louie waded into the mob. Louie was armed only with his fists; Frank swung the baseball bat at every unfamiliar face.

Some of the intruders were already on the run. Carl Clemans led the pursuers, shouting courage to his men. The Wobblies had picked up weapons of wood from the loading dock, but most were discarded as they ran for their lives.

Frank was panting by the time they reached the trestle. Several of the radicals jumped from the near end, rolling down the hillside and into the brush and berry bushes that had sprung up where the trees had been clear-cut.

"Look at them go!" Tom Bassen shouted, pointing at the enemy in retreat. "Solidarity, my ass!"

"Chicken shits!" cried Vern Farnham, leaning on his club.

Frank saw Carl Clemans a few feet away. The mill owner's gaze was fixed on the fleeing Wobblies. There were tears in his eyes as Tom Bassen shook his hand.

"That's the end of them around here," Tom declared, his voice hoarse.

Carl attempted a smile at his foreman. "I hope so. But they're not entirely wrong, you know. They're just not right for Alpine."

Dusk was falling as Frank and the others headed back to the mill. At the loading dock, he noticed patches of blood seeping into the rough planks. Looking around, he saw that some of it had come from his friends and fellow workers. A cut here, a slash there, and bruises that were discoloring almost before his very eyes. But spirits were high. A battle had been fought, a victory won.

Frank looked again at the place on the hill where his at-

tention had been drawn just before he'd almost been clubbed. No one was there now. But earlier, in the path from where the sharp object had been thrown, he had seen two figures standing together and jeering.

Frank had instantly recognized Jonas Iversen, and his own nephew, Vincent Burke.

Chapter Eight

I FORCED MY voice to sound casual as I pointed to the snapshot of the rope hanging from the trestle. "What's the significance of this shot?"

Max leaned over to look while I heard Vida's sharp intake of breath. She coughed rather loudly to mask her surprise.

"Goodness," she exclaimed, "I hope I'm not catching cold." For emphasis, she took a handkerchief from her purse and blew her nose in a loud, buglelike manner.

"I don't know what this picture represents," Max finally said after studying the photo. "I can't see anybody in the background beyond the trestle and the rope, can you?"

I couldn't either, though upon closer inspection, I realized that this photo wasn't taken from the exact same angle as the one that had been enclosed in the threatening letter to Marsha Foster-Klein. The lettering under the snapshot didn't tell me anything I didn't already know: It read GN TRESTLE OVER SKYKOMISH RIVER.

I flipped the page. Another wedding portrait, this time of Per and Susan Iversen. The setting was a church, probably in Ballard, according to the write-up Vida and I had read in *The Blabber*. The couple looked much less solemn and considerably better looking than Trygve and Olga. There followed more kids, more babies, more Christmas trees, and an eight-by-ten photo of a group gathering, probably in the social hall. THANKSGIVING DAY DINNER, 1917 read the caption. The diners appeared well fed and reasonably well dressed.

"May we keep these?" I asked, fingering the two older albums.

"Of course," Max replied with a smile. Now that I noticed, he was better looking than his great-grandparents, too. The only resemblance I saw—besides the beard—was in his eyes. Like Trygve's, they were very keen.

Vida had her hands on the other, newer albums. "May we keep these as well?"

"Go ahead," Max said.

Vida pulled one of the albums in front of her and turned to me. "I have to show you a picture of Max's late wife, Jackie. She was such a beautiful girl." She glanced at Max. "Do you mind?"

Max shook his head, then reached out to slip a finger between two of the last pages. "Our wedding photo is somewhere around here."

Vida found it immediately. It was in black-and-white, taken at First Lutheran in front of the altar. Max wore a beard even then. Of course it was the Seventies when so many men sported facial hair. He was thinner and looked very handsome—and happy—in his tuxedo.

"Jackie," Vida interposed, "was Neeny Doukas's niece. You remember him, of course."

I did. Neeny had been involved in the very first homicide I'd encountered in Alpine. He'd been in the real estate business, and the firm he founded still bore his name.

If Neeny had been a homely old coot, Jackie was his polar opposite. She was a dark-haired beauty whose vibrancy showed through in the photograph. Indeed, she was movie-star gorgeous, and looked like someone I'd like to know—when I got over resenting her good looks.

Despite not having known her, Jackie's image brought tears to my eyes. "Lovely," I murmured, then steeled myself to look straight at Max. "I don't know what to say."

"There's nothing to say," Max said with a shrug. His own

lips trembled, but he held my gaze. "You've had your own terrible loss, I understand."

"Yes."

Vida closed the album. "Your sister, Lynn, was quite lovely, too," she remarked, referring to Max's sister. "Life is so hard."

Max got to his feet. "I really should go. I don't like leaving Ma for too long since I have to go back to Seattle Monday morning. I have a departmental meeting that I shouldn't miss."

Vida and I both stood up, too. "What do you teach?" I asked, again under control.

"American history," Max replied. "My specialty is the era between the world wars."

"Fascinating," I said, probably sounding phony. But I meant it. "I'm kind of a history buff myself. I took three quarters of American history at the U before transferring to Oregon in my senior year. I had an absolutely wonderful professor for all three classes."

Max grinned. "You must mean Tom Pressly. He's still an inspiration for the rest of us."

I nodded. "He certainly inspired me. I loved his description of 'history sense' being like 'tennis sense.' Some people have it, some don't. He had both."

"That's the truth," Max said. "Say, why don't we have dinner tomorrow night and talk about Tom and history and whatever else you need to know for your article?"

All of a sudden I felt giddy. Two out of three nights having dinner with a man who wasn't Milo? "I'd like that," I said simply.

"I must confess," Max said with a deferential air, "I have a motive. I've been working on a book for a couple of years. I'd like to pick your brain a bit. Not only are you a writer, but you seem to have an interest in history."

It wasn't the first time I'd been asked to help with a manuscript. My former ad manager, Ed Bronsky, had prevailed upon me to work with his autobiography. If I could endure hours with Ed and reams of bad writing, I could probably put up with Max's historical treatise.

"I'm no expert," I pointed out.

"But you're a professional writer. I stand in awe of people who write for a living. Then it's settled?" He waited for me to nod my agreement. "Wonderful. I'll call you tomorrow," Max said, then bade us farewell.

"My, my," Vida murmured as Max closed the news room door behind him, "I believe you have a date."

"Shut up, Vida," I snapped, no longer giddy.

"I think it's very nice," she declared.

I didn't respond. I was too embarrassed.

And guilty.

Vida went off to finish her errands, which included buying Roger some additions for his Nintendo Game Boy. She, too, may have been feeling some guilt in case she changed her mind about Buck moving in with her and displacing her precious grandson.

I remained in the newsroom, flipping through the albums. I noted that there were few pictures of Jonas Iversen, and none taken after 1917. It was almost as if he'd ceased to exist.

"Now what?" demanded Milo Dodge as he lumbered through the door. "Have you moved into your office?"

He'd startled me. "Gosh, Milo, are you stalking me?"

"Nope," he replied, sitting down in the chair that Vida had vacated. "I saw your car. You don't usually work weekends."

"We have a special edition coming out Wednesday," I said. "I'm doing some research."

Milo paused to light a cigarette. "No kidding. How come?"

"We need the money," I replied. "Give me one of those things."

He flipped me a Marlboro Light, then offered a match. "As long as you're researching, figure out why that stiff had batteries in his hand."

I stared at Milo. "What stiff? The fire victim?"

The sheriff nodded. "Batteries often explode in a fire, but these didn't. They leaked alkaline instead."

"You didn't mention anything about batteries before," I said in mild rebuke.

"I didn't know about them until we pried open one of the hands," Milo responded, tapping his cigarette into Leo's ashtray. "I've got an idea, though."

"Really?" I tried not to sound sarcastic. "I mean, you don't usually speculate."

"I don't." Milo pushed the chair back and placed both long legs on the table, just missing one of the Frolands' older albums. The sheriff, who was otherwise dressed in his usual civilian garb of flannel shirt and suntan pants, was wearing cowboy boots. He wore his off-duty gun, a Smith & Wesson Chief's Special, tucked in the waistband of his pants.

"But this time," he continued, "I had to wonder why. Who gets burned to death while hanging onto a couple of AA batteries? Why not let go? Wouldn't you want both hands free if you were in the middle of a raging fire?"

I agreed. "So what's your point?"

Milo looked a bit smug. "The victim may already have been dead before the fire started."

"Ah." It was so obvious that I felt stupid. Even then, it took a couple of seconds for the implication to sink in. "You mean this person may have been murdered?"

"Could be." Milo leaned back in the chair and recrossed his legs on the table. It occurred to me that I was supposed to comment on his boots. They were definitely new; the soles were scarcely marred.

"Intriguing," I said, then duly admired the new footgear. "I've never seen you wear cowboy boots before. Is this a fashion statement?"

"What?" Milo feigned surprise as he waggled his feet and gazed at the brown-tooled leather. "Oh, no. Barton's Bootery had these in their window at the mall. I kind of took a liking to them. Clancy Barton talked me into buying a pair. What do you think?"

"I think they're very handsome," I said truthfully. "With those heels, you must stand about six-eight."

"Close to it," Milo replied. "That's not a bad thing for a law enforcement officer."

I'd done my duty. I wanted to get back to business. Rescuing the old album from Milo's boots, I turned to the page that held the snapshot of the railroad trestle. "Look at this. Coincidence, or what?"

Milo looked closely at the photo. "You mean this isn't the same picture you showed me the other day?"

I shook my head. "No. Let me show you the other one." I got up and went into my office to get the snapshot Marsha Foster-Klein had received in the mail. "See? You said you knew the site where this was taken. I drove out there, I could see the rock that looked like somebody's hind end. It's in shadow in the album snapshot, but judging from the photo's format, it looks as if it had been taken by the same camera."

Milo studied both photos. "I wouldn't jump to conclusions about the same camera taking these. Way back, most people only had the one kind of Kodak."

"But it looks like almost exactly the same shot," I countered. "How long would that rope have hung from the trestle?"

Milo shrugged. "How would I know? It would depend on why it was there in the first place. Hey, how come you're so interested in these pictures anyway?"

"I told you," I said, on the defensive, "I'm doing some historical research. We have a special edition coming out."

Milo gave me a curious look. "You're bullshitting me, Emma. You're about the worst liar I ever met. If you ever commit a crime, confess right off the bat."

I felt a faint flush cover my face. "I am doing research," I said doggedly.

The sheriff shrugged again, then removed his legs from the table and stood up. He certainly was tall. His head almost hit the newsroom's low ceiling.

"If you say so," he remarked. "Now I've got to give the M.E. in Everett a big shove. I want to know if our burn victim was killed by something other than the fire."

"I'd like to know that, too," I said, following Milo to the door. "Still no missing persons report?"

"Nope." Milo had to duck to get through the door. I figured he'd be about seven feet tall when he put on his Smoky the Bear hat.

"Let me know about Jack Froland, too," I called after him.

Milo stopped with his hand on the knob of the outside door. "I'm betting there won't be much to tell."

I didn't argue.

I was turning back toward the newsroom when I heard the door reopen. Milo, I thought, forgetting to tell me something. But it was Spencer Fleetwood who leaned in the doorway.

"Working overtime?" he inquired in his smooth, casual voice. "That's very un-Alpinish, isn't it?"

"I'm not a native," I replied. "I don't necessarily follow the local rule of thumb, 'If you can't make it in five, you'll never make it in six,' Anyway, I'm doing research for the special autumn edition."

"Don't forget," Spence remarked, "when you start working on the Halloween edition ads, we're in it together."

"I won't." I waited for Spence to continue on his way, but he lingered.

"I saw Milo Dodge go off in the other direction," Spence said. "Did he bring you a hot news tip?"

I tensed a bit. "We didn't agree to share news. Just ad revenue. But no, Milo stopped in to show off his new cowboy boots."

Spence chuckled. "Which will appear in Vida's 'Scene Around Town' column, right?"

"Right." I told myself to make a note for Vida. Her weekly snippets of gossip were the best-read part of the newspaper.

"I've thought of doing something along those lines," Spence said, now edging into the front office. "In fact, I'm already putting together a kind of 'This Day in Alpine History' thing. Not just Alpine, or we wouldn't have much to say, but what went on everywhere. I may have to bother you for your morgue. Would you mind?"

"No," I replied, wondering why I'd never come up with the idea myself. "Everything's in bound volumes. Kip MacDuff is planning to put at least some of the back issues on disk."

Spence was now all the way past the front desk. "That's a big job. Any chance I could take a peek at those bound volumes now?"

The request was a bit surprising. "Why, no, go ahead. You can work off the table in the newsroom. I'll be in my office."

Gathering up the Froland family albums, I headed for my cubbyhole. Maybe I'd been too abrupt. As a courtesy, I left the door open.

Going through a virtual stranger's pictorial memories is always a bittersweet experience. Usually, family photographs record only happy moments, but a sense of sadness permeates the pages of someone who has died. Except for the rabid genealogist, fifty years from now anyone who looks at the Froland collection won't have known the people in the pictures. The names in the captions may identify them, but they will be little more than that, except for the rare anecdote passed down the years. I've always thought that was an unfortunate commentary on Americans, whose history is so short, and whose memories are often even shorter.

I never found a smiling likeness of Olga Iverson. Maybe she was a melancholy personality; maybe she had bad teeth.

At the beginning of the most recent album, I found photos of Lynn Froland. She had been a pretty blonde girl, tall and athletic-looking. Indeed, one color picture showed her with skis, perhaps at the Stevens Pass summit where she had died in that tragic car accident. Another shot showed her without skis, but in winter togs, sitting with a group of young people outside of what might have the lodge at the summit. I looked closely to see if Max was one of the three young men with his sister and two other girls, but I didn't recognize him. The date was January 1967, the year that Lynn had died.

From the newsroom, a burst of Vida's startled voice made me look up.

"Well!" she cried, "whatever are you doing here?"

"Boning up on Alpine's past," Spence replied in an amused tone. "Is everybody working on Saturday?"

"So it seems," Vida retorted, then marched into my office and closed the door. "What's going on with Mr. Fleetwood?"

I explained about Spence's idea for a radio feature.

Vida sniffed. "Marius Vandeventer did that for years in the *Advocate*. We dropped it not long before he sold the paper to you. It was getting redundant."

"Then," I pointed out, "it's all the more harmless for him to do it over the air."

"Silly," Vida said, sitting down across from me. "Only the very young will learn anything new."

The comment amused me, but Vida was quite serious. She gave herself a shake, then plopped both elbows on my desk. "That's not really why I'm here. After I bought those cute little games for Roger, I went home. The mail had come. You'll never guess what I got." She reached into her purse and drew out a letter-sized envelope. "It's a thank-you from June Froland."

I stared at the address, which was written in a spidery hand. Then I stared at the brief message on the single page.

"Thank you for the lovely flowers. They mean so much at this sad time." The note was simply signed, *June*.

But what I stared at even more than the message was the

envelope and the paper. They were the same as the missive that had been sent to Marsha Foster-Klein.

"What do you make of that?" Vida asked with a glint in her gray eyes.

"It's not the same handwriting," I pointed out.

"True," Vida allowed. "And I'm sure Parker's Pharmacy, for example, sells quite a bit of this stationery. But still . . ." She gave me her owlish look.

"If June's handwriting doesn't match Marsha's letter," I said in an incredulous voice, "did Jack write it? But why?"

"We must try to get a handwriting comparison," Vida declared. "Going through the guest book for the funeral might help. I'll drop in on June tomorrow night while you're out with Max. But there's another thing—which becomes even more curious since I received June's note—that I must discuss with you." She turned to make sure the door was firmly closed. "What about that trestle snapshot in the Froland album? I couldn't say anything while Max was here."

I sat back in my swivel chair. The morning had grown warm, especially in my little office with its low, slanting tin roof. "I've been thinking about that. Most people—at least in my family—might take two or three shots of a single subject, but only one—the best—would go into the album. The others would get stuffed back into their original envelopes or put in a . . ." I clapped a hand to my head. "I forgot to bring the shoe box in here. I'll go get it."

Hurrying into the news office, I discovered it was empty. The shoe box was on the table, but Spencer Fleetwood was gone. It certainly hadn't taken him long to do his research, I thought. In fact, he hadn't quite put away the volume he'd been perusing. It stuck out on the shelf by a good two inches. I gave it a nudge, then looked at the year: 1967. A coincidence, maybe. It was the year that Lynn Froland had died. I pulled the bound newspapers from the shelf, grabbed the shoe box, and returned to my cubbyhole.

"You're right," Vida said as I sat down again. "It's very possible that there are more views of that trestle with June and Jack's other pictures." She noticed the volume of *Advocate*s. "What are you doing with that?"

"Spence had taken it off the shelf," I replied. "I thought I might check out the article on Lynn Froland's fatal accident."

Vida looked suspicious. "Why?"

"Just curious," I said lightly. "Have you ever been curious, Vida?"

Vida harrumphed, then said in a normal voice, "It was late January. I remember, because my youngest daughter, Meg, was born two days later. I wasn't able to attend Lynn's funeral."

The 1967 version of *The Alpine Advocate* looked quite different than the current edition. For one thing, it was a standard-sized newspaper then, rather than the tabloid into which it had evolved during the mid-Seventies. The typefaces for the headlines were different, too—much bolder and blacker thirty-odd years ago. But the main thing missing from the earlier *Advocate* was Vida. She was ten years away from widowhood and working mom status. I could hardly imagine the paper without her.

The Lynn Froland story was in the January twenty-sixth issue, written under Marius Vandeventer's byline. The *Advocate* was published on Thursdays instead of Wednesdays in those days. The accident had occurred on the previous Sunday, with the funeral scheduled for Thursday. Thus, the newspaper was late with the fatality story and early for Lynn's services. I empathized with my predecessor.

"Alpine mourned former Alpine High School prom queen Lynn Froland today, following her tragic death in an automobile accident near the summit of Stevens Pass last Sunday evening," I read aloud. "The daughter of Jack and June Froland died at the scene when the 1960 Plymouth Valiant in which she'd been riding skidded on black ice and rolled down a sixty-foot embankment.

"Lynn had been skiing with friends at the summit. An active, sports-loving young woman, Lynn worked as a checker at the Grocery Basket, and was known to most of Alpine for her friendly manner and high spirits. She had planned to enroll at Western Washington State College in Bellingham this coming fall."

There was more, but I stopped reading. A one-column headshot of Lynn was probably her high school senior picture. The larger front-page photo showed law enforcement officials—identified as the state patrol—looking at the car's wreckage after it had been brought up from the embankment. The tangled mass of metal was a chilling sight.

I closed the book. "Was anyone else hurt?" I asked Vida.

For once, Vida looked vague. "Y-e-s . . . I believe so. But I don't recall. . . . Such a distracting time for me, with the new baby. . . . It should be in the article." She paused. "Yes, as I recall, Lynn was with two or three other young people. The driver wasn't from here, Sultan or Monroe, perhaps. . . . I don't remember the name. You can look it up in here." She tapped the bound volume with a forefinger.

I shook my head. "I was only curious. The car looked like a mess."

"It was," Vida said, "but Lynn was riding in the passenger seat, the dead man's seat, I think it's sometimes called. She took the brunt of the crash. In those days, seat belts were still a novelty. I doubt the car even had them."

As Vida spoke, I'd started going through the shoe box. There were only a few photos inside, and most of them recent. The rest were postcards, including at least a dozen Max had sent while on his honeymoon in the Far East.

"A dutiful son," Vida remarked. "You'll enjoy your dinner with him. He's always been very bright. If only the community college had been built earlier, he wouldn't have had to leave Alpine."

I didn't comment, either on Max's defection or what might have been Vida's attempt to play Cupid. At the bottom of the box, I found Jack and June's certificate of marriage, the birth certificates for both Lynn and Max, the program from Max and Jackie's wedding, and the inevitable clippings about both young women's untimely deaths. There was also a University of Washington commencement program from 1972. I assumed it was the year that Max had gotten his undergraduate degree.

"Yes," Vida said, "he went on to graduate school at Stanford on a Woodrow Wilson fellowship."

"Had Max and Jackie been high school sweethearts?" I asked.

Vida shook her head. "Jackie was four years younger. They'd known each other, of course, but didn't date until he came home on vacation from Palo Alto. They made such a handsome couple. Tsk, tsk."

I replaced the lid on the shoe box. "I'm going to call on Judge Marsha to give her a progress report. I have a feeling she's probably already phoned me once or twice at home."

Vida frowned. "Are you going to accuse the Frolands of sending that letter?"

"Not in so many words," I said. "But I'll point out the coincidence—if that's what it is—of the stationery. Do you mind if I take the note from June with me?"

Vida considered. "You may as well take me with you, too. I've no further plans today, though I thought I'd work in the garden since it's so nice out."

"Okay," I agreed, then reached for the phone. "Maybe I'd better call to see if she's home."

The judge was in. I didn't try to tantalize her, but merely said that Vida and I wanted to give her a progress report.

"Let's hope there's some progress to report," Marsha retorted. "I'll see you in ten minutes."

Vida and I took separate cars, planning to rendezvous at The Pines Village. As I drove along Front Street, I passed Parker's Pharmacy and suddenly remembered the prescription for Paxil. I shrugged. I'd pick it up later. Vida was right behind me in her Buick. If I stopped now, she'd ask all kinds of questions I didn't want to answer.

I expected to pull up in front of the apartment house, but to my surprise, there were no empty parking spaces. I paused at the corner to check out Maple Lane, the short street that ran between The Pines Village and the condos that also faced Alpine Way.

Vida honked. In the rearview mirror, I saw her lean out the window and make a windmill gesture with her arm.

"The Colbys are having a football brunch at their condo," she called out. "I ran an item about it on my page, remember? Go around to the garage entrance. Marsha must have a guest parking place. I'll use the one for that idiot, Ella Hinshaw."

Ella the Idiot was yet another of Vida's shirttail relations. But the suggestion was sound. I followed instructions and found the space marked PENTHOUSE GUEST.

The only problem was that it was already occupied. I recognized the black BMW at once. It belonged to Spencer Fleetwood.

November 1916

The wind blowing in from Puget Sound grew colder as it swirled eastward into the Cascade Mountains. There had been a heavy frost that morning in Alpine. The dark gray clouds covering Mount Baldy and Tonga Ridge promised snow. Winter was coming early this year.

Mary Dawson and her sister, Kate Murphy, watched their footing as they carried buckets to fill from Icicle Creek for the weekly wash. Several other women were already at the creek, but their usual cheerful gossip subsided when the Siegel sisters approached.

Kate nudged Mary. "Are they talking about us?"

Mary shrugged. "Maybe."

Reaching the creek, Kate set her buckets down and called to her sister-in-law Ruby Siegel, who stood with three of the other women. "Well? Cat got your tongue?"

"What do you mean?" Ruby retorted, scowling at Kate.

Kate pointed to one of her eyes. "You don't see any green here, do you? Why did you all stop talking when Mary and I showed up?"

"No reason," Ruby retorted, but she lowered her eyes.

Mary Bassen, the wife of Tom, the woods foreman, laughed. "Oh, good heavens, Kate, we were talking about that horrible mess in Everett. I don't see any reason to keep it a secret." She shot a quick glance at Ruby.

Kate hesitated, then shrugged. "If you say so."

"It makes you feel sorry for those poor Wobblies," Mary

141

Dawson put in. "No matter how crazy they are, shooting them in cold blood isn't right."

"Of course it's not right!" Ruby exclaimed, fire in her eyes. She'd heard at least one eyewitness account; she'd devoured every word in the newspapers. Shortly before Halloween, as the shingle weavers' strike dragged on, some forty I.W.W. members had sailed from Seattle to Everett to break the blockade set up by the mill owners. Sheriff Donald McRae and his deputies had been waiting at the dock. They'd rounded up the Wobblies and hauled them out to a wooded area called Beverly Park. The agitators were forced to run a gauntlet between men wielding gun butts, pickaxes, and blackjacks. Ten days later, two-hundred-and-ninety Wobblies sailed into Everett harbor aboard the passenger ships Verona and Calista. Several thousand onlookers had gathered on a nearby hill to watch the excitement.

"Gruesome," Ruby muttered, as the other women looked at her. "It was those deputies who fired first. They killed that young boy who climbed up the Verona's flagpole to wave to the crowd. There was no call for that. It was like shooting a seagull on a piling. No wonder the Wobblies fired back."

Five radicals had been shot, six more had drowned, thirty-one were wounded. A toll had also been taken on the deputies, with two dead and several others wounded, including Sheriff McRae. When the Verona returned to Seattle, over two hundred Wobblies had been arrested. Seventy-four of them were charged with first-degree murder.

"I don't understand you, Ruby," Kate said to her sister-in-law. "One minute you're all head-up-and-tail-a-flying to crown a Wobbly with your cast-iron skillet, and the next, you're crying crocodile tears because they got their come-uppance."

"A knock on the head isn't the same as a bullet through the heart," Ruby shot back. "Besides, I've said all along those Wobblies have some good arguments. Alpine's an exception. The conditions in other logging camps and mill *towns are deplorable. You've heard about them, you know how badly the workers can be treated. We're just lucky, that's all."*

Kate tipped her head to one side. "You read too much, Ruby. I think I'll ask my brother if you keep a copy of the Communist Manifesto under your pillow."

Like lightning, Ruby's mood shifted. "No fair peeking, Kate," she laughed.

"I wouldn't dream of peeking into your bedroom," Kate said with a droll expression.

"I love to read," Ruby declared as some of the other women began to leave with their heavy buckets in each hand. "Politics and history, they're my favorites. In fact, I read a very interesting article by one of the Wobblies just a few weeks ago."

Kate had bent down to fill one of her buckets. "Oh? About what? How to start a strike?"

"On the economics of the timber industry," Ruby replied. "It was written by Yitzhak Klein, a German immigrant. He made a good case for a conspiracy in the logging business."

"Ha!" Kate exclaimed. "You know what Carl Clemans would say about that!"

The three sisters-in-law were now alone at the creek. Mary Dawson hadn't been listening to the exchange between Kate and Ruby. She'd gotten her water and was standing with the buckets at her feet.

"Ruby," she said, her blue eyes fixed on the other woman's face, "what were you really talking about when we came along?"

Ruby gave a toss of her head. "Oh, Mary . . ."

"Ruby!" Mary spoke softly but sharply. "Out with it."

Once again, Ruby lowered her gaze. "Ohhh . . . You know darned well. . . ."

"That's why I'm asking," Mary asserted. "Don't be a clam. It doesn't suit you."

Ruby looked bleak. "Vincent."

Mary sucked in her breath. "I thought so. What did they say?"

Ruby swallowed hard. "That he's a wrong 'un."

"What else?" Mary persisted.

"That he and the Iversen boy—Jonas—are trouble." Ruby offered Mary a kindly smile. "They blame Jonas more than Vincent. Jonas is the leader, Vincent is the follower."

"High spirits, that's all," Kate put in, then poked Mary in the arm. "Like Billy and Louie last year, before we moved to Alpine. When they set the barn on fire down at the farm in Sultan."

Mary looked askance. "They were scarcely eight years old."

"They were smoking," Kate responded. "They can be full of mischief, too."

"This isn't mischief," Mary said quietly. "Vincent and Jonas are teenagers. They have too much time on their hands. Frank says they started that trouble when the Wobblies came here. Oh, Vincent denied it, he insisted he and Jonas didn't throw any rocks, but Frank knows better."

Ruby wore a pained expression. "One thing leads to another," she said cryptically.

Mary turned on Ruby. "What is that supposed to mean?"

Ruby assumed an air of innocence. "I only know what I hear."

"Well?" Mary demanded, digging in her heels.

"They're up to no good," Ruby replied.

"Such as what?" Mary asked in a trenchant voice.

Ruby flushed. "I don't know. Really, I'm not sure. Those other women . . . They like to talk."

Mary wasn't giving up. "And?"

"Ohhh . . ." Ruby waved an arm. "Honestly, I don't know. One of them said something about . . . unspeakable goings-on."

Kate had also zeroed in on her sister-in-law. The Siegel

sisters were both taller than Ruby, who backpedaled and put one foot in the creek.

"Go on," Kate urged in a chilling voice.

"I swear to God," Ruby said, now lifting a hand toward the heavens, "I don't know. Do you think they'd say anything . . . indecent out loud?"

Mary stepped away. "That," she declared, "makes it all the worse."

Chapter Nine

"Now what do we do?" I asked Vida after she had parked the Buick and walked out of the underground garage to join me in the driveway. "What's Spencer Fleetwood doing at Judge Marsha's?"

Vida looked puzzled. "Maybe he's not at her apartment. He has such cheek, he may be visiting someone else and simply barged into her guest space."

It was possible, but I had my doubts. "Let's wait," I suggested, having pulled the Lexus onto the verge of Maple Lane. "We'll give Spence ten minutes."

"Five," Vida said, holding up the fingers on one hand. "Marsha's expecting us. If Mr. Fleetwood called on her without warning, she can get rid of him."

I agreed. Vida began to prowl the landscaped area between The Pines Village and the condos, curiously named The Baldy Arms. She was thwarted from peeking into the ground level windows, however. The laurel hedges that had been planted along the sides of both buildings were as tall as she was.

"Ridiculous," Vida muttered. "Why don't they clip these branches? They're up over the windowsills in the condos. Surely the residents want to see out."

"There's not much to see," I remarked, waving a hand at the fifteen-foot patch of grass. "Besides, the tenants on both sides may enjoy their privacy."

"Ridiculous," Vida repeated. "What's wrong with people?"

I didn't reply. Vida looked at her watch. "One minute to go."

"You know," I said in a reasonable voice, "I think Marsha would have told us if she had company. If Spence dropped in after I called, then he hasn't been there for more than fifteen minutes."

"Time enough," Vida retorted, though she didn't add for what. Instead, she started counting down the seconds. "Fifty-one, fifty, forty-nine . . ."

She was down to ten when I heard a car start up somewhere in the garage. As we ducked out of sight, Vida stopped counting.

"Aha!" she exclaimed under her breath. "It's Himself."

The black Beamer glided up the driveway, then turned toward Alpine Way. We went into the garage and buzzed Marsha's apartment. At least a half-minute passed before she told us to come up.

"Destroying the evidence?" Vida remarked as we waited for the elevator.

"Of what?" I asked, stepping into the small car. "Rumpled sheets?"

"Don't be coarse," Vida chided. "Cigarette ash, the extra glass or coffee cup, the jacket Spencer Fleetwood might have left behind in his haste to leave."

"He hardly had time to take off his jacket," I said. "Besides, he wasn't wearing one when he stopped by the office."

Marsha didn't appear to be suffering from anxiety when she met us at the door. She was dressed in dark slacks and a baby blue cotton sweater, and looked much improved in health since I'd seen her last.

As soon as we were sitting down, Marsha asked if we'd like coffee. Vida declined, so I did, too. To my surprise, Marsha inquired if we'd prefer sandwiches. It was, she pointed out, lunchtime.

"Why, yes," Vida enthused. "How kind!"

Marsha looked as if she hadn't expected to be taken up on her offer. "Is tuna fish okay?"

"Lovely," Vida said.

I agreed. Marsha disappeared into the kitchen. Vida sprung up from the sofa and began snooping around the living room. She seemed particularly interested in some items on a round mahogany table that held a large bouquet of yellow spider chrysanthemum, bells of Ireland, purple statis, and baby's breath. All the while, she rattled on about the wonderful view of Mount Baldy through the living room's big picture window—except for the charred tree trunks resulting from the fire, which was such a shame, and no doubt so careless of someone.

"You also have an excellent view of Alpine," Vida went on, speaking loudly so that Marsha could hear. "I can see very little from my house. I'm up high enough on the hill, but the neighbors in back of me have some very tall ornamentals. Oh—I'll have a glass of water with the sandwich, please."

"Emma?" called Marsha. "What about you?"

"Water's fine, thanks."

Vida had moved on from the mahogany table to a magazine rack to a stack of books and finally to the cartons that Marsha hadn't bothered to unpack. The judge reappeared with a tray containing our sandwiches and water. If Marsha had a cupboard stocked with condiments, she didn't offer them.

Vida was unruffled. "So difficult to not be certain of your permanent address," she commented, making her way back to the sofa. Marsha, who had made herself a sandwich, sat down in the armchair.

"Okay," Marsha asked, "what's the new lead?"

Vida had already taken a big chunk out of her tuna fish, so I was forced to answer. "By chance, we found an almost identical snapshot of the railroad trestle in Jack and June Froland's family album."

Marsha's jaw dropped. "What?"

I repeated the statement.

Not to be outdone, Vida swallowed and offered her own information. "This morning, I received a thank-you note from June Froland, written on the same kind of stationery as the letter that was sent to you. Not the same handwriting, I might add."

The judge was clearly taken aback. "Good Lord," she murmured. "That's not what I was expecting."

"What were you expecting?" I asked.

Marsha looked startled. "Nothing—I mean, nothing specific. I'm surprised about the Frolands. Are you saying one of them sent the letter and the picture to me?"

"No," I replied. "Anyone could have that brand of stationery. It's the coincidence between that and finding a similar photo in their album." To clarify, I explained how we planned to do an article on the Froland family in the upcoming special edition.

"I don't even know the Frolands," Marsha said, rubbing at her forehead.

"But," Vida put in, "you knew there was a family connection going back to the Iversons."

"A tenuous connection," Marsha pointed out.

"True," Vida allowed, then leaned forward on the sofa. "Marsha, do you have your Aunt Jo's current address or phone number?"

"No," Marsha replied. "Really, I've lost track of her."

"Never mind," Vida said. "I may be able to reach her in Port Angeles. Would you know if she still has her wits about her?"

Marsha shook her head. "I haven't seen her in years, not since my brother's wedding twenty-five years ago." She paused to take a sip of water. "If there is a connection to the Frolands, why would one of them send me a threatening letter? What are they talking about? And what the hell has that railroad trestle got to do with it?"

Vida had winced at the mild profanity but didn't reprimand the judge. "That's what we'll have to find out next," said Vida.

I thought she was whistling in the dark.

"Well?" I asked after we were in the apartment house's elevator. "What did you see of interest among Marsha's possessions?"

"You could see for yourself," she replied, then waited for my enlightenment.

I admitted I didn't know.

"The flowers," Vida said as we exited the elevator on the garage level. "They were fresh as could be, and from Delphine's shop. It's the same arrangement I sent to June Froland. But there was no plastic cardholder, which means they were hand carried to Judge Marsha. There were a few drops of water on the table. I'm not a betting woman, but if I were, I'd say that Spencer Fleetwood brought Marsha those flowers, and she watered them just before we arrived. Hence, the delay in answering the buzzer."

We had reached Vida's Buick in Ella Hinshaw's guest parking slot. "Are you hinting at a romance?"

"Perhaps." Vida's gaze traveled around the bleak concrete walls and ceiling. "You don't bribe a judge with a bouquet."

Before I could head for my car, Vida insisted we return to the office where she intended to telephone Marsha's aunt, Josephine Foster Iverson Bergstrom. Since I didn't have any better ideas, I agreed to go along so that I could listen in on an extension.

Vida sat at her own desk while I used Leo's phone. It took almost half an hour to track down Aunt Jo. There were several retirement and nursing homes in Port Angeles, not to mention another half-dozen in nearby Sequim.

At last, Vida got hold of the old girl who answered in a surprisingly strong voice. I was put off, however, by the fact that Aunt Jo didn't seem to recognize Vida's maiden or married names.

"I'm not from Alpine," Aunt Jo said in an impatient voice. "Now what's this about a newspaper piece? I don't read any more, I've got that macular condition. My eyesight's degenerating. It happens when you get to be eighty-one like I am. How old are you? You don't sound like any spring chicken to me, Mrs. Bunkel."

Maybe Aunt Jo's hearing was degenerating, too. Not to mention her memory, if she didn't know Vida.

Vida ignored the mistake. "Have you heard about Jack Froland's death?"

"Jack Froland?" There was a lengthy silence. "Isn't he a cousin or some such of Burt's?"

"Yes," Vida replied, looking at me and shaking her head. "Burt's father, Per Iverson, and Jack's mother, Karen Iverson, were brother and sister."

"Per," Aunt Jo repeated. "He was my father-in-law. He never got over Burt's getting killed in North Africa. Grandpa Per died about the time the war ended. Poor old coot. Did you know Burt?"

"Slightly," Vida said. "I was very young in those days, though I do recall how everyone praised his heroism."

"You do?" Aunt Jo sounded surprised. "Funny, I don't. Burt was kind of a scaredy-cat. I could never get him to take out the garbage after dark."

Vida rolled her eyes before asking the next question. "Where were you living at the time Burt went into the service?"

"Everett," Aunt Jo replied promptly. "Or was it Marysville? Maybe Mukilteo. What difference does it make? That was way back. I can hardly remember Burt."

"What about your brother, George Foster?" Vida inquired, maintaining her patience. "Do you remember him?"

" 'Course I remember George," Aunt Jo snapped. "You

think I'm senile?" Before Vida could respond, the old woman continued: "George was a year younger than me, and ten times dumber. He married a terrible woman. Never could stand her. Neither could Cap."

Briefly, Vida looked puzzled. "Cap? Oh—your second husband, Cap Bergstrom."

"You knew him?"

"Slightly." Vida tapped a pencil on the edge of her desk. "Why couldn't you stand your sister-in-law?"

"Mouthy," Aunt Jo retorted. "Always on her high horse about something or other. She was one of those . . . what do call them? Radicals, I think. Plus," the old lady went on, "she was a Jew."

"Did her religion cause a problem?" Vida asked somewhat stiffly.

"Not for me," Aunt Jo retorted. "I didn't have much to do with her. Neither did Cap. I think she's dead. So's George. Now what was her name? Cap and I called her The Jew."

I had to cough. I put my hand over the mouthpiece of Leo's phone and turned away.

Vida had winced at Jo's crudity. "I believe her name was Anna Klein."

"Could be. Homely woman. Always going on about the working class. Like we didn't know all about the working class? We *were* the working class."

Vida had taken off her glasses and was rubbing at her eyes. For once, she didn't make her accompanying moaning noise, though I could have sworn I heard her eyeballs squeak.

Apparently, the lull in the conversation confused Aunt Jo. "Hullo? Hullo?" she shouted into the phone. "You still there? Hullo?"

"Of course I'm still here," Vida retorted. "Were Anna and George happy together?"

"How would I know?" Aunt Jo shot back. "I used to tell

Cap, 'How can my brother be happy married to a Jew?' Cap would just shake his head."

Vida cradled the receiver under her chin and held up both hands in a gesture of surrender. "You've been very helpful, Mrs. Iver . . . I mean, Mrs. Bergstrom. You wouldn't have your daughter's phone number handy, would you?"

"Marjorie? 'Course I would. Just a minute . . . I should know it by heart, but I got one of them speedy dial things on this phone, and . . . Here it is. Her married name is Lathrop. They live close, over on Chambers Street."

"How nice for you," Vida said before politely ringing off. "Imbecile," she muttered, already dialing what was presumably Marjorie Iverson Lathrop's number. "Such a bigot. And absolutely dumb as a cedar stump."

I clicked Leo's phone back on as the call rang through to Port Angeles. On the fifth ring, a breathless voice answered.

"Marjorie?" Vida said at her most pleasant, then recited the same tale she'd told to Marjorie's mother. "Dear Jo," Vida went on, suggesting an intimacy that didn't exist and never had, "is getting a bit forgetful. But aren't we all?" Vida uttered the braying cackle that those of us who knew her recognized as both forced and false. I couldn't help but wonder how gullible Marjorie Iverson Lathrop really was.

"Hold it," Marjorie said. "Let me catch my breath. I was outside, picking plums. Why on earth would you be calling my mother about the Froland family? Who did you say had died?"

Vida scowled into the phone. "Your Uncle Jack. He passed on early this past week."

"Uncle Jack?" Marjorie sounded puzzled. "Do you mean the guy who owns a restaurant in Alpine?"

"No," Vida replied, "I do not. Jack Iverson is alive and well. I'm referring to Jack Froland. Didn't you live in Alpine for a time, Marjorie?"

"Not as a kid," Marjorie replied. "Mama and Papa moved

to Marysville after they were married. I don't really remember Papa. He was killed when I was still a baby. I've always thought of my stepdad as my real father." She paused, perhaps mourning both men. "Then about twelve years ago, Bart—my husband—got transferred to Alpine to work in the Snoqualmie National Forest. My stepdad died a year later, and after awhile, we had to put Mama in a nursing home. Bad timing. Wouldn't you know it, Bart got moved a year later to the Olympic National Forest in Port Angeles. He's a Forest Service biologist. But Bart's retiring the first of the year. Mama's going to outlive us yet."

Vida made a face at me. "She sounds very hearty, Marjorie. You should be grateful. But she certainly gives a poor impression of your family."

Marjorie pounced. "What do you mean by that?"

"Oh," Vida lamented, "I shouldn't have said that. But she was quite unkind about some of the other family members, particularly on her side. You'd think she'd speak of them more kindly."

If Vida had overdone her introduction to Marjorie, she was now hitting her stride.

"Who was she bashing this time?" Marjorie demanded. "Bart? She's always mean about my husband."

"No," Vida responded, "I mean on her own side of the family. Uncle George and Aunt Anna, to be specific."

"Oh, them." Marjorie's sigh was audible. "I suppose she was going on about Aunt Anna hyphenating her married name. It was unusual in those days, and Mama was scandalized. Of course Mama never could accept her brother marrying a Jew. I never understood that. Wouldn't you think that a woman whose husband—my poor father—had been killed by the Nazis would be less prejudiced? And don't get her off on the Blacks or the Asians or the Hispanics."

"That's a shame," Vida declared. "I gather you didn't feel so strongly about Aunt Anna?"

"I hardly ever saw her," Marjorie replied, "but she seemed

like a decent woman. Opinionated, yes. She was always talking about politics, and when you're a kid, you don't pay
much attention. I think Mama and Aunt Anna really got into
it during those McCarthy hearings. They had a serious
falling-out. Mama called Aunt Anna a Commie. Aunt Anna
called Mama an ignorant nitwit. Or something like that. It
was right after Uncle George and Aunt Anna got married. I
don't think they ever spoke again. Mama and Aunt Anna, I
mean."

"People should never argue over politics or religion," Vida
declared. "If they must express differing opinions, it's far
better to do so over personal flaws and bad behavior."

I could imagine what chaos Runkel and Blatt family
events had triggered. Bleeding egos for everyone, wounds
that lasted a lifetime. The spark to light yet another family
feud. To be fair, politics and religion often got just as personal, as in ". . . ignorant nitwit." Unfortunately, it sounded
as if Anna Foster-Klein had been right about Josephine Iverson Bergstrom.

"Speaking of families," Vida said in a chatty tone, "I don't
suppose you ever met your cousin, Marsha Foster-Klein.
She's a judge, living here in Alpine."

"A cousin?" Marjorie said.

"A first cousin," Vida responded. "Uncle George and Aunt
Anna's daughter."

Marjorie paused, apparently trying to remember. "Years
ago, we went to a wedding. It wasn't Marsha's, it was one of
the Foster-Klein boys. Gabe. Or Zeke. I don't recall. Anyway,
she was a bridesmaid. That must have been almost twenty-
five years ago. Whichever of the boys it was, the wedding
was in Monroe. Marsha was a bridesmaid. Yes, it's coming
back to me now," Marjorie went on, speaking faster and with
more confidence. "It was definitely Zeke who was the groom.
Gabe was the best man. It was hard to tell them apart, because they both had beards and long hair. Hippies, you know.
Their clothes were all those wild colors—psychedelic, was

what they called them. That's funny—I can't remember the bride at all, except that she had her arm in a cast and a bird on her head. Not a real bird—a stuffed dove."

"Ah!" Vida's eyes lit up as she glanced my way. "I remember that wedding—it was the first one I wrote up for the *Advocate*. The bride had attended Alpine High. Now what was her name . . . ?"

"Ask Marsha," Marjorie put in. "You say Marsha lives in Alpine now?"

Vida, apparently caught up in trying to recall the bride's identity, didn't answer right away. "What? Oh—yes, she's been sitting on the bench for our regular judge who's a bit gaga."

"Excuse me," Marjorie said, "but I'm going to be gaga, too, if I don't pick the rest of those plums before they hit the ground. It's starting to look like rain over here on the Peninsula. You can see the clouds moving down over Vancouver Island."

"Oh, of course," Vida said. "Thanks so much for all your help."

"What help?" retorted Marjorie. "I don't see how I contributed much to your article on the Frolands."

"Connections," Vida said glibly. "Families are all about connections. Isn't it interesting?"

"I guess," Marjorie said in a dubious voice. "Good luck." She hung up.

"If only," Vida grumbled as we left the newspaper office, "we could tie Josephine Foster Etcetera to the threatening letter to Marsha. Aunt Jo is precisely the kind of person who'd do such a silly thing."

"We could try," I said, noting that clouds from the north were descending on Alpine as well as the Olympic Peninsula.

Vida looked at me sharply. "What do you mean?"

I shrugged. "It'd get Marsha off our backs."

"That would be dishonest," Vida declared. "How could you?"

"Because," I said in a fretful tone, "this Judge Marsha thing is a runaround. If she doesn't know of any deep, dark secret in her past, there isn't one. Or if there is, it's so remote that it can't possibly harm her chances for the judgeship. Marsha seems like a smart, practical woman. I'm surprised she hasn't figured it out for herself."

A logging rig rumbled down Front Street, a sure sign that the weather was changing. The fire danger had abated; rain was on its way. My short-sleeved T-shirt and cotton slacks seemed inadequate for what I guessed to be a temperature of fifty-five.

"This isn't like you, Emma," Vida said with a reproachful glint in her eyes. "You always search for truth."

"I've found it," I said. "We're on a wild goose chase. I believe I made that statement at the onset."

Vida heaved a big sigh. "Then you can deliver the news. But if I were you, I'd sleep on it."

"Okay," I agreed. "For that matter, I can wait until Monday to tell Marsha."

Vida had opened her car door. She was about to speak again when she ducked quickly into the car. "Ed," she gasped, and slammed the driver's door shut.

Standing by Vida's Buick, I was too late to escape. Ed Bronsky was already waving his pudgy arms at me. Vida zoomed away just as Ed came within speaking distance.

"Just the person I wanted to see," Ed declared, huffing and puffing. "Do I have news or what?"

"What?" I said facetiously.

Ed didn't catch the irony. "Just when things look grim, something good happens. You know the saying, " 'When one door closes, a window opens up.' "

The quote wasn't accurate, but I didn't bother to correct Ed. "As in . . . ?" I queried.

"As in," Ed said, then stopped to get his breath. "As in you remember how my TV show got cancelled last year?"

"Ed's TV show," as he called it, was an animated cartoon based on his self-published autobiography. It hadn't made it past four weeks of airtime. Ed and his family had turned into a bunch of pigs on the show, which was all too appropriate for the porcine Bronsky family. Even their dog, Carhop, was overweight. While the book had been titled *Mr. Ed*, the TV cartoon had been changed to *Mr. Pig* for obvious reasons. Ed's character had been named Chester White, after a certain breed of pig.

"It's been picked up by Japanese television," Ed announced. "They're going to rework it into an action show. Mr. Ed will become SuperPig. I'll have special powers."

Why not? "Gee," I responded, "that's great. Do you get to wear a cape?"

"I don't know yet," Ed said, very serious. Indeed, in the past few months since his show had been cancelled, he had reverted to his pessimistic, morose role as the ad manager I had known and only occasionally loved. "I'd like to insist on shorts, though," he continued. "Pigs should wear pants on TV."

I'd been edging my way toward the driver's side of the Lexus. "Super heroes should always have a costume," I agreed.

"Shirley's not too happy about it," Ed declared. "There's no Mrs. SuperPig. She thinks that means I'll have love interests."

I found myself struggling to keep a straight face. "Couldn't Shirley be one of them?"

Ed gave a weak shake of his head. "Who knows? It isn't easy dealing with these Japanese TV people. Some of them don't speak much English. Besides, you know what they say—they're pretty inscrutable."

I clicked my door open. "It'll turn out just fine," I

asserted. "Let me know when it's going to air so we can put something in the paper."

Ed gave me a bleak look. "It won't air in Alpine."

"Why? Is it on pay-per-view?"

This time Ed's shake of the head was more pronounced. "Like I said, it's Japanese TV. It's only going to air in Japan."

"Oh." I'd misunderstood. "But you'll still get money, won't you?"

"That's not clear, either," Ed replied. "Skip and Irv are sorting that out now," he added, referring to his vanity publishers-cum-agents who were headquartered in Bellevue, east of Seattle.

Skip and Irv would want their own piece. "I'm sure you'll get something out of this. Why so glum?"

Ed made a face and cracked his knuckles. "I've got no artistic control over this project. Sure, it's exciting, especially when I thought for a while that *Mr. Ed* was dead. Besides, it screws up the sequel to my autobiography, *Mr. Ed Goes Hollywood.*"

Ed had threatened to write a sequel, but I hadn't realized he'd actually started it. I resisted the temptation to ask why he hadn't yet sought my editorial assistance. While composing the original *Mr. Ed* he'd practically camped out on my doorstep. After several rewrites, extensive editing, and proofing, Ed had failed to give me any credit in the book. But I wasn't going to bring that up now for fear that he'd impose on me again.

I'd opened the car door; my rear end was pointed in the direction of the driver's seat. "I'm sure this new situation will give the narrative an international flavor," I said. Like sushi gone bad. "Got to run, Ed."

My original intention had been to walk the single block to Parker's Pharmacy and pick up the Paxil prescription. But Ed's appearance had changed my plans. I decided to drive along Front Street and take a right on Third. I could park alongside the drugstore and nip in from around the corner.

But Ed thwarted me again. In my rearview mirror, I saw him walking toward my destination. Worse yet, as I passed him by, I spotted Mayor Baugh chatting with the Grocery Basket's Jake O'Toole outside of Parker's Pharmacy. Thus, I kept on going and headed home.

One message awaited me. It was Milo, brief and to the point as always.

"Got two T-bones. Should I come over around six?"

The sheriff had called from his home in the Icicle Creek Development. I rang his number, but got his answering machine. I didn't leave a message, but dialed his cell phone instead.

"Dodge," he said.

"You're on for dinner," I replied, hearing voices in the background. "I tried you at home, but you'd left for wherever you are now."

"I'm in Everett," Milo said. "I may be late. Let's say six-thirty, six-forty-five."

"Sure. See you then."

I hung up, wondering what had taken the sheriff to Everett. The phone rang in my hand before I could set it down.

"Maybe we missed something," Vida said without preamble. "What could it be?"

She was referring to the rest of the Froland albums and the shoe box that we'd gone through after returning from Judge Marsha's apartment.

"Like what?" I responded. "There wasn't anything of significance among the souvenirs or the photos."

Vida sighed. "Then I'll have to do some searching of my own when I visit June tomorrow night. They must have other keepsakes in that house. June isn't what I'd call a fussy housekeeper."

The Froland home had looked sufficiently tidy as far as I was concerned. But Vida tends to be fastidious, except when it comes to Roger, who could reduce the place to rubble and not upset his grandmother.

"Do what you can," I said, envisioning Vida wedging her way through crawl spaces in the attic.

"I shall," she promised.

Possibly goaded by Vida's comment about housekeeping, I did some of my own domestic chores for the next two hours. Just before six, I put two potatoes in the oven and opened a can of string beans. It would be a simple dinner, the kind Milo liked best.

An hour later, the potato skins were beginning to wrinkle. I switched off the oven and went out on the front porch to see if Milo was arriving. The rain had just started, dappling the viburnum leaves next to the steps. The sheriff wasn't anywhere in sight.

I wasn't worried, but I was certainly curious. When it came to dinner, Milo was usually on time. I had to wonder what was holding him up in Everett. Or if he was still there. At seven-fifteen, I considered calling his cell phone number, but decided to try his office first.

Deputy Dwight Gould answered. "Dodge stand you up?" he inquired in his dry manner.

"So it seems," I said.

"He's on his way," Dwight replied. "He left here about three minutes ago."

"What held him up?" I asked, heading for the front door.

"New developments," Dwight said. "Ask Dodge."

I assured the deputy that I would do just that and hung up.

I'd stood on the porch for less than a minute when Milo's Grand Cherokee pulled into my driveway. He was still in his civvies as he loped toward me in those cowboy boots that added a good three inches to his six-foot-five frame.

"Sorry," he apologized, giving me a thump on the shoulder and handing over the T-bones. "I had to go to Everett."

"I'll find out why by coaxing you with strong drink," I said. "Luckily, I haven't put the beans on yet."

"Scotch rocks," he said, flopping down into his favorite armchair.

"I know," I responded, then noticed that he looked weary. "Not a very restful day off, I gather."

"No," he said and went silent as I proceeded into the kitchen to make our drinks.

I also put Milo's steak on to cook. He liked it done medium-well; I preferred rare. That was only one of many differences between us. We'd been ill-matched from the start. And yet we could still be friends.

"I hear there are new developments," I said, handing Milo his drink.

"What?" He gave me a quizzical look. "Where'd you hear that?"

"Dwight told me." I perched on the arm of Milo's chair. "Are you going to tell me or do I have to threaten to burn your steak?"

Milo frowned. "I suppose you're worrying because Fleetwood might get hold of the story."

"I always worry about that," I said, "but I can't do much about it on a weekend. There is a story then?"

Milo reached for his cigarettes. I slid off the chair and sat down on the sofa.

"Yeah," he sighed. "There is. There are, maybe I should say. Two stories. One you can't have, but the other's official."

My eyes widened. "Two stories? You'd better give me both of them by Tuesday. What's the one you can tell me now?"

Milo lit a cigarette, took a deep drink of Scotch, and grimaced.

"Just what I didn't need to hear," he said. "Poor old June Froland may have been right. It looks like Jack Froland was poisoned."

December 1916

The joints in Olga Iversen's fingers were stiff with cold as she held up the pair of woolen stockings she'd just finished knitting. Not a single dropped stitch, she thought with satisfaction—red with blue and white stripes, like the Norwegian flag. Olga loved her native land's flag. Her brother had sent her a small replica of it after Norway finally gained its independence from Sweden. Olga wished she had been there for the celebrations.

During the winter, it had been cold and snowy in Trondheim, too. But not so damp as Alpine. The moisture seemed not only to come from the sky, but to ooze out of the ground. And the logging town was so small. . . .

Olga gazed out through the four wavering glass panes that offered the best view of Alpine. The mill, with its huffing-puffing smokestack. The social hall that reminded her of a barn on one of the many farms outside of Trondheim. The bunkhouses, like army barracks. There were no shops, no grand homes, no factories, no harbor, no shipbuilding yards, no scent of the sea.

Most of all, there was no church. Olga missed the great Nidaros Cathedral that soared above Trondheim. Kings were crowned there, near the tomb of King Olaf II, Norway's patron saint. It was where King Haakon VII's coronation had been held eleven years earlier, but Olga hadn't been there to see it. She'd received letters from home, picture postcards, even a souvenir silver spoon that she kept tucked away in her underwear drawer.

Home. How she missed it. How she missed her family, her friends, the festivals, the familiar gathering places for the university students. She had fallen in love with one of them, Bjorn Bjornsen, but his family had insisted that he marry a richer, prettier wife. Olga had thought she'd die of a broken heart when Bjorn returned home to Levanger.

Then Trygve had come back to Trondheim. She'd known him when she was younger, not well, but in the way that a fourteen-year-old girl and a nineteen-year-old man acknowledge each other's presence with a smile and a nod, as if to say, "Some day, perhaps, when we are older . . ."

So, to salve her broken heart, she'd found a safe haven in Trygve's strong arms. Like so many big men, he was gentle with weaker creatures. He had promised a new life in a new world, and at the time, Olga had wanted to flee her shattered dreams.

But that was over twenty years ago, and almost ten since they moved to Alpine. She'd borne four children, three sons and a daughter. That was enough. The youngest, Lars, had been a difficult birth. Olga had almost died. There would be no more babies. There would be no more lying in Trygve's strong arms.

At first, she'd hated Lars, resented him for taking away a part of her life that she'd come to enjoy. But he had been an outgoing child, cheerful, even clownish. Olga didn't laugh often, but when she did, it was because of Lars. He was so funny, so endearing.

It was Jonas who hated Lars. Jonas had been the baby until six years later when Lars replaced him. "Act like a big boy, Jonas," Olga used to admonish him. "You're not a baby any more."

Olga looked again at the stockings. She'd knitted them for Jonas as a Christmas present. He'd hate them, hate them the way he hated Lars, the way he hated her.

The way Olga hated Alpine.

Chapter Ten

I STARED AT Milo. "Are you kidding? Jack Froland was poisoned? How?"

"Yep," Milo replied, taking out a fresh pack of Marlboro Lights. "That's what the M.E. says."

I was incredulous, leaning halfway off the sofa. "How?"

Milo took the first puff from his cigarette. Automatically, I reached into the drawer of the side table and hauled out an ashtray.

"Mushrooms," he replied, taking the ashtray from me.

"Mushrooms? You mean, the poisonous kind?" I asked stupidly.

Milo made a wry face. "That's the kind that kills people."

I knew there were poisonous mushrooms in the woods around Alpine. Carla Steinmetz Talliaferro had done a feature about them several years ago. Only by the grace of God had I realized that she'd misidentified two of them in the cutlines by switching the photos. During her premarriage and premotherhood days with the *Advocate*, Carla had tended to be somewhat careless.

"What kind?" I asked the sheriff.

"*A-ma-ni-tas phall-o-i-des*," Milo replied, slowly and distinctly, obviously having memorized what the M.E. had told him. "You've seen them—they grow in the woods, sometimes along the road. They're the ones with the yellow-orange background and the white dots."

"Yes." I had seen them from time to time, once in my

backyard just below the tree line. Despite their beguiling appearance, I'd beaten them down with a shovel. "I don't get it," I admitted. "I don't see June Froland preparing exotic meals with mushrooms. Have you spoken with her?"

"Not yet," Milo replied. "June's still pretty wiped out. I talked to Max. The news blew him right out of his socks."

"I should think so," I remarked. "Did he have any explanation? I mean, about how his father might have eaten the mushrooms?"

Milo's long face wore an ironic expression. "Yeah, he did. It seems old Jack was a meat-and-potatoes man. His favorite meat was steak—" He paused with a glance in the direction of the kitchen. "—And his favorite thing was to put mushrooms on his steak."

"Good grief." I shook my head. "Had Jack been eating a lot of steak lately?"

Milo nodded. "He'd started feeling better, and I guess his appetite picked up. According to Max, June bought steak every time it was on sale at Safeway. When Jack was feeling lousy, she'd buy it anyway, and put it in the freezer. Max didn't know for sure, but he said his dad had probably eaten steak most nights for the last week or two."

"With mushrooms," I noted.

"With mushrooms."

"Where did they come from?"

"Max wasn't sure," Milo responded. "He thought maybe his folks had gathered them in the woods. They picked berries, wildflowers, and, he thought, probably mushrooms. The Frolands were old school. They foraged off the land."

"School of hard knocks," I murmured. "Depression-era people, who don't spend money unless they have to. Still, you'd think they'd know a poisonous mushroom when they saw one."

"True." Milo chuckled. "That reminds me, a couple of years ago—maybe you remember it from the log—their neighbors filed a complaint. You know May Beth and Jerry Hedstrom?"

"Sure," I said. "She teaches at the grade school and he manages Mountain View Gardens."

"Right." Briefly, Milo looked away. His most recent broken romance had been with a woman who worked at the local nursery. "Anyway," he continued after clearing his throat, "May Beth and Jerry grow a lot of their own produce. It seems the Frolands had a bad habit of sneaking into the Hedstrom garden and stealing everything from pears to pumpkins."

Remembering the report in the police log, I smiled. "Jack and June got off with a warning, right?"

Milo nodded. "They argued that they were old and addled. They thought they were in their own yard, instead of the Hedstroms'. Turns out they'd been swiping stuff for the past couple of years, according to Jerry."

I smiled at the image of Jack and June Froland lugging away bags of contraband beans and broccoli by the dark of the moon. Milo looked as if he could use a refill for his drink, so I went to the kitchen where I also checked on his steak and put mine into the skillet. When I returned to the living room, I had the obvious question for the sheriff. Two of them, in fact.

"Did someone purposely bring poisonous mushrooms to the house? Or was it an accident?"

Milo shrugged. "That's a tough one. You'd think they'd have known better if Jack and June picked those mushrooms up in the woods. If they didn't do it by mistake, who did?"

"June?"

Milo grimaced. "Why? Even if Jack was feeling better, he hadn't licked the cancer. He wasn't going to live forever. Why hurry the poor old fart along?"

"Because he was driving her nuts?" I suggested. "It happens. The caregiver sometimes snaps."

"It's a thought," Milo conceded. "Sam and Dwight are looking for evidence at the Froland house."

I scoured my brain for other options. "Did Max know of anyone else who had been to the house lately?"

"I asked him that," Milo replied, sniffing at the air as the aroma of steak seeped into the living room. "He said they never entertained much. Jack especially didn't like drop-in company."

"They sound like the dullest couple in the world." Wasted lives, wasted time, wasted energy, I thought. Jack at the tavern, June with her needlework. Had they ever possessed any passion, even for each other?

And yet Jack Froland had been poisoned. "You can't really say he was murdered, can you?" I asked Milo.

"That's up to Doc Dewey when he holds the inquest Monday," Milo replied. "That's basing his conclusion on the information he gets from Everett, of course."

In addition to his medical responsibilities, Doc was also the county coroner. But no one expected him to conduct more than a simple autopsy. He had neither the training nor the technical support. Skykomish County couldn't afford a lab or a medical examiner. We were Snohomish County's poor relation. Milo was lucky he could make a decent living as the sheriff.

"Said information being what you already know," I remarked, beckoning for the sheriff to follow me into the kitchen, "what's your call?"

Milo leaned against the counter by the refrigerator. There was a time when I thought he looked as if he belonged there, but that was long past. My eyes darted to the door of the fridge, and for one split second, I acknowledged its barrenness. No primitive drawings by grandchildren, no first-day-of-school pictures, no shiny magnets declaring I LOVE GRANDMA. Vida was right. I faced the stove and turned the steaks.

"Hell," Milo said, oblivious to my sudden burst of self-pity, "I don't know. The M.E. says Jack probably ate the mushrooms for dinner the night he died. I'll be damned glad when June can talk and make sense again."

Did she ever? I wanted to say but kept quiet while I turned on the string beans.

The sheriff also grew silent. When he finally spoke, he said something that caught me off-guard.

"Hey—how come you and Judge Marsha are so chummy all of a sudden?"

I kept my back turned. "What do you mean?"

"When I called the office a week or so ago, Ginny told me you'd already left to see Marsha. What I had to say was no big deal, so I didn't leave a message. Then this morning, Bill Blatt was cruising Alpine Way for speeders and he saw your car pull into The Pines Village. He thought he saw his Aunt Vida's car, too."

I kept my eyes on the kettle, waiting for the beans to boil. "Marsha asked us to do some research on her family. So did Max Froland. On his family, I mean. In fact, way back when, their families intertwined. It could make a good feature for the special edition this week."

Again, the sheriff was silent for a few moments. And again, when he spoke, it was something I didn't want to hear.

"What did I tell you? You're a crappy liar, Emma."

I whirled on Milo, striking the skillet handle with my elbow and almost knocking the steaks onto the floor. "Since when have you been checking on my movements? What if I told you it was none of your damned business?"

"Whoa!" Milo held up his hands as if he thought I were about to attack him. "Hang on. I was just curious. You and Marsha seem like the odd couple."

I'd steadied the skillet and was now waving the steel spatula at the sheriff. "You're never curious. It's not your style. You only ask questions when you're investigating a case."

"Hey!" Milo wiped at his face. Apparently, some of the

grease from the spatula had splattered on him. He was mad. "Knock it off! I was just trying to make conversation."

Poor Milo. He was right, I was wrong. I put the spatula down on the counter and held my head. "I'm sorry. Really, I am. It's just that sometimes . . . sometimes I get . . ." I gave myself a good shake and tried to look Milo in the eye.

"Oh, hell." Milo sighed, then came over to me and gave me a big hug. "It's okay. You're still a mess."

I'd been on the verge of tears, but his down-to-earth comment made me smile. "I guess I am," I murmured against his chest.

He kissed the top of my head and released me. But the expression on his face was very serious. "After dinner, do you want to go to bed? I mean, if it'd make you feel any better. . . ." He raised his big hands in a helpless gesture.

"Oh, Milo," I exclaimed, "what an absolutely dumb idea!" Then, to my horror, I started to cry. He reached out to me again, stopped in his tracks, and looked so stricken that I covered my eyes and said, "Yes."

In the long catalog of foolish things that I have done in my life, going to bed with Milo that night was actually pretty far down on the list. We were both alone as well as lonely. He'd had nothing but bad luck with women ever since I met him, and that included with me.

And for some reason, we talked after we made love. During our romance of several years ago, the only postcoital topics we ever discussed were the Mariners' prospects— both during the regular season and the off-season—and whether he was going to stay the night, and if so, what would he like for breakfast?

But on that drizzly September evening we spoke of other, deeper things. He spoke of the women who'd betrayed him, especially his most recent love who'd used him as well. I talked of Tom, and how I should have guessed that there was more to his life than a crazy wife and a string of small newspapers. It only occurred to me after his death that he'd had a void to fill, and he'd done it with the wrong kind of politics.

And then I confided that I'd been depressed—without mentioning Doc Dewey's Paxil prescription. Milo told me more about his ex-wife. Mulehide, as he called her, and how she'd belittle him, even in front of the children. Milo had complained about her before—the nagging, the endless complaints, and eventually the affair she'd had with one of the other teachers at the high school where she taught English and Spanish. She'd taken their children and robbed him of his pride. He'd never been the same since.

Or, as he put it, "You wouldn't have known me thirty years ago. I was full of piss and vinegar, out to save the world from all the bad guys."

"Maybe," I'd told him, "I wouldn't have liked you half so well."

"Maybe you would," he'd replied. "Maybe then, everything would've been different. For both of us."

Just after ten-thirty, I was about to ask if in fact he wanted to spend the night. But his cell phone rang. It was Dwight Gould, who thought the sheriff should come by the office. Something new had been discovered at the forest fire site. No big deal, but he might want to check it out.

"Did Dwight say what it was?" I inquired, putting on my robe while Milo dressed.

"No," the sheriff replied, fastening the belt with the eagle buckle. I couldn't help but notice that he'd moved down a notch since the last time I'd seen him dress. "You know Dwight—he never says much until he's ready."

"Taciturn," I remarked, then saw that Milo was having a bit of trouble putting on his boots. "Here," I volunteered, "let me help. I've seen it done in the movies."

"I haven't worn them before," he admitted. "I had kind of a time of it this morning."

With my hands on the left boot, I looked up at him where

he'd sat down on the bed. "Milo, has it occurred to you that we might be getting old?"

Milo let out a guffaw. "Hell, yes. But we're not old, we're just hitting our stride in middle age."

"I'll be fifty in November," I said, straining to get the boot in place.

"I'm still ahead of you by a couple of years. Oof."

"I got it," I announced. "Let's do the other one. Unless my back gives out first."

The second boot went on more easily than the first, though I ended up taking a pratfall on the floor and panting slightly.

Milo stood up, then helped me to my feet. "Thanks, Emma." He kissed me on the cheek.

I kissed him back. "Thank you. For everything."

After Mass that morning, I managed to avoid my fellow parishioners by sneaking out during the final stanza of the recessional hymn. I didn't feel like talking to anyone, especially to Ed and Shirley Bronsky, who were in attendance with their five children.

I wasn't feeling antisocial because I was depressed. Rather, I was feeling guilty about having an empty day ahead of me and knowing that I should plunge myself into Judge Marsha's project. The problem was that I didn't know what else I could do. My resources seemed exhausted.

Except for Vida, who was scheduled to call on June Froland that evening. Driving out of the parking lot, I considered a visit to my favorite snoop, but First Presbyterian's services lasted longer than St. Mildred's one-hour liturgy.

I'd turned off Cedar onto Third when I heard a horn honk behind me. Wondering who the crank might be, I looked in the rearview mirror and saw Milo's Grand Cherokee coming up the hill. He honked again. I pulled over at the corner of Cascade and rolled down my window. The sheriff came abreast of the Lexus.

"Want to go for a ride?" he called.

"Where?" I responded.

"Up to the fire site," Milo replied, ignoring the pickup truck and the compact car stuck behind the Grand Cherokee.

I hesitated. It had been raining off and on since I'd gotten up. I wasn't dressed for traipsing around the environs of ro Lake.

"I'll have to change first. Follow me home. It won't take long."

While I slipped into a pair of old slacks, a badly pilled sweater, and my heavy-duty boots, I wondered why the sheriff wanted me to go with him. It wasn't a romantic gesture, I was sure of that. We'd met by chance. Milo didn't act upon whims, so his intentions must be official.

When I climbed into the Cherokee, I immediately inquired why this trip was necessary.

"Evidence, maybe," he said as we started along Fir Street. "Just in case Fleetwood gets wind of it, I didn't want you to feel left out. I was headed for your house. I forgot you'd probably be at church."

"What kind of evidence?" I asked.

"Late yesterday a couple of firefighters found the remnants of some kind of building. That's what Dwight called me about last night. He'd only been notified after the fire crew got back to town and had dinner."

"What about the victim? You didn't mention what the M.E. had to say about corpse number two."

Milo was headed north on Alpine Way, which led out of town and onto Highway 2. "The M.E. hadn't gotten to him yet. We'll probably find out tomorrow or Tuesday. Unidentified burn victims take time."

We crossed the bridge over the Skykomish River. Like all fishermen, Milo glanced in both directions, seeing if there was any action. "Some kid caught a fourteen-pound Humpy yesterday. Not right around here, but down by Sultan."

"That's a big fish," I remarked.

"No good for eating, though," Milo said as we waited at the blinking red light where Alpine Way fed into the cross-state thoroughfare. "The only thing you can do with those Humpies is smoke them."

"They're not bad kippered," I said. The sheriff and I were on the same page. Our romantic interlude hadn't broken the rhythm of our renewed friendship. I was glad.

Sunday traffic was heavy in both directions. As usual, too many drivers were going like a bat out of hell. Only the natives seemed to respect the dangerously slick layer of oil left by other vehicles after a fresh rainfall.

There were two logging roads that led from the highway to the Martin Creek and Embro Lake areas. Getting to either of them required driving two miles west or two miles east. Milo chose the latter direction. We backtracked along the winding road for another two miles, which seemed like at least twice that far because we had to slow to half speed. Finally, as the rain started to come down much harder, we met the fork in the road and turned north toward the fire area. We hadn't gotten very far before we could see the damage. Despite the rain, some of the fallen trees still smoldered. I could smell the smoke, tainted by the chemicals used to put out the flames. I know that forest fires can be our friends, especially those caused by lightning. They keep the ecological cycle moving, Nature's way of replenishment through destruction. Yet I have never liked seeing a burned-out stand of trees, which look like skeletons. There was an eerie quality to the seared mountainside, a desolation that made me feel as if I were back in some prehistoric era before the deer and the chipmunks and the birds made the forest their home.

"We're on DNR property now," Milo said, referring to the Department of Natural Resources. "Let me check the map the firefighters gave Dwight."

The sheriff pulled off at one of the few wide spots in the road, a man-made turnaround. He took the map out of his jacket pocket, lit a cigarette, and rolled down the windows.

I could hear Martin Creek close by, rushing along on its way to join the Tye River. A glimpse of blue gentian assured me that at least some of the Alpine flowers had survived.

I craned my neck to look over Milo's shoulder. The map was crudely drawn, with the fire-damaged areas circled with a black-tipped felt pen.

Milo was using a red pen to make some marks on the map. "Here," he said, pointing to one of the red X's. "That's where the body was found, right at the edge of the DNR property. And about a hundred yards away," he went on, indicating the second X, "is where the building timbers were discovered yesterday. You got a camera?"

"No," I replied in a disgusted voice. "I never have a camera. I get tired of taking pictures of my shoes."

He glanced at my feet. "At least you're wearing boots, because we're going to have to walk from here."

"Great." Giving Milo a grumpy look, I got out of the Cherokee and pulled up the hood on my jacket. "Could it be wetter?"

"The forecast calls for partial sun tomorrow," Milo said as he joined me on the passenger's side. "Let's just hope nobody gets killed out on the highway for the next hour or so. I don't need any interruptions."

If there was a trail, I couldn't see it. But Milo walked purposefully ahead of me, apparently knowing where he was going. The raindrops dripped from my hood and my boots squelched in the ash that was quickly being turned into mud.

"Here," he said, stopping near a fallen cedar tree. "The body was found on the other side." He stared in that direction for almost a minute. "Those damned batteries we found in the victim's hand—what do they mean?"

"You're assuming that the victim either lived in or used the building? Maybe he had a flashlight with him."

"Most flashlights you'd use in the woods don't take AA batteries," Milo said. "Anyway, where is it? The whole thing couldn't have been destroyed."

I studied the ground that had captured the sheriff's attention. There was nothing to see. Milo must have agreed. He trudged ahead, stepping over more fallen trees and branches. With my hands stuffed in the pockets of my jacket, I was wishing I'd worn a pair of gloves when Milo stopped again. As I hurried to catch up with him, I saw about a six-foot length of official yellow tape warning off trespassers.

"The fire crew put that there, just in case," Milo said.

Under the tape were the remnants of what looked like two I-beams. As I bent down, I could also see the remains of a tin roof and some shards of glass.

"It's from some kind of structure," I ventured. "A shack, probably."

Milo gave a nod. "If it weren't for the glass, it might be a shed. In the old days, some people kept cows around here." He turned to peer around me. "Ah. Here come Dustin Fong and Jack Mullins with the evidence kit. I wanted to get them here sooner, but Jack was at church."

Jack Mullins was another deputy and a fellow member of St. Mildred's. I'd seen him at Mass but had avoided him along with everybody else.

Jack looked faintly disgruntled; Dustin, as usual, seemed quietly eager.

Milo addressed them without preamble. "Dwight said nobody on the fire crew messed with this. Let's hope he's right."

"A hell of a way to spend my first day back from vacation," Jack muttered. "Nobody cares that I caught three Kings up at Glacier Bay." He turned to me. "How'd you get stuck up here, Emma?"

"Milo promised me a picnic," I replied, making a mental note to do a short feature on the Mullins's Alaska trip.

"What kind?" Jack asked, his usual humor surfacing. "A barbecue?"

"Everything around here looks too well done for my taste," I said.

Dustin is the youngest of the deputies, and unlike most of his twentysomething peer group, possesses great humility. Perhaps it's his Chinese ancestry, or maybe he's just an exception to the rule. Dustin stood next to the sheriff, virtually at attention. "Have you any idea what we're looking for, sir?"

"Anything that looks like it shouldn't be in a forest," Milo replied. "If this was some kind of hermit's shack, there should be more than just bits of glass, a tin roof, and some burned-up lumber."

Jack gave Milo a questioning look. "Are you tying the victim to this?" he asked, waving a hand over the debris.

"Not yet," Milo said. "But it's a possibility. If it's one of our mountain men, we may never know who he was."

"You keep saying 'he,' " I interjected. "You're sure it's a man?"

"The M.E. thinks so," the sheriff replied, then turned back to his deputies. "You got everything you need?"

"Except a canopy to keep us dry," Jack retorted. "Jeez, couldn't this have waited until tomorrow? The rain's supposed to let up by then."

"I don't believe weather reports," Milo shot back. "I don't believe in waiting, either. I'll be in touch." He turned on his heel—no cowboy boots for him today—and started back toward the road.

I trudged behind him. The wind was picking up, turning the rain into raw, cold pelts. We were well above the three-thousand-foot level, where snow could fall as early as the end of the month. But not now, with the temperature somewhere in the low fifties. With the region's unpredictable climate, it could hit seventy on Monday.

"Sheriff!" Jack's voice cut through the downpour. "We got something!"

"You'd better," Milo muttered, then heeled around and strode back to the evidence site.

I trailed along, wishing that for once I'd brought a camera.

Then it occurred to me that the deputies must have one. Maybe they could save my behind.

"Bottle caps," Jack said, holding out a latex-gloved hand. "Maybe from medicine bottles."

Milo gazed at the half-dozen scorched metal caps, which were all about the size of a nickel. "What else?"

"Hey, we just started," Jack responded, looking put upon. "What do you expect, a smoking gun?"

"Not in this rain," Milo remarked, his eyes now on Dustin who was grubbing around in the dirt. "Where are the bottles?"

Dustin looked up. "We figure they were those plastic kind. But if they were glass, we'll find some sign of them. Hey—what's this?"

The corner of some kind of box was half sunken in the ground and partially covered by a large tree limb. Dustin carefully removed the branch with Jack's help, then they both started brushing away mud, dirt, leaves, and soot.

"It's an icebox," Jack said. "No—it's a small refrigerator. You can see the brand name in the corner. Kenmore. That's a Sears product."

Milo studied the exposed part of the fridge. "You bring shovels?"

"Sure," Jack answered, thumping on a long metal case. "We forgot the forklift, though," he added with a wink for Dustin.

"Get this thing out of here," Milo said, then bent down to put on a pair of latex gloves. "I'll work here, away from the fridge." He tossed a pair of gloves in my direction. "You take that part over there by the cedar tree."

I tried not to look dismayed. "Am I deputized?"

"You got it," Milo replied, not glancing up from the ground.

We worked in silence—except for grunts from Jack and Dustin—for at least ten minutes. Occasionally, the sheriff would pick something up, scrutinize it, and put it into an evidence bag. I, however, seemed to be working a patch that yielded nothing of interest except for a battered Budweiser can. I found two more before the deputies managed to free the fridge.

Luckily for them, it was a small model, the kind you'd put in a den or a motel room. Part of the exterior had melted in the fire. Dustin used a crowbar to open the door. A noxious smell like a stink bomb made me gasp and fall back. The others reeled slightly, too.

"Jesus!" Milo exclaimed. "What the hell is that?"

"Whatever it is," Jack said between coughs, "I hope my wife's not making it for Sunday dinner."

Slowly, the stench dissipated. Milo put a blue-and-white handkerchief over his nose and mouth before looking in the fridge.

"This damned thing blew up," he said in a muffled voice. "It must have been the air getting to the refrigerant chemicals."

Gingerly, I edged up behind Milo. There wasn't much to see from my vantage point except for clumps of what looked like melted plastic.

Milo, however, had a trained eye. "Well, that explains it," he said, standing up and stuffing the handkerchief back in his pocket. "The bottle caps, the fridge, and those batteries the victim had in his hand."

"You're right," Jack agreed. "We should have guessed."

Like an impatient child, I stamped my foot. It got stuck in the mire, ruining the effect. "What are you talking about? What is all this junk?"

Milo gave me a half smile. "What you're looking at, Emma, is what's left of a meth lab."

January 1917

Louie Dawson was afraid, but he didn't show it. Louie wasn't quite nine years old, but he refused to be bullied, even by his teenaged cousin Vincent. To stiffen Louie's backbone, he had Billy, his other cousin, with him. They were the same age, but Billy was as tall as a twelve-year-old.

"Come on, you little brats," Vincent said in his most menacing voice, "fork it over. Both of you owe me twenty-five cents."

"No, we don't." Louie stubbornly shook his head. "You owe each of us twenty-five cents."

"Liars," Vincent said. He glanced furtively around the area by the bunkhouses. The woods were shut down, due to the heavy snowfall between Christmas and New Year's. There was no one in sight on this cold day in early January. No one, that is, except Jonas Iversen, who was slipping and sliding down the snow-covered hill to join the other boys.

"Hey, Jonas!" Vincent called. "Want to meet a couple of welshers?"

"Pipsqueaks is more like it," Jonas replied, skidding to a stop right in front of Louie. "How could these dumb clucks get your goat?"

With another glance at the bunkhouses, Vincent began walking away. Jonas followed him. "I bet these little punks twenty-five cents apiece that Oregon would win the Rose Bowl. Oregon won, and those two won't pay up."

"He's lying!" Billy yelled, his long stride allowing him to

catch up to the older boys. "Louie and I bet on Oregon! I don't even know where Pennsylvania is!"

"It's down the shithouse," Vincent retorted, "so you owe us because you bet on those losers."

Louie, who was chunky if not tall, had hurried along behind Billy. "We know where Oregon is," Louie declared. "Some of the guys around here come from there."

"Fourteen to nothing," Billy said. "You'd have to be a real dope to not know that Pennsylvania couldn't score against Oregon. And we're not dopes, so we bet on Oregon."

Jonas stopped near the railroad tracks. "Tell you what." He gave Vincent a conspiratorial smile. "If you two can walk through the railroad tunnel down the line and not wet your pants, we'll call off the bet."

Louie and Billy exchanged dubious glances. Both boys had been warned repeatedly not to go into the tunnel. It was too dangerous, with unscheduled runs on the short haul lines from the other whistle stops. There was a bend in the tracks only a couple of hundred feet from the tunnel's other side, and a train could come along with almost no warning. Besides, their parents knew, busy little boys preoccupied with their pastimes didn't always hear the whistle.

"You'll go with us?" Billy inquired.

"Hell, no," Jonas replied. "Then it wouldn't be a dare. You go by your chickenshit selves."

Billy leaned down to whisper in Louie's ear. "The four-twenty freight is coming pretty soon. What time is it?"

"I don't know," Louie whispered back. "I heard the four o'clock mill whistle blow a few minutes ago."

"Right." Billy looked up at the heavy gray clouds. At least it wasn't snowing. "So," he asked in his normal voice, "how do we prove we did it?"

Jonas scratched at his chin, which was just beginning to sprout a few signs of stubble. "There's some fusies at the other end," he said, referring to the flares that trains always carried. The youngsters all begged for fusies. They were as

good as firecrackers, almost as good as Roman candles.
"Bring back one of them fusies for each of us. And we gotta
check to see if your pants are dry."

"No, you don't," Billy retorted. "If you can't tell by look-
ing, that's tough. The fusies are the deal."

"We'll see about that," Vincent said, lighting a cigarette.
"Well? What are you waiting for? Santa Claus? He ain't got
no fusies in his big black bag."

Billy started out, but Louie lingered. "Come on," Billy
called. "We don't have much time."

For just one second, Louie looked as if he might cry. Then,
seeing the contempt on the older boys' faces, he started to
run alongside the tracks. Nobody, not even Vincent or Jonas,
would ever call him a chicken.

Both cousins were out of breath by the time they reached
the tunnel. They stopped just inside to look back at their tor-
mentors, who were a good two hundred feet away. Vincent
and Jonas appeared to be falling about with laughter.

"Let's move down a little bit," Billy said, his eyes adjust-
ing to the increasing darkness. "There's a place where we
can stand away from the tracks. We'll be okay."

"But we can't get the fusies," Louie protested.

"Yes, we can." He paused. "I hear the train. Just do what
I do."

Two minutes passed. It was cold and dank inside the tun-
nel. Louie could barely make out the opposite wall with its
stout timbers. He began to shiver just as the train whistle
blew.

Almost immediately, they saw the locomotive's big head-
light coming around the bend on the other side of the tunnel.
It had slowed down as it neared the whistle stop. Billy was
breathing almost as hard as Louie.

Then, as the train slowly approached, Billy started to yell
at the engineer. "Mr. Geerds, throw me a fusie! Throw me a
fusie!" he cried, hoping to be heard above the clamor of the
rails.

Louie joined in. The boys stayed plastered to the side of the tunnel, screaming their lungs out. The locomotive was so close they could feel the heat like a blast from an open oven. At last they saw Harry Geerds, leaning from the cab.

"What the . . . ?" he shouted back. "You shouldn't be here! I'm going to tell your mas!"

"Please." Billy cried, "throw us some fusies!"

"Tell it to the caboose," Harry yelled as the locomotive lumbered out of the tunnel toward town. "They've got 'em back there."

Five, ten, fifteen cars later, the boys could see the red caboose. They began to shout again. A skinny man in overalls stood at the very back of the train.

"Crazy kids!" he laughed. But he threw them a half-dozen fusies.

The train slowed to a stop, with the caboose just clearing the tunnel. Louie and Billy each clutched three fusies, but they didn't run. They sauntered back toward town and remained on the opposite side of the tracks from Vincent and Jonas.

Up ahead at the platform, Harry Geerds was accepting a cup of coffee from Kate Murphy. It was a familiar and welcome break on the run to Leavenworth, though Harry had no time for pie today. Seeing the young boys approach, he pointed at them and wagged a finger.

Kate looked grim as she stared at her son and her nephew. "You're wicked, wicked boys. Foolish and reckless. I've a mind to take a belt to both of you."

"We can explain," Billy said. "We didn't do it to be bad."

Kate's expression softened as it always did when she studied her only son's face. "It'd better be good. Get on home now. You, too, Louie."

"We have something we got to do first," Billy replied, very serious. "Mr. Geerds, would you please come with us? It'll take just a minute."

Puzzled yet intrigued, Harry cradled his coffee mug in his hand. "I guess so. We're running only a couple of minutes behind schedule."

The boys led Harry around the front of the locomotive. Billy pointed to Vincent and Jonas, who were standing by the water tower. "They made us do it," Billy said. "They're bullies. They're always trying to get the younger kids in trouble."

"I never met a bully I didn't want to lick," Harry replied, his bearlike frame indicating he often won, no matter whom he was forced to fight.

Without a word, Billy and Louie walked up to the older boys and dropped the fusies at their feet.

Vincent stared at the fusies; Jonas stared at the cousins.

"You tricked us!" Jonas exclaimed. "You cheated! The bet's off!"

"The bet was," Billy said in an even voice, "that we'd go into the tunnel and get two fusies. We got six." He looked up at Harry. "Did we get these in the tunnel, Mr. Geerds?"

"Sure as shooting," Harry replied, then chuckled as he looked at Vincent and Jonas. "Looks to me as if you'd better pay up, boys. These young'uns beat you fair and square."

Vincent's face was stormy. Jonas looked as if he could strangle both boys with his bare hands.

"We'll bring the money later," Vincent muttered. He nudged Jonas roughly. "Let's go."

With one last searing look at the younger boys, Jonas started up the hill. "Don't worry," he said out of the corner of his mouth. "We'll get those two next time."

Chapter Eleven

I'D HEARD ABOUT meth labs in other parts of the state, but never near Alpine. In a way, that was odd, because the makers of meth were often out-of-work loggers who tucked themselves away in the forest to cook up their illegal substances. So many timber workers suffered from chronic aches and pains in the course of their job that they'd learned how to doctor themselves, and not always in ways that were legal.

"Had you any idea this was going on?" I asked Milo.

"I'd heard rumors," Milo muttered, "but the labs we knew about were always just outside the county line. A couple of them were busted last summer in both Snohomish and Chelan counties, not to mention a bunch further south and west in Pierce, Mason, and Jefferson counties."

The sheriff and I were standing some thirty feet from the burned-out lab site. Jack and Dustin were back at it, carefully sifting through the debris and exhibiting renewed enthusiasm now that they had a real crime scene.

"How do the batteries figure in?" I inquired.

"Part of the mixture for meth—or crank—is the lithium inside AA batteries," Milo replied. "I wondered at the time about those batteries the dead guy had in his hand. But there's no electricity around here to run the equipment to make the meth. I kept my mouth shut, figuring there must be some other explanation for the batteries."

"But there must have been electricity," I pointed out. "How else did they run the fridge?"

"Oh, the power was there," Milo said, taking a last puff from his Marlboro Light and holding the ash out so the rain would douse the butt. "A generator. It's buried somewhere by the shack. Or its parts are, if it blew up." He dropped the cigarette butt and crushed it with his heel. "Remember about a year ago when I went down to Olympia for that law enforcement class on drugs? I learned quite a bit."

I remembered. "You didn't want to go at the time," I remarked. Milo hated classes and conferences. He always protested and complained for at least a month before he finally gave in. But the drug course had really rankled, because it had been scheduled at the same time as the opening of winter steelhead season.

"I thought the class was mostly for city types—you know, gang-related drug stuff," Milo said. "But that wasn't how it turned out. Drugs are just as big a problem in rural areas as they are in the cities."

"I thought you already knew that," I said.

"I did, as far as here in town goes. But I didn't know about all these damned meth labs, and who all had them. I figured it was just gang-related, not poor working stiffs who started out trying to kill their pain. Then they end up making big money and causing a bunch of other people a whole new kind of pain. Including law enforcement agencies." The sheriff meandered over to Dustin and Jack. "Anything new?"

Jack leaned on his shovel and nodded. "I think we got what's left of a microwave oven here."

"That figures," Milo said, then turned back to me. "Those microwaves are part of the process." He paused, tipping back his baseball cap with its Mariners' logo. "Let's go see Garth Wesley."

Mention of the local pharmacist's name made me jump. Had Milo guessed that Doc Dewey had prescribed something for me because I'd admitted to feeling depressed? A small demon inside of me didn't want to admit that I couldn't rally on my own.

"Why?" I asked, a bit breathless.

"Because," Milo replied with a curious look, "I want to find out if he's had a run on pseudoephedrine."

I trotted along after the sheriff as he headed for the gravel road. "Why?"

"Because," he called over his shoulder, "that decongestant is a prime ingredient of meth."

"Oh." I felt relieved. But only for a moment. Once we got to the pharmacy, wouldn't Garth Wesley remind me that I had medication to pick up?

"I won't go through the whole process," Milo said after we'd reached the Grand Cherokee, "but making meth isn't all that hard, once you know what goes into it. The worst of it is, everything that's required is available just about anywhere."

"A mixture of battery acid—or whatever—and decongestant and—what else?—doesn't sound very enticing to me." On the other hand, maybe it'd beat taking Paxil for the next five years.

"The worst of it is," Milo said as we bumped along the uneven road where the potholes now overflowed with rainwater, "much of the stuff these amateur labs turn out is full of impurities. You notice more people than usual around town with rotting teeth?"

"Oh, good grief!" I made a face at Milo. "I don't inspect the locals' mouths. Who do you think I am, Dr. Starr?"

Milo was silent for a moment. "Good idea. He might have some leads. Not to mention dental charts of the deceased."

The rain began to lessen as we neared Highway 2. "So meth—or crank—can ruin your teeth?" I asked.

"You bet," Milo replied. "It doesn't take long. Ah!" He slowed down, pointing to a hemlock snag. "I just saw a Stellar's jay take off from there. Not all the wildlife has been burned out or scared off."

Ten minutes later, we were again crossing the Skykomish River. "Am I still deputized or do I only get to do the dirty work?"

Milo grimaced. "What did you have in mind?"

"Tagging along while you interview Garth Wesley." I gave Milo my most innocent look. "Maybe asking a few questions of my own."

"That's pushing it," Milo declared. He was thoughtful for a few moments as we turned onto Front Street. "You can listen in, okay? I don't like to get sidetracked when I'm doing an interview."

"Okay." Milo's viewpoint was understandable. I didn't like being interrupted when I was after a story. But I wanted to get a word in with Garth first, however. "Before you start, I'd like to ask him something. It's not about the case, it's about a . . . female hormone prescription."

"Sure." The sheriff backed into his usual spot which was just across Third Street from Parker's Pharmacy. He turned off the ignition, removed the key, undid his seat belt, and stared at me. "Now what?"

I resumed my innocent look. "What do you mean?"

Milo slammed his hand on the back of my seat. "Damn! What's with you, Emma? You hardly ever lie. And lately you're hatching tall tales like a chicken laying eggs."

I was annoyed, as much with myself for having told the lies as with the sheriff for seeing through them. "Okay, okay, I guess I've been a bit evasive lately. But not without good reasons. As for the prescription, that's really none of your business, Milo. When I'm ready, I'll tell you."

Milo suddenly looked stricken. "You're not sick, are you? I mean . . . like . . . you know . . ." He fumbled for words.

His obvious concern defused my irritation. "No, no, I don't have anything seriously wrong with me. I just need . . . some fine-tuning."

"Oh." Milo blew out a big breath, "You scared me there for a minute."

I patted his arm. "That's very nice of you. But I'm okay. Really."

Except, of course, I wasn't.

To our disappointment, neither Garth nor his wife, Tara, was on duty that afternoon. We shouldn't have been surprised, since it was a Sunday. Both Wesleys were certified pharmacists who had moved to Alpine ten years ago and bought Parker's Pharmacy. They'd kept the name of the previous owner, Durwood Parker, who, in retirement had managed to polish his image as the worst driver in the county. A common catch phrase was, "Here comes Durwood," followed by the speaker making the sound of a crash, and adding, "There goes Durwood." It was Durwood himself who stood behind the pharmacy counter, luckily nowhere near a moving vehicle, but back at his old stand as the resident pharmacist.

I abandoned my idea of asking for the Paxil prescription. Durwood might mention it to his wife, Dot, who would tell everybody in town. Since Milo had grounded Durwood some years back, and Dot didn't like to drive, they had become real homebodies. Dot spent most of her time on the phone, keeping connected to the rest of the world and spreading enough gossip that Vida often used her as a source.

"Well, well," Durwood said, looking up from some small white paper bags on the counter, "to what do I owe this pleasure on a rainy Sunday afternoon? You aren't here to arrest me again, are you, Sheriff?" Despite many citations, a couple of arrests, and even a night in jail, Durwood held no animosity for the sheriff. Sometimes I wondered if his driving escapades hadn't been a game for him, albeit a reckless one. Fifty-odd years of filling prescriptions didn't allow for a margin of error. Driving did.

"Not as long as you aren't running over sidewalk plants and pedestrians," Milo assured the pharmacist.

Durwood, who was completely bald and had a round face that was emphasized by his round, rimless glasses, chuckled. "No, I haven't driven in quite a spell. Not since I ended up in the display window of Francine's Fine Apparel. I told Dot afterward, that was the closest she'd ever get to a fur-trimmed coat."

A large photo of the incident had graced the *Advocate*'s front page. By coincidence, Scott had been on the scene to take a photo at Posies Unlimited next door to Francine Wells's shop.

Milo was leaning against the partition that guarded the entrance to the pharmacy itself. "You working here much these days?"

"Well . . ." Durwood put a finger to one of his rosy cheeks. "That depends on what you mean by 'much.' I fill in now and then for the Wesleys. Their kiddies are in high school, you know. Aaron plays three sports, and Jessica's involved in all sorts of activities. Garth and Tara like to keep up with them as much as they can. Besides, neither of the kids can drive yet, and I guess they'd rather have me dispensing drugs than giving them a ride." Durwood chuckled some more.

Milo didn't chuckle. "How are pseudoephedrine sales these days?"

Durwood sobered. "We watch who we sell to, Sheriff. We know what goes on with that stuff in the wrong hands."

"Nobody stocking up?" the sheriff inquired.

Durwood shook his head, slowly and certainly. "Garth tracks the sales. I can show you a list of who bought it in the last year." He winked. "Do I get my license back?"

Milo shook his head. "Sorry, Durwood. Not for some time. But I'd still like to see the list."

"Of course." Durwood moved to the computer, which he ran more adeptly than any car he'd ever owned. Moments later, the printer was spewing out pages. "You check with Safeway's pharmacy?" Durwood asked as we waited.

"Not yet," Milo said. "I have a feeling that any big sales would take place somewhere else. Monroe, Everett, even Seattle. More anonymous that way."

Durwood nodded as he handed Milo eight pages of names and dates. "That goes back to September first of last year."

Milo handed me the second page. "See if you find anything odd."

I studied the page, which was for November and part of December. "There are plenty of sales, but not a lot of repeats. Cold and flu season, of course."

"That's right," Durwood agreed. "You'll find more in January and February, then a drop for a month or so until the spring pollen started bothering people."

"Thanks, Durwood," Milo said, taking the second page from me and putting the entire list inside his jacket. "I'll hang onto it just in case."

Durwood made a snappy salute. He'd joined the army when he was seventeen and had served the last few months of World War II driving a tank in Belgium and France. It was a wonder that the Germans hadn't surrendered sooner. Or maybe it was more surprising that Durwood hadn't asked to bring the tank—what was left of it—home with him. "Any time, Sheriff. Always glad to see you when you don't have a warrant for my arrest."

Outside, where the rain had almost stopped, Milo paused in front of the drugstore. "I'll have one of the deputies check out Safeway." He glanced at his watch. "Jeez, it's almost two-thirty! No wonder I'm hungry. You want to go get some lunch?"

I hedged as guilt tugged at my conscience. "I really should go to the office and work on those features for the Wednesday special edition. Besides," I added, "I'm going out to dinner tonight. I don't want to spoil my appetite."

"Oh? Who's your date?" Milo's voice was a little too casual.

"Max Froland," I replied. "He's going to fill me in on some of the family background for the story."

"Oh." The sheriff seemed to relax. "Max is a good guy. I've always felt sorry for him. That family's had more trouble than they deserve."

"Dare I let Max know you told me his father had been poisoned?"

Milo shrugged, his gaze going over my head in the direction of Old Mill Park. "It's official. If you hadn't found out today, you would have known about it tomorrow. Don't mention the meth lab yet, though."

"Okay." I stared at Milo who was still staring down the street. He seemed wistful. "What are you thinking about?"

"Huh?" He gave himself a shake and focussed his hazel eyes on me for a moment, then looked away again. "I was thinking of Lynn."

"Lynn Froland?"

Milo nodded once. "Yeah. I had kind of a crush on her in high school. I was three years ahead of her, but even when she was fifteen, sixteen, she was really something. Out of my league, though. All the athletes and the popular guys wanted to date her."

I couldn't help but smile. There was something endearing about Milo discussing his high school days. He almost seemed to have reverted into a lanky, klutzy teenager. I half-expected him to stumble over his own feet and fall down on the sidewalk.

"I saw some photos of Lynn in one of the family albums," I said. "In fact, one of them may have been taken up at the ski area."

Milo nodded. "Lynn loved to ski. Water-ski, too, swim, rock climb. She did all the outdoor sports."

"Did she also play the field?" I asked with a mischievous smile.

Milo's expression remained serious. "Not really. While I was studying law enforcement in college, I heard she had a steady boyfriend from Monroe. Or maybe Everett. He may have been one of the kids she went skiing with the day she was killed."

"Were you around when the accident happened?"

"No, I was taking classes at Everett Junior College and living off campus. I didn't want to commute from here during the winter. . . ." Milo's head swiveled around. "Goddammit, that guy in the red Mazda just ran the arterial at Fourth. He damned near clipped the O'Tooles in their new Chrysler. Nice car, that." He waved to Jake and Betsy as they drove by, shaking their heads but waving back.

"I didn't recognize the Mazda," I said. "I think they're cute. Sporty, too."

"That's why jerks like him think they can do the Indy 400 in the middle of town," Milo grumbled. "I should have gone after him, but he had too much of a head start. If he's local, I'll nail him next time." The sheriff paused, removing his baseball cap, running his hand through his graying sandy hair and replacing the cap. "That's funny—talking about Lynn, the O'Tooles driving by after seeing that red Mazda. It reminded me of her car, the one she got killed in. She'd just bought it with money she'd saved working at the Grocery Basket. Of course Jake and Betsy didn't own the store then, but I can still see Lynn behind the checkout counter wearing her hair in a ponytail. Anyway, it was a secondhand red Valiant, one of the original 1960 models. Grace Grundle bought that car new, but she didn't like the color. She thought it was too flashy for a schoolteacher, so after awhile, she traded it in on a black Chevy Nova. God, it's weird how certain things trigger your memory, stuff you haven't thought of in over thirty years."

"Like what else?"

"Oh—like seeing Lynn whipping around town with her boyfriend." Milo smiled at the memory. "He was a good-looking guy, tall, blonde, athletic—sort of a mirror image of Lynn. They could have been brother and sister." He stopped and frowned. "Wait a minute—I'm getting mixed up. There was another guy, tall, but dark, good-looking, too, but in a different way. She always let him drive the car. Hunh. She must have had two steadies. At different times, I mean."

"That sounds right for a girl like Lynn at that age," I remarked, starting to take a few steps in the direction of the sheriff's office. "How about giving me a ride home so I can bring my car back down here and get a jump on the special edition?"

"What?" Milo still seemed lost in reverie. "Your car? Oh, sure, let's go. I'll grab lunch at the Burger Barn. I need to do some work."

Twenty minutes later, I was in the newsroom, feeling stupid. I knew I had to do something for Marsha Foster-Klein, but I felt like I'd exhausted all possibilities. Maybe Vida would have some ideas, especially after she had her visit—and scouting expedition—at June Froland's home that evening. On the off chance that Vida might be able to inspire me, I dialed her number. She didn't pick up the phone, which meant she wasn't there. It had taken a long time for her to get an answering machine, and when she did, the message on it was typically Vida: "So pleased you called me. Don't leave your news as a message. I'll need all the details."

Still at a loss, I decided to give in to Milo's case of nostalgia and read more about Lynn Froland's fatal accident. If nothing else, it would prep me for dinner conversation with Max, should the sorry subject come up.

Earlier, I'd only skimmed the article that Marius Vandeventer had written over thirty years ago. Now I read the whole thing, along with a couple of sidebar stories on the front page, including a warning from the state patrol about highway driving in the mountain passes.

It wasn't until I got to the jump of the lead story on page three that I felt I might have struck gold. It was there that Marius took up the account of the accident:

"The driver of the car owned by Lynn," Marius wrote,

"was eighteen-year-old Gabe Foster of Everett. He was taken to Alpine Community Hospital where he is being treated for a broken leg, facial lacerations, and multiple bruises."

Could Gabe Foster be Gabe Foster-Klein, Marsha's brother? I finished the rest of the piece in a rush:

"The other two passengers in the car, Clare Thorstensen, 18, of Alpine, and Terrence Woodson, 19, of Monroe, were treated for multiple cuts and bruises but released from the hospital Monday. Clare, like Lynn, is a 1966 graduate of Alpine High School, and the daughter of Don and Marcella Thorstensen who live on First Hill."

I was finishing the last sentence even as I dialed Judge Marsha's number. She answered on the third ring.

"Any chance you can drop by the *Advocate* office?" I inquired. "I want to show you something."

"Is it important?" she asked in vexed voice. "I'm busy right now."

"Yes, I think it is."

Marsha didn't respond for a few moments. I thought I could hear a muffled voice in the background. A man. What could be more important than Marsha's reputation? Sex? Dubious.

"I'll be there in twenty minutes," she said, and hung up.

March 1917

Ruby Siegel gazed over the top of a two-day-old Seattle Times. *"The czar abdicated," she announced to her husband. "Did you hear about that while you were visiting your Wenzler relations in Seattle?"*

Louie Siegel glanced up from the small cardboard suitcase he was unpacking. "Yes. So what?"

"It's about time," Ruby declared. "Those poor Russians—they're starving. How can they fight the Germans when they're too weak to walk?"

"They spend more time fighting among themselves," Louie retorted.

"Now maybe they'll settle down," Ruby said, still scanning the newspaper with an avid eye. She devoured everything she could read about politics and social change. It annoyed her greatly when the train delivered the paper a day or two late. "I don't think we should get into the war," she went on, noting an article that suggested President Wilson was edging closer to sending troops to Europe. "It's not our kind of conflict. The old order is dying, and it's about time."

"That doesn't have much to do with us," Louie remarked in a disinterested manner. "I'm too old to be soldier."

"There are plenty of younger men here in Alpine," Ruby replied with fervor. "I don't want to see any of them sent to Europe to get slaughtered. Those Wobblies are right—we shouldn't fight a war for the foreign upper classes."

Louie said nothing. He had closed the empty suitcase and put it under the bed. Ruby looked up from the newspaper. Her husband was still on his knees. At last he got to his feet, holding what looked like a train ticket stub.

"When did you go to Wenatchee?" he asked.

"Wenatchee?" Ruby's green eyes widened. "Why, I haven't been there in over a year."

Louie turned the stub over in his hands. "This is dated last week."

"Well," Ruby said dryly, "you were here last week. Did you wave me off to Wenatchee?"

"No." He scrunched up the ticket and tossed it at the wood box. "How do you think it got under the bed, Ruby?"

She shrugged. "How would I know? I suppose one of the boys picked it up some place and dropped it in here. Are you going to nag me about my housekeeping again?"

Louie stood in silence, his eyes darting from his wife to the window where he could see two of their sons pelting each other with snowballs. Their father recognized that they were lively, headstrong boys, and sometimes careless, even disobedient. But, he thought, boys would be boys.

And Ruby would be Ruby. Louie gazed at his wife with an ironic expression.

She put the newspaper aside and stood up, her arms spread wide. "Quit looking as ornery as a bear with a cross-cut saw," she said, embracing her husband. "The boys won't come inside for a while. Why don't I welcome you home in a wifely fashion?"

Louie took Ruby into his arms. With her plump little fig-ure and those dancing green eyes and that mass of red hair, Louie couldn't resist his wife.

The problem was, as he knew too well, other men couldn't resist her, either.

Chapter Twelve

MARSHA FOSTER-KLEIN LOOKED as if she'd thrown her clothes on in great haste. Which, I figured, was exactly what she'd done. The seams in her navy slacks were crooked and the sweatshirt with Mount McKinley on the front was bunched up in the back. Her hair was disheveled and she wore no makeup.

"Well?" she demanded, without so much as a howdy do, "what have you got? It better be good."

"That depends," I replied, determined not to let her rattle me. "Have a seat."

Marsha sat. "What's all this stuff?" she asked, waving a hand at the photo albums piled on the table.

"Never mind those for now," I said. "It's this issue of the *Advocate* I want to show you. The year is 1967." I turned the bound volume around so it faced her. "Read the lead article about Lynn Froland. Skip the sidebars, and go to page three."

Marsha was a quick reader. When she got to the jump, her head jerked up. "Gabe Foster? Jesus."

"Is that your brother?" I asked.

Marsha's face lost some of its usual color. "It could be." She touched her fingers to her lips, as if to keep from blurting out. "Let me think—1967. I was eight, nine years old. Gabe would have been . . . Yes, he would've been the right age." She paused again, apparently still assembling her thoughts in an orderly fashion.

"Did he drop the hyphenate?" I asked after a suitable pause.

"That's what I'm trying to remember." Marsha no longer looked hostile or upset. "Gabe played basketball in high school. The coach thought hyphenated names were pretentious. Gabe had to drop the Klein part, which made my mother so mad she threatened to sue the school system. But Gabe got an athletic scholarship offer from Washington State, and he decided to stick with just the Foster half of his name because he didn't want to cause problems over in the Palouse. They've always been more conservative, as you know. Besides," she added with a faint smile, "he thought a shorter name would help the announcers when they broadcast the games. Basketball's so fast."

I held up a hand, needing a moment to collect my own thoughts. "So you're saying that the Gabe Foster driving Lynn Froland's car could be your brother?" I was incredulous. "When I asked you about the Frolands, you didn't think of this connection?"

Marsha gazed at me with a blank expression. "No. Good God, Emma, that was when? Over thirty years ago? I was nine. My brothers considered me a nuisance; they'd always shoo me away when I tried to tag along. I learned to keep in my place. Do you think I had much interest in what they were up to?"

"You'd know if one of them got into a wreck and landed in the hospital," I noted.

Marsha waved a dismissive hand. "They were always getting into wrecks and banging themselves up. Especially Zeke. He had his license suspended for a year. Besides, Gabe would've been in college in 1967, up at Western Washington in Bellingham. He tore his Achilles tendon when he was a high school senior. He never made it to WSU. The only thing I remember clearly was my parents, shrieking about their car insurance rates."

I thought back to my own youth. I vividly recalled Ben's

first three accidents, all of which occurred within a month after he got his license on his sixteenth birthday. Ben wasn't allowed to drive for six months. In retrospect, I wondered if that wasn't what had driven him—metaphorically, of course—into the seminary. But I'd only been two years younger at the time. That would make a big difference. I was already anticipating my own driver's license. Marsha would still have been playing Barbies—maybe her own version— Judge Barbie, Prosecutor Ken, Bailiff Skipper.

"So you never heard of Lynn or these other two who were in the car?" I asked.

Marsha glanced back at the article. "Clare Thorstensen and Terrence Woodson?" She shook her head. "There's some Thorstensens in town, though. I suppose they're related."

"Probably. Look, Marsha," I said turning the bound volume back around to face me, "even if you don't recall the accident or Lynn Froland, isn't it possible that somebody else does and is threatening you with the fact that your brother drove the car in which Lynn was killed?"

"It's irrelevant," Lynn said in her most judicial tone.

"To you," I said. "Not to the letter writer."

"Then it's also stupid."

"Where's Gabe now?" I asked.

Marsha waved a dismissive hand. "California—Santa Barbara, raising two kids and working for some air-conditioning company."

"And Zeke?"

Marsha scowled at me. "What's Zeke got to do with it?"

"I'm curious, that's all. Isn't that what you want me to be on your behalf?"

Marsha affected indifference. "I suppose."

Her attitude forced me to pry further. "So where's Zeke now?"

She gazed off in the direction of Leo's desk. "I'm not sure. Zeke's always been the family free spirit. The last I heard of him, he was involved in some environmental protest in Texas. My mother would be damned proud of him."

"Has he been arrested?"

"You mean for protesting?" Marsha shrugged again. "Occasionally. He got busted for the first time over at Bangor during an antinuclear submarine protest. I defended him."

I wasn't giving up easily on the Lynn Froland–Gabe Foster–Judge Marsha connection. "I'm sorry, I find it hard to believe that there weren't more problems stemming from the accident at the summit. Are you sure no criminal charges were filed against Gabe?"

"If there were, I never heard about them," Marsha declared.

I felt frustrated, but thought I understood. "If there had been, your parents probably wouldn't have discussed them in front of a nine-year-old."

"Ha!" Marsha looked at me as if I were very dim. "Not in our house. Both my parents, especially my mother, didn't hide anything from the children. In fact, my mother was very vocal about everything, from the mail arriving late to equal pay for women."

I drummed my nails on the tabletop. "I guess I disturbed you for nothing."

Marsha stood up. "I'm afraid you did. Does this mean you've run out of ideas?"

Not wanting to feel like a witness on the stand, I got to my feet, too. "No. There are still some avenues to explore. But I must caution you," I went on, hoping to sound at least semilegal, "that after today, I won't be able to devote much time to your . . . project until after the Wednesday edition is put to bed Tuesday afternoon."

"Great," Marsha said sarcastically. "Then again, I don't see that you've made much progress with time to spare."

"I seldom have time to spare," I snapped. "You might remember that I'm doing this as a favor."

Marsha uttered a laugh that was more of a bark. "And I thought journalists were guardians of truth."

"And I thought judges didn't rush to judgment."

Marsha glared at me, then banged the door as she exited the office.

We had not parted on cordial terms. If we'd been the leaders of two foreign nations, political analysts might have described the meeting as "productive." Which, I had long ago learned to interpret, meant the two parties hadn't killed each other.

I bailed out of the office at precisely four o'clock. When I got home, there were two messages awaiting me. The first was from Ben.

"Out cavorting on the Sabbath," he said, adding a "tsk, tsk." "Call me if you get back by four your time. Which, come to think of it, is ours, too, since we don't go on Daylight Saving Time in Arizona. The sun is always shining here. Dammit."

I took a chance that Ben might not have left right on the hour. To my pleasure, he answered on the fourth ring.

"Going out the door," he said, slightly out of breath. "There's a big barbecue tonight in Tuba City. I'm in charge of the white chilis. Have you made up your mind about Italy?"

I'd forgotten all about Ben's offer. "No," I confessed. "Gosh, that's just a month from now, right? I don't have a passport or anything else I might need to go abroad."

"You've got time," Ben said, then added, "though I suspect you won't go and that you've never intended to."

Despite the lightness of his tone, I caught the reprimand. "Let's face it, I'm not ready to make big decisions, Ben. Are you really going?"

"Yes. The conference sounds worthwhile." He paused. "What if I told you that you had to come under pain of mortal sin?"

"That's coercion. And it's a lie."

"Good God," Ben exclaimed, "since when does a woman have to be coerced into joining her only brother on a wonderful trip? Emma, are you sure you're okay?"

I let out a big sigh. "No, I'm not. Doc Dewey ordered a Paxil prescription for me."

Ben didn't sound surprised. "How's it working?"

"I haven't started taking it yet," I retorted, and knew that I sounded defensive.

"In other words, it's still sitting at the local drugstore. Poor little Paxil."

"It was only Friday that Doc . . ."

"You know, I'm not a medical expert, but if you don't take your medication, it usually doesn't do much good. *You moron.*"

"Okay, okay, I'll pick it up tomorrow." There. I'd promised Ben. I'd have to do it.

"While you're at it, go to the courthouse and apply for a hurry-up passport. Call me tomorrow night after six. Got to run, my chilis await me." Ben hung up.

I'd deal with tomorrow when it came. For now, I had to answer my other message. It was from Max Froland, and it was brief, asking me to call him as soon as I could.

My initial reaction was that he was canceling dinner. As I dialed the Froland number, I felt a surprising sense of disappointment. Was I eager to see Max or did I just want to get out of the house and forget about my own problems?

Max, however, wasn't going to call off dinner. "I couldn't remember what time we'd agreed on," he said. "Or if we'd set a time. It's up to you. Vida has very kindly volunteered to spend the evening with Ma. I guess I'd forgotten what a selfless person she is, especially with Ma nodding off now and then. I hope Vida doesn't get bored to death."

"Oh," I said, "Vida's very resourceful. She'll be just fine. Shall we say six?"

"I'll pick you up then," Max replied. "Meanwhile, I'll make six-thirty reservations at Le Gourmand."

"Oh!" I was surprised. Le Gourmand is pricey, but worth it. I assumed we'd go Dutch. "That's sounds wonderful."

"Good. See you in about ninety minutes."

I hadn't dressed up in months. In fact, not since Tom was alive and we had gone to Le Gourmand. I paused at the sliding door to my closet. Maybe I should have suggested another restaurant. But if Max Froland was in the mood for a real meal, the only other choice was the ski lodge. But Max had made the call. It was stupid to disdain a fine restaurant just because Tom and I had often dined at Le Gourmand. That was then, and this was now. I had to stop moping. I had to.

I'd never worn the moss green pants suit and the butter yellow satin blouse when I was with Tom. Standing in front of the mirror at five to six, I surveyed my image.

The yellow-green combination made my skin look sallow. My brown eyes seemed to have lost their luster—assuming they ever had any. I'd let my brown hair grow out since Tom died, and it was way overdue for a cut or maybe a perm. Admittedly, I looked too thin. At five-foot-four, I needed more weight than my current one hundred and sixteen pounds. Frankly, I looked like a mess.

But I couldn't improve myself in ten minutes, so I left the bedroom and moved out into the living room to wait for Max.

He arrived precisely at six. I wondered if he was that eager to see me or—more likely—that anxious to leave his mother. After I got into his Ford Taurus, I demonstrated my concern by asking after June.

"She's better, I think," Max said. "I'm getting a college student to stay with her for the next couple of weeks. Classes here don't start until the end of the month."

"So you're going back to Seattle tomorrow morning?"

"Yes. All those infernal meetings before fall quarter starts at the U." Max negotiated the turn onto the main highway and headed west. He was wearing the same suit he'd worn for his father's funeral.

We exchanged chitchat about the futility of meetings until we arrived at the restaurant ten minutes later. It had stopped raining, and the clouds seemed to be lifting.

Le Gourmand, which is owned by an expatriate couple from California, is a popular place for diners who come from as far away as Seattle. As usual, the tables were beginning to fill up on a weekend. Max and I were seated under a clutch of gourds, which were suspended from the ceiling to add to the French country atmosphere. Tom had always insisted on a corner table, where there was no danger of falling decor should we have an earthquake during dinner. He was kidding, of course. Or maybe half-kidding. West coast dwellers are accustomed to earthquakes, especially those who've lived in the bay area. Like Tom.

"The last time I was here," Max said as he studied the wine list, "was with my parents for their fiftieth wedding anniversary a couple of years ago." He laughed before continuing. "They couldn't figure out the French words in the menu, thought the prices were outrageous, and both swore they were sick all night."

I had my opening. "What do you think about the medical examiner's opinion as to the cause of your father's death?" I sounded overly formal, but at least the question was phrased more tactfully than asking, "Who popped Pop a poisonous mushroom?"

Max stared up at the gourds. "What can I say? Ma and Pa must have gathered them in the woods. Frankly, I haven't had the heart to pass the news on to Ma. What good would it do? She'd only blame herself—or Pa."

"Gosh," I said, doing my best to sound baffled, "wouldn't you think that after all these years they'd know which mushrooms were edible and which weren't?"

Max looked faintly offended, but his response was polite.

"They probably did, but neither of them could see as well as they used to. It must have been one of those horrible mistakes."

"Then it's probably best not to upset your mother," I remarked. "She did the cooking, I suppose."

Max nodded as the waiter approached. He was Peter, one of the owners' sons who was enrolled at the community college. His twin brother, Paul, had waited on Tom and me the last time we'd dined at Le Gourmand.

Max asked me what wines I preferred, depending, of course, on what entrée I might be considering. I told him frankly that I couldn't tell one wine from another—or from a bottle of mouthwash.

"If you don't mind," I said in an apologetic manner, "I'd just as soon have a bourbon and water."

Max didn't take umbrage at my pedestrian palate. He, however, ordered a pinot gris from a French vintner.

"I've come to appreciate wine over the years," Max said after Peter had departed. "Unlike my sister, Lynn, I never cared much for the outdoors. I was the family bookworm." He smiled faintly. "Jackie—my late wife—was a patron of the arts. She introduced me to classical music, ballet, theater—the whole gamut of good things. She also taught me about wine."

From what I knew of the Doukas family, Jackie's relatives wouldn't have known Bach from boxwood. But I hadn't known Jackie. She sounded like a first-class person. I said so to Max.

"She was," he said softly. "She was bright and beautiful. She played the cello, you know. It always seemed like an awkward instrument for such a delicate woman, but she was very good at it."

"Was Jackie involved in music professionally?" I inquired.

"She played with a chamber group," Max said as Peter returned with our beverages on a pewter tray. My companion tasted the wine, pronounced it acceptable, and lifted his glass. "To Jackie. A wonderful wife and an exceptional woman."

I think I hid my surprise. The toast seemed inappropriate. I couldn't stop glancing to the corner table where Tom and I had sat. Silently, I toasted him as well.

"What," I inquired after taking a big gulp of bourbon, "did Jackie do for a living? I assume she worked."

"Oh, yes." Max smiled fondly. "She was a landscape designer. Not long before her death, several of her gardens over on the Eastside of Seattle were featured in the *Times*. She had a remarkable eye for color and texture."

Heaven help me, I was about to OD on Jackie Doukas Froland. How many years had the woman been dead? Close to fifteen, as I recalled. Did Max put off every woman he met by heaping praise on his deceased wife? No wonder he'd never remarried. I took another swig out of my drink.

"I like gardening," I said in what sounded like a feeble voice. "It's good exercise and a way of working off my frustrations."

"It was the creative process for Jackie," Max replied, picking up the menu. "She liked the research, too. You know—seeking out unusual plantings that fit into the client's idea of what the garden should look like." He chuckled softly. "Of course most clients don't know what they want. Jackie was very good at handholding them through the process. Shall we order an hors d'oeuvre or two?"

"Yes, that's fine," I said, also perusing the menu. "What appeals to you?"

Max was silent for a few moments as he studied the selections. Peter sidled up to our table, informing us that there were some specials, both among the appetizers and the entrees.

"I highly recommend the *sabayon* of pearl tapioca with Similk Bay oysters and caviar," Peter said with a less than perfect French accent.

Max nodded. "That sounds excellent. We'll also try your very tempting smoked sockeye salmon with crème fraîche." He closed the menu and looked at me. "Do you concur, Emma? Or have you got a better choice? Jackie was always one for the patés, especially from the Midi."

"How about a baloney sandwich?" I blurted.

"What?" Max looked startled, but I thought I caught a twitch of Peter's lips. "Oh! You're joking," Max said.

I made the acknowledgment with an inclination of my shaggy head. Along about now, Max probably wished he'd taken me to McDonald's. I didn't drink fine wines, I gardened only for the fun of it, and I'd never touched a cello in my life.

As soon as Peter left, I decided to take the initiative. "I've been going through more of our back issues with references to your family. Whatever happened to the young man—Gabe Foster, I believe his name was—who drove the car when your sister, Lynn, had the accident?"

Max lowered his gaze. "Gabe Foster." He sighed and shook his head. "Now there's a name from the past. I must have purposely chased him from my mind."

"Was the accident his fault?"

Max sipped his wine before answering. "Probably not. The car skidded on black ice. You know how dangerous that can be. You can't even see it under certain conditions. The only thing the state patrol told us was that it was possible the driver was going too fast."

"Had they been drinking up at the summit?"

"That's always a . . ." Max scowled at me. "Why did you bring this up?"

I hadn't meant to broach the subject in such an awkward manner. But the endless eulogy for Jackie had gotten on my nerves. Maybe I'd asked the original question because I wanted payback. This wasn't the rendezvous I'd hoped for, not that I had any romantic illusions regarding Max. But I'd thought we'd discuss some interesting topics such as history or maybe current affairs. Instead, the history had been Jackie's, and the rest was old news.

"I'm sorry," I said. "I tend to overresearch certain kinds of stories." That much was true. "As an historian, you can appreciate that. I have to get a feel for the people I'm writing about."

"Yes," Max said slowly, "yes, I understand. You never know where a path will lead. It's the lure of research, the seeking of the as yet undiscovered."

"Your family has suffered great tragedies," I said, "right up to now, with your father's death. I want to find out how all of you have handled these terrible losses."

Max signaled to Peter who was at the next table. Having caught the young man's attention, he silently pointed at each of our glasses, requesting refills.

"I honestly can't tell you if the accident could have been prevented," Max finally said. "Gabe Foster dated Lynn for two years. I don't recall how they met, since they lived in different towns and went to different high schools. Skiing, maybe. Lynn made friends easily."

"So they were going together at the time of the accident?"

"No." Max drained his wine glass. "They'd broken up. Lynn was dating another boy. Terry Woods or Woodsman, from Monroe."

I recalled what Milo had said about Lynn's two steadies. "So she let her ex drive the car even if they weren't still seeing each other? They must have parted on good terms."

A shadow crossed Max's face. "I guess so. For some reason, she'd always let Gabe drive the Valiant. He may have felt entitled to the privilege."

"They still saw each other," I remarked, "so they must have been friendly after the breakup. That is, they all went skiing together."

"No." Max stopped speaking as Peter returned with our fresh drinks. "Lynn and Terry had gone up by themselves. From what we learned later, Gabe and—what was her name?—the Thorstensen girl, I forget. Anyway, Gabe and his new girlfriend had driven to the ski area with someone else—Terry's brother, or the girl's brother, I don't remember. The other two wanted to leave early, stranding Gabe and the Thorstensen girl. They begged a ride from Lynn and Terry."

I tried to recreate the scene in my imagination. Max would have known if Lynn's romance with Gabe had ended acrimoniously. Thus, I assumed that if the two met occasionally, there were no scenes. Gabe and his new steady had lost their ride back from the summit. If Lynn and Terry had agreed to give them a lift, Gabe might have wanted to show up the new beau by taking the wheel. It would put Terry in his place, demonstrating that Gabe still exerted power over his former girlfriend. A macho move, but typical of a nineteen-year-old star athlete.

Max was eyeing me with suspicion. Or maybe it was merely curiosity. I couldn't tell.

"You seem awfully interested in my sister's accident," he said. "The details, that is. I thought you wanted to know more about the family's reaction and how we dealt with tragedy."

"I do," I said hastily, then added with what was probably a goofy smile, "but we journalists have to get all the facts down first. If we can't be an eyewitness, then we must gather the best information available."

"Oh." Max gave a nod. "That makes sense."

"Speaking of reactions," I went on, "how did you and your parents refrain from going after Gabe Foster?"

Max frowned. "What do you mean?"

"Did you file a wrongful death suit? Did you try to get him arrested? Did you threaten to beat out his brains with a baseball bat?"

Max considered the query as if I were questioning the Army of Northern Virginia's military tactics at Gettysburg. "Pa did talk about revenge," Max finally said. "But in that wild, abstract manner when a person is in shock. The state patrol ruled it an accident."

"Despite the fact Gabe and the others may have been drunk?"

"They weren't drunk," Max replied, "though they may have done some drinking. As for suing Gabe and his family, that required money my parents didn't have. I doubt that it ever entered their minds."

By now, I was certain that Max hadn't made the connection between Gabe and Judge Marsha. Of course he hadn't spent much time in Alpine lately, and Marsha was a relative newcomer. I broached the subject.

"Interesting," Max remarked when I'd finished. He looked up as our appetizers arrived along with a warm baguette in a wicker basket and a small crock of butter. Peter's presentation was a trifle clumsy, the breadbasket almost slipping out of his hands. Max, however, complimented the young man who seemed pleased.

As Peter left us, I waited for Max to continue his comments about the relationship between Marsha and Gabe. But he said no more, concentrating instead on an oyster.

I had an urge to spur him on. "Did you know that your family and the Foster-Kleins are actually related by marriage?"

"What?" Max dabbed at his beard with a linen napkin. "Is that right?" He chuckled. "I'm not surprised. Everybody in Skykomish and Snohomish counties seems to be related somehow."

"But you didn't know that at the time of the accident, I take it." The oysters were indeed worthy of full attention.

"I didn't know it until now. What's the connection?"

I explained. "It's definitely shirttail," I added.

"What did you say Marsha and Gabe's mother's maiden name was?"

"Klein," I replied. "Her father was a radical back in the

first part of the century. He was one of the Wobblies who was arrested after the Everett Massacre."

"Ah." Max put his fork down. "Of course. Yitzhak Klein. He went to prison for a few years. Anna was very vocal during the McCarthy hearings. I don't focus on those years in my area of expertise, but I've still done my research."

"Did Anna follow in her father's footsteps and get arrested, too?"

"No." Max allowed me to finish the last oyster while he polished off the caviar. "Anna engaged in some demonstrations, but mainly she was a letter writer. Later she got involved in women's issues and anti–Vietnam War protests. I can't say that I ever read any of the letters or articles she wrote, but I do know that she was both prolific and vitriolic."

That shot down my theory that Anna had shackled herself to lampposts or taken part in illegal rallies. "I understand her son, Zeke, has been very active in environmental issues."

"Zeke?" Max looked puzzled. "That would be Gabe and the judge's brother? How many children are there?"

"Just those three," I replied, wishing I could pick up the empty smoked salmon plate and lick off the remaining dabs of crème fraîche.

Max shook his head. "I don't know anything about Zeke. But then I didn't realize that Judge Foster-Klein was related to Lynn's former boyfriend." He prodded the breadbasket. "It's still warm."

Max seemed to be dismissing the subject. He suggested we consider our entrees, especially since Peter was coming our way to collect the empty appetizer plates. I didn't need to look at the menu. I usually had the duck. It didn't matter how it was served, it was my sole opportunity to eat duck away from the Big City. Jake O'Toole would special order it only at holiday time when I felt obligated to cook a turkey.

"Duck," Max echoed as Peter hovered over us. "I think I'll have that, too. It's served with a puree of root vegetables and haricot verts. I'll wager the green beans are very tender here." He handed the menus back to Peter. "In that case, I'll have another glass of this." He tapped his almost empty glass, then looked at me. "What about you, Jackie?"

I was taken aback, but tried not to show it. "Ah . . . Okay, I'll nurse another drink with dinner."

With a curious glance in my direction, Peter left us. He knew me only slightly, but well enough to know I wasn't named Jackie.

Max, however, didn't seem to notice his gaffe. "I was tempted by the quail," he remarked. "Jackie didn't care for game birds. Her favorite entrée was veal. She was especially fond of Italian food. Her veal marsala was exquisite."

"A good cook, huh?" I said, sounding like the rube that I was beginning to feel like compared to the incomparable Jackie. To further enhance my lowly image, I reached across the table and dived into the breadbasket.

"An excellent cook," Max replied. "We rarely ate out. Her meals were marvelous. Not that I'm a gourmet," he added modestly.

"Me neither," I replied, slathering butter on a chunk of baguette.

"Not long before she became ill, Jackie took a course in Japanese cooking," Max went on. And on.

Frankly, I drifted. I thought of Tom. I could picture him at the corner table, laughing easily, speaking knowledgably, inquiring about my feelings, soliciting my opinions. A bit too rapidly, I finished my bourbon. Max was still droning on when our fresh drinks arrived. He hadn't quit by the time Peter brought our entrees. Halfway through, he requested a fourth glass of pinot gris and began to discuss his emotional state during his wife's fatal illness. I had tuned out so much of his monologue that I'd forgotten what had caused Jackie's death. Boredom, maybe.

The duck, however, was wonderful. I ate more heartily than I had in months, even asking for a refill of the bread-basket. By the time my plate was clean, Max still had half of his food left. He'd been talking so much that he hadn't had time to eat. Now on his fifth glass of wine, he suddenly stopped.

"I hope I'm not wearing you out with all this conversation about Jackie," he murmured. Or maybe he mumbled. Max sounded strange.

"It's good for people to talk out their feelings," I replied.

"You're a good listener," Max said.

Or that's what I think he said. The words weren't entirely clear. The next thing I knew, Max plunged forward and his face thumped into the haricot verts.

April 1917

Frank Dawson pumped up the lantern next to the kitchen table. It was after eight o'clock, and darkness had descended over Alpine.

"I think we should quit," Tom Murphy announced, one hand holding a deck of pinochle cards. "We've got to finish planning for the annual community play."

Frank glanced at his brother-in-law. Mary Dawson looked at her sister, Kate Murphy. "Well?" Mary said, eyeing each of the men in turn. "Should we let John Barrymore and Enrico Caruso off the hook?"

"No," Kate retorted. "It's early yet. We need one big hand to beat the pants off these two. What's the score? Eleven-hundred to their six-fifty? If we get the bid, we can trounce them like our doughboys will rout the kaiser."

Frank looked at his pocket watch. "All right. We'll play another hand." He resumed his seat opposite Tom, who was shuffling the cards.

"Say," Frank said as Kate cut the deck for her husband, "where are the boys?"

"At our house," Kate replied, "with the big girls. Our Monica's in charge of the boys, Babe and Kate are watching Frances and Tommy."

Mary put a hand to her round belly. "It won't be long before there's another one to watch." She glanced outside where the mill lights shone on the piles of snow along the railroad tracks. "It's officially spring. Won't this snow ever melt?"

"It hasn't snowed since before Billy's birthday," Kate pointed out. "Who wants to bet a nickel that what's left on the ground will be gone by May first?"

"I'll take that bet," Frank replied, sorting his cards. "Everybody gets so excited when the first snow comes. Well, I hope they've all had enough of it by now."

"You'll complain when it gets too hot this summer," Mary shot back. "You should have stayed in England."

"Seattle's like England. It's more temperate, with plenty of nice rain," Frank pointed out. He nodded at each of his in-laws. "These two are smart. They're talking about moving back to Seattle."

Mary uttered a little snort, then looked across the table at her sister. "You haven't left yet, have you?"

"Not yet," Kate answered in a noncommittal tone.

Mary gave Kate a worried look, then assessed the cards in her hand. "I'll open for two-ninety."

"Three-hundred," Frank said in an aggressive voice.

Kate smiled sweetly at her brother-in-law. "Pass."

"Pass," Tom echoed. "I can help you, partner."

"No talking across the table," Kate said severely.

Tom scowled at his wife. "What about feet? You kicked Mary when you passed."

"I was stretching my legs," Kate replied with an innocent look.

"Three-ten," Mary said as the door opened.

The four pinochle players looked up. Monica Murphy, Tom and Kate's elder child, rushed over to her mother. "I can't find the boys," she said, tears glistening in her eyes. "Billy and Louie took Tommy and Frances down to the creek almost an hour ago, but they're not there now! We don't know where they went."

Tom and Frank both rose from the table. Kate's skin paled

as she put her cards down. "How could you lose sight of them? You big girls know better than to let them run around this late."

Frank was lighting another lantern. "We'll go look. They can't be far. The little ones should be in bed." Tommy was the Dawsons' youngest son, having turned two in January; Frances would be five in June. "Why didn't you bring them back over here?"

Monica's pretty face was agonized. "Tommy wanted to throw rocks in the creek. Frances said that if he could go, she could, too."

"Good Lord!" Mary closed her eyes, both hands on her belly.

Frank and Tom didn't bother to put on jackets but hurried out of the house, heading for Icicle Creek. The face of Tonga Ridge was clear-cut all around the town. There were no trees on the hillside, only stumps. The children liked to play on the opposite side of the tracks, near the bunkhouses. If necessary, searchers could be found among the single men who resided there.

"What about Vincent?" Tom asked as they checked the railroad signals, which were on amber for the passenger train that was soon due to pass through town.

"I don't know," Frank replied. "I haven't seen him since supper. He doesn't spend much time in the house now that the weather's warmer."

Tom, whose Irish baritone had great carrying power, shouted his son's name. "Billy! Billy! Billy!"

Frank's voice was not as musical, but almost as loud. "Louie! Louie! Tommy!"

They heard nothing but the echo of their own voices, bouncing off the mountains.

"Goddammit," Frank breathed. "Where are those kids?"

Tom's high forehead was creased with concern. "Monica and your two girls should have gone with them."

"You're right," Frank replied as they followed the creek down past the railroad tracks. "They usually have better sense."

The men paused, shouting their sons' names again. This time a voice called back.

"Murph?"

Frank and Tom spotted the spare figure of a man coming from the creek. He wore only a towel around his waist.

"Roscoe?" Tom said.

"It's me," Roscoe Moyer answered. "You looking for your boys?"

Roscoe, one of the unmarried yard men, pointed at the nearest bunkhouse. "I seen 'em about half an hour ago, when I started out to take a wash in the creek. I was gonna shoo 'em away, but hell, they was havin' fun, so I just went down the hill a piece."

Frank felt the muscles in his body slacken a bit. "Did you see them after that?"

Roscoe shook his head. "I heard 'em hollerin', but they stopped a few minutes later. I figured they'd run off home. It was getting dark."

"Are you sure," Tom asked, "it was Billy and Louie and Frank's two little ones?"

"Oh, yeah," Roscoe replied. "I know them kids sure as I know myself. Billy's tall for his age, and Louie's kinda big the other way. I don't recollect the little ones' names. Sorry." He gave Frank an apologetic look. "I reckon they went off with Jonas and Vincent."

Frank practically pounced on Roscoe. "They were there, too?"

Roscoe took a backward step. It didn't pay to rile either Frank or Tom. Besides, Frank was the mill's slip man, and Tom was the deck man. They deserved respect.

Roscoe gulped. "Jonas and Vince were comin' to the creek when I was headin' down. I didn't see none of 'em after that. I was takin' my wash."

"*Thanks, Roscoe.*" *Tom forced a smile.* "*See you tomorrow.*"

Roscoe was hurrying back to the bunkhouse when Frank grabbed Tom's arm. "*Should we get some of the men to help us search?*"

Tom considered. "*Let's give it another few minutes. Hell, they can't be far.*" *But the Irishman's face was grim.*

Frank started back up the hill. "*Roscoe didn't hear or see them go by. Let's follow the tracks.*" *He glanced at the sky. The stars were coming out, billions of them, so close that they seemed almost within reach. Frank silently cursed Vincent. The boy had been nothing but trouble since he'd come to Alpine.*

When they reached the tracks, Frank and Tom decided to split up. They'd started in opposite directions when they heard Kate calling to them.

"*Have you found the boys yet?*" *she shouted, holding her skirts high as she hurried downhill.*

"*No,*" *Tom shouted back.* "*Stay put.*"

"*I can't,*" *Kate said, her face pale.* "*We have to flag the westbound train when it comes through at ten to nine. Mary's in labor. We have to get her to the doctor in Sultan.*"

Frank, who had waited by the semaphore, swore under his breath.

Kate tapped the small silver watch pinned to the bodice of her dress. "*It's eight-forty now. I'm going to help Mary down to the platform.*" *She stared into the night and wrung her hands.* "*Dear God, where can those boys be?*"

"*We'll find them,*" *Tom said with more confidence than he felt. He gave his wife a pat on the behind.* "*Go help Mary.*"

Kate hesitated, then resumed the uphill climb. She stopped once to look back. Darkness had brought the cold night air down from the mountains. Billy had been wearing only a light jacket. Kate avoided a snowbank and trudged toward the Dawson house.

Frank moved briskly down the line, intermittently calling

Louie's name. He had turned the first bend in the rails when he saw the little group coming toward him. Louie, with Frances in his arms. Billy, carrying Tommy.

"Thank God," Frank said aloud. "Are you all right?" he called to the children even as he heard Frances screaming at the top of her little lungs.

"Yeah," Louie panted as he reached his father. "Just kind of . . . scared."

"Of what?" Frank asked, staring at his youngest daughter's red, blotchy face.

Frances reached out to her father. She stopped screaming when he took her in his arms.

"Scary stuff," Louie replied with a quick glance at Billy.

Frank studied Tommy, who seemed none the worse for the adventure, though there were twigs and leaves in his Dutch boy bob.

"Get down," Tommy said, kicking at Billy. "I wanna get down."

Billy set Tommy on the ground but avoided his uncle's gaze. Frank decided to wait to interrogate the boys until they got back to the house. Or to the platform. Wherever Mary was by now.

As the little group approached, Frank saw Mary. She was lying in a snowbank about twenty feet from the tracks. Kate and her daughter, Monica, were trying to help her get up but the task was made difficult by Mary's bulky body, long full skirt, two petticoats, and heavy wool coat.

Mary saw her children and began to laugh, almost hysterically. "Blessed be God," she gasped, then doubled over with pain.

"Where were they?" Kate demanded, her eyes glistening with tears.

Frank shouted for Tom, who was no longer in sight. "Dammit," he said, "now somebody will have to go get him."

"We will," chorused his older daughters. Young Kate and Babe had appeared from behind the social hall. "We'll stay

together," Babe assured her father. The two long-legged girls started running down the tracks.

Frank had given Frances to his sister-in-law. It was a struggle but he finally got Mary to her feet, just as the locomotive's headlight glowed in the distance.

"Flag it!" Frank shouted.

"I already did!" Tom called back, running toward them with the Dawson girls. Mary leaned against Frank taking brief, shallow breaths. "Such a time," she gasped. "Are the children really all right?"

"They seem fine," Frank replied as the train slouted to a stop.

Kate hugged Billy, then Monica. "I have to go with Aunt Mary to Sultan," she said, picking up the leather suitcase that had been packed the previous week. "Are you sure you're fine, Billy?"

"Yes, Mama. Honest." But Billy's glance at his mother was quick, almost furtive.

By the time the train stopped, at least a dozen other Alpiners had gathered by the tracks.

"What's going on?" Ruby Siegel called.

"The baby's on its way," Frank responded. "Mary and Kate are going to Sultan."

"Good luck, Mary!" Ruby and some of the others shouted.

The two sisters were helped onto the train while the conductor discreetly engaged in some ribald repartee with the men. Then, as everyone waved, the passenger train whistled again and slowly began to pull away from the platform.

Frank heaved a big sigh. "It won't take long to get to Sultan, thank God. Mary should be fine." He looked at his eldest daughter. "Babe, take everybody up to the house. I want Louie and Billy to stay here."

"Yes, Papa," Babe said. She picked up Tommy, who suddenly seemed very tired and willing to be carried. Kate reached for Frances, who backed away.

"I'm walking," she declared, her tears stopped and defiance in her eyes. "I'm not a baby, you big berry-head."

"Then walk between us," Kate snapped, grabbing one of Frances's arms while motioning at her cousin, Monica, to take the other.

As soon as they were out of earshot and the others had headed back to their homes, Frank grasped Louie by the collar of his jacket. "What happened? Why did you boys run off?"

Like Billy, Louie's gaze was evasive. "We didn't mean to."

"But you did." Frank sounded severe. "Why?"

Louie glanced at Billy who was shifting from one foot to the other under his father's hard stare. "It was Vincent. And Jonas. They wanted to show us a bear."

"You've seen a bear before," Frank said. "The bears have gone up into the high country this time of year. Besides, you know better than to go looking for a bear. They can be dangerous if you bother them."

"Vincent said it was the biggest bear anybody'd ever seen," Louie said. "Huge." He spread his arms wide.

"Did you see this bear?" Frank asked.

Louie shook his head. "No."

"Then why didn't you come right back?"

"We wanted to," Louie said. "Vincent and Jonas wouldn't let us."

Frank's head jerked up. "Where are they?"

Louie hung his head. "I don't know. We ran away while they were playing on the rope."

"What rope?" Frank asked sharply.

Louie looked to Billy for help. His cousin obliged, though with obvious reluctance.

"They tied a big rope to the railroad trestle. They swing on it. And . . ." His voice trailed off.

"And what?" Tom cut in.

"Just . . . nothing." Billy looked as if he were about to cry.

"Did you swing on the rope?" Tom demanded.

"No." Billy wiped his mouth with his hand. "Yes. Once."

Frank still held his son by the collar. "Did you?"

"Once."

"What else did you do?" Frank asked, finally letting go of Louie.

"Nothing." Louie looked as miserable as Billy. "We didn't do anything."

"What did Vincent and Jonas do?" Frank persisted.

"They . . ." Louie's face crumpled and he shook his head.

"What were Tommy and Frances doing all this time?" Frank's voice had taken on a frazzled, angry edge.

"Nothing." Louie was shaking, fighting back tears.

Billy, unnerved by his cousin's collapse, threw his arms around his father. "Papa! We hate those boys! They're bad!"

Tom put a hand to his head. "I don't know how bad they are unless you tell us what they did."

Billy finally looked up at his father. "We can't!"

"Why can't you?" Tom asked sternly.

But neither boy would speak of what had gone on by the railroad trestle. It was only a half-hour later when Frank tucked in Frances that he gained an inkling of what the unspeakable might be.

"Guess what, Papa?" Frances said, her blue eyes wide. "I saw Vincent's weewee."

"What do you mean?" Frank spoke harshly, but immediately repented and lightly touched his four year-old's cheek. "Tell Papa."

"Vincent took off his pants," Frances replied. "So did Jonas. Vincent's got dots on his butt, like he has on his face."

Frank didn't ask any more questions that night. Nor did he look for Vincent.

Frank hoped his nephew would never come back.

Vincent never did.

Chapter Thirteen

I CAN'T RECALL a more embarrassing incident, not since I took a bathroom break during my first county commissioners' meeting and returned with four feet of toilet paper attached to my right shoe.

Peter thought we should call 911. I hesitated, but he impressed upon me the liability of his parents in case there was something seriously wrong with Max.

"He didn't eat mushrooms," I said stupidly.

Peter was sufficiently distracted to ignore the remark. I was sufficiently discreet to keep my mouth shut and not say anything about the quantity of wine that Max had consumed in a short time. Peter ought to know. He'd poured each glass. It should dawn on him that Max had simply passed out.

Naturally, there were at least a half-dozen diners that I knew quite well: Clancy and Debra Barton, of Barton's Bootery and St. Mildred's Parish; high school coach Rip Ridley and his wife, Dixie; Cliff and Nancy Stuart who owned Stuart's Stereo. All of them, along with several others, had gathered near the table where Max remained unconscious. Some of the staff had come over to see what was going on, but I didn't spot Peter's parents. The owners must have had the night off.

"Give the guy some air," Coach Ridley shouted. "Get back everybody. It doesn't look serious, but he still needs some space."

Before blowing out his knee, Rip Ridley had played defensive tackle for two years with the Chicago Bears. The gawkers obeyed. At last Max twitched, raised his head a scant inch, and groaned.

Rip, accustomed to injured football players, leaned down to murmur something into Max's ear. Slowly, Max raised his head. Two beans were stuck to his face, one on his forehead, the other in his beard.

"How do you feel?" Rip asked.

"Dizzy," Max replied, then took in his surroundings. "Ohmigod!"

"Relax," Rip urged. "Don't try to get up. Help's on the way."

The sirens announced that help had already arrived. Purse in hand, I backpedaled in Peter's direction. The irony of my situation wasn't lost on me. I'd looked forward to this evening, hoping it might be a step out of the doldrums. Instead, it had turned into a mockery, and it looked as if I was going to pay for the privilege. "Let me settle up with you," I said.

Peter still seemed taken aback by his customer's collapse. "What? Oh—the bill. I'll get it. What's wrong with this guy anyway?"

"Stress," I replied. "His father died very recently."

"Oh." With a last look at Max, Peter headed off to get the tab. I trailed behind him just as the medics and firefighters arrived.

Peter took some time to tote up our items. I steeled myself, aware that the total would be at least a hundred dollars. Dimly, I heard Max arguing with the emergency personnel. Apparently, he thought he was just fine. The EMTs didn't agree.

The tab came to one hundred and thirty-nine dollars. With a twenty percent tip, that was a blow to my Visa account. I had just signed the charge-card slip when Milo Dodge entered the restaurant.

Max was still arguing. The sheriff, after giving a start

when he recognized Max, ordered the medics to take him away in the ambulance. Max finally stopped his protests. I was glad. Frankly, he looked awful.

I had edged up behind Milo. As Max allowed himself to be assisted onto a gurney, I plucked at the sheriff's sleeve.

"Some dinner date, huh?" I whispered.

"Christ." Milo looked down at me. "What'd he do? Drink himself stupid?"

"Kind of," I admitted. "Of course he's been under a strain."

"You're sure you didn't poison him?"

"I felt like it," I confessed. Seeing Milo's puzzled expression, I shrugged. "I'll tell you later."

"Whose car did you come in?" he asked as Max was wheeled out of the restaurant.

"His," I said. "Oh! I'll get the keys so I can drive it back to town."

"I'll ask Sam Heppner to drive it," Milo said, waving to Del Amundson, one of the medics. "I rode with Sam. We'll take his patrol car back."

Five minutes later, the logistics were straightened out. Milo and I were in the patrol car, following the ambulance. The medics didn't use the siren or go beyond the speed limit. Obviously, they didn't feel that Max was in any danger.

"So," Milo said in amusement, "your big date was a washout."

"A passout's more like it," I replied, and related how Max had dwelled on his late wife's virtues until I'd wanted to scream. "Fifteen years later, he's still wallowing in the loss of his perfect wife." I turned to Milo. "God, am I doing that with Tom?"

Milo shrugged as he turned off Highway 2. "It's only been fifteen months, not years."

That wasn't the answer I wanted to hear. Milo was no help. I changed the subject. "Why are you out cruising on a Sunday night?"

"Got another break in the fire case," he said, guiding the patrol car across the bridge. "The National Forest Service chipped in with the news that somebody's cut down three four-hundred-year-old cedar trees on the other side of Martin Creek."

"What?" I was aghast. "You mean on public land?"

"Yep. Real giants, Western red cedars seven-feet in diameter." Milo made a disgusted face. "They were cut less than a mile from where the fire started. It might tie in."

"How? With what?"

"With the meth lab," Milo said. "I heard about how these nuts illegally cut down old trees and sell them to support their habit as well as the meth labs. It's been going on for quite awhile, and it's almost impossible to police the forests. They're too damned vast."

"How do they get the trees out?" I asked as we drove along Front Street.

"They don't take the whole tree," Milo replied, pulling into a parking place by his headquarters. "Oh." He paused with his hand on the ignition key. "Did you want to go home?"

"No," I said, "I want to hear more about this. Tell me now, before we go inside and confusion reigns. Why don't they take the entire tree?"

"They have to work fast," Milo explained, "so they cut out the best parts, like choice chunks of meat. They load a truck and head off to a shingle mill. Or maybe some place that makes musical instruments. Cedar's in demand for stuff like that. Anyway, they get four, five-hundred bucks for an average load. They've been doing it over on the Olympic Peninsula for years."

"Good grief." I stared out through the car window. It was well after seven, and getting dark. "So there's some of the trees left on the ground? I should get Scott to take some photos."

"That's not all."

"What?"

Milo put a cigarette in his mouth and rolled down the window on his side of the patrol car. "The firefighters have pinpointed the starting place. Like I figured, it was the meth lab. It virtually blew up, probably with the victim in it."

"An accident?"

Milo shrugged. "Maybe. It depends on how the guy died. We may never know. Tomorrow we're going to try to match dental charts with dentists in SkyCo and the surrounding counties. It'll take some time."

"Anything else I should know?"

"Not that I can think of," Milo responded.

Despite the open window, the cigarette smoke was getting to me. Even in my smoking days—not that they appeared to be over yet—I never smoked in the car. The confines were too close, and it made me cough. I started to get out, then stopped.

"Maybe you should take me home," I said. "Do you mind?"

"No, it's a five-minute round trip." Milo turned the ignition key.

"Wait." I saw Milo look slightly exasperated. "Drop me off at the Frolands'. Please?"

"They were taking Max to the hospital," Milo replied.

"Oh." I should have realized that. I stared out the passenger window, thinking. Suddenly I realized that the car parked next to us belonged to Spencer Fleetwood. "What's he doing here?" I asked, gesturing with my thumb.

Milo looked around me. "Is that Fleetwood's Beamer? He probably picked up the 911 call on his scanner."

"Rats!" Scooped again, and on my own date. Not to mention that he'd probably put the fire and the tree-cutting stories on the hour-turn news. "I suppose Spence has already heard the latest."

"That can't be helped," Milo said. "It's a matter of record. Sorry."

"On second thought," I said, "take me to the Froland house anyway. Vida's staying with June. I'll get a ride home from her when she leaves."

Milo started to scowl at me, then chuckled. "You're avoiding Fleetwood? I thought the two of you might have something going. Dinner at the ski lodge? A candlelit table for two?"

"All the tables in the ski lodge bar have candles," I shot back, "as you damned well know. As far as a romantic evening with Spence is concerned, they might as well have floodlighted the place."

The sheriff pulled out onto Front Street. "Fleetwood seems okay to me," he remarked. "You make him out be some kind of monster because he's the competition."

"Of course," I said. "But actually, we're going to try to pool our resources and come up with some promotions and ad campaigns that'll benefit both of us. That's why we had dinner the other night."

"I can't say I really like him," Milo said as we passed by the newspaper office and the Whistling Marmot Movie Theatre. "He's not my kind of guy. Too slick. But maybe that's not all his fault. He reminds me of somebody I knew when I was in high school."

"Who was that?" I asked idly.

Milo didn't answer right away. "Come to think of it, he wasn't a Bucker, he was from another high school. I knew him from 4-H Club when we had regional meetings with other students."

We'd gone by Harvey's Hardware and Francine's Fine Apparel. Milo turned right on Sixth, heading up the hill to Spruce. "What did the guy do?" I inquired. "Ruin your egg-hatching project?"

"City girls," he sneered. "You don't know dick about 4-H. Everybody joined it in high school. What did you do for activities? Hustle bums in Pioneer Square bars?"

"In case you've forgotten, I went to a Catholic school," I

said primly. "We dispensed Christian charity and beat the crap out of the public schools in sports. Say," I said, recalling something Milo had mentioned earlier in the day, "did Sam and Dwight find anything at the Froland house?"

"You mean in the kitchen?" Milo shook his head. "Somebody'd already cleaned out the fridge. Go figure."

John Engstrom Park, honoring one of Alpine's early mill superintendents, was dark, but the lights were on in the houses that marched up the face of Tonga Ridge. Milo turned the corner and pulled up alongside Vida's Buick.

As I started for the house, the sheriff called after me: "Tell Vida she needs a search warrant if she's going through the Frolands' closets and cupboards."

"Ha!" I kept walking toward the door.

Vida let me in. "June's sleeping," she said, with a finger to her lips. "Where's Max?" She stepped out onto the porch, rubbernecking around the street. "Is that a sheriff's car? What's going on?"

I explained. Vida was appalled.

"Haven't I often warned against hard liquor?"

"It wasn't hard liquor," I countered as we moved into the Froland living room. "It was wine. I was the one drinking the hard stuff."

"It's still alcohol," Vida huffed. "How very embarrassing. For you both." She plopped down on an old brown-and-white plaid sofa. "So Max was taken to the ER?"

"Best place for him," I said. "How's June when she's not asleep?"

"Addled," Vida replied. A sly look surfaced in her gray eyes. "It's certain. Jack Froland wrote that letter to Judge Marsha."

"No kidding!" Despite our earlier suspicions, I was surprised. "You're sure?"

"Oh, yes. I found the stationery as well as samples of Jack's handwriting. Marsha should relax now. I questioned June discreetly to find out if she knew anything about the letter. She not only didn't know who Marsha is, she thought Judge Penguin was still on the bench."

I considered the ramifications of Jack Froland's threatening letter. "Did you ask June about the picture of the rope?"

"Yes," Vida replied. "She had no idea, not even when I reminded her that a similar photo was in one of the family albums. Really, Emma, the woman is a nitwit. I've always said as much."

"At least we can get Marsha off our backs," I said. "I don't suppose June mentioned who might have poisoned Jack."

Vida sniffed. "June refused to discuss how Jack died."

Again, I was silent for a few moments. "This doesn't make sense. For some bizarre reason, Jack sends a threatening letter to Marsha about her past. Jack dies a few days later, allegedly poisoned by someone, possibly by his own hand. Regret?"

"Hardly," Vida retorted. "Jack Froland wasn't smart enough to have regrets."

"If," I suggested, "Marsha actually knew who sent the letter and the reason for it, she'd have a motive for killing Jack."

"Nonsense," Vida snapped. "Marsha wouldn't have come to you if she knew the writer's identity. Furthermore, she doesn't know the Frolands, shirttail relations or not."

I admitted I was grasping at straws.

Vida's silence seemed to signal agreement. I started relating Milo's news about the fire and the hacking down of the ancient cedars. June's cries for Vida interrupted me in the middle of explaining how the perps disposed of the felled trees' choicest wood.

As Vida tromped into the bedroom, I trailed along behind her. June took one look at me and scowled. "Where's Max?"

Vida answered for me. "Max has been delayed, June dear. Look, Emma Lord came to see you. Isn't that nice?" Vida shoved me toward the bed and exited the room just as the phone rang. I'll get that," she called.

"Busybody," June murmured, then cocked an eye at me. "Aren't you the one Max was taking to dinner tonight? Why isn't he here? I don't believe a word that Runkel woman says."

Truth seemed my best ally. "Max had a . . . little dizzy spell at the restaurant. He's having Doc Dewey check on him."

The scowl deepened on June's pudgy face. "You went to that fancy French place out on the highway, didn't you? Serves Max right. Too rich. He took us there once. I didn't know what I was eating half the time. And the prices!" June fanned herself with one hand. "Jack said he could have bought a whole cow for what Max paid for dinner."

I felt like saying that I could have bought at least a hoof or two for what *I'd* paid for dinner. But I kept my mouth shut.

"Where is she?" June leaned forward in the bed. "What's she doing now in my house now? Who called?"

Vida reappeared like a genie let out of a bottle. "Max will be home shortly. He . . ."

"How's his stomach?" I interrupted.

"His . . . ? Well," Vida said, catching on, "Dr. Sung told him he should probably eat bland foods for a day or two."

"Dr. Sung?" echoed June. "That Chinaman? What does he know!"

"He knows," Vida said clearly, "that he's not a Chinaman. He's from Hawaii. I believe he's mainly Korean."

June threw up her hands. "Korean! What difference does it make?"

I heard the knock on the door first and beat Vida to see who was outside. It was Sam Heppner, who'd returned the Taurus and was holding Max's car keys.

"He needs an oil change," Sam said, dropping the keys in my hand. The deputy, in typical taciturn fashion, tipped his regulation hat and left.

When I returned to the bedroom, Vida and June were arguing about what constituted a bland diet.

"Jell-o!" June exclaimed. "Max wouldn't eat Jell-o when
he was a kid. Why would he eat it now? Jack was supposed
to be on a bland diet for a while a couple of months ago. I
gave him chicken noodle soup one night and he poured it
down the sink. Stopped up the drain, and we had to call the
plumber."

"You certainly don't have much in your refrigerator," Vida
shot back. "It's empty. I hope you have cans of soup for
Max."

"What do you mean, the fridge's empty?" June demanded.
"That's crazy. It wasn't the last time I looked."

Vida gave June her gimlet eye. "Which was when?"

June seemed taken aback. "Well. Let me think. I've been
off my feet the last few days. A week ago, maybe? The night
Jack died?"

"That's over a week," Vida noted with an expression of
disapproval. "Isn't it time you were up and doing?"

"I'm not well," June asserted with a pout. "It's my nerves.
They're shot. I don't see how Max can leave me so soon."

"He may not," Vida responded. "But if he's unwell, you
may have to take care of him instead of the other way
'round."

June looked alarmed. "I can't do that. I'm too weak. All
those months I had to take care of Jack . . ." She stopped and
perked up a bit. "Max has a girl coming in to do for us. She
can take over. I hope she's not some flibbertigibbet. You
know what young people are like these days. Lazy, with no
sense of responsibility."

While Vida might agree, she didn't give June the satisfaction. "Emma and I must go. Max should be back very soon."

"He'd better be," June grumbled. "I'm hungry now."

Vida looked exasperated. "You weren't hungry two hours
ago when I offered to fix you a meal."

"That's right," June said. "I wasn't. Anyways, everybody knows you can't cook. You don't fool me with all those fancy recipes you run in the newspaper, Vida Runkel."

"*I beg your pardon!*" As Vida took umbrage, her bust puffed up like a grouse's breast.

"You're right, Vida," I said, making agitated gestures with my hands and feet. "We really must go."

"What?" Vida stared at me, then recognized the ruse. "Oh. Yes, you're right. We really must."

June didn't protest, so we left with only the briefest of farewells. After we got into the Buick, Vida let out an enormous sigh. "That woman's a trial. I marvel that Jack didn't poison her years ago. Of course, he was such a windbag. And no brains between them. However did those two have a son like Max? Or do they allow nitwits to teach at the university these days?"

"I believe they do," I replied. "That is, if Max can qualify as a nitwit for passing out in his green beans."

Vida was looking in the rearview mirror. "Here comes a car. Maybe it's Max. Someone must be dropping him off. Let's get out of here. I can't stand another minute inside the Froland house. Besides, it'd be embarrassing for you."

"I'm not the one who made a fool of myself," I remarked as Vida pulled out from the curb. "But you're right, I don't need any more Frolands tonight." I was silent as Vida headed down Spruce Street. The Froland house was only a few blocks from my little log home. We turned on Fifth, which dead-ends in the forest. But when we reached Fir, instead of slowing down for my place, Vida picked up speed.

"Hey, where are we going?" I asked as we went right past my house.

"To call on Judge Marsha, of course," Vida replied. "Aren't you anxious to relieve yourself of responsibility for her letter?"

"Yes," I said, sounding uncertain. "I suppose I am. You're absolutely positive it was written by Jack Froland?"

"Of course." Vida turned on Alpine Way, heading straight for the parking garage under Marsha's building. "There were samples all over the house. Someone—probably Max—had put Jack's personal effects into one of the bedroom drawers. Driver's license, AARP card, Medicare, Medicaid, credit cards. His signature was everywhere. Not to mention little notes he'd written to himself. Jack wasn't a very tidy person."

"But why?" I asked in my most earnest voice.

"Why write the letter to Marsha? We may never know," Vida replied, pulling into Ella Hinshaw's guest parking space. "Not that I don't want to. But as far as Marsha is concerned, she wanted to learn the letter writer's identity. Period."

Vida was right. Furthermore, I should have been relieved.

Marsha sounded truculent when Vida announced our arrival over the intercom. But she buzzed us in and was waiting at the door when we reached the so-called penthouse.

"We have news," Vida declared, bustling past Marsha and going straight to the sofa. "Jack Froland wrote that letter."

"What?" Marsha stared at Vida. "Jack Froland? Are you kidding? I want proof."

Vida rummaged in her purse. I remained standing. I hoped we weren't in for a lengthy visit.

"Here," Vida said, handing a worn slip of paper to the judge. "This is a note Jack wrote to himself. It's some sort of reminder about taking his medication."

Marsha switched her gaze to me. "Where's the letter?"

"At the office," I replied. "We came directly from the Frolands'."

"I'll have to compare the handwriting myself," Marsha said with a scowl. "Can you get it now?"

I should have thought to pick up the damned letter before we called on Marsha. "I can, but I'd rather wait until tomorrow morning. I can run it over to the court house first thing."

Marsha was studying the note. "It looks similar. But I still need to see the letter to make sure. All right, get to me right after eight."

I said I would, then started edging toward the door. But Vida had made herself comfortable and appeared to be in for the long haul.

"It would be interesting, Marsha," Vida began, "if you could think of some reason why Jack Froland would have sent you such a letter in the first place. Frankly, I find this whole thing a box of bees."

Marsha, who was standing halfway between the sofa and the door, pounded a fist against the wall. I suspect she wished she had her gavel.

"How do I know? He was nuts, maybe," Marsha retorted. "What difference does it make now? He's dead, I have no idea what he was talking about, and for all I know, he often sent letters like that to public officials. Maybe it made him feel important."

That was a good an explanation as any I could come up with. Maybe it was time to let go. We'd done our job. If Marsha wanted to pry further, she could do it on her own time.

Vida, however, wasn't satisfied. "Why send that old photo with the letter?"

"Because he was crazy," Marsha said impatiently. She was reaching for the doorknob. I almost hoped she'd try to put the bum's rush on Vida. The spectacle would definitely fit in with the rest of my bizarre evening.

"Furthermore," Vida continued calmly, "if Jack had been sending such letters, why haven't we heard about them? Most people would go to the police. The complaint would show up in the log. I'm assuming, of course, that the threats would be as groundless in other cases as they are in yours."

"I can't explain that," Marsha responded. "Look, it's late, I'm tired. We'll finish this thing off in the morning when I compare that note with the letter. Okay?"

Vida glanced at her watch. "It's not quite nine. Goodness, I didn't realize you were such an early bird." She rose deliberately, smoothing her skirts, straightening her coat, adjusting her blue bowler hat. "I guess we'd better be on our way."

"Yes." Marsha opened the door. Vida practically strolled out of the condo, humming to herself.

"Were you just trying to annoy Her Honor?" I inquired after we were in the elevator.

"Not exactly," Vida replied, "but I find this all very queer. Marsha learns who wrote the letter, evinces some disbelief—for which I don't blame her—and never even says 'thank you.' I kept waiting to hear some form of appreciation, didn't you?"

"Marsha lacks social skills," I said as we exited into the garage.

"Marsha is not a happy woman," Vida noted. "I wonder why not?"

"Lots of people aren't happy," I said. "I'm not very happy, either."

"You still have manners," Vida pointed out as we got into the Buick. "Besides, you have a good reason to feel sad. What is Marsha's?"

"Her husband died," I said, "though that was years ago."

Vida began backing out of the parking space. "Y-e-s, that's so. My, so many dead people, especially people who died young, seem to have crossed our path lately."

"Tom was too young," I said, unable to keep the bitterness out of my voice.

"Tom was middle-aged," Vida said. "I'm referring to Marsha's husband, Max's wife, Max's sister, and . . . have I left anyone out?"

"What?" I was still brooding about Tom. "No, I don't think so. Jack Froland was old."

"Some people have more than their share of grief," Vida said, turning onto Fir Street from Alpine Way. "You know," she continued, slowing down as we neared my house, "Ernest was eight years younger than Tom when he died."

I turned to stare at Vida. Somehow, in all my grief, even

in Vida's references to her husband's death, I'd never considered that her loss was as great—maybe greater—than mine.

"I'd never calculated Ernest's age," I admitted.

"He was forty-nine," Vida said, bringing the car to an easy stop by my driveway. "We'd planned to go to Europe that fall. We'd never been there. I still haven't gone." She paused, gazing through the windshield. "I couldn't bear to see Europe without him."

"Oh, Vida!" I put my arm around her. "I've been too damned self-absorbed!"

"That's perfectly understandable," she said, dry-eyed but with a slight tremor in her voice. "And mind your language."

All the years that I'd waited for Tom, all the frustrations I'd suffered, all the faults I found with him for not spending his life with me had never altered Vida's convictions about what a fine man he really was. She'd called him "Tommy" and whenever she spoke of the two of us, those big glasses of hers took on a rosy tint. I'd often found her attitude annoying, but now I realized that she'd been vicariously living her romantic dreams with Ernest.

"Is that the real reason you don't want Buck moving in with you?" I asked softly. "You feel you'd be betraying Ernest?"

"Perhaps." She sighed and straightened her shoulders. "It simply feels wrong. I can't explain it to Buck. Then he gets angry. I really don't blame him."

"I gather Buck doesn't feel the same way," I remarked. "I mean, he's been able to get beyond his wife's death."

"You know what men are like," Vida said with a touch of asperity. "Wife out, wife in. So to speak. They look at things differently. Maybe they're more . . . practical."

"Not Max Froland," I pointed out.

"No." Vida shook her head. "Not Max. Jackie became an obsession with him."

"Did you know her?" I asked. "Was she really so wonderful?"

Vida sighed. "Jackie was very pretty and she was smart enough. I suppose she had a certain sparkle to her. But I never knew her well. The Doukases were a bit standoffish in those days. First Hill was the place to live before The Pines development was built. Of course First Hill is a bit rundown now. But then, if you lived there thirty years ago as the Doukases did—two families of them in big houses—you looked down on the rest of Alpine, both literally and figuratively."

I glanced quickly at Vida. She seemed like her old self, which was a relief. "One last thing," I said, releasing my seat belt. "Do you think June deliberately poisoned Jack?"

"Certainly not," Vida replied. "It must have been accidental."

"Probably," I said, opening the car door. "But I'm puzzled."

"By what?"

"Who cleaned out the Frolands' refrigerator?"

Vida wore a quirky expression. "You mean, in case there were more mushrooms?"

"Exactly," I said.

A large camper had turned off of Alpine Way and was plodding down Fir Street. I told Vida not to wait for me to get into the house. I didn't want her to get sideswiped by the wide vehicle. Thus, she drove off, and I went up to my porch where I searched for my keys.

Digging deep into the big leather satchel, I couldn't find them. The RV rumbled by, perhaps a family coming home from a trip. Maybe they actually had keys to their house. If not, they could sleep in the camper.

Suddenly, I remembered that a couple of years ago I'd hidden a spare key in the woodpile. It should still be there.

Fortunately, I'd turned on the light outside the kitchen door. I went around the Lexus to where the wood was stacked. If I'd driven, I would have made sure I had my keys with me. But in what must have been a more excited state than I realized, I'd searched my purse for a mascara wand. Like everything else in the satchel, it had fallen to the bottom. I'd removed my keys and left them on the arm of the sofa.

I stared at the woodpile. Where had I put the damned key? Down low, as I remembered. Squatting on the carport floor, I ran my hand under the wood. Finally, almost at the end of the row, I felt flat metal.

I had the key in my grasp when I sensed that I wasn't alone. Slowly, I secured the key, stood up, and turned around.

A man was standing in the shadows of the carport.

I screamed.

August 1917

Olga Iversen looked out through the window at the front of her house. Mary Dawson was coming up the path, carrying a basket. Olga ducked out of sight, holding her breath. Despite the heat of the midday sun, the door was closed. Maybe Mary hadn't seen her. Olga decided not to answer her visitor's knock.

"Mrs. Iversen!" Mary called in her pleasant voice. "Olga! I've brought you a present."

Olga didn't want any presents, not from Mary, not from anybody. She stood flat against the door, between the two windows at the front of the house. Most of the other wives in the camp were Americans. They spoke so fast that Olga seldom understood them. They seemed to laugh a great deal, too, though what they found amusing about their hard life in Alpine was beyond Olga's comprehension.

Mary knocked again and called Olga's name. And then, because nobody locked up their houses in the town, Mary gave the door a nudge. Although Olga was a sturdy woman, she was caught off-balance. She staggered to one side as Mary poked her head in.

"There you are," Mary said with a big smile. "Are you hiding from me?"

"Hidink? Oh—no. I vas . . ." Olga fumbled for the right words. ". . . busy."

Mary set her basket down on the table and removed a hand-embroidered tea towel to reveal three small glass jars.

"I brought you some blackberry jelly, fresh made. My sister,
Kate, and I made jelly this morning, before it got too warm
to keep the cookstove going. The berries are lovely this season, especially up on First Hill. I suppose it was the long,
cold winter."

The only part that Olga understood was the jelly, the
berries, and "the long, cold winter." Bitterly cold, and
scarcely a day of sun from November until March. Olga
swore she could still feel the damp in her bones.

"T'ank you," she said politely. "No lingonberries here.
Best yelly, the lingonberries."

"You can get them in Seattle," Mary noted, "down in the
Public Market."

"Ya?" Olga looked wistful.

"When we lived in Seattle several years ago," Mary said,
placing the three glass jars on the table, "I'd take the trolley
to the market two or three times a week. It was such fun to
shop among the stalls, so much to choose from." Mary was
getting a bit wistful herself. "You should take the train to
Seattle some time. It's good to get out and see some new
sights." Noting Olga's empty expression, Mary went on.
"There's a very large Norwegian community in Seattle.
You'd enjoy that. I'm sure they'd sell lingonberries there,
too." Seeing Olga's eyes showing a faint spark of interest,
Mary kept talking. "Of course we have many Norwegians in
Alpine, too. It's nice that you can speak to some of them like
Cap Toney in your own language."

"Ya," Olga said. "Cap Toney. Nice man. Norvegian man."

As she always did, Mary felt like she was fighting an uphill battle trying to befriend Olga Iversen. If only the woman
would try to learn English, Mary thought to herself.

"I must get back home to see how little Helen is doing,"
Mary said. "She's such a busy little baby. How are your children doing? They seem to get taller every time I see them."

Olga put both hands on her breast. "My children? Good,
nice."

"That's what counts," Mary said, stepping toward the open door. "Oh!" she exclaimed, batting at the air. "You're right to keep the door closed. Those deer flies are a pesky nuisance this time of year. So are the no-see-ums. Good-bye, Olga." Mary departed with a friendly smile.

Olga firmly closed the door. Mary's six children were all well behaved, which annoyed Olga. What was worse, Mary seemed to enjoy them. How could you enjoy children, she asked herself, when there was nothing to keep them occupied? How could you enjoy a child like Jonas who caused so much trouble?

At least Vincent Burke was gone. Olga believed he'd been a bad influence on Jonas. She looked out the window. Mary was halfway down the path, laughing and waving to someone Olga couldn't see.

Mary shouldn't laugh so much, Olga thought. Even if Vincent had been Mary's nephew and not her son, he was nothing to laugh about. Olga doubted that Mary had enjoyed him. The boy had been gone for over three months. Nobody seemed to know what had happened to him. He'd simply run away.

Sometimes Olga wished that Jonas would run away, too. Sometimes she wished he'd find a job in another town and not live with the family any more. Sometimes she wished that he'd join the army and use up his anger on the Germans. Sometimes, especially on those dreary gray days that played Alpine, she wished that Jonas was . . .

Olga caught herself. She mustn't wish that on anyone, especially her own son.

But sometimes Olga couldn't help but wish that Jonas was dead.

Chapter Fourteen

M Y SCREAM WAS echoed by a laugh and a shout.
"Emma! It's me, Spence."

I caught my breath as he moved into the light. "You scared the wits out of me," I gasped.

"Sorry," he apologized, coming close enough to put a hand on my arm. "Didn't you hear me pull up in the driveway?"

I looked beyond him. Sure enough, the Beamer was parked on my property, a good ten feet from the street. "No," I admitted. "I was concentrating on finding my spare house key. I left all my other keys locked inside when I went out this evening."

"Anticipating a big thrill?" Spence inquired with a small chuckle.

"No," I barked, "I was not." I stomped past Spence and headed for the front porch. "Nor was I expecting my companion to pass out during dinner." My fright had been replaced by annoyance; I was having trouble making the key turn in the lock. "Why aren't you at the radio station, getting the jump on me with the late-breaking news?"

"I've already done that," Spence said, lolling against one of the pine poles that held up the little roof over the porch. "Your key's probably rusty. Want me to try it?"

I hated to ask, but I wasn't adroit at keys and locks under any circumstances. "Here," I snapped, and handed over the key.

244

A twist of the wrist was all it took for Spence to open the door. "After you, madam," he said with a courtly bow.

I managed to enter the house without tripping over my own feet. The keys lay on the sofa arm, just where I remembered I'd left them.

"What are you doing here?" I demanded, the manners that Vida had attributed to me going out the window. "Why aren't you at the station?"

Without being invited, Spence sat down in the nearest armchair. "I did the eight o'clock news. You know—about the cedar trees and the rest of it." He paused just long enough to make sure I was suffering. "Ordinarily, I don't go on the air Sundays. I turn the programs over to Tim Rafferty or one of the college students."

"You also use a bunch of canned reverends, most of whom sound like they're broadcasting from a revival tent," I retorted. "Where do you get that stuff?"

A flicker of annoyance crossed Spence's face. "KSKY is a small station, on a limited budget. The canned features we air are always of general interest to our listeners, and often they have a local angle that hits home. We use low-cost resources the same way a small weekly newspaper in a small town does," he added with bite in his usually mellow voice.

"Touché," I murmured. The *Advocate* ran its share of wire service filler. "So why are you here?"

Spence shrugged. He was wearing his customary cashmere sweater—this one in maroon—under a black leather jacket. "I was curious. What really happened with Max Froland tonight?"

"What do you mean?" I was still cranky, and didn't try to hide it. "Do you think I poisoned him?"

Spence chuckled. "Relax, Emma. If we're going to work together on co-op advertising, you can't be jumping down my throat every time we see each other."

Spence was right, but I still felt mulish. "This has been a bad day."

"I know that." Spence's dark eyes were very steady as he watched my face. Along with that eagle beak of his, he looked like a bird of prey, considering a weaker creature. "Was he really sick or was he drunk?"

"If he'd been drunk," I replied, trying to become less fractious, "you wouldn't put that on the air."

"Of course not. I have the same policy as you do, citing people for drunkenness only if they break the law. Good God, if I broadcast the names of everybody in town who got loaded and passed out, I'd get a lot more crank letters than I do now."

"You probably get letters from the same people I do," I said, my temper coming under control. "How about Caspar, Captain of the Underworld? Or Red Whiteandblue?"

"I've missed them," Spence said. "My favorite is the one who always addresses me as 'Spawn of Satan'. He—I presume it's a he—hates any music that was recorded after 1950. He never signs his name, though, not even a phony one."

"By now, I know who most of them are," I replied. "Somehow, I can still smile and nod when I see them on the street or in the grocery store."

"It's the threats to blow up the station I don't much like," Spence said, stretching out his long legs. I suspected he hoped I'd ask him to take off his jacket or offer him a drink. I wasn't feeling quite that hospitable yet.

"Do you report the threats to the police?" I inquired.

"Do you?" Spence shot back. "I don't take any of it very seriously. It's more like a nuisance. I assume you get the same threats, too."

"The ones I get want to set fire to the *Advocate*," I responded. "You may have a more sophisticated audience than I do if they know how to make a bomb."

"It's the price of doing business and being in the public eye. Or ear," he added. "There's no point in reporting that kind of nonsense. Dodge has better things to do than chase after a bunch of loonies who are actually harmless."

"I agree." My conscience was nagging me. "Would you like to take off your coat and have something to drink?"

Spence shook his head. "I should check in at the station one more time tonight before we sign off at midnight. I was wondering—does the sheriff think there's a tie-in between the meth lab fire and the fallen cedars?"

"I don't know," I said, refusing to mention the sheriff's liking for the possible connection. "Milo never thinks. I mean," I added hastily, "he doesn't speculate."

"What's your guess?"

"It's just a guess. Maybe, but when were they cut? Before or after the fire? They were away from all the damage," I went on, "so if they were hacked down before, nobody would have noticed. Did you inquire at the sheriff's headquarters?"

"Yes. But they weren't talking, maybe because they hadn't figured it out yet." Spence paused, stroking his chin. "They should be able to tell from the weather. The rain came after the fire. My own guess is that they were cut in the last twenty-four hours, after most of the fire crews had left the area. I figure it was a separate operation."

"You may be right," I said, wondering why Spence was drawing out the conversation. I supposed it was his way of forging a bond between us—a pair of newshounds, on the scent. Thus, I changed the subject to our professional common ground. "It looks like you and Leo have come up with some good co-op ads."

"Leo's a great salesman," Spence acknowledged. "He uses different tactics than I do. Leo cajoles, coaxes, nudges, and always makes the client laugh. I tend to be more . . . subtle."

"Smooth" was the word I figured Spence really meant. "At any rate, I'm pleased with how this issue is shaping up."

"Good," Spence said with the grin that flashed all those big white teeth. *The better to eat you with, my dear.* "By the way, do you think Dodge will be able to come up with an ID on the fire victim?"

"Only if he gets lucky and finds a dentist who can match records with what's left of the body," I said. "Frankly, I don't like the odds."

"No, you're probably right." Spence paused again.

I made another offer of a drink. It was a tactic I used to get a guest to either fish or cut bait.

Spence chose the latter. "I'm going to hit the road." He stood up; so did I. "Is Max Froland a drinker?"

"I don't know," I said walking him to the door. "I have a feeling he just sort of had a letdown tonight. You can't blame him, really."

"No," Spence agreed. "He's been through a lot of crap."

"It happens."

"Yes." For just a moment, he looked grim. "It does." Spence started to open the door, then stopped. "Speaking of letters, did you get one a couple of weeks ago threatening to reveal your darkest secret?"

"What?" I think I actually gave a start.

"That one creeped me out a bit," Spence said. "Whoever wrote it threatened to take out an ad in the *Advocate*, telling all. I thought maybe you'd gotten one like it, only threatening to take out an ad on KSKY."

"No." I tried not to stare at Spence. "Was it signed?"

Spence shook his head. "It was handwritten and mailed here in town. Judging from the penmanship, I'd say it was an older person."

"Did you keep it?"

"No. What's the use? It just struck me as a little weirder than most." Spence opened the door.

"Do you have any dark secrets?" I inquired as he headed onto the porch.

He turned and gave me an ironic look. "If I did, would I tell you?"

Spencer Fleetwood went down the steps and walked to his car. He didn't seem to have his usual swagger.

I wondered why.

. . .

In the morning, I considered calling Max to see how he was feeling. But I'd probably wake him—along with June—so I decided to wait. As good as my word to Judge Marsha, I made a quick stop at the office to collect her letter and then trotted over to the courthouse.

The judge wasn't in, so I gave the letter to the bailiff, a short, stocky man named Gus Tolberg. Gus looked put upon, as he always did, even in court. Maybe he should have remained on the Tolberg farm that his family owned just outside of town. He was trustworthy, however, and I knew it was safe to leave the letter—and the photo—with him. I was just damned glad to be rid of the thing. But I wondered if I should tell the sheriff about it. If Jack Froland had written that letter, and if his death wasn't accidental, then the letter might be evidence.

I was halfway through the rotunda when I remembered that I'd promised Ben I'd apply for a passport. I hesitated, then decided to do it. Obtaining a passport didn't mean I'd actually have to go to Italy. I could make up my mind later.

The county clerk wasn't in yet either, but I was informed that I couldn't apply at the courthouse. I'd have to go to the post office on my lunch break.

By the time I returned to the office, Vida and Leo were arguing about the amount of space she'd have in the special edition.

"Look, Duchess," Leo said, waving a couple of ad mockups at her, "are you complaining because I'm bringing in too much revenue? You've got a thirty-five—sixty-five split. You should be happy. It's less work."

"I counted on a forty—sixty split," Vida said, "which is what I usually get for my page. For this issue, I have two

extra pages besides the regular section. That means I lose fifteen percent of my copy."

"Yes, it does," Leo replied amiably. "Which also means
that we get fifteen percent more revenue. Hey, talk to the
boss." He turned to me. "I hear your date lost his head in the
vegetables last night."

As usual, the grapevine was fast and extensive. "That's
old news," I said, making a face at Leo. "Vida, don't argue
about more ads than copy. What are you thinking of?"

"The Froland story," she retorted, looking out of sorts. "I
organized it in my head last night when I wasn't trying to
carry on a sensible conversation with June. I trust you
wanted me to write it for my page?"

"Yes," I said, as always deferring to Vida when it came to
Alpine's history. "We can jump it to another page if you need
more space."

"Very well." Reaching for her background materials, Vida
turned her back on both Leo and me.

We were all busy that morning, trying to fill the special
edition. I sent Scott to get pictures of the savaged cedar
trees. I'd let him write the story since he handled the police
log as part of his regular beat. Meanwhile, I'd handle all the
other hard news—which I fervently wished would include
the identity of the fire victim.

As of noon, Milo hadn't heard from any of the local dentists—including Dr. Starr—who could match the dead man's
teeth to an X-ray. However, the sheriff asked if I wanted to
meet him at the Venison Inn, which had reopened that morning.

"I should run errands," I said, thinking of the post office
and the pharmacy. "But I skimped on breakfast. Is noon
okay?"

Milo said it was. I was almost late because Vida put out a
call for "Scene Around Town Items" at five to twelve.

I'd already given Vida a note about Milo's cowboy boots.
"Durwood Parker subbing for the Wesleys," I volunteered.

"Betsy O'Toole searching for Jake's birthday present at the mall," Ginny put in.

"The Peabody brothers carrying an eighteen-wheeler down Railroad Avenue," said Leo.

Vida gave Leo a stern look. "The Peabody brothers are strong, but not that strong. Come, come, Leo—what were they really hauling?"

Leo grinned at Vida. "Almost had you that time, Duchess. They were using their tow truck to take a busted pickup to Cal Vickers's Texaco station."

"Very well." Vida was not amused. "I need at least two more items."

Unfortunately, Scott was still at the tree-cutting site. The rest of us seemed to have run out of local sightings. No Averill Fairbanks claiming that Texaco's regular delivery to Cal Vickers's gas station was really an invading space ship from Pluto, no Crazy Eights Neffel sneaking into Francine's Fine Apparel and putting on a Donna Karan evening gown in the display window, no Grace Grundle complaining that her cats had been attacked by mice wearing party hats. But we were saved by Kip MacDuff, who breezed into the newsroom just as Vida was giving Leo, Ginny, and me the evil eye.

"Girl Scouts at Old Mill Park Saturday," Kip said. "They were having some kind of picnic. The Reverend Otis Poole fell off his bicycle outside the Baptist Church yesterday afternoon. I was driving by, asked if he was okay, he said he was fine, just embarrassed."

"Excellent," Vida declared. "You're very observant, Kip. Thank goodness someone is." She let her evil eye linger on the rest of us for another second or two.

I arrived at the Venison Inn five minutes late, but Milo had already commandeered a booth for us. It was lucky that he was on time, because it seemed as if everyone in town had turned out for the restaurant's reopening.

Gone was the fake knotty pine paneling, the lamps on wagon wheels suspended from the ceiling, the work of local artists (including two paint-by-the-numbers), a framed jig-saw puzzle of Glacier Peak, various varnished wooden clocks, and a farmhouse scene rendered in tempera on a rusty saw. All of this small-town decor had been replaced by pale blue paint, dark blue tile flooring, and gray faux leather booths. The only art work was a Buddy Bayard studio portrait of restaurant founder Jack Iverson that hung by the cash register.

I hated it.

"It's kind of bland," Milo allowed. "Harder to keep clean, too."

"It even smells different. The grease buildup is gone," I complained, opening the new menus that consisted of four blue and white laminated plastic pages. "They've changed some of the entrees and raised the prices."

"You can't blame Fred and Opal for that," Milo remarked. "They haven't upped prices in years. All this new stuff has to be paid for."

"They should have spent more and hired a good interior decorator," I huffed. "I'll bet Opal designed this herself."

"We'll get used to it," Milo said, giving me a benevolent smile. "The last remodel was . . ." He was interrupted by his cell phone.

I watched the sheriff expectantly as he listened to the caller on the other end.

"No kidding . . . that's a big break. Okay, I'll be back in about thirty minutes. Thanks, Bill."

"Well?" I said to Milo who looked pleased. "Is the news worth spreading?"

"Not yet," the sheriff replied. "That was Bill Blatt, saying that a dentist in Monroe had matched the X-rays to the fire victim."

"Not a local, then," I said. "Why can't you tell me now?"

"I can tell you," Milo answered slowly, "but I don't want the name to get out until I've talked to the family. If there is a family."

"Who is he?"

"Some guy named Terry Woodson." Milo picked up the menu again. "At least they still have cheeseburgers."

"Terry Woodson?" I echoed. "That sounds familiar."

Milo looked up from the menu. "Yeah? You're right, it does."

I stared off into space, the space that was just to the left of Milo's head. The crinkly old brown upholstery had far more character—not to mention tears and holes—than the gormless gray. I was so lost in thought that I jumped when Beverly Iverson spoke to me.

"How do you like it, Ms. Lord?" she asked, obviously well-pleased with her parents' improvements to the family establishment.

"It's . . . fresh. And lighter," I said, hoping my smile wasn't as phony as it felt.

"We've expanded the menu, too," Beverly said, "with eight different burgers and several varieties of pasta. Would you like to hear our luncheon specials?"

I politely declined. So did Milo. Boring, in a rut, with no imagination, we both ordered our standard burgers, fries, and salad; coffee for the sheriff; Pepsi for me.

"You look distracted," Milo remarked after Beverly had left. "What's up?"

"That name," I said. "Terry Woodson. I know it from somewhere. Think, Milo."

Milo, however, shrugged. "It doesn't ring any real bells with me. We'll check to see if he had any priors. Maybe you remember his name from the log."

Faintly, I heard my cell phone ring in my purse. As usual, I had trouble digging it out. I managed to catch the call on the fourth ring. The connection was bad, as it often is in Alpine where the mountains interfere with reception.

"Who?" I all but shouted, unable to make out more than a couple of words and a lot of crackle and zap.

"Max." The single syllable came through. But the next

words were mangled. I slipped out of the booth and moved to the rear of the restaurant. Max was still talking. ". . . next time."

"Sorry, I didn't hear most of what you said," I told Max.

There was a pause on the other end. Maybe Max was re-thinking what he'd said the first time. "I'm heading for Seat-tle. I called you at the office but they said you'd gone to lunch. I got your cell phone number. Can you hear me now?"

"Yes, much better." I nodded at Heather Bardeen who was heading for the rest room. "How do you feel, Max?"

"Better. But foolish. I guess everything just came over me at once. I wanted to apologize and let you know that if you'll let me, I'll do better next time I'm in Alpine."

"That's okay, Max," I said. "I understand."

"Thank you. I realize it must have been embarrassing. I must ring off now, I'm approaching the 405 interchange to Seattle."

I clicked off the phone and returned to the table. Beverly had delivered our beverages. Milo was smoking and study-ing the ceiling with its recessed lighting. I told him about Max's call.

"Did he promise not to talk your ear off next time about his wife?" Milo asked with a wry expression.

I shook my head. "No. He probably doesn't even realize he's doing it. Or maybe he'll switch the subject to his sister, Lynn. You made her sound like a teenaged queen."

"That's because I had a crush on her," Milo said. "Hell, she *was* a queen, the homecoming queen. But I'd graduated by then. Anyway, I never had a chance with . . ." He stopped and frowned. "You're right," he said, sitting up straight. "I remember now. The name of the guy who went with Lynn after she dumped the Foster kid was Terry Woodson."

"Of course!" I locked gazes with Milo. "That's why I know the name. He was mentioned in the article about the accident that killed Lynn."

Putting out his cigarette, Milo's long face looked incredulous. "Jeez, life's weird, huh? I mean, Terry Woodson was the most wholesome, all-American good-looking guy you could imagine. And he ends up getting burned to death in a meth lab. I'll be damned."

"That was over thirty years ago," I pointed out. "You said yourself the other day you'd changed so much that I wouldn't know you."

Milo didn't argue. "I wonder if his folks are still around in Monroe." Suddenly looking impatient, the sheriff's eyes shot over to the service counter. "Are those our orders waiting under the damned warming lights?"

I had to laugh. At least six orders sat on the counter. Despite the new menu, it appeared that the old customers still wanted their burgers and fries. "Could be," I said.

"Beverly better hustle her butt over here," Milo grumbled as she popped up an aisle away. "Hey!" The sheriff waved a long arm to catch her attention.

The indecision that had been nagging me since joining Milo for lunch now came to the forefront of my mind. Maybe if I hadn't been angry with Marsha Foster-Klein for her lack of manners and roughshod attitude, I would have kept my mouth shut. I suppose I wanted to retaliate in some way. As soon as our meals arrived, I told Milo about the letter and the photo.

"Jesus," he said when I'd finished. "You and Vida think Jack Froland mailed that stuff just before he died?"

"We do," I replied. "Vida compared the handwriting. It certainly looks like Jack's."

Milo shrugged. "Jack Froland was pretty despondent awhile back. Maybe he wrote a bunch of letters like that to public officials. You know—to make other people feel bad, too."

I gave Milo a sideways look. "He may have written at least one other. Spencer Fleetwood told me he'd gotten one like it. He volunteered the information. I didn't tell him about Marsha."

Milo shrugged again, then reached for the catsup. "See? It's a wonder you and I didn't get one. Poor old Jack was on the peck."

All the time that Vida and I had invested in Marsha's letter seemed to have been wasted. "If that's the case," I grumbled, "he wasn't much of a letter writer."

"Oh?" Milo was amused. "You're just pissed because you didn't get a letter. Maybe Jack wrote his own obituary notice. At least that showed some imagination. I thought 'Come see Jack-in-the-box' was pretty damned funny."

"Not to mention in poor taste," I retorted. But Milo's comment made me think. "I wonder—who did write that notice?"

"June, I suppose," Milo said, dipping a couple of fat French fries into the catsup.

"No." I shook my head. "Not June. She has neither the wit nor the imagination. Max—despite his propensity for passing out in public places—wouldn't have turned in anything so crass. Not to mention that the phrasing wasn't exactly impeccable."

"You said the handwriting on the judge's letter was Jack's," Milo pointed out.

"That's true. But someone else may have told him what to write."

Milo pushed his empty plate aside and nodded to Beverly who was across the aisle waiting on a couple who looked like tourists. "That could be. What difference does it make? Do you still think Jack may have been poisoned on purpose?"

I sighed. "Not really. Unless it was June, performing a mercy killing. It just seems strange that after so many years of foraging, Jack and June would make such a terrible mistake and pick the wrong kind of mushrooms."

Beverly handed us separate checks. "Did I hear you say mushrooms?" she asked in her chirpy little voice. "You should try our new mushroom burger next time. It's unbe-lievable."

"Magic mushrooms, huh?" Milo gave Beverly his lop-sided grin.

"Well . . ." Beverly's fair skin turned pink. "Not those kind. But they're really incredible mushrooms. We get them all the way from Tacoma."

Innocently, I smiled at Beverly. "You don't pick the local ones?"

Beverly shook her head. "They're too seasonal. And tricky. Some of them are poisonous. In fact," she leaned closer and spoke in a whisper. "I heard that Uncle Jack—Uncle Jack Froland, I mean—ate some just before he died and they killed him. Isn't that awful?"

"Who told you that?" I asked, trying to sound casual.

"My dad," Beverly replied, still whispering. "He heard it from Uncle Fred who found out just today after he and Aunt Opal got back from vacation. I think Uncle Max told him."

Apparently, Beverly hadn't made the connection between Max's information and its source, who was sitting right in front of her with a toothpick in his mouth.

"But," Beverly went on, "my mom says it's a good thing. This way, Uncle Jack—Uncle Jack Froland—didn't have to suffer any more."

"True," I said. "Uncle Jack"—I omitted the clarification between the two Jacks—"is at peace."

"Yes," Beverly said, then turned as the tourists summoned her back over to their booth.

When she was out of hearing range, I spoke softly to Milo. "The grapevine runneth. But I had a thought."

"Which is?" Milo inquired, putting a dollar bill and two quarters down for Beverly's tip.

"Magic mushrooms," I said, digging into my wallet to pay my share. "If Terry Woodson was a doper, wouldn't he enjoy a magic mushroom now and then?"

"Maybe." Milo stood up, obviously anxious to be on his way. "So what?"

"Well . . ." I paused as I got out of the booth. "I don't know," I admitted as Milo put a paw in the middle of my back to hustle me down the aisle. "I guess I was having a little fantasy."

"Save it for one of your editorials," Milo retorted.

We paid our bills, then exited into bright sunlight. I made the sheriff promise to let me know what he found out about Terry Woodson. "Survivors, especially," I said, hurrying to catch up with his long stride. "I might interview them."

Milo didn't respond. He was already loping past the *Advocate* entrance while I trailed behind.

Vida was at her desk, nibbling on those infernal carrot and celery sticks. "I hear they've identified the fire victim," she said before I could get all the way inside the newsroom. "Billy told me a few minutes ago."

I gave Vida a dubious look. "How long did you have to hold your poor nephew's head underwater?"

Vida looked askance. "He volunteered, of course. I just happened to stop in at the sheriff's office on my way back from the bank."

I stood in front of Vida's desk. "I suppose," I said with a touch of sarcasm, "you've already spoken with Terry Woodson's surviving kin."

"Of course." She peered at me from behind her big glasses. "Terry Woodson's mother, Irma, is in a nursing home in Monroe. Her brain is completely gone, from drink, I gather. Her liver's not far behind. Terry's father—his name was Elmer—died last spring, but after he and Irma divorced twenty-five years or so ago, he remarried. The second wife's name is Lorena. She's somewhat younger and seemingly sober. I got all this information from her. A pleasant woman, if somewhat dim."

I absorbed all this data with what was no doubt a slightly

stunned expression. "Did Mrs. Woodson tell you how her stepson went wrong?"

"Yes." Vida didn't bother to hide a smug expression. "He was led astray by another youth. It was what caused the breakup of Elmer Woodson's first marriage. Terry got mixed up with drugs. So typical, so foolish. He led what Lorena Woodson called an 'alternate lifestyle.' Indeed." Vida made a face. "He left home, wandered about, returned—a pattern oft repeated. Finally, he ended up living in the woods. Lorena didn't know where. It was too late to care, as she put it. And Terry still let this other fellow hold a heavy influence over him."

I could tell from the sly look in Vida's eyes that she was holding something back.

I had to ask. "Okay—who's the evil genius?"

The smug look turned downright catlike. "Zeke Foster-Klein. Now isn't that interesting?"

September 1917

Olga Iversen jumped when a woman's voice called her name. Hurriedly, she struck a wooden match and touched off the crumpled paper in the cast-iron cookstove.

"Goodness!" Ruby Siegel exclaimed as she bounded through the open front door. "Isn't it a bit warm for a fire? Or are you getting an early start on supper?"

"Ja, ja." Olga nodded nervously. "Supper. Fresh trout. Per caught many trout."

Ruby thought Olga looked as if she were guarding the stove. Indeed, Ruby mused that if the other woman got any closer, she'd set her rear end on fire.

"I came by to see if you'd come to the Red Cross meeting tonight," Ruby said. "Did you know that we netted almost seven hundred dollars at the bazaar?"

Olga moved a few inches from the stove. The kindling was crackling; the disgusting drawings had no doubt already burned into ash. Horrible visions ravaged Olga's brain. Ash, like what covered hell. There must be ash everywhere, with all that fire. It would serve Jonas right if he went to hell. That's where he belonged.

"Ah . . ." Olga put her plump fingers to her chin. "No, I stay home tonight."

Ruby tried to hide her exasperation. "But don't you want to help America win the war? Don't you want to knit warm stockings and balaclava helmets for our doughboys? You do wonderful needlework. Doesn't your heart bleed for them *when the troop trains pass through Alpine? They all look so young."*

"I stay home." Olga's face was set. "Norvay not in var."

Ruby's patience snapped. "You aren't living in Norway." You stupid cow. *"You're living in America." She paused to rein in her temper. "I have my own reservations about this foreign war, but I'm going to do everything in my power to help us win. They say this will be the war to end all wars."*

"You knit," Olga replied, her expression unchanged. "I stay home."

"What if your boys were over there, crawling around in those terrible trenches?"

"My boys are here." Olga wished otherwise. She wished that Jonas would go into the army and be sent far, far away. That awful Vincent had left town months ago—for good, it seemed. Maybe he was a soldier by now. Olga didn't like Vincent, but she knew that Jonas missed his friend, even if the boy wouldn't admit it.

"Fine. Stay home." With a swish of her long skirts, Ruby stomped out of the house. Olga Iversen was impossible. What was wrong with the woman? Maybe, Ruby thought darkly, she drank.

Maybe, Ruby thought with a touch of compassion, Olga had good reason to drink. If one of her own boys turned out like that wretched Jonas, Ruby might resort to the bottle, too. Jonas was incorrigible, Ruby was sure of it. But what he did—what Ruby thought he did—was too unspeakable to say out loud.

Chapter Fifteen

"I CAN'T QUITE BELIEVE this," I said to Vida, who was still looking smug. "Are you positive?"

"Certainly," Vida retorted, "though it was like pulling teeth to get the information out of Lorena Woodson. You wouldn't believe the coaxing and the soft soap I had to use."

Actually, I would, having had many years of experience with Vida's methods of extracting the deepest secrets from other people.

"I keep trying to tell you," Vida said as Scott entered the newsroom, "that this is a very small town. There is no such thing as coincidence."

"But Terry Woodson's from Monroe, and the Foster-Kleins were Everett people," I pointed out.

"I'm speaking of the entire Highway 2 corridor, from the summit to the sound," Vida asserted. "I'm also talking about connections that have their roots many years ago. The population was much smaller then. Thirty, twenty, even ten years ago Monroe and Everett were just a fraction the size of what they are now."

Vida's statement was correct. Seattle had sprawled so much in the past few decades that Monroe and Everett were considered suburbs. Even Alpine had grown since the advent of the community college.

Scott stood beside me. "Are we doing a census story in this issue, too?" he inquired. "I thought we had too much copy."

I told my reporter that the census wasn't a story, just passing conversation.

"Good," Scott said. "I'm working on all my stuff this afternoon, especially the mulching piece. There's a lot more to it than you realize."

For some perverse reason, I refused to mulch. Maybe it sounded more complicated than it really was, but I wasn't interested in devoting my life to carrot peelings and dried leaves. "Did you get some good pictures of the cedars?"

"I think so," Scott replied, going to his desk. "I dropped the roll off at Buddy Bayard's. Man, those trees were awesome."

"A terrible crime," Vida murmured. "It's so sad that the forests can't be patrolled more easily."

"For sure," Scott said, facing his computer monitor. "But it's just about impossible to . . ."

I left Vida and Scott to their ruminations about protecting old growth. In my absence, Ginny had taken three phone messages for me. One was from Jeannie Clay, Dr. Starr's dental assistant, reminding me of a cleaning Thursday morning. The second was from Judge Marsha, marked ASAP. She would have been my priority, except that last, but certainly not least, was a message from Adam. My son still came first. Ginny had made a notation that Adam would be in the rectory until two o'clock, our time. It was now five to one, three hours later than St. Mary's, Alaska.

The radio relay made its usual strange, disconcerting sounds. Then I heard Adam's voice, an echo that I assumed bounced off some satellite before reaching my ear.

"It's me," I said, "Mom." My own voice sounded hollow.

A pause. I tried to picture my son in the Quonset hut that served as St. Mary's rectory.

"Are you okay, Mom?"

"I'm fine. How are you?"

Pause.

"Good. It's cold, rainy, and the wind's blowing in from the

sea. I'm getting used to it, though. It's nothing, I'm told, compared to the whiteouts when the snow never stops."

"How are your parishioners?"

Pause.

"Hearty. They're mostly Inuit, good people. I admire their fortitude."

Pause. But Adam wasn't done speaking; he was collecting his thoughts. "Are you sure you're okay? I mean, better than before?"

I winced as I remembered the Paxil prescription, still waiting on the shelf at Parker's Pharmacy. "I honestly think I am," I said after a pause of my own. "The last week or two have been really busy. It takes my mind off of me."

Pause. If Adam had felt compelled to serve in a remote location from Alpine, why not Maine? I was sure they had real telephones in Maine.

"Same here. Death can come suddenly, violently. The whiteouts, the bears, the sea. These people deal with it better than we do, I think. They accept death as part of life. They don't bitch about the unfairness. They don't blame God. Death happens. I'm learning from them, Mom."

"I'm so proud of you. You've exceeded all my expectations." They had been very low for years, as Adam switched majors and changed colleges. I'd considered him flighty, immature, self-serving. I couldn't have been more wrong. "Do you need anything?"

Pause.

"Books," Adam replied. "Fiction, real page turners. You know me, I like spies."

"I'll get some. What about warm clothes?"

A loud humming filled my ear. I hoped Adam hadn't been swept away by a tsunami or swallowed by a whale.

"No, I'm good with gear. Just the books. Can you hear me?" he shouted over the interference.

"Barely. Should we hang up?"

More noise, another pause. "I guess so. Love you, Mom. 'Bye."

"Be careful. Please." Reluctantly, I disconnected the phone. For several moments, I sat at my desk, staring at the state department of fish and wildlife calendar on the opposite wall. For September, the color photograph was a huge king salmon, leaping out of the water. It seemed symbolic. Without Tom, I felt like a fish out of water. But the salmon could dive back in. Maybe, some day, I could, too. Maybe my son could teach his mother how to move on.

I didn't remember Marsha's message until Ginny stood in my office door. "The judge is on hold. Do you want to talk to her or call her back? She sounds kind of wigged out."

I told Ginny I'd take the call. The connection was perfect, but the person on the other end wasn't someone I wanted to hear.

"I need to see you right away, before I go back on the bench at two o'clock," Marsha said in a strident voice. "Can you get over to the courthouse in about thirty seconds?"

Under ordinary circumstances, I would have been extremely curious. But I was still wrapped up in thinking about Adam. And Tom.

"I could if I had jet shoes," I retorted. "What's the rush? It's only ten after one."

"I can't talk over the phone. Get your butt over here, Emma. This could be important to you, too."

Ah. Marsha was appealing to my self-interest. Had she heard about Terry Woodson and the connection with her brother, Zeke? It was possible, though I doubted that even Milo knew about it yet.

"I'll be there in a few minutes," I said and hung up. In the newsroom, I approached Vida, who was putting on a bright orange cardigan sweater. "Where are you going?" I inquired.

"To call on the sheriff," she said. "He needs to be informed."

"That's just what I was thinking." I grinned at Vida. "You appear to be ahead of him on this one."

"Men are so poor at eliciting the facts," she declared with a sad shake of her head. "Even when it's their job."

Scott and Leo looked up. "Why are we getting bashed now, Duchess?" Leo asked.

"Never mind," Vida huffed. "It's not entirely your fault as a sex. It's just that you're so lacking in certain skills." Adjusting her duck-billed velour cap, she departed the newsroom.

Leo looked at me. "Is something afoot?"

"Yes," I replied, slinging my handbag over my shoulder. "I'll tell you both later. I'm going to the courthouse now."

Judge Marsha was pacing her chambers when I arrived. "What's going on? Dodge called me about fifteen minutes ago and said he'd be over with a warrant for somebody's arrest. I asked who, and he wouldn't say. Do you know anything about it?"

"Gosh," I said, looking innocent, "I thought you'd called me here to thank me for everything I did about your letter. Or aren't you interested in your new appointment any more?"

"Screw the letter," Marsha shot back. "It's a bunch of crap. The old fart who wrote it is dead. Who cares? It was just a joke, and a stupid one at that. Come on, out with it. You and that goofball Vida seem to know so damned much."

"Don't you dare call Vida a goofball!" I shouted. Marsha had gone too far. "Apologize, or I'm going right back through that door."

"Okay, okay." Marsha ran a hand through her usually neat blonde coiffure. Indeed, she looked unusually frazzled. "I'm sorry, but I'm upset. The last couple of weeks haven't been easy for me." She sat down behind her big oak desk. "Take a seat. And thanks for what you and that . . . Vida did. It just turned out be such a dumb stunt on Jack Froland's part. I hope he's turning in his grave."

I ignored the remark. "What do you want to know? I can't read Milo's mind."

"I heard you had lunch with him."

I tried to keep calm. "So what?"

She leaned forward, fists on the clean beige blotter. Maybe Marsha never made mistakes. But she did now. "You're screwing him, aren't you? Isn't he your backup for Cavanaugh?"

I froze in the oak chair. It took me a moment to gather my composure. I threw discretion to the wind. "Where's Zeke?" I asked in a dead calm voice.

Marsha gave a start, then took in my arctic expression. Briefly, she averted her gaze. "Zeke? My brother? Who knows? He follows the wind and the next protest against government outrage."

"No, he doesn't," I said, still calm. "He leads, not follows. Does the name Terry Woodson ring a bell?"

The puzzlement on the judge's face deepened. "Terry Woodson? I don't think so." She lowered her gaze. "Maybe, faintly. Who is he?"

"Who *was* he," I said. "He's the guy who was dating Lynn Froland when she got killed in the wreck at the summit. He was in the car with your other brother, Gabe, when the accident took place." I leaned forward in the chair. "He's also the guy who got burned up in the meth lab. The drug outfit that your brother Zeke got him into."

Marsha had turned pale. "This is crazy," she said through gritted teeth. "My brother is nowhere around here, he hasn't been for years."

"That's not what Terry Woodson's stepmother says." For the first time, I noticed that Marsha had lost some of her usual arrogance. I couldn't resist needling her. "After you hand out a couple of divorces and put some deadbeat dads into work-release programs, why don't we visit Lorena Woodson in Monroe? Vida would be glad to join us."

"I don't have time for nonsense," Marsha snapped, but she

sounded shaken. "The last I heard of Zeke, he was in Texas. Or maybe Oklahoma. He planned to protest Timothy McVeigh's execution."

I was rubbing my hands together, as if in glee. It was an inappropriate gesture. I put both hands in my lap and tried to stare down Judge Marsha. "Is this the secret you kept? That your brother was a druggie?"

"Of course he's a druggie!" Marsha exclaimed. "He's always done pot. Big deal. It should be legalized anyway."

"I don't mean just a user. I mean that he dealt. Not only dealt but made the drugs, along with Terry Woodson."

"I don't have to listen to this," Marsha declared, her face gone stiff. "Please leave, or I'll have the bailiff throw you out of my chambers."

Frankly, I would have enjoyed haranguing Marsha just a little longer, but I didn't relish having the glum—and strong—Gus Tolberg throw me out onto Front Street. "Okay." I got up. "Mrs. Woodson's probably too busy to see us anyway. I imagine she's having a nice long talk with the sheriff."

Marsha didn't say a word as I made my exit.

"When I came through the *Advocate*'s front door Vida was barring my passage. "Well? What did Marsha say? How did she react? Did she know about her brother's criminal habits?"

I managed to edge past Vida to reach the reception counter where Ginny sat, exhibiting her usual placid calm.

"The judge is in denial," I replied. "I'll reveal all in my office."

Vida, however, had other ideas. She grabbed my arm and steered me back to the front door. "You can tell me on the way to the sheriff's. According to Billy, Milo's expecting Mrs. Woodson any minute."

"We can't sit in on the interview," I protested, disengaging myself and taking a backward step.

"We won't," Vida replied. "We'll get to her first."

"We can't do that, either." I gave Vida an exasperated look. "Besides, you've already spoken with her on the phone."

"That's hardly enough," Vida huffed. "Much better, in person. Come along, we don't want to miss her. It's a long drive from Monroe, and Lorena would probably enjoy a nice cup of tea."

I was still protesting even as Vida virtually dragged me down Front Street. Maybe we could use the incident for "Scene." VIRTUOUS NEWSPAPER PUBLISHER HAULED AWAY AGAINST HER WILL BY UNSCRUPULOUS HOUSE & HOME EDITOR. I had a mind to sneak it into Vida's column just before press time.

"How will we know her when we see her?" I demanded as Vida forced me to lurk in the doorway of the Sears catalog outlet across Third Street from the sheriff's office.

"We'll know," Vida assured me in her stage whisper.

We waited. At least three people came and went from Sears, having to edge around Vida's imposing figure. She knew them all, and they knew Vida. Nobody complained about the inconvenience she was causing.

"Ah!" Vida cried as a brown compact car crept along Front Street. "A woman's driving, and she's obviously looking for something. There's room two parking places down from Milo's car. Oh! She didn't see it!"

The compact's driver kept going, right by us. The woman behind the wheel had short platinum blonde hair, swept into waves that looked like an exotic bird's plumage. She wore glasses and a dark jacket or sweater. I noticed a Masonic emblem on the rear bumper as she drove by Parker's Pharmacy.

"There are two spaces in front of the drugstore," Vida murmured. "Why didn't she take one of them? Oh, my—she's pulling in next to your car. Let's go."

Holding onto her velour cap, Vida virtually ran the rest of the block, crossed Fourth without looking, and reached the compact just as the driver got out. I trailed behind, but heard Vida's piercing voice inquire if the woman was lost.

She was. I reached Vida's side just in time to hear the woman say she couldn't find the Skykomish county sheriff's headquarters.

"The young man—he sounded young—who gave me the directions said to go by city hall with the dome on the right and that the sheriff's office was in the next block," the woman explained in a fretful voice. "But it's not." She gestured across the street to the Clemans Building, which faced Milo's digs. "I saw the newspaper sign, so I'm going to ask someone there where the sheriff is. I hope they have more sense than that Blatt person who gave me the wrong directions."

Vida puffed out her cheeks. "You must have misunderstood. The Blatt person is my nephew, and," she went on with a munificent gesture that included me, "we *are* the newspaper."

"Oh!" The woman looked startled. "My goodness. Well, I'm Lorena Woodson. You must be the person I talked to on the phone." She held out an uncertain hand. "Mrs . . . Blatt?"

Vida took Lorena's hand and gave it a firm shake. "I was *Miss* Blatt forty-odd years ago. I'm Mrs. Runkel now." She gave the other woman a toothy grin. "But call me Vida. Why don't you come into the office and have a cup of tea first? It's rather a long drive from Monroe."

"Well . . ." Lorena seemed unsure of what to do. She glanced at the *Advocate*'s entrance, back to Vida, and then down the street. "I should go straight to the sheriff. I told him I'd be there by two-thirty."

It took me two nudges to remind Vida of my existence. After the introduction, Lorena seemed puzzled over who worked for whom. It was a common source of confusion, even among Alpine old-timers.

If Lorena was pleased to meet me, she didn't show it. "I'll be going now. Just point the way."

"We'll walk you to the sheriff's office," Vida declared, linking her arm through Lorena's, "but not until you've had a chance to catch your breath. After all," she continued as our visitor dug in her heels, "it's my nephew's fault that you got mixed up. It won't take a minute to make tea. The water's already hot."

"Well . . . really, I shouldn't . . ."

After a tug or two from Vida, Lorena somehow got through the door. Ginny looked up from her desk. She has a knack for sensing awkwardness in other people. "Hi, Emma, Vida," she said, standing up. "You're back already. No calls." She gazed at Lorena, who still looked dubious. "I'm Ginny Erlandson. Would you like some coffee?"

Vida spoke for our guest. "Mrs. Woodson would like a nice cup of hot tea, Ginny dear. Thank you so much."

The newsroom was empty, but Vida headed for my cubbyhole. I half-expected her to commandeer my chair, but she didn't. Instead, she guided Lorena into one of the visitor's chairs.'

"First," I said, sitting down in my rightful place, "let me express my sympathy for the loss of your stepson, Terry."

Lorena looked at her hands, which were fidgeting on her desk. "I shouldn't be here." She started to get up.

"Now, now," Vida said from the chair next to Lorena, "you mustn't rush off. You wouldn't want Ginny to make tea for no reason."

Lorena scowled, though not at Vida, but into the space between us. "Well . . . If I'm going to sit for a minute, do you mind if I smoke?"

"Heavens no!" I broke in before Vida could object. "We'll both smoke." I got out the ashtray that I kept in a desk drawer and managed to find a pack of Basic Ultra Lights that had two cigarettes left in it.

Lorena looked relieved as we both lit up. In a majority of nonsmokers, she had found an ally, a friend, a boon companion. Vida glared at me as Ginny arrived with the tea.

"Terry was no real loss," Lorena said after the first puff. "Ever since I met his father, Terry was nothing but trouble. Elmer used to get so upset—he insisted that Terry should have had a bright future. I guess he squandered it on drugs. So many people do. It's a crying shame."

Without staring. I looked closely at Lorena Woodson, who I estimated to be in her mid-sixties. The blond hair was dyed and sprayed into brittle peaks on the top of her head. Her lean face was lined, with broken capillaries on the cheeks and nose. Like Elmer's first wife, Irma, his second choice probably enjoyed her liquor, too. I suspected that all of the Woodsons had their own ways of coping with life.

"You mentioned to Vida," I began, "that Terry had a friend, Zeke Foster-Klein. Do you know where he is?"

Lorena tipped her head to one side. "What did you say his name was?"

I repeated it. "Maybe," I added, "he went only by Zeke Foster. I think his brother, Gabe, dropped the second name at some point."

Lorena's mouth turned down. "Zeke! Of course I know him. I mean, I only met him once or twice, but he was a bad influence on Terry. Zeke should have been locked up a long time ago. A bad hat, if there ever was one. His brother wasn't much better. What was his name? Greg? No, Gary. That's not right." Lorena frowned.

"Gabe," I put in.

The other woman's face brightened. "That's it—Gabe. Anyway, Elmer told me Gabe almost got Terry killed in a car accident."

"Really?" Vida feigned surprise. "How did that happen?"

"Showing off," Lorena said, after blowing on her tea, "according to Elmer. The car went off the road up at the pass and killed the poor girl Terry was dating. That smart aleck Gabe never went to jail, either. Bribes, probably. Elmer said the sheriff up here back then was crooked. I hope you got a better one now."

"We do," I said staunchly.

"Let's hope so." Lorena glanced at her watch. "Good Lord—it's after two-thirty. I'd better run."

"But you haven't finished your tea," Vida protested. "Or your"—she winced—"cigarette."

"I'll save it," Lorena said, putting the long Virginia Slim out in the ashtray. "Elmer figured both those Foster boys were headed for big trouble. He told me Zeke and Gabe became hippies, with long hair, beards, the whole thing. Disgusting, dirty creatures if you ask me." Lorena had gotten out of the chair. "If the sheriff's close by, I can walk from where I parked."

Vida escorted Lorena out of my office. I had an editorial to write, and our visitor had given me an idea. While Front Street wasn't exactly congested, except in our mild rush hour, parking could be a problem. The idea to make Front and Railroad Avenue one-way streets wasn't new, but maybe it was time to resurrect it.

"It's time to resurrect the one-way street proposal," I typed. And stopped. Lorena Woodson had given me some other ideas, too. I swung away from the computer screen and put pen to tablet. I was jotting down some thoughts when Vida returned.

"What did you make of all that?" she asked, flopping down in the chair she'd just vacated. "Do you get the feeling that too many things are tied together and that Judge Marsha—or at least her family—may be at the core?"

I tapped the tablet on my desk. "Just what I was thinking. Everything seems to have a link to Lynn Froland's fatal accident. I made some notes. Here, take a look." I turned the tablet so Vida could see it.

"Lynn dates Gabe Foster-Klein, Lynn dumps Gabe, Lynn takes up with Terry Woodson, Lynn dies in car wreck though both boys and Clare Thorstensen survive," she read aloud, then stared at me. "Why haven't we talked to the Thorstensens? Don't they live by you?"

"They do," I said, "but they're elderly and keep to themselves. I hardly ever see any visitors over there."

Vida chewed on her lower lip. "That would be Tilly and Erwin. They must be ninety if they're a day. Let me think—their son was Don, Clare's father. Yes, they're the Thorstensens who used to live on First Hill but moved out to Ptarmigan Tract."

"We should call them," I said, "though I'm not sure why."

Vida didn't say anything. She was clearly lost in her own thoughts. Abruptly, she got out of the chair and left the office. I was looking up the Thorstensens' number in the phone book when Vida came back a minute later carrying a bound volume of the *Advocate*.

"This," she said, putting the big book on the desk, "is from my first year on the paper. Do you remember, I mentioned that the Zeke Foster wedding was the first one I covered?"

Vaguely, I recalled the phone conversation between Vida and Marjorie Iverson Lathrop in Port Angeles. "Something about a bird on the bride's head," I remarked.

Vida was flipping through the pages. "I started in May of that year. I believe the wedding occurred a couple of weeks later. Ah!" Vida shot me a triumphant look and passed the volume to me. "Here she is, the bride with a bird on her head and her arm in a cast. May I present Clare Thorstensen, who became Mrs. Ezekiel Foster-Klein."

November 1917

Harriet Clemans surveyed the festive social hall with approval. Evergreen boughs accented the red, white, and blue streamers hanging from the rafters. Fruit baskets sat on long trestle tables, piled high with oranges, apples, grapes, bananas, and pears. The bare lightbulbs that illuminated the big room had literally been dressed up with colorful strips of paper that Harriet thought looked like hula skirts.

"Everything looks lovely," she declared. "We should have a wonderful Thanksgiving dinner. I've written a song for the occasion."

Ruby Siegel was impressed. She knew that the mill owner's wife was an accomplished woman, about to become a college graduate, in fact. But Ruby hadn't realized that musical composition was one of Mrs. Clemans's talents.

"What's the song called?" Ruby inquired.

Harriet shrugged, a playful smile on her lips. "It's very simple. The Alpine Song, in C Major. I wouldn't know what to do with all those sharps and flats."

"Would you sing it now?" Ruby asked, nodding at the upright piano across the hall.

Harriet's smile had become strained. "You play, don't you, Ruby?"

"A little." Ruby made a face. "I'm sure you're better than I am."

"I'm speaking of the piano," Harriet said softly.

"Of course." Ruby tried not to look startled at the remark.

275

"I've done the accompaniment for several of the community plays."

"I know. So following the after-dinner toasts and speeches, you play the music and I'll sing the song," Harriet decreed. "Maybe we should practice now. Do you have a few minutes?"

"Yes," Ruby replied, "now that the decorations are up. Mary and Kate threw me out of the kitchen." She looked Harriet straight in the eye. "According to my sisters-in-law, my talents don't include cooking."

"Nor mine," Harriet responded. She waved a hand at the piano. "Shall we?"

Ruby was about to answer when her husband hurried into the social hall. Louie Siegel doffed his snap-brim cap at Harriet. "Excuse me, Mrs. Clemans," he said, his voice taut, "may I speak to my wife alone for just a moment?"

"Of course," Harriet replied. "I'll check on the cooking crew, though Mr. Patterson seems to have everything well under control," she added, referring to the camp's head cook.

"What is it?" Ruby hissed when Harriet was out of hearing range. "You look agitated."

"I am," Louie said, "but I'm worried, too. I just hauled Jack and Georgie back from that damned railroad trestle."

"They know better than to go there," Ruby exclaimed, alarm over her two older sons' adventurous spirits written large on her face. "Especially this time of year! Were they alone?"

"They were when I got there," Louie said, "but they finally told me that Jonas Iversen and Hiram Rix had been with them. Hiram took off back home, I guess, but Georgie and Jack stayed with Jonas. I'm damned sure I heard Jonas run off when I came calling for our boys. I could see his big boot prints in the snow, going the other way."

"Are the boys all right? Had they been on the rope?" Ruby asked, a hand to her breast. Georgie was only six and Jack was barely eight, a year younger than the Rix boy.

"They had," Louie replied, "though it took a couple of swats to get it out of them. Dammit, something's got to be done about that Jonas. I've tried speaking to Tryg Iversen, but he just scoffs and pretends his English isn't so good. After dinner tonight, I'm going to get together with Frank and Tom and Earl Rix. We'll talk to Mr. Clemans. We've got to sort this Jonas thing out once and for all."

"What can Mr. Clemans do?" Ruby asked with a helpless gesture. "Fire Trygve Iversen?"

Louie frowned. "I don't want that. Tryg still has Lars at home, along with Jonas. Lars is only ten. And I think Tryg helps out with both Per and Karen, even if they have gotten married."

"I know," Ruby said. "Per and his wife Susan lost one of the twins just before the baby's first birthday. But they're expecting again in the new year. That will make two little ones for them. As for the Iversens' daughter, Karen, I wouldn't be surprised if the stork wasn't due one of these days at the Frolands' house. Karen and Gus have been married for over two years."

"Don't give me moonshine where the Iversens are concerned," Louie said with unaccustomed sternness. "Tryg has to do something about Jonas, and that's that. The boy's a predator."

Ruby flinched at the word. "Don't say that!"

Louie's chin jutted. "It's true, Ruby. We can't pussyfoot around Jonas's doings. He's immoral, he has no conscience. If," Louie went on, lowering his voice as Monica Murphy and Kate Dawson came into the social hall, "Trygve can't stop Jonas, somebody else will have to."

Chapter Sixteen

DESPITE HER BRIEF display of triumph, Vida was castigating herself. "I can't believe I'd forgotten the bride's name," she lamented. "Am I getting senile?"

"Vida," I consoled her, "the Thorstensen-Foster wedding was a quarter of a century ago. Even you can't remember everything."

"But it was my first wedding assignment!"

Leo, who had come into the newsroom, came up behind Vida, who was holding her head.

"What's up, Duchess?" Leo inquired, knowing better than to be concerned at Vida's histrionics. "Did you catch Crazy Eights Neffel wearing some of your hats?"

"Don't be beastly," Vida cried, whipping off her glasses and torturing her eyes. "Ooooh . . . I'm such a ninny!"

Bemused, Leo glanced at me. "Why this self-flagellation? Shall we buy the Duchess a hair shirt?"

I explained that Vida had forgotten the bride's name from a wedding she'd covered back in the Seventies.

"Hey," Leo said, with a pat for Vida's back, "I've been known to forget my own name. And that's when I haven't been drinking."

"Bother!" Vida snapped, putting her glasses back on. "That's not the same. I take great pride in my powers of recollection."

Leo made a bow. "We stand in awe." He grinned at me and

278

placed several ad mockups on the desk. "Have a look. It's shaping up better than I expected."

I, too, was pleased. "You think this co-op venture with KSKY could work long-term?"

"We'll see," Leo said as Vida stalked out of my cubby-hole. "Spence has to get out in the trenches more instead of using those college kids to solicit ads. He used to be more of a presence. I don't want him leaning on us to bring in revenue. What does he do with his time? How many hours a day can you spend stringing a bunch of tapes together?"

I didn't know. But I agreed with Leo. "This has to be fifty-fifty," I said as the phone rang. "It's early days, though. Let's see how he does next week."

Leo picked up the ads, gave me the high sign, and went back into the newsroom. Milo was on the other end of the line, sounding grumpy.

"It's pretty damned tough to get a warrant for the judge's brother," he groused. "Marsha insisted I had no probable cause. No warrant. Hell, it's not my fault Zeke Foster's a creep. Marsha acts like we've got it all wrong, her brother's just a flake. She should know better after all these years on the freaking bench."

"Maybe she didn't know what Zeke was up to," I said. "Any idea of where you can find him?"

"No known address," Milo said, still grouchy. "The last one was a P. O. box from eight years ago in Corte Madera, California."

"He married Clare Thorstensen in his younger days," I said. "Did you know that?"

"Clare Thorstensen. Hunh. Is she related to Vic Thorstensen, the EMT? Or the Thorstensens out in Ptarmigan Tract? I think they're Vic's cousins."

I explained what I knew of Clare's background, including the fatal car accident. "I was going to call her parents myself. Do you remember her?"

"Vaguely. She was younger than me. Hey, I have to run.

That lamebrained Woodson woman's finally showed up. She's fifteen minutes late. How can you get lost in Alpine?"

I'd forgotten about Vic Thorstensen, one of the medics. I decided to call him first on the off chance that he wasn't on duty. I'd barely glimpsed him at Le Gourmand in the wake of Max Froland's collapse.

Vic was home but sounded half-asleep. I apologized for rousing him, then inquired about Clare.

Vic yawned before he answered. "Clare? She's my cousin, Don and Marcella's daughter. She got married and moved away. That must be twenty years ago. I haven't seen her except once or twice since. Why are you asking about Clare?"

"The man she married is wanted for questioning in the meth lab fire."

"Huh?" Vic yawned again. "I don't believe it. They live in Chicago or somewhere around there. Are you sure? Darryl—or is it Derek?—anyway, he's a minister. Dodge must be nuts."

I took a deep breath. "I thought his name was Zeke."

Vic laughed. "That was the first husband. It lasted about six months. God only knows where that bird is now."

"What happened?"

"Oh—you know. It was the Seventies, Clare was into the whole hippie scene." Vic stopped. "Why do you need to know?"

I felt like saying that journalists always needed to know. "I'm following the story, of course. Deadline's tomorrow. If the sheriff picks up Zeke, I'll need some background."

Having seen me at disaster scenes over the years, Vic must have felt I had credibility. "You wouldn't believe it with Clare if you saw her as the minister's wife now, but back then she was kind of wild. She'd met Zeke skiing a few years earlier, when they were dating other people. In fact, Clare was dating about every warm body she could find. Anyway, she and Zeke hooked up again one winter on the slopes. On the last day of ski season, she crashed and broke her arm.

They got married a couple of months later. Clare really got into the funny stuff with Zeke, but that wasn't his only hippie habit. He believed in free love. Clare didn't, not once she got married. They split right before Christmas that year. It was a wakeup call for Clare. She straightened herself out after that."

"And Zeke? Did she completely lose track of him after the divorce?"

Another yawn from Vic. "She wanted to lose him, period. Clare went off to Concordia College. She met her future husband there. Dirk, that's his first name. We exchange Christmas cards. That's about it."

"Do you think her parents would know more about Zeke?"

"I doubt it. He wasn't Don and Marcella's kind. Hey, how much did that Froland guy drink the other night?"

"Enough," I said.

"Wine, huh? You'd think . . ." Vic stopped. "Hey, got a call, see if I'm needed." He hung up.

The other Thorstensens weren't home, but they had an answering machine. I asked them to call me back at their earliest convenience.

For the moment, I was stymied. I saw that Vida was out, so there was no one to speculate with. The sheriff was tied up with Lorena Woodson. After he finished interviewing her, he'd plunge deeper into the investigation. Surely he was trying to find buyers who had dealt with Terry Woodson or Zeke Foster-Klein. But most of all, I had a newspaper to put out, and a fat issue at that. I tried to put the whole Froland/Foster-Klein/Woodson mess out of mind and concentrate on work.

A few minutes later, Ginny poked her head into my office. "You were on the phone when Vida left. She said to tell you she'd been called over to June Froland's house."

"Why?"

"She didn't say."

"Okay. Thanks, Ginny." I returned to my article on the meth lab fire. I was writing it backward, hoping that Milo would pick up Zeke Foster-Klein before deadline and give me the hot lead paragraph for the front page.

Shortly before four o'clock, I checked on Scott, who often needed prodding to get his stories in on time. But on this mid-September afternoon, he was in high gear, his long, lean fingers flying across the keyboard.

"Big date tonight," he said, still typing. "Tammy has a fifty-dollar gift certificate to the Union Square Grill in Seattle, but it isn't good on weekends, so we're going tonight. I have to get out of here at five on the dot. Tammy's a stickler for being on time. Oops." He stared at the monitor. "Gosh, that last line is gibberish. I better pay more attention to what I write."

I was still trying to get used to Professor Tamara Rostova being called "Tammy." With her tall, angular figure and classic features she didn't quite fit the mold.

I'd just gone back into my cubbyhole when Marcella Thorstensen called. She and Dan had just gotten back from a weekend of staying with friends on the Kitsap Peninsula. They had visited a couple of exotic nurseries during their stay and were planting their treasures before it started to rain again. Marcella asked if I could stop by about seven-thirty.

I'd hoped to dispose of the Thorstensens over the phone, but Marcella sounded as if she were in a hurry. I had no other plans for the evening—certainly not a big date at the Union Square Grill—so I agreed to come calling.

The phone rang again.

"It's incredible!" Vida cried as I took the call. "Come quick, to the Frolands!"

"What is it?" I asked in a startled voice. But Vida had hung up.

It was clouding over when I went out to the car. In the distance, I heard sirens. I wondered if they had triggered Vida's frantic call. Perhaps Vic Thorstensen had been called to duty.

Five minutes later, I was on Spruce Street, where I could see Vida standing by the curb, waving her arms. I could also see an EMT van parked in front of the Froland house. Pulling up a full space away from the medics' vehicle, I jumped out of the car as Vida hurried to meet me.

"You'll never guess what June did!" she shouted.

"No, I wouldn't. So tell me."

"She tried to commit suicide! Before my eyes, she took all the sleeping pills Doc Dewey gave her. She was so quick, I couldn't stop her."

"Is she alive?" I asked as we all but galloped toward the front door.

"She was when I called 911," Vida replied, now a bit breathless. "But that's not the worst of it."

I was getting confused. "What?"

"Wait." Vida led the way down the all-too-familiar passage to June's bedroom. Vic Thorstensen wasn't among the medics who firmly waved us off. We retreated into the living room where Vida paced the floor. "June asked me to come over, she said it was an emergency. Naturally, I was disturbed—and curious. For a moment, I thought that the college girl Max had hired to stay with his mother hadn't worked out. But even though the girl wasn't here when I arrived, that wasn't the case." Vida took a big breath.

From the rear of the house, I could hear the medics' ministrations. If they were still working on June, she must be alive.

Vida sat down next to me on the sofa. She cleared her throat and looked me in the eye. "June admitted that she cooked those mushrooms to poison Jack."

"What?"

Vida nodded so hard that the velour cap slipped down to meet the top of her glasses. "Yes, she did. She knew they were poisonous. It's true that Jack's sight was failing, but hers wasn't. She still did needlework, remember?" Vida paused to adjust the cap, but it left her glasses cockeyed. "June claims it was a mercy killing, but I wonder."

"Why?" I sounded a little breathless myself.

"Think about it." Vida stopped, listening to what was going on in the other room. The medics' voices were an inaudible murmur. "Jack was better, not worse," Vida went on. "He didn't seem to be suffering. Jack and June haven't gotten along for years; they led separate lives for the most part. I think June thought that Jack might recover and she'd be stuck with him for another five, ten years at least. She murdered him, and that's that."

I wasn't convinced that June's motive was entirely selfish. Jack had suffered for quite a while. June had been his sole caregiver. I knew how hard that role could be. "Why did she tell you this?"

Vida shrugged. "She thinks she's dying. Or that God is going to punish her for poisoning Jack. After he died, she went to pieces. You saw that for yourself. She tried to tell Max, she asked for Pastor Nielsen to come, but he was out of town this weekend, officiating at a niece's wedding in Iowa. I suppose she called on me because . . ." Vida faltered, perhaps from modesty, though I doubted it. "Because I'd spent time with her recently. She has no close friends."

I grew thoughtful for a moment before speaking again. "What are you going to do about it?"

"I don't know. Nothing, perhaps. This is a dreadful moral dilemma." Vida yanked off her glasses, but apparently she was beyond her customary grinding of her eyes. Instead, she set the glasses down in her lap, removed her cap, and ran both hands through her hair until it stood on end. "I don't know when I've been in such a quandary!"

"It's more than difficult," I allowed, aware that I was now a party to Vida's problem. Another siren sounded and then died down outside the house before I could voice my own concerns.

Vida leaped to her feet and looked out the front window.

"Ambulance," she announced. "They must be taking June to the hospital. I wonder why they're not transporting her in the EMT van?"

The answer came swiftly: June was moaning like a deranged ghost, a much lower key than the shrieking she'd dished out after Jack's death. The ambulance attendants must be considered more experienced in dealing with thorny cases.

Vida held her head. "I find this all very depressing. Why does life have to come to this? Why can't people get along? Especially married people. I don't approve of divorce, but it's certainly better than murder. I think."

For the next few minutes, we kept out of the way as we lived through June's hysteria as she was unwillingly propelled out of her house. The experience seemed unreal.

"I should call Max," Vida murmured as the gurney was rolled down the walk. "Poor man. How can he bear it?" She squared her shoulders and tromped to the telephone.

I watched out the window while June was loaded into the ambulance. Vida had gotten through to Max who apparently was still on campus.

"Vida Runkel here," she began, sounding more like her usual self with a phone in hand and news to dispense. "No, no . . . Not so serious, but your mother has had a . . . setback. . . . Yes, she's going to the hospital now, but just to make sure everything is . . . No, Max, please don't come. I'm sure she'll be fine. . . . Yes. I'll keep you posted. . . . Certainly. I plan on going to the hospital as soon as she gets . . . settled. . . . Of course I will. Now don't worry too much, please. Good-bye, Max. I'll talk to you soon."

As soon as Vida hung up, she let out a yelp. "Good grief! I forgot to ask Max who was staying with his mother. The girl should be notified. Maybe I can find her name around here some place."

I offered my help, but Vida insisted that I run along. She wanted to straighten things up before she went to the hospital. I suspected that she also wanted to make another, more thorough search of the house, though at this point, I wasn't sure why. Maybe it was just because she could snoop in an unfettered atmosphere.

"Such a nuisance," Vida declared as I made my exit. "Really, it would almost have been better if June had succeeded in killing herself."

"Vida!" I was aghast.

"I'm merely being practical," she asserted. "What's going to happen to her?"

"That depends," I said, "on whether or not you turn her over to the sheriff."

"Yes." She tapped her fingers against her cheek. "I suppose it does. Oh, dear."

I left Vida in her quandary. To take my mind off June Froland's dilemma, I turned the radio on as I drove back to the office. It was almost five, but I was determined to finish my half-baked editorial. As I listened to a trio of Oldies But Goodies—all of which I'd hated when they were popular thirty years ago, all of which were still as Irene and I remembered—I realized that I shouldn't be writing about one-way streets. Plundering old growth trees and selling drugs out of meth labs were not only timely, but far more worthy. But the trees and the meth lab would require some research. If I hadn't squandered so much time on Marsha's stupid project, I would have gotten a head start on this week's issue.

A youthful male voice identified the singers and the songs on the tiresome three-pack. "This is Rick Corrolla, sitting in on the drive-home show for our good buddy, Spencer Fleetwood. It's four-fifty-eight, and we'll be back with the latest news after a word from our sponsors."

I was pulling into my parking place when the commercials for Alpine Toyota, Barton's Bootery, Safeway, and Stuart's Stereo concluded. Rick came back live with the news, so I waited to turn off the ignition.

"Only minutes ago," Rick began after the brief intro,

"longtime resident June Froland was taken to Alpine Hospital by ambulance after a severe stomach upset. Mrs. Froland is the widow of Jack Froland who died barely two weeks ago. Medics referred KSKY to the hospital staff to learn the cause of her complaint. We have a reporter on the scene, and will keep our listeners informed with breaking news. Meanwhile, at Blackwell Mill, a study is underway to . . ."

I turned off the car and the radio. I knew about the mill study, which had been in the works for some time. Jack Blackwell was trying to expand, perhaps to add a paper mill. Except for Jack and a few of his employees, nobody else was for it because paper mills smell bad.

As I walked to the *Advocate*'s front door, I saw Milo out of the corner of my eye.

"Wait up," he called as a few drops of rain began to fall.

Typical Puget Sounder that I am, I ignored the rain as it began to fall harder. "What's new?" I asked as Milo joined me.

"Saw you pull in just as I was coming out of the drugstore," Milo said. "I ran out of cigarettes. It's been a crazy day."

Cigarettes from the drugstore. Maybe they'd do me more good than the Paxil that still awaited me. Maybe they'd do more harm than good. Maybe Paxil would, too. There were side effects. Maybe the medicine would make me want to smoke again.

"What happened with Lorena Woodson?" I inquired.

Milo gave me a knowing look. "Probably what happened when you and Vida grilled her. "Terry was nothing but trouble, Lorena hardly knew him, never kept up with the guy, bitched because she supposed they'd have to pay for a funeral."

"He's already half-cremated," I remarked. "Maybe Al Driggers will give her a discount."

Milo uttered a halfhearted chuckle. "I doubt it. What I wanted to tell you—to keep you onboard—is that we rounded up a couple of local kids who bought meth from Zeke Foster-Klein or whatever he calls himself these days."

"Here?" I saw Milo nod. "No names, of course."

"Right. They're under age. Even if they weren't, I couldn't tell you because . . ."

". . . Because it's part of an ongoing investigation," I finished. "Are the kids sure it was Zeke and not Terry?"

"Pretty sure. They said the guy was dark. Terry was fair. Of course there could be a third party involved," Milo added as the rain came down harder.

"When was this?"

"A month ago. Dwight Gould picked the kids up for speeding on River Road after school this afternoon. They had a bunch of outstanding warrants, not to mention a half-ounce of pot in the car. Dwight and I made them an offer they couldn't refuse."

The outstanding warrants meant that I could check the police reports in the paper and probably learn the kids' identities for myself. But that didn't seem necessary at this point. Milo would handle the drug-related part of the case.

"So Zeke's been in Alpine recently," I mused.

"He's probably been working the whole Highway 2 corridor." Milo glanced up at the sky. "This is just a squall. It's brightening over Baldy."

My hair was damp, but I wasn't cold. Typical weather, fifty-odd degrees and raining. "Keep me posted," I said. "I'm going to see the Don Thorstensens tonight."

"They won't know anything about Zeke's whereabouts," Milo said over his shoulder. "Save yourself a trip."

The sheriff was probably right. But I'd told Marcella Thorstensen I was coming, so I had to keep my word. Besides, I could work another hour or so, pick up Chinese at the mall, and then go out to Ptarmigan Tract before I called it a day.

Before I could step inside the office, Milo shouted at me. "Hey!" He loped back down the sidewalk. "What's the deal with June Froland? We got an emergency call about a half-hour ago."

I hesitated. "June had to be taken to the hospital. Give Vida a call. She's probably there with her by now. Or I'll have her paged and tell her to call you."

Milo looked suspicious. "You're not telling me everything."

"I can't." I looked apologetic. "As you would say, it's part of an ongoing investigation."

"Sounds weird to me," he muttered. "You sure you can't say?"

I let out a big sigh. Milo would know soon enough about June's suicide attempt. "June deliberately took an overdose of sleeping pills. Vida was there when she did it. Get the rest of it from her. Please."

"Jesus! What next?" Milo shook his head, but gave in. "Good thing Vida likes to talk," he said as he started on his way again.

But would she? I wondered. Vida could also be discreet. She loved gossip but she kept secrets. It was a big part of her maven's magic. It was also the reason that so many people—such as June Froland—confided in her.

It was seven o'clock when I finally turned away from my computer. Since it was after-hours, I couldn't call the state department of forestry in Olympia, so I decided against the tree piracy for this week. Instead, I concentrated on the meth lab, piecing together the facts I'd acquired so far as well as some research I gleaned off the Internet. All my other stories were pending, so I'd finish them tomorrow in time for deadline.

I picked up the usual mediocre Chinese food at the mall but decided to save it until I got home. The rain was still coming down, and it was getting dark, earlier than usual for mid-September. I passed KSKY on my way to Ptarmigan Tract. Spence's Beamer was parked outside, along with two other vehicles I didn't recognize.

Marcella Thorstensen met me at the door of their neat cookie-cutter house, where I noted that an exotic-looking evergreen and a couple of other shrubs looked as if they'd just been put in the ground. She introduced me to her husband, Don, who was watching Monday night football. They were both well into middle age, and I realized that I had indeed seen them, not only around town, but a couple of times at Don's parents' house across the street from me.

Marcella offered cider. "We bought it over on the peninsula," she said. "Our friends live at Kingston. We love going to the nurseries around there. They have so many unusual plants." She turned to Don, who had his eyes glued to the TV. "We got our new babies in the ground just in time, didn't we, Don?"

"Unh," Don replied as the Forty-Niner quarterback got sacked.

"I could spend hours going through those places," Marcella said with a sigh that was almost orgasmic. "Fronds are my favorite. We got six new ones, all for out back. Aren't they gorgeous, Don?"

"Enh," said Don as the Niners punted.

"Now what can we do for you, Ms. Lord?" Marcella asked just before I began to wonder if I was going to spend hours listening to a recital from the catalogs of the Kitsap Peninsula's nurseries.

I explained—gently—how their former son-in-law was wanted for questioning in the meth lab fire. Marcella expressed shock; Don expressed displeasure over two broken tackles on a first-and-ten play.

"That Zeke!" Marcella exclaimed. She was a small, rail-thin woman who looked as if she spent most of her time outdoors. "We never could stand him, even though we tried. And how we warned Clare that she should never marry him! You won't believe the hard feelings it caused back then. Didn't we try to tell her what Zeke was really like, Don?"

"Aargh," Don said as the Niners failed to recover a fumble at midfield.

The rest of the conversation went nowhere, right along with the Forty-Niners. Just as they tried to stop a field goal from their own thirty-yard line, I heard what sounded like a sonic boom. Maybe, I thought, it was Don imploding.

Marcella apparently didn't notice the loud noise. She'd gotten off onto what a successful marriage Clare now enjoyed with her minister husband. The next thing I knew, I was looking at pictures of three grown grandchildren. It was half time at the football game. Don got up and left the room, presumably to get a refill of the Doritos he'd been munching.

"The pity is," Marcella was saying as my eyes glazed over a high-school graduation photo of a happy young man who looked like he'd slam-dunked his SATs, "with Clare and Dirk's involvement with their parish, they don't get out to see us often. We'd go back to Chicago more, but the weather there is so bad in the winter, and when it's nice here, I like to work in the garden. Do you garden, Ms. Lord?"

I was afraid she'd ask me next if I mulched. But my cell phone rang, sparing me an immediate reply.

"Emma?" It was Milo, and he sounded unusually excited. "Where are you?"

Briefly, I told him.

"Then you got a big story right down the road," Milo said as I heard his siren turn on. "Somebody just blew up the radio station."

December 1917

Mary Dawson tipped her head to one side, then the other. "It's crooked," she announced to her husband, Frank. "That tree needs to go a bit to the left, and don't be such a cross-patch about fixing it."

"The tree's fine," Frank countered, eyeing the six-foot Douglas fir with dislike. "I've already moved it four times."

"You've only moved it three," Mary retorted, "and that's because you butchered the top. It had a perfect top before you got at it."

"It had two tops," Frank declared. "You can't have two tops."

"Then you should have left one of them," Mary said. "Honestly, Frank, every year we go through this. Why do you have to take a perfectly good Christmas tree and . . ."

"It wasn't perfectly good," Frank interrupted, snatching up his pipe from the kitchen table. "The ones that Tom and I cut down yesterday were better than this one or that other shrubby thing you and Kate hauled out of the woods."

Mary tried not to laugh. Every year, it was the same. Frank and Tom would cut down their families' trees, their wives would criticize their selections, and the next day Mary and Kate would go out and harvest what they considered a superior fir. Neither of the Siegel sisters could figure out why their husbands made such poor choices year after year.

"All right," Mary said. "Leave it be. I'll straighten it before we start decorating after the kiddies are in bed. Right *now, I'm going to get Kate and find some pine boughs. It's not snowing, so it shouldn't take long if we climb up a ways on Tonga Ridge."*

"For God's sake, be careful," Frank cautioned as he managed to light his pipe on the second attempt.

Ten minutes later, the sisters were walking up Icicle Creek, their sturdy boots leaving impressions six inches deep. With the temperature above freezing, the creek was running high from the melting snow on the ridge. The river was also up on its banks, but there was no fear of flooding. Yet.

"Billy's so excited for Christmas Eve," Kate said, her chronic asthma shortening her breath. "Monica is too old to admit she's agog, but I can tell otherwise." She stopped, coughing a half-dozen times.

"Let's stop going uphill," Mary said. "You're going to wear yourself out before you get the tree decorated. I think there's some pine trees closer to the train tracks that have branches low enough to cut."

Kate didn't argue. The women turned right, carefully picking their way to avoid objects hidden by the snow. "How far down the line?" Kate asked as the tracks came into view.

"Just before the trestle," Mary answered, sniffing at the wood smoke that hung in the air. "Maybe it'll be nice tomorrow for Christmas. I'm glad they're sending a priest up here to say Mass."

"Yes," Kate agreed as they walked along the tracks, where the snow had been cleared away in a three-foot swath. "I hope we get Father McDermot. . . ." She stopped again as a sharp crack sounded nearby. "What was that? A power line snapping?"

Mary shook her head. "They usually only do that when they're frozen. It sounded more like a gun to me."

"A hunter, maybe, going after venison for Christmas dinner." Kate shrugged and kept walking.

Turning a bend in the tracks, they saw the trestle up ahead where Burl Creek tumbled into the Skykomish River. Like Icicle Creek, Burl was running high. Brush, logs, even small trees were being swept along on the swift current.

"The pine trees are just above the creek," Mary said, "maybe twenty feet up. . . ." This time Mary stopped speaking. "Did you see that?" she asked, taking Kate by the arm. "Someone just ran up through the trees."

But Kate hadn't seen anything. "Our hunter, maybe," she said. "Let's hope he doesn't think we look like a deer. Maybe we should start yelling so he knows we're here."

"A good idea," Mary replied. "Yoo-hoo! Yoo-hoo!"

"Hey!" Kate shouted. "Hallooo . . ." She began to cough again. "Drat. Let's hope he heard you."

Staying on the alert, the women moved to the creek. Kate noticed fresh footprints in the snow. "Somebody's been here, all right. Look."

Mary stared at two sets of footprints, one large, one not so large. They led down from the hill to the edge of the creek. "Oh, my God!" Mary cried. "Is this blood?"

Crimson spots spattered the snow next to the rushing waters. Kate flinched and put a hand to her breast. Then her eyes followed the smaller set of prints back up the hill. "Two people were here. Only one left."

Mary stared at the prints. "What do you think happened?"

Kate gazed in horror at the creek, running full spate. A person could get swept away downstream. Especially if that person had been shot. "Forget the pine. Let's follow these single prints back up the hill."

"You'll get out of breath," Mary protested. "Besides, whoever it is may have a gun."

"It could be a woman," Kate said. "The prints are small enough." She straightened her shoulders. "If we go slow. I'll be all right."

"I'd rather you didn't try," Mary said, looking up at the trestle. "That's odd. The rope's gone."

"Good," Kate declared, her face grim. Then she turned a worried face to her sister. "My God, Mary, what do you think happened here?"

"I'd rather not think about it," Mary responded bleakly. "But we have to do something. We can't stand around here all day."

"Then let's go," Kate said, her expression now determined. She started up the hill, heedless of her wet skirts and petticoats.

"Oh, Kate," Mary said in a wretched voice, "I don't know if we . . ."

But Kate was already several yards away. With a shake of her head, Mary followed.

Within another ten yards, the footprints turned back toward town. At one point, it looked as if their prey had fallen. Mary and Kate now moved faster along the more even ground. It was beginning to get dark and it felt as if the temperature was dropping. Coming out into the open at the edge of the forest, Mary looked up. Heavy clouds had begun to move in. Across the valley, Baldy was already half-hidden.

The footprints began to mingle with those of other people. On Christmas Eve, Alpine was a-bustle. Rufus Kager was hauling a Sitka blue spruce on a horse-drawn wagon. Tom Bassen was nailing a cedar wreath to his front door. Harriet Clemans was delivering a basket of her famous potato rolls to the Rix family. Somewhere voices were raised in the third verse of "O Come All Ye Faithful."

It should have been a perfect holiday scene.

But Mary and Kate felt sick at heart as they sorted out the most recent footprints and realized that they led to the Iversen home.

"Mother of God," Kate whispered as she looked at the darkened house. "Now what do we do?"

Mary didn't answer for a long time. Finally, she heaved a sigh that was almost a wail. "Nothing."

"But Mary," Kate objected, "we can't just let things go."

"Yes, we can," Mary insisted. "It's none of our business. And it's Christmas. Maybe," she went on slowly as she turned her back on the Iversen house, "it's all for the best."

"You're a Pollyanna," Kate burst out. "You always were!"

Mary didn't reply, but kept walking.

Kate stood in place for a few moments. Maybe Mary was right.

It was Christmas.

Chapter Seventeen

W<small>ITH ONLY THE</small> briefest of explanations to the Thorstensens, I raced out of their house and drove away as if Satan himself were in pursuit. It took me less than five minutes to reach the radio station site. All the emergency vehicles were roaring to the spot. I slowed down within about fifty feet and surveyed what was left of KSKY.

Frankly, I couldn't see much through the smoke and flames. The clearing was alight as the fire raged. I flinched as a couple of small explosions went off somewhere inside the inferno. I could barely make out the rear part of the building that had been left standing. Not that Spence had built himself a broadcasting Taj Mahal—KSKY was a small cinder-block edifice consisting of a half-dozen cramped rooms. Some fifty feet away from the building, I noted that the radio tower was still intact. Apparently whoever had bombed the station had wanted to destroy the people, along with the place.

As the firefighters uncoiled their hoses, I spotted Milo pulling up behind the engines. The other emergency vehicles were arriving, including a state patrol car and a Forest Service truck, as well as Alpine's medics and ambulance crew, who were having a busy day. As I hurried toward the sheriff, the smoke made me cough and my eyes began smarting.

I stopped short of Milo as I saw him confer with one of the firefighters. Then I caught sight of a huddled figure leaning against a tree while another person paced close by.

"Hey!" The pacer called to the medics. "Over here! Craig's hurt!"

Milo turned, shouting to the man who had asked for help. "Anybody else inside the building?"

"No," answered the man, who I now could see was young and fair-haired and might have been in shock. He stopped pacing, then held his head as if reconsidering his answer. "No." He sounded more confident the second time around. "Craig was the only one in the station. I was outside having a smoke during a canned feature."

The medics were tending to Craig, whose head was bleeding and who seemed to be in some pain. If memory served, Craig was an older college student who served as KSKY's engineer. I guessed that the younger man was Rick Corrolla, the D.J. I'd heard a few hours earlier.

"Where's Fleetwood?" Milo yelled as the fire hoses began to douse the blaze.

"What?" Rick—assuming it was Rick—looked at the sheriff in a dazed manner.

Naturally, I didn't have a camera with me. Scott had gone to Seattle. Maybe Vida was home by now. I dialed her number, but she didn't answer. In desperation, I called Leo, who was at his apartment, watching the same football game that had so enthralled Don Thorstensen.

"Jesus," Leo said in wonder when I hurriedly told him what had happened. "I'll grab a camera and be right there. Anybody killed?"

"No, but the engineer is hurt. Hurry." I clicked off.

The rain was helping to put out the fire. Fortunately, it hadn't gone beyond the clearing, where flames or sparks might have touched off the surrounding trees and brush. Craig was attempting to get to his feet, but the medics wouldn't let him. They had a gurney and apparently were trying to talk Rick into going to the hospital, too. Rick, however, had resumed pacing and was shaking his head.

I figured this was my only chance to get a firsthand interview. "Rick?" I called. "What happened?"

Rick stopped moving, but was still having trouble focusing. "I don't know."

"You were outside?"

He nodded. "I was having a smoke. Jeez, smoking probably saved my life. The studio must be gone. Poor Craig, he got the worst of it."

"He looks like he'll be okay," I said gently. "So somebody threw a bomb into the station?"

"I guess so." He paused, reaching for his cigarettes. His hands shook as he tried to light up. "I was standing out back and then I heard this huge noise. Wham!" He held out his arms to indicate the enormity of the blast. "It lit up everything like it was daytime. In fact, I guess it knocked me down." The cigarette was finally aglow. Rick paused to take a deep puff. "I looked around, and the whole place was starting to go up. What was left of it, I mean. The rear part of the building wasn't hit so hard, not at first. I went through the back door and got Craig. He was half out of it. God. What a mess."

"Do you know where Spence is?" I asked as one of the medics took Rick by the arm.

Rick shook his head. "He left, maybe half an hour ago. Somebody called and he had to run."

I stepped aside as the medics took Rick to the aid car. Craig was being put in the ambulance, which had its lights flashing. Milo was now concentrating on the fire that was mercifully sputtering out.

"I hope Fleetwood's got insurance," the sheriff said, walking over to join me. "I put out an APB on him. He's out of business for awhile."

"That depends," I said. "He can broadcast from a pup tent."

"Had he gotten any threats lately?" Milo asked.

"Not that I know of." I wiped my eyes with a Kleenex. "He did get a letter a couple of weeks ago that sounded sort of like the one Judge Marsha got."

"But no threat of violence?"

"I don't think so. But," I continued, remembering a remark Spence had made, "he mentioned getting the occasional bomb threat. It didn't sound like it worried him."

"Maybe it should have," said Milo.

"Rick told me Spence got a phone call about a half-hour ago that seemed to make him tear out of the studio," I said.

"Hunh." Milo surveyed the cloud of white smoke that was settling among the radio station's ruins. "That's odd. You wouldn't get a bomb threat and go off without the other guys. Who would want to blow up KSKY," he went on with a sly glance at me, "besides you?"

"Very funny," I retorted as Leo's car came down the road just as the ambulance and the medic van drove off. My ad manager pulled up on the verge where the medical emergency vehicles had been parked. The area was still crowded with at least a dozen other cars and trucks that had stopped to take in the excitement.

With camera in hand, Leo waved at the sheriff and me. "Did I miss a bloody victim photo-op?"

"Actually," I said, "you did. But that's okay. We've still got smoke. And what's left of the station."

Leo didn't waste any time. He finished the first roll in a couple of minutes, then reloaded and began taking pictures of Milo, the two state patrol officers, and Wes Amundson from the Forest Service.

"I'm leaving," I announced. "My eyes are driving me nuts. Thanks, Leo."

"No problem." Leo was still shooting film.

Back inside my car. I sat very still for a few moments. I was tired. It had been a long, harrowing day. The rain was letting up. I'd go home, change into my robe, zap the Chinese takeout, and collapse in front of the TV. It was a travel day for the Mariners, so there was no baseball. Maybe I'd catch the end of the football game instead.

I will never really know why I did what I did next. Some might call it fate. Others might say it was perversity. I'd like to think it was simply journalistic curiosity along with a need to get the smoke and the chemicals out of my eyes and lungs. Maybe I wanted to close the circle on Marsha Foster-Klein and go back to the site of the photo that had sent Vida and me on a wild goose chase.

Whatever the reason, I found myself driving past the college's computer lab and pulling off by Burl Creek where the railroad trestle is located. I got out of the Lexus and walked into the clearing. The clouds were moving swiftly across the sky. The three-quarter moon was on the rise, illuminating the trestle.

I looked up in disbelief. A rope fell from the railroad tracks above the creek.

And a man dangled from the rope.

I was too horrified to scream.

There was no need to panic. The sheriff was less than half a mile away. I was a hardened journalist. Assuming the man on the rope was dead—and from what I could tell, he definitely was—there was no immediate danger.

Steeling myself, I looked closer at the figure that swayed some fifteen feet above the ground. The moon disappeared for a moment, hampering my sight. Burl Creek offered the sound of sedate water burbling toward the river. I could still catch a faint whiff of the smoke from the fire, but it mingled with the pine trees on the hill behind me. When the clouds rolled on, I peered upward again.

The dead man was middle-aged, dressed in jeans, a sweatshirt, and a denim jacket. His long dark hair may have had some gray in it. The beard did not. I couldn't help but wondering if I was looking at the body of Ezekiel Foster-Klein.

My nerves had settled. I reached for my purse to get the

cell phone. As usual, it had fallen to the bottom. The clouds had once again covered the moon. Looking in my purse was like peering into a deep well. I swore out loud as I felt every other item—notebook, keys, compact, hairbrush, wallet, checkbook, sunglasses case, eyeliner, lipsticks, Kleenex, and what seemed like a dozen pens. Finally, I located the damned phone. I was extracting it from the rest of the rubble when a strong hand gripped my forearm.

"I wouldn't call the sheriff if I were you," said the voice that despite its ragged edge I recognized as belonging to Spencer Fleetwood.

I gasped and tried to turn around. Spence yanked the phone out of my hand. He looked dreadful, his sharp features haggard and his brown eyes darting in every direction.

"Move," Spence ordered, still holding my arm tight and adding a nudge with his knee for emphasis. "Come on, Emma, don't make this any harder than it already is."

It would do no good to scream. The road was too far away and there wasn't a house within a hundred yards. I had no choice but to obey. Spence was steering me toward his Beamer, parked about thirty feet beyond my Lexus. If it had been there when I arrived, I hadn't seen it in the dark.

Spence opened the rear door on the driver's side and told me to get in. At least, I thought dismally, he wasn't going to stuff me into the trunk. Not yet, anyway.

Spence moved in beside me. I wondered if he had a gun. He seemed to be breathing rather hard, and for the first time I noticed that there was a cut on his cheek and his knuckles were badly bruised.

"I wish to God you hadn't come along just now," he said. "Why, Emma? What brought you here?"

Since I wasn't really sure and in no mental shape for reflection, I gave a halfhearted shrug. "Curiosity, I guess."

"God!" Spence's jaw clamped shut. He was staring straight ahead into the darkened car. "Now what do I do about it?"

"About . . . what?" My voice sounded feeble.

He turned to face me. His eyes seemed to throw sparks even in the almost nonexistent light. "Why did it have to be you?" The words were ground out of his mouth, almost unrecognizable from his usual smooth, mellow radio voice. He squeezed my chin between his thumb and forefinger. "*Why?*"

"I . . . don't . . . know." It wasn't easy to talk with my lower jaw immobilized.

Spence's free hand moved to the back of my neck. He let go of my chin and placed his fingers on my throat. I tried to pull away, but he had me pinned against the car door. If only I could reach behind me, maybe I could open the door if it wasn't locked. . . .

I twisted myself around as best I could, my right hand groping for the lever. It wouldn't take much for Spence to snuff the life out of me. I couldn't see his face; it was too close; now his cheek was against mine. I felt a switch of some kind. Was it the door or the window? I pressed it, but nothing happened. The door must be locked.

I was so terrified, so caught up in trying to escape that it didn't dawn on me that I wasn't being strangled. It was the soft, whimpering noise that got my attention. Spence's hands had dropped behind me, his head was on my shoulder, and he was crying.

What sounded like grief brought me to my senses and restored my vocal cords. "Spence! What's wrong?"

He didn't answer right away but continued to sob. Finally, he looked at me, then sat up, removed his hands, and wiped his eyes.

"Christ. I can't believe this is happening!"

"You mean the bomb? Or . . ." I wasn't sure who the hanged man was, so I merely said, ". . . the body over the creek?"

"Both!" Spence leaned back against the soft leather upholstery. "This is just a nightmare. I've lost everything. It was supposed to turn out so different."

My fears in abeyance, I managed to recover some compassion. "I honestly don't know what you're talking about. Is there somewhere you can start?"

Spence took a handkerchief out of his pocket. The blood on his cheek was dry, but a few droplets still oozed from his knuckles. He wiped his hands again, then patted at the bloody hand. "I don't know if I should."

My next question took some courage. "Are you going to kill me?"

A hint of amusement crossed Spence's face. "Kill you? What made you think I was going to kill you?"

"You were kind of rough with me," I replied slowly. "You scared the hell out of me."

Spence sighed. "That was panic. I just wanted to get out of that place with . . . Zeke."

"I thought it was Zeke Foster-Klein. Did you know him?"

Spence regarded me with a strange expression I couldn't fathom. "Know him? Of course I knew Zeke. He was my brother."

I could hardly believe that Spencer Fleetwood was really Gabe Foster-Klein. But it was true. I should have guessed he wasn't Spencer Fleetwood. It was so obviously a made-up radio name.

"So you're not living with your family in Santa Barbara and hustling air-conditioning," I finally said after the shock had ebbed.

Taking out a pack of cigarettes from his pocket, Spence frowned. "Is that what Marsha told you?"

I nodded and gratefully accepted the offer of a Balkan Sobranie. "She also told me she had no idea where Zeke was."

"She knew, because I told her," Spence said, rubbing gingerly at his chin, which I noticed was also bruised. "But she found out only in the past couple of weeks."

I thought back to my suspicions about Spence visiting Marsha. He'd brought flowers, which seemed to indicate a romance. It never occurred to me that the relationship might be very different.

"What happened with Zeke?" I asked. "I mean, I assume he committed suicide." I hoped so. I didn't much like the idea of Spence hanging his own brother.

"I tried to stop him," Spence said, looking down at his bruised knuckles. "He thought I was going to turn him in, but I wasn't. Marsha and I were hoping to work something out with him. A plea bargain, maybe. Zeke wouldn't hear of it. His brain was all messed up with drugs." Spence paused, shaking his head. "Anyway, he was paranoid, he believed we were against him. As a judge, Marsha had become part of the establishment he hated so much. Oh, yes, he had strong political convictions in the beginning while he was in college. Antiwar during Vietnam, antigovernment, antievery-thing. Zeke had been all over the country, to Europe and Australia and Thailand. But he always came back to this area. The first I knew of him being around Alpine was six months ago. I ran into him and Terry Woodson at a restau-rant in Sultan. They were both high, and even though they didn't say so outright, they dropped a bunch of hints about what they were up to."

"You didn't investigate?"

"No. That was one news story I didn't want." Spence gave me a halfhearted grin. "Not even to scoop you."

I smiled weakly. "Could we open a window? It's stuffy in here."

"Sure." Spence pressed a button; the window slid down smoothly. "Better?"

"Yes. Thanks," I said. "Did you see Zeke after that en-counter?"

"Once, a month or so ago when I was doing a remote broadcast from Skykomish." Spence looked at his knuckles again, saw that they weren't bleeding any more, and pock-eted the handkerchief. "I didn't see him again until tonight. He called me at the station and made all kinds of wild threats, including blowing us up. I figured it was just drug talk, but I agreed to meet him. He chose the spot, which was here." He stopped speaking again, this time to stare out into the darkness. "I was waiting in the car when I heard the explosion. I knew right away what he'd done. I couldn't believe it. I thought of going back to the station, but before I could make up my mind, he came roaring along in his pickup." Spence pointed off to our left. "He ploughed the damned thing right through the woods. It's still there."

"Did Zeke admit bombing KSKY?" I asked as Spence again fingered his chin.

"Of course. He bragged about it, said he wished he'd killed me. Then he began to rant and say that Marsha and I would never bring him in alive. I tried to tell him we didn't intend to bring him in at all, that we'd try to help him. But Zeke said he'd already killed one man—Terry—and maybe more at the station. He wasn't going down for murder one. We really got into it then and started fighting. Zeke had plenty of adrenaline going for him. From the drugs, I suppose. Anyway, he knocked me out just as the Amtrak passenger train went through. I don't think I was unconscious for more than a couple of minutes, but when I came to, Zeke was up on the trestle with a rope. I knew what he was going to do. I begged him to stop, but he went ahead and . . . he did it." Spence shuddered and his head drooped. "Good God, I couldn't believe it. I came back to the car and was going to call for help when you came along. I didn't want you seeing that . . . gruesome sight, but I couldn't stop you fast enough. I was a mess. I'm sorry if I scared you."

"You did," I asserted. "I was absolutely terrified."

"I may have been in shock," Spence said. "Maybe I still am. Tell me about Rick and Craig. Are they okay?"

I related what I knew of Spence's employees. He sighed with relief. "Thank God. But the station's . . . gone?"

"Pretty much," I said. "The tower's still there, though."

"Good." He was suddenly lost in thought. "Shall we call

Dodge or just go back to town?" Spence seemed oddly help-less.

"Let's call now," I said. "You have my cell phone."

"What? Oh." His expression was rueful. "Sorry." He reached down to the floor and found the cell. "Here. You call."

I did, reaching Bill Blatt. I tried to be succinct, saying that there was a suicide at the Burl Creek trestle. Bill asked me to wait. I told him that Spence was with me. I didn't say it was his brother who had died.

"Thanks, Emma," Spence said after I rang off.

"Sure." Puffing on the cigarette, I tried to relax. "Did you choose your radio name in honor of Fleetwood Mac?"

Spence shook his head. "I was never a fan. I chose it be-cause of the car, the old Cadillac. I always wanted one as a kid. I had it legalized not long after I moved from Everett."

"You must have gone into radio right away," I remarked. "Gabriel Foster-Klein would have been a mouthful."

"That isn't why I changed my name." Spence's sharp pro-file looked severe.

"Oh? Why then?"

He looked me in the eye. "I didn't just move away, I ran away." He lowered his gaze, focusing on his bruised knuck-les. "Zeke isn't the only one who took human life. I was the one who got Lynn Froland killed in the accident up at the summit."

Dumbfounded, I wondered how many more shocks I could take in one day.

"You mean," I said, "you were driving the car."

"Driving like an idiot," Spence retorted. He put a hand up to shield his eyes. No doubt he could still see the tragedy un-fold. "I was showing off, being the macho man who could still get my ex-squeeze to let me drive her car. I wanted to show Terry Woodson—of all people—that I was still nu-mero uno. But Lynn got mad when I started doing a zigzag thing on the highway. She tried to grab the wheel. I pushed her away and lost control of the car. I might as well have stabbed her to the heart."

"That's incredibly sad," I responded for lack of anything better to offer.

"I've spent my life regretting it," Spence asserted. "Maybe that's why I've never married. I'm not Catholic, but I've done my share of penance."

"Why did you come to Alpine?" I asked.

He shrugged. "I had some money saved up from a Chicago station that changed its format and offered me a nice package. Like Zeke, this area was always home for me. That stretch of Highway 2 from Everett to the other side of the mountains gets a hold of you. It's so beautiful, still so primeval. Radio's a tough business. I'd had my share of the big city rat race, not to mention the desolate small towns of Texas and Oklahoma and Nebraska. I wanted to put my roots down in the good, sweet earth of the central Cascades."

"Weren't you afraid you'd be recognized?"

Spence laughed sharply. "In a way, I didn't care. But the last anybody had seen me around Everett—let alone Alpine—I had long hair and a beard. Not to mention that I was thirty years younger. And," he went on with a shake of his head, "the only one who spotted me was that old coot, Jack Froland. I suppose you don't ever forget the face of the person who was responsible for getting your daughter killed."

"I can see that," I allowed. "Plus, when Marsha came to town a year or so ago, he may have made the connection between you."

"Probably. We're supposed to be related to the Frolands in some shirttail manner. In any event, I'm sure that's why he wrote those letters to Marsha and me. Not that I blame him."

"The one you got was just like Marsha's?"

"Yes. When I got mine. I tossed it, thinking it was one

more crank," Spence said. "But just the other day, Marsha finally told me about hers. When she asked for your help, she
didn't know I'd gotten a letter, too."

"So that explains why she suddenly seemed to lose interest," I murmured. "The terrible secret wasn't hers, it was
yours. Come to think of it, her letter didn't accuse her of
anything, only of something in her past that could jeopard-
ize her chances with the Court of Appeals appointment."

"It wouldn't have," Spence said firmly. "But since Marsha
didn't know what Jack was talking about, she got scared."

Headlights illuminated our parking area. I turned to look
out the rear window. A sheriff's car was coming to a stop.
The moon had nipped out from behind the clouds. I could
see Bill Blatt and Dustin Fong get out of the car.

We got out of the Beamer. I stepped back. This was
Spence's story to tell. If he could get back on the air in the
next few hours. I'd let him scoop me.

Besides, I didn't have a camera.

Vida, agog with my account of all that had happened, kept
me up until after midnight. She was waiting on my doorstep
when I finally got home a little after ten. Naturally, Vida had
enormous regrets that she hadn't been on hand for at least
some of the traumatic experiences. But, as she finally revealed, she'd had a big surprise, too.

"It may sound silly," she said over her sixth cup of tea,
"but I hadn't made a truly thorough search of the Froland
house. I don't know why I thought it was necessary at this
point. Duty, I suppose."

That wasn't the word I would have chosen, but it sounded
better than "snoopy." "What did you find?"

"An unfinished manuscript written by Max Froland," Vida
replied. "It was in a shoe box in the spare bedroom's closet."

I remembered that Max had told me he was writing a
book. "Is it a history text?"

Vida's eyes sparkled. "Not exactly. That is, there's history, but it's written as a novel. And it's all about Alpine's early days. There are," she added, suddenly breathless, "even things I didn't know!"

"Good grief!" I exclaimed, half-serious. "That's hard to believe."

Across the kitchen table, she leaned closer and lowered her voice. "Some of these things are rather shocking. It's no wonder they didn't get handed down, especially in those days when people didn't talk about child molesting."

"Child molesting?" I grimaced. "Does Max name names?"

"He does indeed." Vida sat up straight again. "You would never guess who the major molester was."

"Is that a military title?"

Vida gave me her gimlet eye. "It's not funny. It's terrible. The perpetrator was a teenager named Jonas Iversen."

"You're right," I said, "I'd never guess it was him since I haven't the foggiest idea who he is. Was."

"Jonas was one of Trygve and Olga Iversen's sons. Trygve, as you'll recall if you've read my story on the Fro-lands, was the assistant mill superintendent in Alpine's early days. All I knew was that Jonas had disappeared toward the end of 1917, just like another boy—Vincent Burke—had done a bit earlier. But according to Max's account, Jonas may have been murdered by his own mother!" Vida slapped her hand on the table. "What do you think of *that*?"

I stared at Vida. "You're right, it's shocking. What became of the mother?"

"Nothing. I got the impression it was like a mercy killing. Trygve couldn't stop the boy, it seems, and Olga couldn't go on with the horror. Not to mention the legal consequences if Jonas was arrested and the shame that would follow. Olga lived to be an old lady, dying during World War II, I believe. But Trygve couldn't stand it. *He hanged himself from the railroad trestle a year later.*"

I could scarcely believe it. "You didn't know about the suicide? That might have been talked about and handed down."

But Vida shook her head. "Not in those days. Suicide was a disgrace, too. I'd always heard that Trygve had been killed in a railroad accident. Anyway, that's why the Iversens changed the spelling of their name. It was Per, the eldest son's idea, though what good it did when part of the family stayed in Alpine, I couldn't say. It sounds more like a gesture to me."

"Where did Max get all this information?" I asked, still amazed at the contents of Vida's discovery.

"Max has written a dedication to his father," Vida replied, finishing off her tea. "Jack Froland was Trygve and Olga's grandson and the son of Karen Iverson Froland. By the way, Jack Iverson wrote the obituary for his uncle. I found a draft of it and a note from him to June. I should have known. Jack's a dunderhead."

"Hunh." I sat with my elbows on the table, propping up my face with my hands. I was exhausted, but I was still able to think. "So why would Jack send that old picture of the trestle along with his letter to Marsha?"

Vida shrugged. "Who knows? Jack may have had some crazy notion because that was the place where Jonas did . . . whatever he did with those youngsters, and because his grandfather committed suicide there. I found several old photos with the manuscript. I'll show it all to you tomorrow. Frankly, I've only skimmed the book."

"You kept it?" I asked in some surprise.

Vida wore an air of innocence. "Of course. June won't be home from the hospital for a day or two."

"What are you going to do about June?" I asked as Vida finally got to her feet.

"I've been thinking about that," she said, very solemn. "What good would it do to let on? June's not in her right mind, she probably hasn't been for some time." Vida had moved into the living room, where she picked up her coat and purse. "Maybe it really was an accident." Vida put on her coat, then went to the door. "Let's call it a mercy killing."

When Evergreen Cemetery in Everett opened a century ago, no one could have foreseen that Interstate 5 would pass by so close that you could almost read the headstones from your car.

Autumn had officially arrived on the Friday that Zeke Foster-Klein was buried next to his parents. I'd worn my winter coat for the first time since March, and although the sun was shining, I felt the hint of decay in the air as I stood near the open grave.

There had been no other service except for what was being held now by a young Unitarian minister who was one of Marsha's clients. Just out from under the green canopy, I noticed a handsome tombstone for Phillip Andrew Barr. Marsha's husband had been only twenty-five when he'd died of a brain tumor. He hadn't lived half as long as Tom.

I'd also seen the markers for George Foster and Anna Foster-Klein. George's was simple, but Anna's had an additional inscription: SOLIDARITY. Apparently, the matriarch of the Foster-Klein brood had never renounced her father's belief in the good fight.

I'd arrived late, having been caught in the usual traffic slowdown between Sultan and Monroe. Amazingly, Vida hadn't joined me. Roger had broken his toe that morning when he kicked his boom box because it had run out of batteries.

I wasn't really sure why I had come. It was the first funeral I'd attended since Tom's. Furthermore, Marsha hadn't endeared herself to me over the past few weeks, and I retained a certain wariness about Spence, who had somehow managed to get back on the air after only forty-eight hours. Of course he'd done it too late for us to get the full story in Wednesday's paper.

But there I was, looking out over the farmland across the freeway where strip malls were slowly snuffing out the fields and barns. The Cascades rose in their early autumn splendor, with the trees in the foothills turning to gold.

I'd gotten to the grave just as the minister had begun his eulogy. A free spirit, he said of Zeke, a traveler who had taken the path less traveled. That was one way of putting it.

But there was no mistake about the grief of brother and sister. They were the only other mourners in attendance. Marsha sobbed and leaned on Spence as the casket was lowered into the ground. Spence looked pale, older, still haggard. He removed his Gucci sunglasses to wipe his eyes. There was probably guilt mingled with the sorrow. Like the Frolands, the Foster-Kleins were no strangers to tragedy.

The brief service concluded. Marsha gathered her composure and went over to speak with the minister. Spence made a comment to the funeral director, then noticed me, apparently for the first time.

"Emma!" he said in surprise as he held out a hand. "I didn't expect you to come."

"Well, I did." I forced a smile. "I thought you might need some moral support."

He put his sunglasses back on and hugged me. "Thank you. Thank you very much." Stepping back, he looked down at me with a serious expression. "I know this couldn't have been easy for you. But one of the reasons I offered to go the co-op route for advertising was because I admire you. You've managed to overcome a horrendous tragedy in your life and keep emotionally grounded. I don't know how you do it."

Momentarily, I was speechless. "But . . . I really haven't . . . I mean . . . I've had all sorts of . . ."

Spence put a finger to my lips. "I know, you've had some ups and downs. But you've carried on, and you haven't become bitter, at least not that anyone can tell. You're very brave, Emma. How do you do it? Is it your faith?"

"Yes, I suppose it is, and . . ." I paused, glancing at Marsha, who was still talking to the minister. "It's family, my son and my brother. Ben, especially. He's very direct." *Blunt* was what I meant. Or maybe it was *honest.*

"That's good." Spence managed a smile. "Marsha is very direct, too. Excuse me, I should say something to Pastor Nirvana, too."

He walked away, joining the minister. And Marsha.

Right after lunch, I called Ben. Luckily, he was in.

"Hi, Stench," I said. "Still want me to join you in nude bathing at the Trevi Fountain?"

Ben said yes.